PRAISE FOR J.B. CURRY

"Sexy, saucy, and sultry, *Bad Keys* is a mystery/romance that recalls Carl Hiaasen's novels and the TV series *Moonlighting*."

BLUEINK REVIEW

"Sometimes profane and often delightful, this caper finds absurdity even in moments of danger. . .Bad Keys is an unusual mystery and romance. Beneath its wild chase lies optimistic belief in what people can do when they act with conviction."

KAREN RIGBY, ***FOREWORD CLARION REVIEW***

"A scintillating mystery and steamy romance rolled into one fast-paced romp. A lush setting and laugh-out-loud characters will have readers coming back for more from J.B. Curry."

CARYN SHAFFER, ***SAN FRANCISCO BOOK REVIEW***

BAD KEYS

DISCARDED

BAD KEYS

J.B. CURRY

Bad Keys

ISBN: 978-1-7327900-0-1

Copyright © 2019 by J.B. Curry

All rights reserved.

No part of this book may be reproduced in any form or by any electronic or mechanical means, including information storage and retrieval systems, without written permission from the author, except for the use of brief quotations in a book review.

This is a work of fiction. Names, characters, businesses, places, events, locales, and incidents are either the products of the author's imagination or used in a fictitious manner. Any resemblance to actual persons, living or dead, or actual events is purely coincidental.

Published by Arcanic Media
jbcurry.com

Cover design and proofreading by Ebook Launch

Editing by Marla Daniels

For my family

1

IT WASN'T THE MONEY. It was the theft of the Minneapolis Piano Tuners Guild seal that finally made Luke Hansen crack.

Other recent stressors had already put hairline fractures in Luke's usually stoic temperament, priming it for this final, shattering blow. For instance, the eight-month anniversary of closing his piano repair shop had recently come and gone. As had the six-month anniversary of his ex-wife boot scootin' off with a rodeo cowboy from Sioux Falls. Then of course there was the five-month anniversary of the foreclosure on his remodeled split-level in Edina.

And just this evening he had walked into his moldering studio apartment to find his latest goldfish floating lifeless in its tank, one bulbous eye goggling reproachfully in his direction as if to say, "I knew it would end like this."

"Quitter," he said to the fish as he tore open the handful of mail that had found its way to his mailbox. Bills, mercifully small. Credit card offers, easily ignored. Advertisements for penis enlargers, completely unnecessary for a six-foot-eight-inch-tall man, if he did say so himself.

And one thick envelope from the Treasurer of the Minneapolis Piano Tuners Guild, Brett Kowalski. It contained a spreadsheet and a document titled "Prospectus," informing him that Brett Kowalski had emptied out the Guild's bank account, intending to use his loot to finance the purchase of two hundred slightly damaged off-brand Chinese-manufactured pianos from a Miami company called Castillo Imports. The plan, it seemed, was to pass off these junkers as quality instruments and overcharge the chumps who bought them by obscene amounts.

Luke, a proud son of the Guild, was furious, naturally. But not surprised. Nope, he'd smelled this buttfuck coming a mile away.

When Brett Kowalski had moved his piano showroom from White Plains, New York to the borderlands of the Mall of America a few months ago, the Minneapolis piano tuners had quickly succumbed to the spell of his salesman's patter and New York mystique and elected him guild treasurer.

Even though Luke had been next in line for the office. Even though Luke's father had been treasurer for years and had expected to pass the position down to his son when he retired.

Even though, when the new treasurer flashed his cap-toothed smile at him and reached up a pudgy hand for a back slap, Luke could sense he was in the presence of a shitweasel *cum laude*.

Luke scanned the document in his hands with cynical resignation until he noticed the bleary stamp at the bottom of the last page next to Kowalski's florid signature. It was a circle containing a crossed tuning fork and tuning hammer, the tools of the piano technician's trade. The Piano Tuners Guild official seal.

He stared at the stamp for a second. Then he grabbed the envelope to check the postmark—Miami, Florida.

An electric current shot up his spine, crackling in his fingertips and blazing behind his eyes in unutterable fury.

He stole the seal.

Ripping off the money was one thing, but stealing the seal? The symbol of the pride and honor of a musical tradition hundreds of years old?

That was a mortal fucking insult.

Luke was aware that his reaction was less than rational. He knew the seal had no real value to non-tuners.

Sure, it looked imposing, with its polished handle and its brass head, like something a medieval monarch would stamp on a royal decree. When Luke's father had been the treasurer of the Guild, he had kept it displayed on his own beautifully tuned piano with great reverence. Seven-year-old Luke had been duly impressed. Whenever he sat at the keys to practice his lessons, he never dared to so much as touch it.

But by the time he followed his father's footsteps into the piano-tuning life, he had come to understand that to non-tuners the seal was only an odd relic. A leftover from a long, long time ago when piano tuners had been—well, not important, but at least useful. But those days were as extinct as the wooly mammoth.

Fewer people actually played their pianos anymore. Mostly they just used them as cocktail tables. And who bothered to get their cocktail table tuned?

No, to civilians the Piano Tuners Guild seal might not matter a whole lot. But to Luke, leaving it in Kowalski's slimy little rat paws felt like a betrayal. And he simply couldn't stand it.

He tossed the papers down on the dinette and yanked

his phone out of his pocket. The dipshit ex-treasurer wouldn't have changed his number yet. A man who would mail out a typed itemization of his crimes was not a man trying to hide.

As the phone rang and rang, Luke scrubbed his hand over his wedge of a jaw and up through his neatly combed hair until it was standing up in thick blond spikes.

Finally, the call picked up with a fumbling sound. Hairband guitar blared in his ear. The stripper anthem "Pour Some Sugar On Me," if he wasn't mistaken. A voice slurred, "H'lo?"

Luke unlocked his jaw. "Brett, this is Luke Hansen. I—"

"Hey hey hey! Luke, my brother, how's it hangin'? Hold on a sec, would ya?" He dimly heard Kowalski's muffled voice say, "Crystal, baby, I'll be right back. Gotta take this call. Damn, girl! Owwww!"

Happy hour at the titty bar. Outstanding. Luke loosened his necktie and breathed deeply.

A few seconds later, the music dimmed and Kowalski came back on the line. "Luke, I'm glad you called, bro!" he said, unleashing singular talent—his smooth, warmly authoritative voice. Even on the point of inebriation, it had a pure, honest timbre, without a note of guile.

At this moment, nothing could have been better calculated to pitch Luke into a state of rage like he'd never felt before.

Kowalski continued, "Did you get my prospectus?"

"Yes," Luke managed.

"Sweet deal, right? My contacts in New York tipped me off about it. I wanted to go over the numbers with you before I left, but I had to jump on the flight for Miami so I could get in with Castillo before everyone else. Negotiations like these need the personal touch. *Mano e mano.* You know how it is in the high-end trade."

Luke ignored the Master of the Universe spiel. "Are you saying this importer hasn't actually sold you the pianos yet?"

"Relax, I told you, we got an agreement. Fact, I'm meeting one of Castillo's guys in a few minutes. He told me that Castillo's own daughter is working on this deal. And he says she's *very* anxious to do business with us, know what I mean? And Luke, bro, this girl is hot. Like, *hot*. Total babe. Name's Esmeralda, can you believe it? Real porno name, right? She's a swimsuit model, the guy says. He sent me some pictures of her, and she—"

"I don't want to hear about your bimbo, Brett."

"Fine, then she's all mine. Anyways, as soon as Esmeralda clears up this problem with the Feds for us, we'll be good to go."

A new dread curdled Luke's gut. "Exactly what problem with the Feds?"

"Just a little misunderstanding. See, this Chinese company, it makes a couple hundred pianos and then it goes kaput. So Castillo sees his chance and buys them up real cheap. Only, when he ships them over here it turns out they have ivory key tops. Real ivory, like, from elephants."

Luke could only bow his head and groan. Elephant ivory key tops were to a piano business like garlic to a vampire. They'd been banned in most of the world for decades, but there were still plenty of international oligarchs and sweatshop barons in the market for luxury goods who didn't scruple about killing the poor elephants, or the reputation of the Piano Tuners Guild.

Kowalski blithely went on, "So US Fish and Wildlife finds out about the ivory, and they take the keys off so they can destroy 'em. And now Castillo has these fucked-up pianos on his hands he wants to get rid of quick, which is where we come in."

"We?"

"You and me, bro! You're gonna be my junior partner. That's why I sent you the prospectus."

"And just why did you pick me for this honor?"

The irony in Luke's tone sailed right over Kowalski's receding hairline. "Because I knew you were the kind of guy who'd back me up one hundred and ten percent. Dependable, that's you, Luke. You just need someone with vision to give you direction. That's me."

The news that he had been assessed as a prime stooge did nothing to improve Luke's temper.

"Plus, someone's got to put new keys on the pianos. You make these babies look pretty, slap a Steinway label on them, I mark them way the hell up and push them on the customers, and we'll make a killing, Luke, a killing! Smart, don't you think?"

"I think, you tone-deaf troglodyte, that you've just outlined the lamest attempt at fraud I ever heard of. You disappoint me, Brett. You know what else disappoints me? We're not going to be able to rent the Pinewood Beer Hall for the Guild's spring banquet now that you've spent all our money sucking up to shady importers in a Miami strip joint."

There was a pause as Kowalski finally cottoned on to Luke's lack of enthusiasm for his brilliant scheme. "You have questions. That's totally understandable—"

"No, Brett, I have diatribes and threats, but no questions, except one. Are you going to use UPS or FedEx to send the seal back?"

"Seal?" Kowalski sounded blank.

"The Guild seal you swiped on your way out of Minnesota. I want it back."

"Oh. That. I have to keep the seal for now, Luke." The rich, confident voice took on the beginnings of a whine. "I'm the treasurer. I have to put it on all my documentation to make sure it's totally legit. Gotta dot those t's and cross those i's."

"Let's make one thing clear, here, Brett. You aren't the treasurer anymore. You're an embezzler, among other things. Embezzlers don't get to be treasurers."

"You don't understand," Kowalski said, whine at full flow. "This deal is practically done! Ironclad! The money is absolutely safe, I swear. And when the Guild sees what a great investment this is, they'll vote me treasurer for life. No, president!"

That did it. Luke's lid, blown. "Listen Mister President, you better send me that seal back, or so help me I will hunt you down like a duck and shake it out of your carcass!"

There was a sullen silence. Then, "Look, it'll be fine. Trust me, okay? *Ciao.*" The line went dead.

Luke placed his phone in his pocket and stood thinking for a moment, still vibrating with the electric force that had charged him when he first saw the evidence of the stolen seal.

The money Kowalski had filched would clearly be gone by tomorrow night at the latest, vanished into the G-strings of strippers and equally unsavory places. But the seal. That would stay in the erstwhile treasurer's possession for as long as he imagined he might get some use out of it.

So what was he going to do about it?

Hunt Kowalski down and shake the seal out of him, like he'd told him he would? No, that was crazy.

Wasn't it?

He knew what his mother and his five older siblings would say if he asked them what he should do. Some variation on the old theme of *stop being an idiot and get a real job*.

His fellow piano tuners in the Guild would make some crotchety and probably fruitless complaints to the police, but that was about it.

His ex-wife was too busy knocking boots with her rodeo cowboy to express any opinion on the matter.

And his friends ... well, he didn't have any at the moment, since he'd lost all his single friends when he got married and all his married friends when he got divorced.

His gaze fell on the dead goldfish. "Well, any advice?"

The fish bobbed up and down a little, like it was saying, "Look, buddy, I've got my own problems."

Seemed he had to make this decision on his own.

2

THREE DAYS LATER, Esmeralda Castillo nearly sprayed a mouthful of lime Perrier over a hairstylist, a makeup artist, and a photographer's assistant before she managed to get it down and splutter into the phone, "This Brett Kowalski guy did *what?*"

"He offered me a bribe to give him the ivory piano keys, on behalf of the Piano Tuners Guild of Minneapolis," repeated Special Agent Alistair Truitt on the other end of the line.

Esmeralda promptly launched into a torrent of Spanish profanity, which had Marco, the photographer's assistant, snickering and the other two flunkies looking confused.

A few yards away, the high-strung photographer turned a scowl in her direction as he made adjustments to his camera. She ignored him. They were minutes away from starting her photo shoot, another swimsuit thing on Miami Beach—white sand, turquoise ocean, expensive car to lounge around on, *etcetera* and so forth—but at that moment, Esmeralda couldn't give a *mierda*.

All the effort it had taken to turn those piano keys over

to US Fish and Wildlife, all the trouble they had made for her family and Castillo Imports, and now some moron from Montana or wherever thought he could just sleaze off with the remains of dozens of murdered elephants? Over her thong-clad dead body.

When she finally finished swearing, Esmeralda said, "I hope you arrested him, Al."

"Uh, n-no," stuttered the bilingual and easily shocked Agent Truitt. "We only spoke on the phone. And he was cagey enough to avoid saying anything actually incriminating. But I think he could be a valuable informant. From what he implied, he has contacts in the black market up north not just for ivory piano keys, but for all kinds of high-end smuggled merchandise."

"Could be," she said. "I think my cousin Roddy mentioned this guy. He sounded desperate for any deal he could get. He *must* be desperate, to approach you like that."

"In this case, desperate is good. We could get a lot more information about the ivory trade out of him if we play this right."

"Play what? And who's this 'we'?" she said, setting her Perrier down on the refreshment table with a thump.

"Esmeralda." A wheedling tone entered Truitt's voice. "How would you like to serve your government?"

"What a horrible question to ask someone."

"I have a plan," said Truitt, undaunted. "I let Kowalski believe that I was open to his offer, and then I implied you were my middleman. Er, middlewoman."

"Me? I'm the one who blew the whistle on the ivory in the first place," she said. She was the one who'd convinced her cousin Roddy to let her take the problem to Fish and Wildlife when he could have done a shady deal exactly like this instead.

"Kowalski doesn't know that," Truitt said. "Now listen, I've already supplied him with your contact information. When he calls you, you ask to talk to him face-to-face. I'll fit you with a transmitter before you meet with him. You get him to make an offer for the keys and brag about his clients, and boom! We catch him in the act of buying illegal ivory *and* we get the goods on his accomplices."

It sounded easy enough. And she couldn't say she wouldn't love to take a pound of flesh off someone trying to turn a profit on poached elephants. But ...

"I don't get it, Al. You could get this information from Kowalski by yourself. Why involve me?" Though she could guess why. Poor Agent Al had been coming up with reasons for calling her for the last two years, ever since she had turned down his marriage proposal. Which he had made the day she had first met him. A not-unusual occurrence in her life, sad to say.

But Al said smoothly, "Kowalski is never going to spill his information to a federal agent, even one he thinks is corrupt. If he senses a trap, we could lose him. But you won't raise his suspicions. You should be able to get him to talk with no trouble."

Undeniably true. Esmeralda had never yet met a man who could resist the urge to tell her every excruciatingly boring detail about himself if given a hint of encouragement. In fact, all she usually had to do was stand in one place long enough.

"You'll be perfectly safe if you take this meeting," he coaxed. "I would keep covert surveillance on you at all times."

Esmeralda was about to tell Truitt that she would prefer not to have him watching her from the bushes, but at that moment a cream-colored Porsche convertible rolled into position on the beach, the morning sunlight gleaming on the hood. She winced. In a few minutes she was going to have to spread herself out on all that rapidly heating metal and make "O" faces at the camera.

Never again, Esmeralda vowed to herself. *After this shoot, never again will I incur first-degree burns from a hot Porsche for the benefit of the jackoff community of South Florida.*

When Esmeralda had first gotten into modeling at the age of eighteen, she had had hopes of making a modest place for herself in the more respectable quarters of the fashion industry. But she quickly came to realize that she had two irredeemable flaws barring her from the catwalks of New York or Paris.

First, at a mere five feet eight inches in height, she was positively runtish among the attenuated sisterhood of models.

Second, she had an immutable aversion to plastic surgery, and was thus in possession of possibly the last unaltered nose south of Palm Beach.

Her hair might be long and glossy black, her skin golden and flawless, her eyes liquid, and her bone structure striking, but her nose, with its slight bump at the bridge and tiny dimple on the tip, would never be anything other than cute. And she might as well be Cyrano de Bergerac in a bikini for all the good a cute nose would do her.

So a mere swimsuit model she was, but only for a little while longer. One way or another, this job was almost over. She was twenty-four now, which equaled about one hundred eighty-seven in model years. She would have maybe one or two more seasons in front of the cameras, and then, if she wasn't smart, the usual post-modeling career of concubinage and/or trophy wifedom.

Fortunately, she was smart. She'd worked her ass off to launch her other career, her real life's work. One lousy phone call from the grant-writers at Nagarhole National Park in India, and she could shuck the modeling life like last season's La Perla, she reminded herself. She'd have the funds to run wild and free. She just had to grind through the next few hours without getting annoyed to death.

"Hang on, Al," she said into the phone before tucking it against her shoulder. She shot an evil look at the makeup artist and the hairdresser, who were making darting motions at her head with mascara wands and curling irons. "Do you mind? I'm on the phone with the Feds here. Have some respect for the United States Constitution."

"Oh, my scrumptious little mango," said Marco, as he held a light meter next to her face. "Don't you know we only owe allegiance to the kingdom of Louis Vuitton?"

Resisting the urge to swat them all like Zika-infested mosquitos, she returned her phone to her ear and said, "Look, Al, I'm working right now. I'll think about it and call you back around six or so."

"You're at the zoo?" Truitt asked. "Why don't I stop by there and we can talk in person?"

"No, it's my other job."

"You mean you're ... modeling today?" A strange note crept into his voice. "Is it— is it a bikini ad?"

Out of the corner of her eye she saw the photographer making furious hand gestures at her, which loosely translated to, "Get your ass over here and onto this car before I fire it." Distracted, Esmeralda said, "No, it's a one-piece thong."

A stifled moan came over the line.

She rolled her eyes and said, "Six, okay? Bye, Al." She hit the end button and started to put the phone away in her purse. Then she paused, tapping it against her chin in thought. She had to warn Anita. Technically, Anita was just her father's housekeeper, but in reality she was the boss of her father's family. If anyone could chase off trouble that came sniffing around the house, she could. Ignoring the photographer's spasmodic flailing, she made the call.

When a familiar, motherly female voice answered, she said in Spanish, "Anita, it's me. Listen, a guy named Brett Kowalski might be calling the house. He's a piano salesman from Minnesota. Or Missouri. Some godforsaken place like that. What? Yeah, those damn pianos again. Yes, Anita. I'm sorry about my language. Anyway, I need to talk to this piano man myself, but it's important that he doesn't upset Papa. So if you hear from him, just get his phone number and call me right away, okay? Thanks."

Ending the call, she tossed her phone into her bag and her bag under the water table. Then she fluffed her boobs inside the swimsuit and strode off to fry her butt cheeks on top of yet another overpriced car.

3

THAT SAME MORNING found Luke just south of downtown Miami, staking out the Castillo Imports office building in his elderly Ford F150 truck.

The office was on a street lined with what seemed to be the Miami standard Art Deco architecture and palm trees. But the neighborhood's better days were rapidly receding, leaving a few low-end storefronts and a couple of half-renovated buildings in their wake. Luke had parked in a spot half a block away from the Castillo building and was examining it with some puzzlement.

The building itself was a typical glass-and-concrete corporate affair two stories tall, the entrance set atop a broad flight of shallow steps to lend it grandeur. The odd thing about it was the seven-foot grand piano sitting on the sidewalk at the foot of the stairs.

Not that many people other than Luke would be able to tell that it was a piano. It was resting vertically on its long side. The legs and pedal lyre had been removed and packed in a box in the curve of the rim. And it was entirely wrapped in foamy plastic. It looked like a big flat rectangle to the untrained eye, in fact. But to Luke, it was obviously a brand new parlor grand taken out of its shipping crate.

Was this one of the pianos that Kowalski thought were such a great investment opportunity? If so, what was this one doing abandoned on the sidewalk?

A quick Google on his way south had told him that Castillo Imports was a highly rated import company dealing in furnishings and *objets d'art* for high-end retailers. For thirty years it had been owned and operated by a man named Eduardo Castillo. If Kowalski's interest in the shipment of Chinese pianos wasn't a total fabrication, the importer might be Luke's best lead on him.

Actually, Castillo was his only lead. If he couldn't trace Kowalski here, he would be left to comb through Miami-Dade's population of transient sleazeballs by hand, which didn't bear thinking about.

Luke considered his next move. The direct approach? Just go in and ask where Kowalski was? He couldn't assume these people were criminal scumbags just because they were under federal investigation. And even if they were, they might be overjoyed to hand Kowalski over.

"Well," he said to his truck, "what do you think?"

The truck's cooling engine gave an exhausted tick and a bing. It had rattled southward for three straight days without breaking down even once. Past Orlando it had battled through befuddled tourists in Dodges, wobbly Alzheimer's patients in Cadillacs, and suicidal commuters in Hondas. He figured it had earned the right to bask in the Florida sunshine like every other American senior citizen.

He got out of the truck and the swampy heat of a Miami morning promptly socked him in the face. His shirt instantly plastered itself to his skin, and he nearly crawled back inside to huddle against the feeble air conditioning.

Instead he crossed the street to the office, skirting the forlorn piano. He went up the stairs and through the door, where a blast of arctic air engulfed him. He examined the room as he recovered from the thermal shock.

The building's lobby was an airy space two stories tall, lit by a stack of long, thin, horizontal windows up the front. A second-story balcony extended across the back of the room, a chest-high glass barrier running along its edge. The second-story wall was pierced by a few doors, but most of it was taken up with paintings, hangings, and display cases containing expensive-looking doodads. The fruits of the import business, he assumed.

A stone-and-glass staircase ran up along the right side of the lobby to the mezzanine level. On the ground floor, groups of potted plants and larger sculptures were scattered around on the polished stone tiles. A curving glass reception desk took up the left side of the floor, with doors and hallways leading back from that.

Behind the desk was an attractive fortyish woman in business casual talking on the phone. She was speaking in a low, agitated murmur, but when she looked up as he approached he could see that her face was strangely immobile. Botox, he bet. Not one muscle so much as twitched as she snapped down the receiver and said crisply, "May I help you?" She kept her hand hovering near the phone, probably ready to snatch it up again the second she got rid of him.

Luke put on his best expression of professional friendliness. It made no impact whatsoever. He plunged ahead. "Hi, my name is Luke Hansen. I'd like to talk to Mr. Castillo."

"Do you have an appointment?" she asked in a voice as inert as her forehead.

"No, but it's very important. I need to discuss a mutual acquaintance named Brett Kowalski."

No reaction to the name. "I'm afraid you'll have to make an appointment."

"Please. I've come a very long way. I won't take more than a few minutes of Mr. Castillo's time. Could you call up and ask if he'll see me?"

"I'm sorry, but Mr. Castillo isn't in the office today."

"Could I talk to his secretary or assistant?"

"His assistant is out as well."

"Can you give me an address or phone number where I can reach Mr. Castillo?"

"No, that's not possible. If you leave your name and contact information, I'll let him know you stopped by."

Luke decided not to hear the hint to get lost. "Would you happen to know if Brett Kowalski called or came here?"

"No such person has been here."

"Are you sure?"

"Yes."

They exchanged glares of mutual frustration.

"Is there anything else I can help you with?" she said between her teeth.

"Yes," Luke said. "Can you tell me why there's a piano sitting on your sidewalk?"

"Because the warehouse staff decided to pull one last stunt before they quit. They were told to bring the piano to the office, so they did, and then they just left it out there! So even though I have a million other things to do, I've been stuck on the phone all morning trying to find someone who can move that damn thing inside before we get a citation, which is the very last thing we need right now on top of all the other trouble because of Mr. Castillo's daughter ..." Her voice trailed off and she went a little white around the eyes as she realized she was ranting about her employer's embarrassing HR problems to some dude off the street.

Scenting blood in the water, Luke smiled. "I believe I can solve your problem for you." He took a business card out of his wallet and handed it over.

"Full-Service Piano Technology," she read off the card. "What does that mean exactly?"

"It means I can move that piano wherever you want it, for a reasonable fee." He quoted his usual moving price.

The receptionist, suspicious but with a dawning spark of hope in her eyes, said, "And you can do it this morning?"

"Sure."

"How soon can your moving crew get here?"

"I am the moving crew."

She ran her eyes up and down and all around him, until he'd been thoroughly inspected. Then, for the first time, she smiled, ratcheting up her mouth muscles. "Now that I can believe," she said, a new, throaty tone in her voice. "I'll cut you a check as soon as the piano is in place."

"I'll also need you to do me one other favor," he said, feeling crafty. "I want Mr. Castillo's address and phone number."

"Honey, if you can deliver the goods, I'll do you any favor you want," she purred.

"Right. So where do you want me to put it?"

She sashayed around the desk and up to his side, threading her arm through his. Tipping him a peek of cleavage, which he suspected was mostly silicone, she pointed at the display gallery on the balcony sixteen feet above their heads. "I want you to put it right up there. Come on, I'll show you."

With a firm hold on his arm, she led him into the corridor behind her desk to a bank of elevators. "Can you can get it in here?" she asked as they stepped into the service elevator.

"Sure. It'll be tight, but I can do it," Luke replied.

She looked delighted at his answer.

As they ascended to the second floor, Luke thought over this exchange, wondering if he had stumbled into a RedTube video without noticing.

They inspected the balcony where the piano was going, Luke mapping out the path he had to take to get it there as he went along. Easy enough. He could do this move one-handed. Which he might have to try if the receptionist didn't stop clutching his bicep.

As she walked him back to the lobby, it occurred to him that this office was a little too calm and quiet for a weekday morning. The usual shuffle and mumble of a building full of industrious worker bees was at only half volume, if that.

From what he could see, and from what the receptionist had let slip earlier, Castillo Imports was in serious trouble. He started to wonder if he was going to get paid for this job. *Maybe it'll be worth it anyway, if it helps me find Kowalski.*

He cast an eye at the receptionist plastered to his side. *Maybe.*

He decided to try a delicate probe. "You mentioned Mr. Castillo's daughter before. I think my acquaintance, Mr. Kowalski, knows her too."

The receptionist's lips tried to wrinkle up. "Esmeralda knows all sorts of men."

There really was an Esmeralda? Luke had half thought she was a figment of Kowalski's skeevy imagination.

"But let's not talk about her," the receptionist said. "Let's talk about you. You're very tall, aren't you?"

"So I've been informed. About Esmeralda—"

She tittered and squeezed his arm like she was testing a cantaloupe in the supermarket. "How'd you get so strong?"

"I was bitten by a radioactive pro wrestler," he said, giving up.

He managed to scrape the lady off at her desk, then he plunged back out into the heat of the morning to unload his equipment from his truck. He set up ramps and braced open doors along his route. When everything was ready, he grabbed a wheeled dolly and approached the piano.

He examined it carefully, noting that the plastic wrapping had been cut open, then crudely taped back together. Under the plastic, it was a typical new parlor grand, seven feet long and about eight hundred pounds. Not in the same league as a nine-foot, half-ton concert grand, but still plenty large enough to intimidate civilians.

Fortunately, whoever had dumped it here had left it strapped to a supporting skidboard. That would save him some effort. He set the dolly at his feet and crouched down at the keyboard end, working his fingers under the corner of the board. He hoisted the end of the piano up and kicked the dolly underneath. Then he lowered the instrument, letting it lever itself up onto the dolly as it went down.

He rolled the piano to the ramp he had set up on the entrance stairs and braced his shoulder against it. One step at a time, he shoved eight hundred pounds of wood and cast iron up the ramp to the top of the steps, sweating like a mule the whole way.

When he bumped it over the end of the ramp and onto the landing, a faint thud and twang sounded from inside the case. Probably one of the bags of moisture-absorbing desiccant had gotten loose in there and was banging against the lid and strings.

He pushed the piano through the open doors and into

the blessed air conditioning. Through the lobby and corridor, into the elevator, then out and onto the mezzanine. Occasional thumps and pings sounded from inside the case as it rolled along.

He positioned the piano near the middle of the balcony, close to the glass railing where it would be out of the way of traffic, and lifted it off the dolly. Technically, his job was done.

But I've got to see this disaster with my own eyes.

He unbuckled the skidboard straps, then took out his multipurpose pocket tool and cut the tape holding the thick plastic wrapping together. He pulled the plastic away and bundled it to the side. He took the cardboard box containing the legs and pedal lyre down from the curve of the instrument's rim and set that aside too. Then he stood back a little to look over the case.

It had a decent finish job, sleek and black and only a little dusty from its travels. He opened up the fall board to look at the keys and winced. "Poor piano. Look what those philistines did."

The key tops had been stripped without any finesse, leaving a mess of glue and damaged wood as raw as a gnawed cuticle. He looked closer. Then he saw it. Here and there a chip of white gleamed among the splinters. He knew what that meant.

He ran a fingertip over one, and felt the unmistakable silky hardness of elephant ivory.

He shook his head and shut the fall board. Then he reached up to cut the thin plastic strap holding the lid closed. He opened up the lid, and a desiccant bag fell out of the case at his feet.

Piano manufacturers always put a couple of bags of desiccant granules in their instruments to soak up any moisture in the air and keep the felt and wood innards from mildewing. About the size of a paperback book, they could be tucked into spare corners inside the case and forgotten until a piano tuner came along to throw them away.

Luke bent to pick up the bag, and frowned a little. There was something different about it. The cheap gray fabric pouch was printed with the standard "Dessicant—Do Not Eat" warning in English, French, Spanish, and Chinese. But the stuff inside was heavier and packed tighter than usual. After a second, Luke shrugged and tossed the bag into the pile of wrapping and other junk. He looked inside the case and frowned again.

There were more desiccant bags piled up along the rim. A lot more—at least twenty. China must be terrified of mildew.

Luke scooped out the bags and dumped them in the trash pile. Then he scanned the strings and action, the glue joints in the bridge and soundboard. All fairly standard. He gently closed the lid with a little pat. He felt sorry for the poor beast. It wasn't the best instrument. Not a Steinway, or even a Kawai. Still, with enough time and effort, he thought he could get a respectable tone out of it.

He carried the heavy bundle of packaging junk to the nearest maintenance closet and stuffed it in a trash bin. Then he collected his ramps and pads and packed them away in his truck.

When he came back inside the building, he found the receptionist standing at her desk with a small cluster of other people. Well-dressed, slightly flabby office-worker types. A couple of the women giggled and fluttered. The men attempted to suck in their guts. All of them were staring at him with wide eyes.

They had been watching him this entire time, he realized. He must have put on quite a show. He had the urge to take a bow.

"That was amazing," the receptionist said. "It took four guys just to get that thing off the truck, and you moved it around like it was Styrofoam."

Luke shrugged. "It's all a matter of leverage."

"Oh, don't be so modest." She leaned her boobs toward him. "It's also a matter of muscle."

He moved his biceps out of clutching range. "Right. Could I have my check now, please?"

She glanced up at the gallery. "But you haven't finished the job yet. It's still on its side."

"Well, that part I do need some help with. I can put on the first two legs by myself, but someone has to hold the corner of the piano up while I crawl underneath and attach the third leg." He turned toward the office workers. "Maybe a volunteer ..."

At those magic words, his small crowd of admirers vanished into thin air.

"I guess not. I'll have to find a partner and make separate arrangements to come set it up. Anyway, the piano is in place, as we agreed."

The receptionist licked her frozen lips. "Why don't we discuss your payment over lunch? I'm due for a long," she ran a fondling gaze over his chest and stomach, landing on his crotch, "lunch."

"I'm not the slightest bit hungry," Luke said steadily. In fact, he was starving, but he had the distinct impression that food was not on the proposed agenda here.

"Not even a nibble?"

"I'm actually considering bulimia."

Fuming, she finally wrote him out a check.

He put the check in his wallet, resolving to cash it right

away on the off chance it wouldn't bounce. Then he looked at the receptionist expectantly.

The receptionist stared back.

He said, "I've done my part. Now how about Mr. Castillo's address and phone number?"

"Yes, about that. I've reconsidered," she said, once again the ice-cold professional. "It wouldn't be appropriate to give out that information. But I'd be happy to give Mr. Castillo a message to call you as soon as he can."

Luke reached out and drummed his fingers on the desk, once, slowly. "You know, I could put that piano right back on the street where I found it."

Thirty seconds later, he was out on the steaming sidewalk, the address for Eduardo Castillo safely entered into the GPS on his phone. He roused the truck and rattled off, headed for a place called Di Lido.

4

DI LIDO TURNED out to be one of a chain of man-made islands strung across Biscayne Bay. Or were islands in Florida called keys? Luke kind of thought they were.

As his truck rumbled over the toll bridge and out over the absurdly blue water, he saw the first of the perfectly oval landmasses shimmering ahead, crowded with white mansions and ringed with sleek boats. They looked very glamorous and civilized, but he wasn't letting his guard down. Like past explorers of strange tropical islands, he intended to proceed with extreme caution, in case the natives proved hostile.

But apart from a few appalled stares at the truck from passing BMW and Lexus drivers, he forged through to the interior of Di Lido with no trouble. He followed a palm-lined street around the southern curve of the island to the address marked by the GPS flag on his phone, and shuddered to a stop at the side of the road. He got out of the truck and walked to the head of the glass-smooth driveway, pausing to give the place a once-over.

Luke's work had taken him to plenty of McMansions,

the natural habitat of the piano. But the Castillo residence would make the lakeside villas of Minnesota hide their porticoes in shame.

It was a massive Spanish Mediterranean pile of white stucco and red tile. A shadowy veranda ran along the front and extended into a deep carport to one side of the house, where a Bentley sat in aristocratic repose. On the other side, a wrought iron gate caged in a teeming tropical garden.

Past the looming house he caught a dreamy glimpse of the Miami skyline far across the turquoise plane of Biscayne Bay.

The ocean breeze hissed and waved among the palm trees, but the house itself was quiet and still, the windows shadowed holes in the white façade. They gave him the twitchy sensation of being watched out of deep eye sockets.

A furtive movement attracted his attention back to the garden beside the house, and he discovered he wasn't paranoid after all. He really *was* being watched. An elderly lady was staring at him out of the foliage.

"Hello?" Luke called out, starting up the driveway to the garden gate. She didn't move or speak as he approached.

Luke stopped at the gate and studied her over the scrolling ironwork. With her shapeless and colorless housedress, sturdy shoes, and neat bun of silver hair, she could have been an illustration for the term "housekeeper." But the shrewd little black eyes in her walnut of a face were not the least bit servile.

Along with McMansions, Luke's work had put him into contact with plenty of little old ladies, the natural companions of the piano. And for some reason they usually liked him, fluttering and flirting in a motherly sort of way. So he smiled easily and said, "Good morning, ma'am. Is this the Castillo residence?"

No response, except for a further wrinkling around the mouth. She weighed him up for a long, unnerving moment, and unleashed a storm of Spanish.

Luke was at a total loss. His only experience with foreign languages was dozing through German class in high school. But then he heard *"el piano"* amid the jumble of vowels and rolling "r"s.

"Excuse me, did you say *piano?*"

The old lady paused and gave him another purse-lipped, measuring look. More Spanish. This time he heard the words *Brett* and *Kowalski*.

Luke nearly waggled around like a bloodhound catching a scent. "Yes, I'd like to talk to Mr. Castillo about Brett Kowalski and the pianos, ma'am."

She was already vanishing into the garden, tossing an order to *"venga conmigo"* over her shoulder.

"Ma'am?" Luke pushed open the gate and stepped into the garden. He cast an unsettled glance at the spiky, shiny leaves and flowers crowding around him. The soundtrack to *Little Shop of Horrors* looped through his head.

He hurried after the housekeeper down a path through the rampant jungle and emerged onto a long, tiled veranda along the side of the house where three sets of French doors led into the dim interior. He glimpsed the old lady's hem swishing through the shadows of the first door, which stood ajar. He called out, "Ma'am?"

"El piano está aquí," her voice drifted out to him.

Shooting a last suspicious glare at an encroaching wax myrtle, Luke followed her into the house.

When his eyes had adjusted to the dim light, he saw he was in a large room that resembled nothing so much as King Tut's treasure chamber. Chairs, tables, cabinets, pillows, bowls, boxes, statues, rugs, hangings, paintings, fans, screens, baskets, trinkets, tchotchkes, and thingamabobs surrounded him in a horde of overwhelming colors and textures. And every single item looked obscenely expensive.

When he managed to pick out the housekeeper amid the riotous mass of stuff, he found she was gesturing grandly to something half-hidden behind a painted screen.

Luke waded through a scattering of ottomans and pushed aside the screen. Kowalski, Castillo, and the Chinese pianos instantly vanished from his mind.

Before him stood a 1935 special edition Mason and Hamlin grand piano with a walnut case and ornately turned William and Mary style legs. He moved closer, entranced. "Aren't you a beauty," he breathed. He reached out to run his hand over the closed fall board and touched the satiny finish over a burled inlaid medallion.

The old lady was saying something else, something that sounded like "Esmeralda." He barely heard her. He lifted the fall board and saw with relief that the original ivory key tops had been replaced with modern plastic. He set his fingertips on them and stroked lightly. Dusty.

He played an arpeggio and winced. It was at least a half step out of tune and the action was sticky. It probably hadn't been touched in years.

He walked around to open the lid. He found more dust, but it was otherwise immaculate, a model of the fine craftsmanship of the early twentieth century. "How long have you had this piano?" he asked as he bent over to examine the pin block.

There was no response.

"Ma'am?" Tearing his gaze away from the Mason and Hamlin, he raised his head, thinking he'd take another shot at communicating with the old lady.

She'd vanished. He looked around the room carefully,

in case she'd camouflaged herself under a pile of cushions, or maybe fallen into an oversized pot, but it appeared that she really had left.

For a wistful moment, he held out the hope that she'd gone to get him a plate of fresh-baked cookies. She had the cookie-pusher look about her. And, aside from a quick and dirty calorie refuel at a drive-through back in downtown Miami, he hadn't eaten much lately.

It's more likely she went to tell Mr. Castillo that you're here, he told himself sternly. And that's what he should be focusing on, wasn't it? He couldn't get distracted by baked goods or pianos in distress.

He reluctantly closed up the lid and fall board. He excavated a sofa from a pile of pillows and sat on it for a bit, but soon he was up again, wandering back through the treasure trove to moon over the Mason and Hamlin.

God, I would love to play you, he thought, running his fingers over the fall board again.

It had been a long time since he had played. He'd lost his own piano at the same time as he'd lost his house. Not that he could have fit it into his new studio apartment. Except for occasionally sneaking a little one-on-one time with his clients' pianos, he'd been out of luck for more than six months. Times like this, when he saw an instrument this fine, he missed his music even worse than usual.

He could just imagine what the Mason and Hamlin sounded like when it was well tuned and regulated. Round, warm, expressive notes filled his mind, something from Liszt, maybe, until he could almost hear the music shimmering through the silent room.

Until he just couldn't take it anymore.

He slipped through the French doors and hurried back through the garden and up the driveway to his truck. He got his tool kit out of the cab, then trotted back around the house and entered the treasure room again.

A careful look around told him that it was still as quiet as a pharaoh's tomb. He was free to indulge in a little vigilante piano tuning.

He lifted the lid and fall board, called up the tuning app on his phone, and placed it above the keyboard where he could see it easily.

He got his tuning hammer out of his tool case and took his place in front of the keys. He leaned over to place the hammer tenderly on the first pin. "Don't worry," he murmured. "I'm going to take good care of you."

5

ESMERALDA SHIFTED to a new position on the hood of the Porsche, the skin on her hip and elbow sizzling as the photographer lined up another shot. Beyond the green privacy fence screening them off from the rest of the beach, she could hear the caterwauling of a pack of fratboys on permanent spring break. Having sniffed out a swimsuit shoot, they'd been working themselves up to a loud lather for the past half hour.

She wondered how long they'd be kept at bay by the middle-aged bodybuilder in charge of the studio's security. Sometimes the beefhead would take a break from eyeballing Esmeralda to cast a desultory warning glance at the fratboys from between the screens. But mostly he busied himself sitting on a stool and scratching his 'roid rash.

Esmeralda had been busy lolling around on the car, then rolling on the sand, then frolicking in the ocean. Now she was back on the car again, and nearly at the end of her already micron-thin rope.

She sent a bitchy look at the camera just as the shot

clicked. It would probably turn out to be the best photo of the bunch, with her luck.

Under the refreshment table, an air-raid siren suddenly went off in her purse. She bolted upright. Anita's special ringtone. It had sounded only three or four times before. Anita didn't like mobile phones and wouldn't even call one unless it was an emergency on the order of a massive coronary or a military intervention in Cuba.

Heart suddenly racing, she yelled, "Water break," and darted off the car to the refreshment table, deaf to the photographer's swearing.

She barreled past Marco, who had been lounging by the ice bucket and lazily texting. Snatching up her purse, she pulled her phone out. "Anita? What is it? Is something wrong with Papa?" she said in Spanish.

"No, no, Maria Esmeralda," Anita said soothingly. "It's nothing like that. It's the piano man you called me about. He came to see your papa."

"What? Brett Kowalski showed up at the house?" *¡Pendejo!*

"That was the name he said. He's in the library."

"You mean he's still there? You let him in the house? *Why?*"

Anita was silent for a moment. "I thought you needed to speak to him. It is what you wanted, isn't it? And I can't talk to him myself. The poor man doesn't know Spanish." Anita heartily pitied anyone too uncivilized to speak Spanish.

"Is he upsetting Papa?"

"No, *niña*, your papa is still resting."

Esmeralda thought fast. "Okay, good. I'm coming home to talk to him. I'll be there in a few minutes. Just keep him busy for a little while, all right?"

"Oh, he's busy enough," Anita said mysteriously.

As she ended the call, Marco, the shameless eavesdropper, said, "Listen, *fruitabomba*, far be it from me to give you advice—"

"Not too far, obviously."

"Running off in the middle of a shoot is going to give you a reputation as a flake, and flakes don't get primo modeling gigs like this one. This might end your career."

"You think?" she said hopefully, dragging her sandals out of her bag and shoving them onto her feet. She had already wound down her social media profile, and if she was forced to officially retire early because of this, well, whatthefuckever. "Thanks for worrying about me, Marco, but I gotta do what I gotta do. And right now, I gotta go change. Tell your boss I'm going to lunch, will you?"

Just then, the flimsy green fabric of the privacy screen bulged and split with a loud rip. A beery fratboy flopped through the opening onto the sand in front of them like a beached walrus. He caught sight of Esmeralda and let out a bellow. The rest of his pack immediately piled through the fence after him.

"*Cojeme*," she said, and sprinted for the parking lot.

"*Chao pescao*, sugarbun," Marco called, waving her off.

The photographer squalled in outrage at her escape and gave chase, brandishing his camera. Behind him the fratboys rallied a quick pursuit, and the useless bouncer finally got off his stool and lumbered along at the rear.

Esmeralda raced ahead of the cavalcade toward the nearby hotel parking lot where her snappy red-and-white-striped Mini Cooper gleamed cheerily amid the sea of convertibles and SUVs. She dove into her car, cranked the engine, and squealed off at Daytona speed, leaving the fratboys staggering hopelessly in her tailwind as the photographer shook his fist in her rearview mirror.

"Baby, Vin Diesel's got nothing on you," she crowed to her reflection in the mirror as she whipped out onto the A1A.

But by the time she pulled into the carport at the house twenty minutes later, the triumph of her successful getaway had bubbled off and her original fury at Brett Kowalski was rushing back in to take its place.

She got out of the Mini and steamed up to the front door, ready to drag the invader out by any convenient body part. Anita opened the door just as she got there. The housekeeper was wearing an odd, speculative expression.

"Is he still here?" Esmeralda asked in Spanish as she stepped into the dim front hall.

Anita nodded. "In the library. He's tuning the piano."

"He's what? We have a piano?"

"Yes, child. You had lessons when you were six, remember?"

"Oh, yeah." With some effort, she called up a memory of a despairing teacher drooping over the music for "Mary Had a Little Lamb." Not one of her father's better investments, that piano. "What on earth is he tuning it for?"

Anita shrugged. "It's keeping him busy, like you said to."

Esmeralda heard a faint musical sound echoing along the tiled hallway. One single note, then a pause, then the same note again. Then again. Then *again*.

Unfortunately she could also hear a querulous voice drifting down the sweeping staircase from the second floor. *Mierda*. Papa was awake. He'd be down to investigate the noise soon. She had to get this presumptuous slimeball out of the house immediately.

"Keep Papa busy while I deal with this, would you?" she said to Anita. Then she hustled down the hall to the library, Anita's suggestion that she, "Put on some clothes, *por Dios,*" echoing behind her.

The library door was cracked open, and she stopped to peek through the gap before going in. She saw a man in profile, leaning over the forgotten grand piano. He was so caught up in his task he didn't notice her sudden appearance, so she had plenty of time to size him up. And she had a lot of sizing to do, because everything she was seeing was the exact opposite of what she'd expected.

She had spitefully envisioned someone weedy, weak-chinned, and potbellied. But this guy was actually handsome, with sandy blond hair and fine Scandinavian features. Maybe a larger jaw than strictly necessary, but undoubtedly good-looking. And he was gigantic, more than six and a half feet tall and strong as a rhinoceros, if she didn't miss her guess.

Esmeralda's years of modeling had made her an excellent judge of physique, and she could tell that what he had under his white button-down shirt, khaki pants, and brown tie wasn't the carefully sculpted lumpiness that came from a pill bottle and a Nautilus machine. Instead he was packed with the kind of solid muscle that denoted pure brute power.

Her side view showed her a wide neck easing down into massive shoulders, a lean waist, long, sinewy arms and legs, and a rock-hard butt, which happened to be presented very nicely at the moment as he bent over the instrument.

One broad, long-fingered hand delicately touched the keys, the other grasped a wrench-like thing attached to the innards of the piano. She watched in silence as he played a note, his gaze intent on the screen of the phone set on the ledge above the keyboard. He tweaked the wrench and played the note again, tipping his ear toward the strings, his face turning toward her. What he heard must have pleased him, because his finely cut mouth curved in a little smile.

And Esmeralda's lips parted in something more than astonishment. That smile instantly vaulted him from handsome to dangerously sexy.

Okay, enough of that crap. Dangerously sexy? Are you kidding? The man was here trying to peddle elephant parts. Not a thing sexy about that. But he might be more dangerous than she expected.

She just had to think of him as a big, strong animal in a really bad tie. And she knew exactly how to handle big, strong animals.

The first rule of animal training was to let them know that you were not to be fucked with. So as soon as she got her strangely rapid pulse back to normal she knocked open the door, strode through the room to stand next to the piano, and said, "What the hell do you think you're doing here?"

6

LUKE, at that moment leaning over a recalcitrant pin in the treble range, turned his bent head toward the imperious question and came eyeball-to-nipple with the most spectacular pair of breasts he had ever seen in real life. Or on a screen. Or even in his fevered imagination.

Cupped tenderly in a pink-and-blue confection of a bathing suit, the breasts, of perfect silky skin and buoyant firmness, heaved with angry breathing. Above the breasts, a husky voice went on, "I expected you to call, but showing up at my house uninvited is off limits."

"Uh—"

"If you want to do business, you'll need to extend me some basic professional courtesy. You'll need to respect my family's privacy."

"Ah—"

"You'll also need to stop staring at my tits for a minute."

"Trying," he said.

With a mighty effort, he yanked his eyes upward and focused them on a gorgeous scowling face. Tumbled waves of shining black hair, deep-brown eyes smoky with anger and eyeshadow, full red frowning lips, and an adorable, fiercely scrunched nose. Beautiful. No, *beautiful* was too insipid a word for this woman, who charged the air around her with energy. She was magnificent. Splendid. He stared, entranced.

"Are you having a stroke?" she asked.

"No! No stroke. Sorry. I'm so sorry, I'm … just not used to the way people dress here in Miami. I'm from Minnesota, and it's still really cold there, in April. Snow on the ground, you know. Slush, really, but still, not swimsuit weather at all."

She let him finish babbling, then lifted a smooth black eyebrow. "Really? The weather? That's the excuse you're going with?"

"Okay, no excuses. I'm really, just really— very sorry." He tried a deep, calming breath, but that only invited her tantalizing scent of hot skin, sea salt, and tropical lotion to weave through his lungs. He fought off a wave of intoxication.

Luke straightened to his full height. Adjusted his tie. Cleared his throat. Then he stuck out his hand for a handshake, before realizing he was still holding his tuning hammer. He put the hammer down on the piano bench next to him and tried again. "My name is—"

"I know who you are, and I know why you're here."

The treacherous receptionist must have called ahead to warn them he was coming. He put his hand down. "Well, I'd certainly like to say the same about you."

She blinked, an expression that might have been humor flashing across her face. Then her delicate jaw hardened. "I'm Esmeralda Castillo, of course."

Esmeralda. He tasted the name on his tongue. Beautiful. He knew that name. She was—

"I'm here," she continued, "because you have made me very unhappy."

Luke was confused. His ex-wife had taught him that he was fully capable of making women unhappy, but surely he hadn't been around this particular woman long enough to do his worst.

Then he remembered how he'd driven several clients clean out of their houses with the repetitive *plink ... plink ... plink* of a tuning. To some people, having to listen to that for hours on end was a form of torture fit for Guantanamo Bay.

"Is it the tuning that's upsetting you? I know it can get annoying, but you really have to play each note several times to get the partials right, and that's not even counting the pitch raise—"

"No, it is not the tuning that's upsetting me," she cut in, enunciating each word like she was talking to an imbecile. She paused, then asked, "Why *are* you messing with that piano, by the way?"

He managed to take his eyes off her long enough to glance at the open case. "Because it needed it. It's such a beautiful instrument I thought— I guess I thought it should sound beautiful too."

She watched him quizzically.

He blundered on. "I certainly didn't mean to presume on you, or Mr. Castillo. He's your—" He risked a quick peek down at her slender left hand. No ring. "Father?"

"That's right."

Father. Not husband. Luke nearly sagged in relief. Then he made himself recall that this was the shady-sounding female Kowalski had mentioned during that last phone call. What had he called her? *Hot.* And *very anxious to do a deal.* And the receptionist at the office said she was *trouble*.

She said, "You can't talk to Papa. Papa's retired. Roddy's in charge of the company now."

"Roddy?"

"Rodrigo Castillo. My cousin."

"Oh."

"And Roddy has already closed with another offer. He must have told you."

"Well—"

She shifted toward him slightly. "But you and I can still negotiate a deal of our own," she said, her whiskey voice a touch lower.

Luke swallowed, his heart starting to pound against his sternum. "We— we can?"

"I heard from a reliable source that you're interested in some related merchandise we have on hand. Something we'd need to keep strictly unofficial."

"Ah," he said, at sea once again.

"I'm the one you're going to want to talk to about that, not my cousin. The less he knows, the better. Look, this isn't the time or place for this discussion. We'll set up an appointment for tomorrow to discuss prices and distribution and so on, all right?"

Prices? Distribution? Luke tried to gather his swimsuit-addled thoughts together. "Lady, I think there's been some kind of misunderstanding—"

"Shh!" She whipped her head around to the hall door. Voices were drifting in from the hallway. She stilled, listening. Then she prowled over to the door, every movement lithe and sure.

Luke watched her, helpless to do anything else. Her limbs were long and smooth, her waist tiny, bottom high and curving. Her proportions were of such mathematical perfection that the equation could have been written by Euclid's dick. And they were only barely concealed by the swimsuit, which, as she leaned to peek through the door into the hall, was revealed to be a thong. He nearly swallowed his tongue.

She pulled her head back into the room and spun around to pierce him with her dark, fiery gaze. He found he couldn't breathe. She was simply too gorgeous to be real, a nymph fallen from Olympus.

"Shit," the divinity said, "he's coming downstairs. Quick, out the back door! Move your ass!" She hurried toward him, making shooing motions with her hands, trying to herd him back through the French doors behind him.

"Who?" he croaked.

"Papa!"

"But—"

"I told you, he can't see you, Mr. Kowalski," she hissed. "You have my number, so text me tonight and we'll set something up. Now scram."

Comprehension finally dawned. "You think— but I'm not—"

"Hey, Ez," came a voice from the patio door.

They both turned. A muscular, good-looking young man in his early twenties with brown skin, thick black hair, and a dark expression stood silhouetted in the open doorway. When he had their attention, he swaggered into the room. He was dressed in a suit that had to have cost more than Luke's entire wardrobe.

"Roddy," Esmeralda said, a wary note entering her voice.

So this was the cousin who had apparently reneged on the deal with Kowalski, Luke thought.

Another man appeared behind Roddy, this one equally well dressed but looking softer, slicker, and closer to Luke's age of twenty-eight, or possibly older. His quick, dark eyes ran over them, pausing for an infinitesimal moment on Luke before moving on to Esmeralda. An oil slick of a grin immediately spread over his face. "Easy, baby! Working hard, I see. Love the swimsuit. Is that a thong?"

Esmeralda's adorable nose wrinkled like a sewer line had just ruptured. "Juan," she said curtly, and turned back to her cousin. "What's he doing here, Roddy? And what are *you* doing here? I thought you were at the port all day today."

"We were, until Anita called us about our visitor," he said, jutting his chin toward Luke. "We had to skip lunch to come deal with this situation."

Esmeralda pressed her lips together. "Well it wasn't necessary. I had things under control." She glanced back toward the inner door.

"Yeah, no, I don't think so." Then his eyes raked Luke up and down. "So you're Brett Kowalski."

Now, Luke had a decision to make. Did he clear up the misunderstanding now, and get a few embarrassed laughs and a quick shove out the door? Or did he just run with this mistaken identity thing and see where it might lead?

The Castillos had obviously never met Kowalski. And just as obviously his "ironclad" deal with them had been more of an aluminum-foil-clad deal. They wouldn't be able to tell him where to find the guy even if he just asked them plainly.

But Esmeralda had said she'd been expecting Kowalski to contact her. And she'd hinted that she had another arrangement with him in the works, one that sounded perfectly underhanded and that she didn't want her family to know about.

If she learned she'd been blabbing about her schemes to a total stranger, she might clam up entirely, and his best chance to find Brett Kowalski and get back the Piano Tuners Guild seal and the money would be gone. But if he went along with her mistake, he could stick close to her until his quarry showed himself. And he could find out what quasi-legal shenanigans the former treasurer had embroiled the Guild in while he was at it.

He wasn't lying, he told himself. It was going undercover. Suppressing his relentlessly Lutheran upbringing, he held out his hand to Roddy and said, "Yes, I'm Brett Kowalski. You must be Rodrigo Castillo."

After a significant pause, Roddy took his hand, shook it once, and did a dead rat drop. He expression, like Esmeralda's had been, was a fine blend of anger and contempt. Which Luke understood perfectly now, since it was the same grimace he wore himself whenever he thought of Kowalski.

"This is Juan Hernandez, my consultant." Roddy tilted his chin toward the man by his side. "I believe you've talked to him before."

Juan peeled his eyes off Esmeralda and considered Luke for a long moment. His smug smile widened. "That's right. We've spoken a time or two, haven't we, Brett?"

"As you say," Luke replied warily. How much, he wondered, did Juan actually know about Kowalski? And what he might tell his boss? There was a sly glint in his eyes that Luke didn't like at all.

But whatever Juan's thoughts were, he was keeping them to himself for now. With a final smirk, he shambled off to sprawl on a nearby sofa and resumed leering at Esmeralda.

"If you're here to talk me into selling you the pianos, you're wasting your time," Roddy said. "I've accepted another offer."

Luke glanced at Esmeralda, but she was ignoring her cousin in favor of anxiously watching the hallway door. "Yes. So I've heard. But Ms. Castillo and I were just discussing something related—"

"There's nothing more to discuss. I'm the one who makes the decisions around here, no matter what Ez might have told you." He shot his cousin a resentful glare that Luke, who had siblings of his own, had no difficulty interpreting.

Juan clicked his tongue. "Going behind our backs, Easy? Bad girl."

"We can talk about it later. Mr. Kowalski was just leaving." She turned a glare on him like lasers shooting out of her eyes.

"No, not later," Roddy said. "I want to get this resolved now. I have important business in the next few days, if you haven't forgotten, and I don't need to clean up any more of your messes. So—"

"What's going on here?" a well-worn voice growled from the hallway.

Everyone turned toward the man who had appeared at the inner door and was raking them all with a commanding stare.

"Papa," Esmeralda said, her voice tight.

Here, then, was Eduardo Castillo.

He was a moderately tall, handsome man of about sixty-five, with thick black hair streaked silver at the temples. He wore a light-colored suit even classier than his nephew's, and an expression of kingly displeasure.

Behind him in the doorway loomed another man, this one younger and shorter but twice as wide. He had a good-but-not-great suit awkwardly draped over his slabby muscle, and small, alert eyes in a broad, brown face.

Together the boss man and his bodyguard made quite a striking sight. At first.

As they walked slowly into the room, a few incongruous details struck warning notes. Castillo's shirt, for instance, was buttoned crooked. There were shadows of old stains on the front and sleeves of his beautiful suit. His cheeks showed patches of stubble his razor had missed. And his arrogant mask was slipping, muddled anxiety leaking around the edges. The bodyguard hovered close by, his eyes on his boss, his attitude not so much protective as supportive.

A suspicion bloomed in Luke's mind. He glanced around at the others in the room, gauging their reactions. Juan had on the same look of contemptuous amusement he'd worn from the start, Roddy looked tense and worried, and Esmeralda looked afraid. Not afraid *of* her father, he suddenly saw. Afraid *for* him.

"I was watching those fools on the ... the ..." Castillo gestured shakily, "picture ... box ... *la tele* ..." He drifted off, his eyes vague.

Luke's suspicion grew to a certainty.

"You were watching TV, Papa?" Esmeralda said in a gentler tone than Luke had yet heard her use.

Castillo looked back at her, but his gaze remained blurred. "*Sí*. I heard voices and ... noises. I said to Ignacio, 'Who is in my home?' but *el tonto* said he didn't know." He paused to frown at the man by his shoulder, who stayed as still and inscrutable as an Easter Island head.

The old man turned his frown on the rest of them. "You think you can ... can fool me, but I will find out what is going on here." His wandering gaze fell on Luke. "And who might you be?"

No one said anything, so Luke stepped forward and

reached out his hand once again. Castillo shook it, a fine tremor in his withered fingers. "Brett Kowalski, sir," Luke said, the lie curdling on his tongue. *Tricking a dementia sufferer? Low, Hansen. Very, very low.* But he was well in the hole now, and had to keep on digging.

Castillo's face sharpened, and he favored Luke with a steely perusal that must have been daunting once. "Kowalski? What kind of name is that? Do you have business with me?"

Out of the corner of his eye, he could see Esmeralda glaring at him again. But this time there was a desperate plea in her look.

"No," Luke said quietly. "I only came to discuss something with Ms. Castillo. It wasn't very important."

"Ms. Castillo ... oh. Her." The old man cast a dismissive glance at his daughter, and seemed to lose interest in the subject.

But then Juan said loudly from the couch, "That's right, not important at all. Just those pianos in the last shipment from Cartagena. You remember. The Chinese pianos with the bad keys." He smiled up at the older man, his long-lashed eyes wide and innocent.

A strange tension suddenly charged the air. Roddy and Ignacio stiffened and Esmeralda sucked in a sharp breath.

Castillo himself just stared at Juan for a long moment, his mouth falling open in a soft, confused wobble. "The keys," he mumbled. "The keys. The keys, the keys thekeysthekeysthekeys—" His voice rose to a high, keening pitch. He balled his hands and brought them up to pound clumsily at the sides of his head.

"Papa," Esmeralda said, an anguished note in her voice. She reached for her father, but he stumbled away from her, arms flailing. He knocked over a spindly lamp and lurched into a solid wooden table, half muttering, half yelling in Spanish. He grabbed at the objects sitting on the table and flung them away.

"*¡Matones!*" he yelled. "*¡Asesinos!*" He hurled a carved figurine and a candlestick to the ground and was lunging for a silver box when Ignacio appeared beside him and gently took it out of his hand, speaking Spanish to him in a low, calm voice.

Luke retreated to a spot a few feet away and sank down onto an ottoman, trying to make himself invisible.

Ignacio continued talking in that same lulling ripple as Castillo's agitated movements slowed, and he started listing over wearily, leaning on the table. A trail of saliva leaked from his mouth.

"Papa, let me help you back upstairs," Esmeralda said, reaching out to her father.

The old man didn't answer but swatted at her irritably. "Rodrigo, *hijo* ..."

Roddy rushed forward. As he pushed past his cousin he hissed, "Just stay back. Haven't you done enough?" To his uncle he said, "I'm here, *Tio*." He took the trembling hand held out to him and let the old man lean on his arm as they slowly made their way out the door. Ignacio followed behind. Esmeralda watched the door click shut behind them, her eyes huge and her cheeks pale under her makeup.

Luke desperately searched his stock of platitudes for something that might dispel the cloud of unhappiness smothering her. But Juan was the first to break the silence.

With a leisurely motion, the consultant shot the cuff of his Italian suit and glanced down at his heavy gold watch. "You'd better not let the old man keep Roddy too long, Easy. We have a meeting with the Zapata people in an hour." He got to his feet.

Esmeralda turned on him, the banked energy in her flaring to life again. She shot a look at Juan hot enough to incinerate him on the spot. "You did that on purpose! You know what happens whenever someone mentions those *carajo* pianos to him."

Juan smiled easily and nastily. "Now, how would I know that? Just because he threw that temper tantrum a couple of weeks ago? I thought the whole incident would have rotted right out of his brain by now."

"*Comemierda*," she hissed. "How dare you talk about my father like that? Who the hell do you think you are?"

"I think I'm the man who's pulling your family's company out of the shitter after your crazy Papa drove it in there. Do you think you could still afford to live in this fancy house and flash your ass all over Miami Beach if it weren't for me? You ought to be down on your knees thanking me, Easy. In fact, I can't think of any better place for you to be. How about we go to my car so you can show me how grateful you are? Finally give you something useful to do with that mouth of yours." He stepped toward her and lifted a hand to fondle a lock of her hair, or maybe grab her boob.

Esmeralda folded her arms across her chest. Not defensively. More like she was Mr. Clean and she was about to use Juan for a scrubbie sponge. "Remember what I said would happen the next time you tried to put your hands on me?"

Juan instantly dropped his hands in front of his crotch. "Bitch. You think you're too good for me? You're going to regret it, I fucking promise."

"That's enough!"

Juan and Esmeralda jumped and turned toward him. That was when Luke realized that the voice that had barked out the order was in fact his own.

The other two had apparently forgotten he was there, because they stared, confounded, as if the ottoman he was sitting on had leapt to life and started speaking Sanskrit.

Juan flushed. "You have something to say, Mr. *Kowalski*?"

He stood up, not taking his eyes off the little twizzleprick. "Don't talk to the lady like that."

Juan started to look nervous. "This is none of your business."

True. Nevertheless, he took a long step forward to loom over the smaller man.

Luke knew he could look imposing when he chose. Around age sixteen, after getting a few terrified shrieks from small children, he had developed the habit of trying to look unthreatening, which involved speaking quietly, moving carefully, and sitting down a lot. But there had been a time or two in high school and college when he had averted drunken scuffles just by straightening his shoulders and frowning.

So he straightened, frowned, and said, "Apologize. Now."

It worked better than he could have hoped. Usually in situations like this, guys would bluster and snarl before backing down, just to save face. Not Juan. The creep crumpled faster than an empty can of Red Bull.

He stared up at Luke, the blood draining from his face, and gave a froglike gulp. He turned to Esmeralda with a sickly smile. "Sorry, Easy. Just joking around. Ha, ha. No hard feelings, right?"

Esmeralda was staring at Luke, an odd look in her eyes. But she spared Juan a disdainful glance. "Fine. Now get out."

"I'm waiting for Roddy," he whined.

"Then wait for him outside. I've got to talk to Mr. Kowalski about something."

Juan's eyes darted to Luke, then slid away. A strange smile flickered on his face. "Yeah. Right. You and Mr. *Kowalski* have a nice talk," he said, managing to imbue every single word with a sneering insinuation. But he slunk out the patio entrance without any more trouble.

Esmeralda stomped after him, slammed the door shut and locked it. Then she spun on Luke, a glint in her eye.

Luke braced himself.

7

IT WAS clear to Esmeralda that she was going to have to muster up some finesse to deal with the large and overmastering presence in her house, since brute force had failed so far. In spite of all her efforts to prevent it, this Kowalski guy had entangled himself in a sticky family situation, and now she had to unstick him, one way or another.

And then she would get him to spill his guts about trading in poached elephant ivory. She owed it to the US Fish and Wildlife Service, who had asked for her help. More importantly, she owed it to the dead elephants, who couldn't ask.

But first, damage control. She said, "I'm sorry you had to get involved in that."

"I'm not. After what he said to you, I would have been happy to pick him up and bounce him out the door."

She waved a dismissive hand. "Don't worry about Juan. It was really nice of you to stand up for me like that ..." She paused to reflect on the novelty of having a guy try to protect her. She scoured her memory for the last time one had, and came up with zilch.

Shrugging that away, she continued. "But it wasn't necessary. I can handle Juan. I have a lot of experience with that sort of thing."

He looked faintly horrified.

She felt compelled to explain. "Some guys just get that way when they finally figure out that I'm never going to sleep with them." She leveled a look at him to make sure he got the point.

Wisely, all he said was, "Oh." Only his North Woods accent made it sound more like "oo."

Esmeralda almost smiled. It was like talking to an escapee from season two of *Fargo*. "Anyway, I wasn't talking about that idiot Juan. I was referring to what happened with my father."

"Oo," he said again. "Yah, I'm sorry about that, too. I never would have come here and bothered him if I had known about his, uh, condition. Alzheimers?"

She nodded. "Early onset. And there's no reason why you would know about it. The family is keeping it quiet for now." She let a hard warning note creep into her voice. "Can I assume you won't discuss what happened today with anyone?"

He looked offended that she would even ask. "Of course. I don't gossip about people's personal problems. Or anything else, actually."

She nodded. He'd had a chance to cause trouble before and hadn't taken it. She'd give him the benefit of the doubt, on this at any rate.

"Will Mr. Castillo be all right?" he asked.

At this gentle question, a too-familiar sensation burned behind her eyes and tightened the back of her throat. Keeping her voice steady, she said, "He should be. His episodes don't last long, and he'll forget it happened soon enough. Roddy's presence always helps. He'll stay with him until he's calm again."

"Why did mentioning those pianos trigger an— an episode?"

"We don't know, and we certainly can't ask him." She could hear the bewilderment in her own voice. Sometimes it was so hard to adjust to the change in her father. In the old days when he'd had to field problems with Customs, he might have grumbled over "excessive regulation by the socialist *carajos* in government," but he wouldn't fly into a rage. He'd had a good relationship with law enforcement, always operating strictly by the book.

But everything had gone sideways two weeks ago, after the cargo ship carrying the pianos came in to port. After she discovered the ivory problem and took it to her contact in Fish and Wildlife.

Frustrated by Roddy's foot-dragging and attempts to shuffle off responsibility, she'd felt she had no choice but to take matters into her own hands. Off she'd gone to interview with Alistair Truitt, only to return to find her father heavily medicated, his home office trashed, a family freak-out in progress, and the blame for it all laid at her door.

She passed a hand over her hair. "This business has been *jodido* from the very start. I almost think I shouldn't have—" She shut her mouth and scowled at her visitor. Sneaky bastard. A few sympathetic questions delivered in that quiet, rumbly voice of his, and he almost had her ready to sob out her secrets to him.

He smiled slightly. "Is that why you were trying so hard to get rid of me? You were protecting your father?"

"That was one of many reasons," she said in an acid tone. But her heart wasn't in it.

Not quite able to meet his steady gaze, her eyes faltered

downward and caught on the objects her father had thrown on the floor. She knelt to pick them up while she marshaled her thoughts. Time to redirect. Focus on the intelligence-gathering mission, not her family drama. Elephants. Ivory. Right.

Now, what was the best approach to take with this man, who stubbornly refused to be crammed back in her mental box marked "fourth string player?"

She cast a glance up at him through her lashes, trying to figure him out. It wasn't easy. His face was naturally austere, his expressions subtle. His eyes, which she couldn't help but notice were a rather beautiful shade of blue-gray, had a certain amused detachment in them.

Except sometimes when he looked at her, like now. As he stared down at her on the floor in front of him, color burned over his hard cheekbones and his eyes turned distinctly glassy. Anyone who couldn't guess what he thinking would have to be in a coma.

Realizing he was in danger of sliding into another cleavage-induced trance, she swiftly got to her feet. On the way up she sneaked a tiny peek at the front of his pants, and, yep, it was getting tight down there. She deposited the collected knick-knacks back on the table and said briskly, "Like I was saying before, we need to set up an appointment for tomorrow to talk things over. Right now I have to get back to my job, assuming I still have one."

He shook himself. "Job? You have a job?"

"Of course I have a job. I do swimsuit modeling. Catalogs, ads, that kind of thing."

"Oo. That explains ..."

Her resident devil poked her with his tiny pitchfork, making her say, "Explains what?"

"The, uh ..."

"Yes?"

"The ..." He gestured feebly.

"The swimsuit?"

"Right."

"Fabulous, isn't it? It's on loan from a top designer. I had to rush off in the middle of an ad shoot when I heard you were here at the house. Didn't have time to change." *Poke, poke* went the tiny pitchfork. "I have to get it back to its owners soon, before they chase me down and strip it off me," she added with a little purr.

"I see." His color deepened, and he stared resolutely at a point above her left shoulder.

She bit down on a smile. She really shouldn't enjoy busting his balls like this. But his valiant attempts to be gentlemanly were just so ... cute.

And there she went again, thinking hot and squishy thoughts about an ivory salesman. He might be cute, he might be kindly toward her father and gallant toward herself, but he was still an ivory salesman.

Annoyed afresh, she went to the hall door and opened it sharply. "I'll see you out."

By the time they had reached the front door, she saw he had resumed his Stoic The Viking expression. "When will you be available to talk about our business agreement?" he said.

She stopped and faced him square on. Or as square on as she could with her neck craned up. "Can you meet tomorrow at nine o'clock?"

"Sure. Where?"

"I have a certain place in mind. It would be better if I drove you there myself."

His eyes narrowed. "Where is this place?"

She unleashed one of her best camera-ready smiles on

him—slow, provocative, and mysterious, *à la* Mona Lisa. "I'll tell you tomorrow."

The smile worked. He looked down into her face, gray eyes now wide and dazzled, and said, "Okay." The way he said it made it sound like "oo-kee."

Cute. The thought intruded before she ruthlessly squashed it. "I'll come pick you up, then. Where are you staying?" she asked, businesslike again.

He blinked. "Ah, why don't I call you and give you the address tonight?"

"Text me," she said firmly.

He took his phone out of his pocket. "I'll need your phone number."

"I thought our mutual acquaintance gave you my number."

After the slightest pause, he said, "I'm afraid he overlooked it."

Dammit, Al. She rattled off her number, which he rather enthusiastically entered into his phone.

She found the purse she'd tossed onto the table near the door and got out her own phone. "You'd better give me your number too."

He did, with alacrity. Nothing then remained but to open the door and shepherd him through it. She caught the scent of soap and wood and the spice of clean sweat as he passed. *Sexy*, she thought before she could stop herself.

She followed him out onto the front step, where they exchanged goodbyes, and stood to see him off the property.

He took a few steps up the walkway, stopped, and turned back. "Listen, if I happen to call you before we meet tomorrow—" He shook his head. "Never mind."

If I happen to call you? There was something strange

about that phrasing. "No, wait," she said as he started to turn away. "What were you going to say?"

He looked back, and then he smiled at her, a full-face grin made up of one part boyish mischief and ten parts animal heat.

Her breath stopped. Amazingly, flame sparked low in her body and rushed upward to lick over her face. Good lord. Who knew she still had it in her to blush?

"I'll tell you tomorrow," he said, echoing her words from earlier.

"Okay," she whispered.

While she regained her balance, he walked up the driveway to a beater truck parked on the street, got in and drove off.

When he was out of sight she went back inside the house to get her bag, thinking hard. At some point in the last half-hour, she had decided to give Kowalski a chance to redeem himself. He had earned that much consideration. He would have the opportunity to reform his ways and spill every dirty ivory-trading secret to the authorities of his own free will.

But if he didn't take advantage of her generosity, then screw him. She would wring the information out of him another way and hang him out to dry without compunction, no matter how panty-melting his smile was.

She took out her phone again and hit a contact button. When the line picked up, she said, "Hi Al, it's Esmeralda. Listen, about this sting operation on Kowalski. I'm in. But we have to do things my way."

She listened for a minute, then sighed. "Yes, Al, I'm still wearing the thong. Now, what I want to do is this ..."

8

AFTER THE GRIM consumption of another drive-through burger, Luke found a motel for the night in a warren of streets and parking lots off Biscayne Boulevard in North Miami.

The place had one single virtue—it was cheap enough not to put further stress on his already traumatized wallet. But his fastidious soul winced as he carried his bags into his assigned room and looked around.

Everything he saw was chipped, cracked, or stained with fluids of unknown origin. A concoction of smoke, mold, and urine wafted through the atmosphere. The air conditioner was on its last gasp and there was no television. There was, however, a cockroach the size of a hamster in the bathroom sink.

Have I gone completely off my rocker? Luke wondered as he stared at the roach. A week ago he had been a normal guy living a normal life, and now he was in hot sheets hell, impersonating a con artist so that a filthy rich bikini babe would try to entice him into some nebulous criminal enterprise. "I barely recognize myself anymore," he said aloud.

The bug gave him a snooty twitch of its antennae, so Luke washed it down the gargling drain and went to text Esmeralda Castillo the motel's address.

He settled gingerly on the sagging bed with his phone and spent the next ten minutes typing and deleting such phrases as, "It was so wonderful meeting you" and "Counting down until I see you again," punctuated with emoticons.

And what in the name of all sanity do you think you're doing? he wondered as he erased another fatuous smiley face. This was a business meeting, not a date.

A date. With Esmeralda Castillo. The idea choked a laugh out of him, it was so inconceivable.

He hadn't gotten involved with many women over the years, but enough to know that Esmeralda Castillo was definitely not his type. He had always gone for calm, sensible females who fit well into his quiet and orderly life and who appreciated music as much as he did.

Like his ex-wife, for example, a paragon of propriety and levelheadedness. Or so he had thought before she rode off into the sunset on her rodeo cowboy. Hey, at least she was a proficient keyboardist.

Esmeralda was another order of being entirely. She was temperamental, switching from avenging goddess to tragic waif to sex kitten with a flicker of her long eyelashes. She was without an ounce of musical ability, judging by her abandoned piano. And as for her morals ... well, anyone who would voluntarily have dealings with the likes of Brett Kowalski would have to be either bent or stupid, and Esmeralda was certainly not stupid.

So, no, she was definitely not the right kind of woman for him. At all.

And that is nothing but sour grapes bullshit, a caustic voice whispered inside his head.

A woman like Esmeralda could get a date with any man in the world if she wanted to. Any man. She probably had a standing line of movie stars and billionaires and presidents of small countries ready to fling themselves at her dainty feet. So what chance was there that out of all her teaming, swarming masses of lovestruck dudes she would choose Luke Hansen, piano tuner? None. None whatsoever.

In the end, he merely sent the motel's address, his room number, and a terse "@ nine tomorrow." Then he tossed his phone onto the rickety nightstand and started his nighttime routine, resolving to put his nonexistent personal relationship with Esmeralda out of his mind.

It wasn't like he didn't have more important issues to worry about, he reminded himself as he brushed his teeth. Issues like where she was planning on taking him tomorrow and what kind of illegal goatfuck he would find when he got there.

He could only hope to learn something useful before the real Brett Kowalski contacted Esmeralda and blew his clumsy deception to smithereens. He had tried to think of some way to head off the possibility as he was leaving that afternoon, but his ingenuity simply didn't stretch that far. He always had been a lousy liar. If he sustained the charade all the way through the meeting tomorrow he'd be astounded.

He undressed down to his briefs, put his clothes away neatly, and rolled into bed with the feeling that he was in for an uneasy night.

He was right. The night was abysmal, and not just because of his worries or the bedspring digging into his back. For one thing, sunset at Roach Motel signaled the beginning of a symphony of roaring engines, screams, moans, and heavy bass woofers, with the gasping rattle of the air conditioner providing counterpoint.

But more disturbing than the racket, or even the anxiety about tomorrow, was the persistent ache in his balls that had been dogging him since the first second he had set eyes on Esmeralda.

Damn. Now he'd gone and done it. He'd avoided thinking about her for an entire two minutes, but here she was, back again. He lay stiffly in bed, eyes screwed shut, making a forlorn attempt to barricade his mind against her.

No use. She barged right on in and hit the replay button on his memory deck.

Over and over again her mindboggling breasts bounced and swayed one good lean away from his face. Her whiskey voice scolded him. Her perfectly sculpted butt cheeks wiggled away. Her smile seared into him. Over and over and over.

God almighty. His eyes snapped open and he glared down the length of his body to where his adamantine dick was now tenting the sheet. "Cut it out right now. She will never, in a hundred thousand million billion years, want you. So forget about her and go to sleep."

Stupid bastard didn't listen, bobbing insistently against his stomach. He ran the heel of his hand up the shaft, tempted to pull it out and convince it to relax with his own hairy palm.

But he really, truly, did not want to add to the astronomical sperm count that must already be contained in this motel room. A man had to maintain some standards.

So instead he stuffed his earbuds in and called up Debussy on his phone, turning the volume up as loud as he could. Then he rolled over on top of his surly cock and let the tender notes of the *Preludes* jackhammer into his eardrums until he was too addled to think at all.

By morning Luke was too tired to try to sleep anymore, so he risked a shower in the crusty bathroom, shaved, dressed, and stepped out of his door to forage for breakfast.

The air had once again draped itself over the stucco and asphalt of the city like a gigantic soaking wet blanket. Either the heat or the past night's frolics must have worn his neighbors out, because the motel was finally silent. The only signs of human habitation were the piles of bottles and cans, the used condoms and needles, and the puddles of vomit he could see wherever he looked.

He ducked his head against the pounding sunlight and made ready to trek through the drifts of trash in the parking lot to the fast food restaurant on the other side.

As he stepped onto the walkway, his gaze fell on an alligator lawn ornament someone had placed on the strip of cigarette-speckled dirt next to his door.

Kind of a strange landscaping choice, he thought hazily. Funny he hadn't noticed it last night. He bent down to examine it, and the lawn ornament blinked nictitating eyelids and opened an enormous set of yellowish teeth.

In an instant he was diving back into his room with an agility that would have dropped the jaw of his high school basketball coach. He slammed the door shut and leaned his entire two hundred forty pounds against it while he panted through one bitch of an adrenaline dump.

Now, now. It's only a slavering primordial beast trying to take your face off. No need to overreact.

He could handle this. He was an Eagle Scout, for God's sake. And he'd had close encounters with all kinds of Minnesota wildlife before. Bears, coyotes, and once even a bull moose. Not one of those critters had made him do more than raise his eyebrows. This was the same thing, only the Florida version. Down here they were probably used to alligators running around on all their public streets, like squirrels. There was no reason to be a wussy about a ... big ... scaly, green ... squirrel. Right?

He cautiously opened the door, then yipped and slammed it shut again. The thing had followed him onto the walkway, and was now sitting in front of his door and grinning. Grinning!

Okay, so he was a wussy. He'd analyze this humiliating character defect later, after he'd escaped being eaten by a giant lizard.

When his hands were steady enough, he stumbled to the room phone and punched in the number for the motel's highly strung and heavily Spanish-accented manager. One inarticulate conversation later, he had a promise of rescue. Or of pizza delivery, he wasn't sure which. But either would work, he thought. He could make a break for it while the alligator was devouring the delivery guy.

After he hung up he paced the grungy carpet for what felt like hours. But it was actually only about fifteen minutes before he heard the sound of an engine pulling up in front of his room. He took a deep, steadying breath, cracked the door and looked through.

A white van stenciled with "Joe Bob's Discount Gators, Inc." was backing into a parking space nearby.

The alligator on his doorstep, sublimely indifferent, kept on basking in the saturated morning sunshine.

The engine shut off and the driver's door opened. From inside the van a beer belly appeared, followed by the rest of what was presumably Joe Bob.

The guy thumped onto the pavement and stretched, looking around. He caught sight of Luke's eyeball through the crack in the door and bobbed a scruffy chin at him. "Mornin'. Hear you got a gator problem?"

Luke poked a finger out of the door to point at the animal dozing three feet away.

Joe Bob did an elaborate double take and let out a guffaw, the bastard. "This little feller? I almost didn't notice him."

He ambled to the van's rear doors and opened them up. Then he went over to the alligator, bent down, and squinted at it. It didn't so much as twitch its knobby tail.

"Well," he said, the word sounding like "way-ell." "Ain't you tasty lookin'? Yessir, I could make some nice steaks outta you." He darted out a meaty hand and grabbed the beast's ferocious-looking snout. With his other hand he took a roll of electrician's tape off his belt and deftly wrapped its jaws. Then he picked the alligator up and tucked it under his arm like a violin case.

Aside from one flail of a webbed foot, the creature made no protest at this treatment, but went right back to sleep.

Luke risked opening the door a little wider. "You're not really going to eat that thing, are you?"

The gator-catcher squinted at him. "Naw. Not yet, anyways. This ain't nothin' but a four-footer. It's them six-footers make good eatin'."

"So ... what are you going to do with it?"

"Way-ell, there's a golf course up north needs somethin' special for the water hazard." He winked, then he shut the alligator up in the back of the van, heaved himself into the driver's seat, and rumbled away.

"Yanking my chain," Luke said to himself as he once again stepped out into the soggy Miami morning. "This entire city is just yanking my chain."

9

BREAKFAST, when Luke finally acquired it from the fast food joint across the parking lot, was almost as harrowing an experience as facing down the alligator. But he consumed the biscuit and egg-like substance with fortitude.

Back in his room, he took out his phone and started looking up numbers for Miami-Dade's piano tuners. Kowalski might have contacted some of them in hopes of finding a new set of suckers to swindle, he thought. Couldn't hurt to call around and ask questions.

But no one he talked to had heard of Brett Kowalski. And though the Florida piano tuners seemed a somewhat smarmier bunch than their Minnesota brethren, he didn't get the sense that any of them were lying.

Strangely, none of them had heard about two hundred keyless grand pianos coming on the market either. A rumor like that should definitely have made the narrow rounds of the piano world by now. Unless someone was deliberately keeping the news quiet. But why would they? Were the Castillos that embarrassed about the affair? Or was it their mysterious buyer who was playing mum?

He sat on the bed, pondering, until a quick rap sounded on his door. He started, and checked the time on his phone. Nine o'clock exactly. It was *her*.

He got up and straightened his tie. Ran a hand over his hair. Tried to calm his hammering pulse. Failed. He took a step toward the door and then looked around his room with a prickle of shame. He should have told her to meet him someplace else. Someplace she might find more impressive.

As if there was any way he could possibly impress a woman like her. Snorting at himself, he went to open the door.

And there she stood before him. Last night's fantasy in the flesh. Though she didn't exactly have a fantasy outfit on. He wasn't sure what he had expected her to be wearing—*a string bikini, maybe?* But it wasn't this. Today the swimsuit goddess was apparently trying to disguise herself as a mere mortal.

Work boots encased her little feet. Khaki shorts clung for dear life to the curves of her hips. The buttons of a green polo shirt strained over her breasts. Her hair was drawn straight back in a glossy black ponytail. Her stunning face was nude of all makeup. The only colorful thing about her was the enormous bright orange purse hooked over her shoulder.

Luke had never realized until this moment that plain and beige were so outrageously sexy. He had to work hard to keep himself from panting.

Fortunately for him, she was turned slightly away from his door, scanning the motel through a pair of gigantic sunglasses. He had time to wrestle down his incipient erection and school his expression into something less ravenous.

"Hi," he eventually managed to say.

She turned to face him and whipped off the shades,

giving the motel a single disgusted flick of her dark eyes. "This place," she announced, "is a rat hole."

"Good morning to you, too. Want to come in?" he asked politely.

"Not without a hazmat suit. Couldn't you find anything ... not revolting?"

"Well, I briefly considered The Four Seasons penthouse suite, but it didn't have the same rustic charm."

There it was again, the flash of laughter in her eyes, quickly concealed. "Ah, rustic charm. Is that what I smell?"

"No, I think that's the restaurant across the street."

This time, he almost got a grin. *Bonding over my shitty accommodations. Awesome.*

She adjusted the strap of her purse. "You ready? I want to get out of here before I catch something." She spun on her heel and marched back toward the parking lot.

Bonding moment over. After shutting the door behind him, Luke followed her. "So are you going to tell me where we're going?"

"I'm taking you to meet someone."

"Who?"

"It'll be easier just to show you. Come on, my car's right here." She moseyed toward a Mini Cooper parked a few spaces away from his truck.

"Oh lord," he said. Why did it have to be a Mini? She was rich and presumably self-indulgent. Why couldn't she drive something big and expensive, like ... like that flashy Range Rover pulling up to the drive-through at the restaurant? Why?

Esmeralda got in the driver's side and started up the engine. Then she stuck her head out the window and said, "Well? What do you want, a public service announcement? Get in."

For a fraction of a second, Luke's former cautiousness tried to resurrect itself. Should he really be letting this possibly criminal female take him to an unknown location to meet with her possibly criminal associates? By all reason, he ought to refuse, and end this game here and now. Find Kowalski some other way.

But then the inherited wisdom of thousands of generations of male ancestors rose up within him and said with one voice, *When a swimsuit model drives up and tells you to get in her car, you get in the damn car!*

With that precept ringing through his mind, Luke circled around the minuscule front bumper and opened the passenger-side door. Then he bent way down to look inside and contemplated the physics of inserting his six-foot-eight-inch body into the available space. It was a tough problem, to be sure. But, Luke reminded himself, he had once moved a baby grand piano up a spiral staircase. This couldn't be too much more difficult, could it?

He met Esmeralda's eyes and saw the humorous gleam shining there, though she kept the rest of her face admirably straight. "Okay, I'm coming in," he warned her, and stuck a foot inside. The rest of him followed, piece by piece.

By the time he had his butt positioned on the red leather seat and the door closed, he had achieved a pose that would do a yoga master proud, with one knee wedged under the dashboard, the other by his chest, and his arms folded under his chin.

"It's like watching someone do life-size origami," Esmeralda said as she put the car in gear.

"Laugh all you want, just don't take too long to get wherever we're going. I'm losing circulation in my feet."

"That won't be a problem. Grab the Jesus handle."

"Grab the what?"

Esmeralda grinned, gunned the engine, and whipped the car into a tight U-turn out of the parking lot, narrowly missing an oncoming bus.

"Jesus!" Luke extracted an arm and lunged for the handle above his window as the tiny car zipped down the road at a velocity that plastered him against his seat. A few blood-curdling turns later, and they were on Biscayne, hurtling south into the depths of the city.

10

"THE ZOO? We're going to the zoo?" Esmeralda's passenger asked as he watched a big green and yellow sign filled with animal shapes fly past the car.

"That's right."

"*Why* are we going to the zoo?"

"You'll see."

Out of the corner of her eye, she saw his massive jaw clench as he ground his teeth, but he said no more. She had to admit, he was being a remarkably good sport about this entire situation.

He was unique among chiselers, for sure. The ones she had met before—and as a model she had met plenty—were much whinier. Much flashier, too. She would have expected a high-end goods smuggler to hole up in a five-star hotel, whether he could afford it or not. Instead, he was staying in what could be charitably described as a landfill. And to top it off, the twist in his lips when he had greeted her at the door had told her that he found his circumstances more amusing than not.

So he was laid back, not pretentious, and in possession of a sense of humor. And hot, couldn't forget hot. She could almost see herself starting to like the guy. Her hopes of turning him to the good side of the Force were rising. She might convince him to go to the authorities about his ivory-smuggling contacts with no trouble at all. But she wasn't going to risk enlightening him about the point of this excursion until she had him exactly where she wanted him.

She turned into the zoo's giant semicircular parking lot and zipped all the way up to the very first row right in front of the entrance gates. Luckily it was a weekday, and there were only a few cars full of early arrivals scattered around.

She whipped into a primo spot and killed the engine. She grabbed her bag and hopped out onto the pavement. Then she got to enjoy the spectacle of her oversized companion wrestling his way out of the Mini. By the time he got free, he was looking a little rumpled and shell-shocked. Good. He was softening up nicely. With a wide smile, she beckoned him toward the entry. "This way."

He cast her a narrow-eyed glance as he absently straightened his tie, another ghastly brownish specimen like the one he had had on yesterday. He looked around at the deserted turnstiles and at the parked cars full of bored families surrounding them. "I don't think the place is open yet."

"Nope," she said, and strode toward the plaza.

She heard him huff something under his breath, and then he fell into step beside her. She blew right past the still-empty ticket booth and led him towards the gray aluminum-clad administration building to one side of the gates.

When they got to the glass door, he reached one long arm past her to pull it open, then politely stood aside and held it so that she could enter first.

As she walked through the door, she felt a big, warm hand lightly touch her back to help her navigate the treacherous passage. She stiffened, expecting the hand to attempt a slide south for the "accidental" ass grope. But instead, the touch simply vanished, leaving a not-unpleasant tingle in its wake. Weird.

She brushed the incident aside and strode into the main office, nodding good morning to a couple admins and security guards as she passed. She went to the security desk, where she picked up a visitor pass.

"Here, put this on." She handed her guest the pass, a little laminated square with an alligator clip.

He took it, looking at her in puzzlement. "Where's your visitor pass?"

"I don't need one. I work here."

"Why does a zoo employ a swimsuit model?"

With admirable forbearance, she explained, "The zoo doesn't employ me as a model, it employs me as a zookeeper. Though actually I'm only an intern and I don't get paid. Which is why I'm doing the modeling for a side job while I finish up my PhD in biology. Clear enough?" She turned on her heel and marched away.

After a moment, he appeared beside her again with a chagrined look on his face, the visitor pass attached to his shirt pocket.

After a brief stop to stow her bag in her locker, she led him through the building and out the back entrance. They walked down a paved area to the mule corral, where the electric carts the zookeepers used to get around the zoo, the "mules," were parked. She swung behind the wheel of the nearest one and started it up. "Jump in."

He stopped short. "Oh, no. Not again."

"Don't be a weenie. These things only go twelve miles an hour."

"That doesn't make me feel much better," he grumbled. But he wedged himself into the seat next to her and braced his arms on the dash.

She stepped on the accelerator and they puttered out of the corral and onto an access path hidden from the public part of the zoo by thick plantings of shrubs and trees.

After a moment, her passenger said, "So, a PhD?"

"Threw you for a loop, didn't it?"

"I'm sorry I assumed you worked here as a model."

"Don't worry about it. I'm used to people not seeing past the swimsuit."

"It's kind of an unusual day job for an aspiring biologist," he said delicately.

"I know. I more or less stumbled into it. I happened to have contacts in the industry who helped me get some good gigs in spite of my flaws."

"Flaws? What flaws?"

"My nose, for one."

"What about it?"

"It's cute."

"Yeah? So?"

"It's *only* cute. It's what makes me not quite beautiful enough to be a star."

"That's crazy. You're the most beautiful woman in the world."

She took her eyes off the road to stare at him. His tone wasn't leering or pining. It was merely matter-of-fact, with a touch of exasperation that he had to state the obvious. The ocean is wet, Florida is hot, you're the most beautiful woman in the world. Duh.

Esmeralda had thought she was immune to flattery by now, but she was blushing anyway. *Carajo*, how did he keep doing that to her? She hastily put her guard back up. In her experience, whenever the extravagant compliments started flowing there was a proposal of one sort or another headed down the pipeline. She said carefully, "That's very nice of you—"

"You're also the worst driver in the world! Look out!"

She glanced back at the path and casually swerved to avoid plowing down a stand of oleander. "I'll have you know I've never once gotten a traffic ticket."

"I'm not surprised. I doubt there's a traffic cop on earth who would give you a ticket. But how many times have you been pulled over?"

She stuck her chin in the air. "That is immaterial."

"Uh-huh."

"Buck up, your ordeal is almost over. We're here," she said.

She turned off the path into a wide clear area surrounded on three sides by more thick hedges. The fourth side was taken up by a huge barnlike building, though instead of solid wood the walls were made of widely spaced bars as thick as a human arm. Past the bars, part of the open space of the animal habitat was visible, but its occupant was out of view at the moment.

Next to the barn, a woman was busy raking hay out of a cart. She was a solidly built straw-blond in her fifties, wearing the same khaki-shorts-and-green-polo outfit Esmeralda had on. She straightened and leaned on her rake as they pulled up nearby, a slight smile on her weather-beaten face. "There you are, Cuban Barbie."

"Hi, Celeste." Esmeralda shut off the mule and got out,

then gestured to her companion, who was unwinding himself from his seat. "This is Brett Kowalski. Mr. Kowalski, this is Celeste Rubenstein, my boss."

Celeste looked him up and down with a frank stare. "So you're the special guest?"

"More of a kidnap victim," he replied, frowning at the wall of bars.

"No one's keeping you, unless you want to stay," Celeste said. "So, you want to stay?"

He turned his rather intimidating frown on Celeste. "If it's worth my time."

She twinkled at him. "How much is your time worth, hon? Dollar amounts, now."

He didn't rise to the bait. He merely said, "I take it you're the contact I'm supposed to be meeting today?"

The older woman let out a belly laugh. "Not even close."

That was apparently the last straw. He rounded on Esmeralda, putting his back to the barn. "All right, Ms. Castillo. Tell me what this is all about." His gray eyes were steely, his jaw as hard as granite.

Coño, he's cute when he gets masterful. She corralled her unruly thoughts and looked him in the eye. "It's about facing the true cost of your actions."

"What?"

"Think of it as a subject of meditation. A zen koan. Or a fortune cookie."

He briefly closed his eyes, seeming to muster patience. "Okay. How about we start simply. Does this person you dragged me out here to meet actually exist?"

"Oh, he exists all right."

"Where is he, then?"

Esmeralda looked over his shoulder into the barn

behind him. Right on cue, a big, familiar shape was moving silently through the shadows under the long roof, coming to stand at the wall of bars. There he was, the love of her life, watching them with deep, knowing eyes.

She smiled at Kowalski. "He's right behind you."

11

LUKE SPUN around and came face to face with an enormous bull elephant.

"Holy shitbucket," he yelled, leaping backwards. "Where did he come from?"

He heard Esmeralda's rich chuckle. "He moves quietly, doesn't he?"

Luke didn't reply, absorbing the shock of the animal's presence. He'd never had much to do with animals before, except for his hapless goldfish. His family hadn't been zoo-goers, hadn't kept pets. He'd certainly never seen an elephant this close before.

At this range, he could see every wrinkle of the tough gray skin, every vein in the folded-back flaps of his ears. He saw tufts of wiry brown hair covering the back and the double-domed head and growing in neat rows down the massive trunk. His gaze caught for a moment on the magnificent set of tusks, each nearly as long as Luke was tall, which swept from the huge head to almost brush the ground. Then he had to stare at the gigantic feet, as big as platters and tipped with thick wedges of toenails.

He looked back up to find a dark, thickly lashed eye cocked at him. To his shock he realized that while he had been looking over the elephant, he himself was being evaluated just as thoroughly. A sly intelligence was moving in that eye, alien and yet perfectly understandable. It was a look that said, "If the mood strikes me, I might use you for a tennis ball."

Then Esmeralda brushed past him, striding toward the bars. Luke instinctively reached out a hand to pull her back to safety, but the corrugated trunk had already uncoiled to meet her, the finger-like thing at the tip brushing softly over her hair before the entire muscular length settled around her shoulders in a strange hug.

She laughed again, wrapping an arm around the trunk. She tipped her head up toward the great beast, and the look on her face stole Luke's breath away. She looked radiant with love, as beatific as a saint in a stained-glass window.

She said, "This is Raj. Raj, this is my friend. Be nice to him."

Raj stared at Luke some more. He did not look inclined to be nice.

"Here," said Celeste, popping in at Luke's elbow and nearly making him jump again. She held a bowl full of leafy green stuff out to Esmeralda. "Might as well make yourself useful and feed him his kale while I go clean out the habitat. Hey, watch it there," she said, pointing at the muscular trunk, which had escaped Esmeralda's embrace and was weaving slyly through the bars toward Luke.

Esmeralda quickly intercepted the trunk and shoved it in a different direction. Then she took the bowl of leaves. "Don't worry, I've got things under control."

"I can see that." Celeste slid a little smile at Luke. "You and your boyfriend have fun."

Luke said, "Me? I'm— I'm not—"

Celeste cut him off with a loud snort. "I wasn't talking about you, kid. I was talking about him," she said, nodding toward the elephant. She tossed a shovel and a rake into a nearby hand truck and started wheeling it past the barn toward the larger habitat. Then she paused. "Heard anything about that India money?" she said to Esmeralda.

"Not yet. Any day now, though."

"I hope you're right. You've worked hard for this grant. Raj and me are proud of you, aren't we, Raj?"

Raj snuffled agreeably.

"But don't think I'm giving you any slack before you go off to get your fancy degree. See you tomorrow bright and early, Cuban Barbie." She pushed the truck forward again and disappeared around the corner of the barn.

"Cuban Barbie?" Luke said. "That's kind of insulting."

"Eh. She hasn't meant anything by it since she watched me shovel my first ton of elephant shit."

While she was talking, Raj's trunk had wandered a little too close to him again, and she shoved it away with a playful slap. "You might want to stand back a little farther. He's liable to grab your ankle and yank it out from under you. His idea of a practical joke."

Luke hastily backed up. "He has one lousy sense of humor."

"Careful. He's very intelligent and he understands nearly everything you say."

He saw Raj glance at him lazily, and Luke could almost hear him say, "You bet your puny ass I do."

Luke swallowed.

Esmeralda went on. "He's a little temperamental, but he has reason to be. Forty-some years ago when he was a calf he was an attraction at a third-rate carnival. Bad scene, back then. Beatings, starvation, cold filthy little cage. You've probably heard the stories. It left a mark. He doesn't warm up to people very well."

"He seems to get along with you well enough."

"We've known each other for a long time, and he's used to me." She picked a leaf out of the bowl and held it up to the elephant. "Want some kale, Raj?"

The huge trunk curled high in the air and the long lower lip fell open beneath it. Esmeralda delicately placed the leaf inside the big pink mouth. The lip closed, the trunk fell, and the great jaws slowly worked as the creature savored his greens with the aplomb of a gourmand.

Luke thought for a moment while he watched Raj munch kale. He still had no idea what he was doing here, and Esmeralda wasn't hurrying to explain, wrapped up as she was in her gigantic buddy. Unless ... "What is this India money your boss was talking about? What does it have to do with me?"

"Not a thing. You see, for my dissertation I'm going to do two years of field research on reintroducing captive elephants to the wild. As soon as my fellowship grant with the World Elephant Foundation gets final approval from their Indian partner organization, I'm off to Nagarhole National Park in India." She smiled a breathtaking smile into the distance, maybe looking at a vision of her golden future.

"India. Wow. That's ... that's far away."

"Yes, it will be an incredible adventure."

"Are you thinking you're going to reintroduce Raj here to the wild?"

"No, unfortunately he's too old. He could never adjust to life on his own now. He'd starve. That's if poachers didn't murder him for his tusks first." She reached a hand through the bars to brush down the softly glowing length of ivory. "Even now, after everything I've seen, I still can't understand how people would actually kill intelligent creatures like Raj just to yank out their teeth and turn them into things like piano keys. It makes me crazy." She watched him out of the corner of her eyes, judging the effect of her words.

Luke finally felt an inkling of what this whole expedition was about creeping up on him.

She went on. "But I can't blame the poachers too much. Most of them are just poor and desperate. The ones I blame are the ivory traders. Those *hijos de puta*. They're the ones who have the most blood on their hands. They have to be made to understand that an elephant's life is worth more than a few useless trinkets." She met his eyes. "Which brings me to the reason for our visit here today."

"Ms. Castillo, I'm going to take a wild stab in the dark and guess that you think I am one of these *hi ... hijos ...*" He gave up. "That I am an ivory trader."

She gave him a cold look. "Don't try to be coy, Mr. Kowalski. I know that the Fish and Wildlife agent you approached told you I could sell the ivory key tops to you. I know that's why you came to see me after my cousin wouldn't let you have the pianos. But I didn't bring you out here to work a deal. I wanted to show you what you're destroying every time you exchange ivory for money."

The puzzle clicked together in his mind. Kowalski, the stupid slimy moron, had apparently tried to add corrupting Federal agents and dealing in contraband to his criminal enterprises. This was infuriating, though not surprising.

What was surprising was the overpowering relief he felt. Relief and chagrin.

Relief because Esmeralda Castillo was not a crook. She was exactly what she appeared to be, an idealistic grad-student-slash-bikini-babe. And chagrin because he was an idiot for misreading the situation so completely.

And now he had to tell her the truth. But how? How to say he had been deliberately tricking her since nearly the moment they met?

Man up and spill it, Hansen. She already thinks you're an elephant murderer. Her opinion of you can't possibly get any lower. "Look, I have a confession to make," he said as she dumped the rest of the kale on top of the mattress-sized pile of hay near their feet, picked up a rake, and shoved it all through the bars.

"What confession?" She leaned on her rake and looked at him expectantly, her dark eyes shining with earnestness. Her soft lips were parted slightly, giving her a look both ravishing and innocent. A beam of sunlight caught on the particles of chaff floating in the air, making a golden halo around her.

Crap. I've been lying to an angel. He rubbed a hand over his face, searching for the right phrase.

Behind her the elephant lazily grabbed up a trunkful of hay and tucked it into his mouth. It gave Luke an idea, if not how to explain, at least how to stall. "Why don't we go get something to eat first? Are you hungry? I'm hungry. I'm so hungry I could eat that kale."

At those words, the thick trunk froze in the act of grabbing up more hay. Slowly it lifted and turned toward Luke, the little finger at the end pointing straight between his eyes.

"Not that I would," Luke hastily said. "I'm not really into fiber."

12

ESMERALDA DROVE him in the mule back to the entrance plaza. The zoo had opened while they were at the elephant barn, and a few tourists were milling about. After they parked, she guided him through the light crowd to a food court.

Hungry though he was, he had to strain to muster up some enthusiasm for another hamburger. He'd had so much fast food lately he could feel his arteries hardening by the second.

Esmeralda saw him looking over the menu placard above the counter with what must have been a forlorn expression, because she said, "Try the pulled pork tacos. I hear they're good."

"You haven't tried one yourself?"

She shook her head. "Vegetarian."

Of course she's vegetarian, he thought wryly. But he took her advice and ordered the tacos.

When they got their food and bottles of water, Esmeralda led him down a short stretch of walkway to a bench across from one of the animal habitats.

Luke looked out across the fence and ditch separating them from the enclosure, scanning the artfully scattered rocks and trees. "Where's the animal?"

"Still eating his snack, I assume," Esmeralda said. She sat down and took a dainty little bite of her salad.

"This is Raj's compound?" Luke said, joining her on the bench.

"Yep. The barn we were just at is hidden behind that low hill there." She pointed to one corner of the lot. "Raj should be coming out to see us soon, now that he's sure you're not going to try to steal his kale."

Luke grinned and bit into a taco. She was right, it was good.

They ate in silence for a while, both seemingly content to enjoy the peaceful morning. The sun was hot but not brutally so, and the air was soft. The only sound was a gentle squeak as a family of four pedaled past on a canopied vehicle that looked like the mutant offspring of a golf cart and a bicycle. Nearby, a couple of white birds with long, thin legs and beaks fluttered elegantly. If he wasn't dreading coming clean to the beautiful woman next to him, he'd almost count himself as happy.

One of the birds was edging up to the bench, its wrinkly eye cocked at Luke's French fries. As he tried to compose a graceful explanation—all right, excuse—for his behavior in his head, he absently plucked out a fry and aimed it. "What are these birds called?" he asked Esmeralda.

"No, don't!" she said as the fry left his fingers.

Before it even hit the ground, an explosion of white feathers had detonated around Luke as seemingly every bird in the zoo converged on him—the brand new sucker in their midst.

"Uh oh," he said.

She shook her head, looking disgusted. "Those are ibises. And now you'll never get rid of them for as long as you live. When I was six, I gave one part of my ice-cream cone and I swear some of them still follow me around to this day." She waved a foot halfheartedly at a nearby ibis, which nimbly sidestepped her before taking up its station again.

"You've been coming here since you were six?"

"Mm-hm. When I was little I kept pestering my father for a pet, but he would never allow it. Anita was the one who really raised me, though, so when she couldn't stand my begging any more, she started bringing me here. That was when I first met Raj. And that was it. I was in love."

"Why an elephant? I thought little girls usually fell in love with horses." All of his sisters had, anyway.

She looked a little shy. "I can't explain it. But I don't think you ever can explain love, can you? It's a mystery by nature."

He said, "I know I've never been able to figure it out." *Just ask my ex-wife.*

"Anyway, the instant I saw Raj, I decided then and there that I was going to be an elephant caretaker when I grew up. I came back here every chance I could get just to be with him. I'd sit on this very bench and tell him about everything that had happened to me since I had last seen him. And after a while, he started coming to stand at the edge of the moat to listen to me. It sometimes seemed like he understood me better than any of the humans in my life. Seems that way now, actually."

"Why are you leaving him to go to India, then?"

"I have a calling," she said simply. "Elephants are the most magnificent creatures on earth and I have to do whatever I can to save them. Do you understand?"

"I guess ... no. I mean, don't take this the wrong way—"

"Watch it. No one ever said anything inoffensive after starting a sentence like that."

"—but you seem to have a very idealized notion of these animals."

She shrugged, sipping her water. "It may sound like it, but trust me, I've studied the reality of them extensively. I've spent years learning their anatomy and behavior. I've fed them, bathed them, and shoveled up tons—literally tons—of their dung. You don't maintain many illusions about anything after that. And yet, the love remains. Like I said, it's a mystery."

Suddenly, her body went taut with the same vibrant emotion as before, at the barn. She reached out and grasped his hand.

A tiny bolt of lightning raced up his arm from where her delicate fingers clasped his big, callused paw, striking deep in his chest. He stared down at her stupidly, almost drunk from the feeling. This was the first time she had ever touched him, and just this, a simple handhold, was the most amazing sensation in his memory.

She pointed to the habitat. "Look, there he is. Do you see him? Do you see?"

In a daze, Luke followed her finger out across the dusty length of the enclosure. There was Raj coming around the low hill, as vast, gray, and silent as a thundercloud. And for a moment, caught in her spell as he was, he saw what Esmeralda must see—a rare and wonderful being both needing and commanding devotion. A feeling as sublime as a Bach fugue rippled over his skin. He watched the elephant move with a ponderous majesty to stand across the moat from them, regarding them over the fence with an age-old awareness.

Esmeralda said softly, "You seem to be a good man. You do understand, don't you?"

As if in a dream, he looked down into her glowing face. "Yes."

She smiled. "Then, will you tell me something?"

Anything. He managed to nod.

"Will you tell me who you plan on selling the ivory key tops to?"

He blinked down at her. "Huh?"

"What I want more than anything in this world is to stop the killing of elephants for their tusks. You can help me by telling me everything you know about the ivory trade. I have contacts in law enforcement. We can go to them together and give information that will shut the network down. I can promise you won't be prosecuted. You'd be doing a great service to your country, and the world." She gripped his hand tighter. "Will you do it? For Raj? For me, Mr. Kowalski?"

Kowalski. The name was like a crack to the face, snapping him right out of the enchantment she had been weaving.

The truth fell out of him with a thud. "I'm not Brett Kowalski."

She stared at him for a full ten seconds. Then she snatched her hand back like he'd said, "I have Ebola."

"What?" she said.

It all came rushing out—the prospectus, the money, the Pinewood beer hall, the phone conversation from the strip joint, and the Piano Tuners Guild seal. Eventually the flood of words trickled to a halt, and he closed his lips and prepared to be obliterated.

She leapt to her feet, her eyes glittering with fury. "You lied to me?" If her voice weren't so beautiful, he would call it screeching. Her fingers clenched around her water bottle, denting the plastic. Luke suspected that he was only a hairsbreadth away from getting a face full of Polar Springs.

Raj shifted slightly, and at that moment Luke knew two things. First, that the elephant really did understand when Esmeralda was unhappy. And second, that he was very lucky that there was a ditch and a fence between him and Raj.

"I'm sorry. I should have told you much earlier." He got to his feet as well.

"You should have told me the second I met you, Mr. Whoever-the-hell-you-really-are."

"Luke Hansen. My name is Luke Hansen. And you didn't let me introduce myself, if you recall. You made an assumption about who I was, and I simply let you."

"Sophistry, Mr. Hansen. And if *you* recall, you deliberately gave a false name to my cousin and my father. My father, an Alzheimer's patient!"

Luke winced.

"You should have told me who you were, and that Kowalski owed you money."

"It's not the money. It's the Piano Tuners Guild seal—"

"Are you kidding me? You expect me to believe that you came all the way down here and concocted this elaborate scam—"

"I wouldn't say it was elaborate—"

"—over a *seal*? A big *stamp*?"

"It's the truth. I don't expect to find the money, but I want that seal back for personal reasons."

"And how was lying to me going to help you with that? Or were you just amusing yourself? Thought it would be fun to play a round of Fool The Bimbo?" Something like hurt tinged the anger in her voice.

"No! I just figured you could lead me to Kowalski, or the people he was dealing with. I was going undercover."

"Undercover," she repeated in an odd, muted voice.

"I didn't know if I could trust you. The way you were talking to me yesterday made it sound like Kowalski was your partner in some shady business deal. And you must admit you didn't give me much reason to think you were being honest. Abducting me to the zoo under false pretenses and so on."

She watched him for a beat, and then her mouth took on an ironic tilt. "You're right. I haven't been totally honest with you, Mr. P— Hansen. But I will be, now."

"Well. That sounds ominous."

"I have someone else here you need to meet."

"Not this again," Luke said, exasperated. "What do I have to talk to now? A white rhino? A giraffe?"

"No, something even more exotic. A federal agent." She tipped her head down toward her chest and said loudly, "Okay, Agent Truitt, you can come out now."

Luke had just enough time to wonder if that was what she called her bosoms and, if so, why she was telling them to come out, when he heard a rustle nearby. He turned his head to see a man stepping out from behind a planter full of weird tropical foliage a few dozen yards away. With a ferocious glower at Luke, he stalked across the pavement to stand near Esmeralda. Much too near.

"Luke Hansen, meet Special Agent Alistair Truitt, of the US Fish and Wildlife Service," she said.

"Special Agent, huh," Luke said, sizing the guy up. His clothes looked like they would blend in nicely on the ninth green, except for the gun bulge under his light jacket. He was tall, but not freakishly so. And he had classic all-American features, shining dark hair, and baby blue eyes. Looked kind of like Superman.

Luke instantly hated his guts.

The feeling seemed to be mutual. "That's right, I'm US law enforcement. And I'm trying to think of one good reason not to charge you with interfering in a federal investigation, Mr. *Hansen*," he growled.

Luke looked at Esmeralda. "I think I like your other friend better."

13

"YOU WERE FOLLOWING ME? RECORDING ME?" Outrage vibrated through Luke's body as he stared Truitt down.

The three of them—Agent Truitt, Esmeralda, and Luke—were crowded into an office in the administration building that Truitt had commandeered from some luckless admin so that they could sort out this debacle in private. Esmeralda was turned away from them, busily fishing a spy transmitter out of her bra. Apparently, Truitt had planted it on her earlier that morning before she met with Luke. Then he had followed her from Luke's motel to the zoo, listening to their conversation the entire time.

By unspoken mutual agreement, Luke and Truitt were keeping their eyes locked on each other so that they wouldn't stare at Esmeralda's undulating back.

"We wouldn't have recorded you if you hadn't stolen Kowalski's identity," Truitt said coolly.

"Now hang on just a damn minute—"

"Never mind all that," Esmeralda said as she turned around. In her mercurial fashion, she seemed to have entirely gotten over her mad. Now she was bubbling with an alarming level of new enthusiasm. "We all need to kiss and make up so we can concentrate on the real Kowalski."

She handed the transmitter over to Truitt, the nickel-sized gadget still warm from where it had been nestled between her breasts, Luke imagined. From the way Truitt ran his thumb over the thing, his imagination wasn't far off. The agent cleared his throat. "Mr. Hansen is not part of the 'we.' He is interfering in a federal investigation."

"Oh, come on. You can't seriously think Kowalski could interest the Feds," Luke said. "He's all talk, and not very good talk."

"Brett Kowalski is a possible link in the flow of smuggled ivory out of Florida," Truitt said stiffly. "We're building up an important case here, and you might have just shot it to hell."

Luke raised a skeptical eyebrow. He strongly suspected that the main object of this "important case" was to give Truitt an excuse to stick things in Esmeralda's bra. But all he said was, "If Kowalski has any information about black market channels for ivory, I'm a ballerina."

"You might very well be a ballerina for all we know," Truitt blustered. "You've already lied to us once. Who's to say you're not lying now?"

"Al, he's not a ballerina," Esmeralda said soothingly. "I believe him. I think he's truly just a simple piano tuner blundering into a situation beyond his depth."

"Thanks a lot," Luke said.

"But," she went on, "he can still be useful to us if we let him. He knows Kowalski, and we don't. And he has a stake in finding him too. A really weird stake, but if it works for him, it works."

"I'm not going to even consider the possibility of

involving him until I've done a thorough background check on him. I'll need your identification." He held out an imperious hand to Luke.

Luke took out his driver's license and handed it over, saying, "Check all you want. You'll see I've never had so much as a parking ticket. Oh, while you're at it, why don't you do a background check on Kowalski, too? That way, at least you'll know what he looks like. Which is nothing like me, by the way."

Truitt paused in taking down his information to send him a look of pure dislike. "We've tried. We haven't found him on our databases yet, and there are no pictures of him on the web under the name Kowalski. It's an alias. He's a lot trickier than you're giving him credit for."

That gave Luke pause. Now that he thought about it, he realized he never had seen any pictures of Kowalski. His store website and social media mostly featured stock photos of children happily practicing piano, and other such improbable images. In fact, he really knew nothing about the man other than what he had told the Guild himself. So it was technically possible that he was a career criminal who had infiltrated the Guild for nefarious reasons of his own.

On the other hand, he patently lacked the brains to smuggle so much as a packet of sugar off a buffet table. But trying to explain that to Truitt and Esmeralda was clearly a waste of time. They were too invested in their ivory theory.

And on further reflection, Luke decided he didn't care whether Kowalski was being pursued by the Feds or not. As long as Luke could get the seal back without involving the Guild in any way, the entire US government could use the guy for a chew toy as far as Luke was concerned.

"So what does he look like?" Esmeralda asked.

Luke thought for a minute, summing up Kowalski's

measurements like he would a particularly cheap spinet piano. "Five feet five inches tall, one hundred eighty pounds, fifty-five inches around the middle."

"I knew it," Esmeralda crowed. "I knew he'd be a turnip of a guy. What else?"

"Brown hair, thinning on top. Hazel eyes. Good teeth. And he has a really great voice."

"That's true," Truitt grudgingly said. "He had a very good phone presence when I spoke to him."

"Funny you didn't notice the difference in our voices when you were eavesdropping on me," Luke said.

Truitt flushed.

"There, you see, Al?" Esmeralda said, ignoring the byplay. "Mr. Hansen has already provided us with some important information. I vote we keep him." She reached up and patted him on the shoulder, causing Luke to go speechless and Truitt to frown darkly.

"Like I said, I'll wait until the background check comes in before I make any decisions," the agent said, handing Luke back his license.

"In that case, I'm going to take Mr. Hansen back to his motel."

"I'll follow you there."

"No, please. No more following. I don't know about Mr. Hansen, but I've had enough of this cloak-and-dagger stuff for one day."

Luke, still incapable of speech, nodded vigorously.

Truitt turned his shoulder to Luke and said in a low voice to Esmeralda, "I don't want to leave you alone with this guy. We know nothing about him."

"Al, don't be paranoid."

"I'm being responsible. I wish you would, too."

"Listen, if there's one thing I know, it's how to spot a creep. He isn't one. Trust me."

Truitt was flushing dangerously red. "You cannot go off with him alone, and that's final."

"Is it? Are you planning on arresting one or both of us, Al?" she said, an edge in her voice. "Because unless you are, you don't get to tell me what I can and can't do."

Truitt let out a frustrated noise between his teeth. But he seemed to realize he had gone too far, because he eventually said, "All right. But I'll be calling to check up on you later."

"If you have to. Come on, Mr. Hansen. Bye, Al." With a swish of her black ponytail, she disappeared through the office door.

Before Luke could follow her, Truitt raked him with an ice-cold stare. "I'll be checking up on you too. Don't leave town."

"Don't worry. I'm not going anywhere."

Esmeralda collected her purse from her locker and then she and Luke walked out of the building and into the middle of a flock of ibises. They had apparently been massing outside the door in hopes that Luke would reappear. They milled around him in a white fluttery mass, avaricious little eyes on the watch for more French fries.

"I feel like I'm in a Hitchcock movie," he said.

Esmeralda paused in the act of taking a pair of enormous sunglasses out of her purse and smiled at him quizzically. "You like old movies?"

"I have a fondness for the classics. You?"

"Try me. Which movie do you think you're in?" she asked as they waded through the ibises toward the parking lot.

"A combination of *The Birds* and *North By Northwest*, I guess."

"Are you reluctant secret agent Carey Grant or that blond who gets driven insane?"

"That's yet to be determined."

14

"SO, how do you know Agent Truitt?" Luke Hansen asked.

Esmeralda glanced over at the passenger seat of her car, where he had once again crammed himself. "I met Al through work. US Fish and Wildlife has jurisdiction over exotic zoo animals, so Al is the one in charge of making sure we zookeepers are up on our Federal rules and regs."

They were speeding back up the expressway toward Biscayne Boulevard and Luke's motel. They had maintained an awkward silence until now, each of them brooding on recent revelations.

He said, "You two seem ... close."

Her thoughts still on elephants and slippery ivory dealers, she had to struggle to refocus on Luke's ever-so-delicate probe. Which she really should have seen coming. But she decided she didn't much mind getting probed by this guy. His cute factor had gone up about a thousand percent since she'd found out he wasn't dealing in elephant parts.

Cutting to the chase, she said, "No, I'm not sleeping with Agent Al. Or anyone else at the moment." In fact, she'd been too focused on her work to bother with masculine nuisances for nearly a year now.

A pause. "Okay."

"Not for lack of trying on Al's part. But he blew his chance at a relationship with me the day we met."

"Why? What did he do?"

"He proposed marriage. I hate it when that happens."

She heard something creak alarmingly, and shot Luke a glance. He was clenching the handle above the door so hard he looked like he was going to tear it off. He stared straight ahead, his jaw doing that bulging thing again. "Does that happen to you a lot?"

"Instant proposals? You'd be surprised. It's super annoying, because the guys build up these fantasies of me that have nothing to do with reality. Take Al, for instance. He doesn't want a zookeeper on her way to India, which is what I am. In his heart he wants someone who'll take care of his house on the golf course and laugh at his office party jokes and cart Al Junior to soccer practice in the Volvo." She couldn't repress a shudder.

"You don't want any of that stuff? Marriage, kids?"

"Maybe. But not with Al, and certainly not right now. I'm only twenty-four, *por Dios*. Twenty-four is way too young to get married."

"That's how old I was when I got married," he said in a low voice.

"You're married?" A sensation as unpleasant as it was weird knotted her stomach.

"Divorced."

"Oh." The knot unraveled, but left an equally unwelcome feeling of relief behind. "So, why'd you get divorced?" she asked brightly.

"Do you have any boundaries, Ms. Castillo?"

"Sure, when I want them. So? Your divorce?"

"I'd rather not discuss it."

"Come on. You conned me into baring my soul about my lonely childhood at the zoo. The least you can do to make up for it is tell me why your marriage imploded."

"Fine," he huffed. "She played Hammond organ at a country-western joint in Saint Paul. One night, the World's Roughest Rodeo blew through the bar, and the next thing I knew, my wife was headed to South Dakota in a horse hauler with a bareback bronco rider named Rafe."

"Wow."

"Yeah. I couldn't believe it at first. It didn't make any sense. I thought everything was fine with us. That is ... you know ... I'd recently lost my piano repair shop, and we weren't talking or ... or anything very much, but ... I thought it was the ordinary ups and downs of a relationship. Our life seemed so normal. She was a nice girl. We lived in a nice house with a really nice yard I worked on every Sunday ..."

"Sounds, ah, nice."

"Yeah, well. She sent me a Dear John email and divorce papers from Sioux Falls, and I never saw her again."

"What was in the Dear John email?"

"Really, Ms. Castillo!"

"If you don't tell me, I'm going to assume it was a complaint about your bizarre sexual kinks involving dental care products."

"I don't have any sexual kinks," he ground out. "I'm normal. I'm boring, in fact. Which is exactly what my ex-wife complained about in her email."

She turned to stare at him, incredulous. "Mr. Hansen, you left everything in your life behind to chase a guy thousands of miles across the country on the most ridiculous pretext I've ever heard, and you're telling me your ex thought you were boring? Did she ever even meet you?"

"Jeez, watch the road!"

She turned back in time to see a yellow light, and jammed up the speed in time to rip through the intersection just as the light turned red. "Sounds to me like your ex did you an enormous favor."

"By dumping me in front of our friends and family and sticking me with a mortgage I couldn't afford on my own?"

"By freeing you from a lifestyle you obviously aren't suited for."

"I liked my lifestyle."

"As a suburban drone? Really? Men your age usually hate turning into suburban drones. You're what, thirty-three?"

"I'm twenty-eight!"

"There, see? All that lawn care has aged you beyond your years. You should have beat feet out of Milwaukee—"

"Minneapolis. Milwaukee is in Wisconsin."

"Whatever. Point is, a man like you should have gotten out of there a long time ago, but you were trapped by all your responsibilities and *mierda* like that. You were lucky your ex released you back into the wild so you could follow your bliss down here."

"I'm not following any bliss. I'm just looking for Kowalski."

"Then maybe you owe him too, much as I hate to say it. Since he gave you an excuse to bust out of Manitoba."

"Minnesota! Manitoba is in Canada!"

"Whatever."

"Are you done analyzing my personal life?"

"We're back at your gross disgusting flophouse, so I guess I am." She screeched into the motel parking lot under the vulturish scrutiny of two shirtless drunks and a rail-thin and itchy prostitute lurking in their respective motel doorways. She parked as far from the unsavory observers as possible and shut off the Mini.

Maybe Luke would invite her into his room again, she thought. Maybe this time she would accept. She grabbed her purse before she hopped out of the car and shut the door.

Luke extracted himself a bit more slowly and stood looking at her over the hood. "Well, Ms. Castillo, it's been an interesting morning."

She leaned her crossed arms on the car and smiled at him. "That it has. And you've been a good sport. Thanks for putting up with Raj and me, and Al. Wasn't quite what you were hoping for, was it?"

"No. But it was kind of fun," he said, sounding surprised. He paused, then blurted out, "I really am sorry. For lying." He looked so earnest, she couldn't help but smile more.

"Don't worry about it. If it's any consolation, you make a terrible crook. I had you pegged as a decent guy nearly from the start."

He blinked at her, then grinned. Once again that damned hot and fluttery feeling invaded her nether regions.

"You know, you have the most amazing way of complimenting me and insulting me at the same time," he said.

"I can't help it. You're just too cute when you get all dignified."

"Cute? I'm not cute."

"Yes, you are. You're a seven-foot-tall Viking teddy bear."

He did a double take and laughed aloud, his gray eyes

sparkling. The invading forces of arousal made a lunge to claim more territory in her lower body.

She cleared her throat. "If you get a lead on Kowalski, you'll let me know?"

"You betcha. And you'll do the same?"

"Sure."

"Well, then."

"Well."

"I'll be seeing you," he said.

"Right," she said.

He gave an abrupt nod and walked off across the parking lot toward his motel room.

She watched him go with an odd sense of disappointment. For a moment she considered calling him back, asking him if he'd like to get a cup of coffee, maybe talk over some strategies for nailing Kowalski. Or convince him to move to a different hotel. It didn't feel right, just leaving him all alone in what amounted to a demilitarized zone.

But he was a grown man. A huge, if rather sweet and innocent, grown man. He didn't need her interference any more than she needed his.

She was about to get back into her car when she saw him stop in his tracks, his whole big body going tight. Instinct sizzled over her skin, the same feeling she got when something was wrong with Raj.

"Mr. Hansen? Luke?" She moved around the car and hurried toward him. "What—?"

He shoved out an arm to stop her. That was when she saw it. The door to his room was creaking on its hinges, the knob hanging drunkenly from a couple of bolts and splintered wood.

15

LUKE SHOT a glance around at the other motel doors. None of them had been tampered with. And the residents who had been standing in the doorways and watching them had vanished like smoke.

"Stay here," he said to Esmeralda. He strode to the door.

"No, don't! The guy could still be in there," she whispered frantically.

Luke paid no attention. He slammed the door open. If the guy was still in there, he could grab him and ... *And what? Give him a stern lecture?*

It didn't matter what he would have done. The room was empty except for the wreckage.

The place looked like it had been attacked by a pack of rabid beavers. The chipboard furniture was in splinters. The mattress was lying half off the box springs, slashed up and leaking fluff. His bags had been dumped out, the contents tossed and trampled on the floor. His tool case gaped open, his once carefully organized tools now a heap of chisels and glue bottles.

He looked into the bathroom. The lid of the toilet tank

had been smashed, the shower curtain torn down. The only thing that was the same as he had left it this morning was the bathroom sink. Which, he saw, had been reoccupied by the cockroach.

Behind him, he heard Esmeralda's light step. She looked around his shoulder into the room and said something elaborate in Spanish.

He had no idea what she said, but the vicious tone was about right.

He moved further into the room, detritus crunching under his shoes. He looked down at the torn-up bed. "Looks like I need to find a new place to sleep," he said dully.

Esmeralda delicately picked her way over to what was left of the bedside table and sifted through the debris until she found the room phone, miraculously in one piece and still plugged into the wall. She held the receiver to her ear and clicked the call buttons.

"I'm calling the manager," Esmeralda said.

Luke didn't object. He barely even heard her. He was too busy quelling a strong impulse to pound what was left of the furniture into tiny splinters. He bent to pick up a formerly crisp white shirt, now wrinkled and sporting a muddy footprint on the front. He found his newly torn nylon suitcase, folded the shirt and put it inside.

He became dimly aware that Esmeralda's voice had risen to a strident pitch. She listened for a moment, then slammed the receiver back into the cradle and tossed the whole phone onto the pile of rubble that used to be the nightstand. *"Que un cabron."*

"Problem?"

"The guy doesn't want to call the cops. He says you're a troublemaker. And he kept yammering on about an alligator." She sent him a quizzical look.

"I have no idea what he's talking about," Luke promptly lied.

She arched an eyebrow at that, but let it go. "Well, he's coming here now. He'll figure out that this is no prank pretty quick."

Just as she finished talking, the sticklike motel desk clerk himself appeared in the open doorway. He had apparently run all the way from the office, because sweat was rolling off his face and into the collar of his nicotine-stained guayabera. He looked around wildly at the destruction, his lips gaping. Then his gaze found Luke. He gave a bronchial wheeze, and started yammering in Spanish and waving his arms.

When he paused to pant for breath, Luke said, "I didn't understand a word of that, but I have a feeling it isn't good."

Esmeralda, who had been looking at the guy with the same expression she might use on the roach in the sink, said, "This man-shaped toenail fungus doesn't want the cops here, for what reasons I can only guess. He says if you call them he'll tell them you broke the door and trashed the room yourself. And he wants you to leave right away."

The manager, who had finally caught his breath, bleated, "You make trouble! You call about the gator, now you bust up the room! You go now. You go or I tell the police you make trouble."

Esmeralda sneered at the clerk, then said to Luke, "Obviously, that's a bunch of *mierda*. You have a federal agent to back up your side of the story, for crying out loud. But ..."

"But?"

She shrugged. "I don't think the cops are going to do you much good."

Luke's gaze moved from the twitchy clerk to the ruin all

around him, and he exhaled slowly as the reality of the situation sank in. She was right. Involving the cops would be completely pointless.

They would never find the oinking shitheels who did this, and getting into a dispute with the manager and the local police over a couple hundred dollars of ruined stuff just wasn't worth the hassle. He knew it, the manager knew it, and Esmeralda knew it. Hell, even the roach in the sink probably knew it.

"All right. No cops. I'll be out of here as soon as I'm packed."

The manager let out a self-righteous snort and stomped off. Esmeralda glared after him, but said nothing.

"Well," Luke said, "It appears I'm fucked." Then he looked at Esmeralda guiltily. "Excuse my language."

"No, 'fucked' is the only appropriate English word for this situation. Though I could teach you some Spanish ones sometime. For a little extra oomph."

"Thanks, but I don't think spewing profanity is a good way to convince the motel manager that I'm not a vandal." He picked up a pair of pants and folded them.

"Forget that *come mierda*. He doesn't matter."

"I booked this room for a week, and he's not going to give me back my deposit."

"So, you'll be out twelve bucks."

He was silent, trying to calculate how long it would be before he was sleeping in his truck.

She bent and picked up one of his neckties that had been tangled in the fluff of the slashed-up mattress. What kind of bastard sons of camels desecrated a man's ties?

"Look," Esmeralda said, holding out the tie to him, "If you need a loan—"

"No!" He all but snatched it away from her.

She drew her hand back and pressed her lips together, her cheeks going red.

Luke struggled for composure. "No, thank you. I don't need charity, Ms. Castillo."

"Of course not," she said. But her eyes were filled with pity.

It was acid on his flayed pride, and he couldn't bear it one more second. "I have to pack up now. So, if you'll excuse me?" He stuffed the tie into his suitcase.

"Oh. All right. I'll just ... go." She went to the door and stood there, clutching the straps of her purse.

Luke avoided her gaze, bending to scoop socks into his bag.

"Goodbye, Mr. Hansen," she said. She walked out of the room, pulling the door shut behind her.

In the silence she left behind, he heard the roach in the sink buzz its wings derisively.

"What do you know about it," he said as he shoved underwear into his bag. "You have a nice cozy drain pipe to live in. No girl roaches feeling sorry for you."

Still, maybe he should call Esmeralda and apologize later, after he found a new motel. She'd want to know where he was staying, anyway. Since she was still going to work with him to find Kowalski. If he hadn't completely blown his chances just now.

Shitnozzle. I ought to kick my ass.

The door creaked open again. He looked up swiftly, but it was only the breeze, not Esmeralda coming back.

Then he looked through the opening. What he saw froze his breath into icy shards in his lungs.

A green Range Rover had pulled up behind Esmeralda as she was walking across the parking lot to her car. Two men were out of the big car and were backing her up against the side of her Mini. One of them said something to her in Spanish.

Luke didn't need a translator to understand what was happening. The menacing postures and the vicious smirks on their faces told him everything.

One of them raised his hand to touch a black curl that had escaped her ponytail, and she flinched away. He saw her hand slip into her purse, her eyes never leaving the goons in front of her.

"Shit!" Luke said. They could grab her, shove her into the Range Rover and be gone in less than five seconds. He had to do something. He had to do it now.

And he was going to have to use stronger methods than his usual straightening-and-frowning routine. These guys would be harder to intimidate than Lutheran college boys on a spree.

He looked frantically around the room, his gaze skating over pillow fluff and chipboard. There were his tools, still heaped on the floor. He darted over to them and seized his tuning hammer, telescoping the handle out to its full twelve-inch length. Then he slammed through the door and strode out to the parking lot, his heart pounding steadily in his ears.

At the bang of the door the two men fell silent and turned slightly to watch him approach. They didn't exactly stiffen, but he saw a new wariness in their attitudes. Aside from darting one glance at him, Esmeralda didn't take her eyes off them.

When Luke got to the front of the Range Rover, he stopped and sized them up. They were wearing loud shirts, designer jeans, and athletic shoes that looked brand new and expensive. But their faces didn't match the clothes or the car. They weren't very old, early twenties at most, and they had a well-gnawed quality that told of rough childhoods and bad diets.

Luke filed all that away for later. The only important thing about these two right now was that they were standing between him and Esmeralda. He said, "Is there a problem here, gentlemen?"

They exchanged glances, and then one of them, meatier than the other, said, "We ain't got no problem. *La cuca*, she is fiiine, you know? We got to find out how much for her to party with us, you know?" He rubbed his fingers and thumb together in the international sleazeball sign for money, and added a leer, displaying a snaggle of yellow teeth.

"Her worth is far above rubies or pearls. Which is more than you two can afford, I'm thinking."

Apparently the punks were unfamiliar with Proverbs, because their evil smiles got a little confused. "*¿Que?*" the skinnier one said.

The fatter one said, "Man, we can afford anything. Forget about the jewels. White gold, you know?" He flicked his nose.

"I meant, she's not a hooker," Luke patiently explained. "And she doesn't want to talk to you, do you, ma'am?"

"No, I don't," Esmeralda said.

"There you go. So why don't you guys move along?"

The leers slid completely off their faces, to be replaced by even uglier expressions. "Hey, *cacorro*, this ain't your business. We want a bitch, we get the bitch. You fuck with us, you get fucked up. That's how it is. You gonna get fucked up?" the leader said. He squared up to Luke, flexing his hands, pumping up his muscles. The other one edged closer to Esmeralda, hissing something in Spanish.

Esmeralda hissed back.

Luke barely heard them. Something strange was

happening. The sounds of traffic and far away voices faded, the unimportant details of the world around him dimmed. His body went cool and still. Time froze into a single frame. All at once he could see the angles and distances between Esmeralda, the cars, the two men, and himself as sharp and clear as a diagram. And he could see how moving one object would move the others. Just like moving a piano. It was all a matter of pivot points and leverage.

Calmly, almost slowly, he stepped sideways, putting the front end of the idling Range Rover between himself and the men. Then he raised his arm up high, letting the sunlight gleam on the steel head of the tuning hammer in his fist.

He could slam it into the hood to tear up the lovingly polished finish and dent the metal, or he could spiderweb the windshield with one tap. He heard his voice say, "Let me ask you something. How much can you afford to pay your body repair guy?"

The men started toward him, panic and fury on their faces and Spanish insults he was grateful he couldn't understand spewing from their mouths.

He had chosen his position perfectly. Instead of splitting up to come at him from two sides, they both scrambled around the front end in their hurry to get at him.

"Luke!" Esmeralda's voice was tense as a wire.

He didn't take his eyes off the men. When they were almost on him, he spun against the side of the car and ran around the rear end. He dashed in front of Esmeralda and pivoted to face the two thugs, the hammer raised high.

"Get in the car," he ordered her over his shoulder.

"No way," she shot back.

The men rounded the end of the Range Rover and stopped short, finding Luke ready for them. He watched the realization dawn that he had played them, reversing their positions and blocking them from their quarry. They stilled, considering their next move for a long, dangerous moment. The fatter one delved a hand inside his pants pocket.

"I wouldn't, if I were you," Luke said. "I'll crush your wrist with this hammer before you get your hand out of your pocket." In this cold state of awareness, he could see exactly how he had to move his tool to pulverize their bones. A clean strike at the wrist joint, the point of the jaw, the short ribs. It would be easy.

"We already called the cops," Esmeralda yelled from behind his shoulder. "They'll be here any minute!"

The bastards started to look worried. The skinnier one stole a small, telling look at Luke's motel room.

Another second stretched to breaking point. No one moved. Then, the fatter one snarled, *"¡Despégala pues!"* He'd been outmaneuvered, and he knew it.

Flinging out Spanish vituperation and obscene hand gestures, the thugs went back to their car and slammed themselves inside. Their feral eyes gleamed at them from behind the windshield.

Keeping his tool up, Luke shouldered Esmeralda behind the barrier of the Mini in case the bastards tried to take a run at them.

The powerful engine growled, and then the big car shot out of the parking lot and roared down the street.

Luke watched until the last green gleam was out of sight. Slowly, he lowered his hand, letting the hammer dangle at his side.

"Coño," Esmeralda said, sounding shaky. "How crazy was that?"

Luke didn't answer, as he was working hard not to throw up. The world around him slammed back into normal mode, leaving him awash in adrenaline and rattled to his core.

Esmeralda moved out from behind him, circling around and looking up into his face. "Thank you for chasing those guys off. They were starting to worry me a little bit."

"*You* were worried?" he said, his voice cracking. "Why didn't you get in the car?"

"What good would I do in there if you needed backup?"

"Backup, huh." He gestured to her purse with his hammer. Her hand was still inside, gripping something. "Do you have pepper spray in there?"

"Yep. And also brass knuckles," she said, drawing her hand out. Sure enough, she had a massive chunk of gleaming metal wrapped around her little fist.

Luke blinked. "Holy crap!"

She let out a small grin. "Yeah, a lot of guys can't believe a girl would actually have one of these things. So, while they're standing there thinking about it, you sock them in the solar plexus," she said, making a little jab in the air near his midriff.

"You mean you've used those before?"

"Well, no. Not as such. Usually guys will just run away when I take the knuckles out."

"I don't blame them. You know, sometimes you scare me, Esmeralda."

She gave him an arch look as she slipped the knuckles off and shoved them into her bag. Then her expression changed like quicksilver into something warm and intent. "Oh, I don't think anything scares you, Luke. You're very, um, brave," she said, her cheeks glowing.

"Thanks." He made a mental note to never tell her about that morning's alligator incident.

They fell silent, looking at each other. Her eyes darkened, going so deep and velvety that he started to list forward, like he was falling into them. His nausea vanished, the battle-ready tautness of his nerves changing to a different kind of tension.

He tore his eyes away from her. "You were pretty brave yourself," he said gruffly.

After the tiniest pause, she said, "Not so much. I wasn't the one in danger."

"Esmeralda, those guys had you cornered. They could have grabbed you and taken you to who knows where. If they had pulled guns or knives ..." His mouth went dry just thinking about it.

She brushed his words aside. "They weren't actually interested in me. They were asking me questions about you."

16

"*WHAT?* What do you mean, they were asking about me? How did they know who I am?"

"They didn't. They wanted to know what your name was, and what you were doing in Miami. Who you were working for. That was what was making me nervous, to tell you the truth."

"But why ...?" His neck bristled with awareness. "It was them. Those were the guys who broke into my room."

Esmeralda's brows snapped together. "But—"

"That's why they believed your bluff about the cops," he said, remembering the glance one of the thugs had shot at his motel door. "They already knew about the break-in. They must have realized there was a good chance I would have reported it."

"But—"

"And I've seen that green Range Rover before. This morning, when you were picking me up, it was at the drive-through in the restaurant over there." He pointed at the grease trap where he had gotten breakfast.

"But—"

"I can't be sure it was the same one," he went on, "but how many Range Rovers could possibly show up at a place like this?" He glanced around at the cars in the parking lot, all of which appeared to be one pothole away from the scrap heap.

"But Luke," Esmeralda said, determined, "why would the thieves hang around here after they had robbed the place?"

"Because they didn't get what they were looking for. That's why they were asking questions about me. They were after information from whatever source they could find ..." A thought struck him.

He ran across the parking lot to his truck, which he had parked a few spaces away from his motel door. He let out a breath when he saw that the doors were still locked, the windows undamaged.

He heard Esmeralda's light steps come up behind him. He said, "They must not have known what I was driving, or they would have broken into the truck too."

"But why would they target you specifically? Who would do something like that just to get information on you?"

He started to turn around to face her when he suddenly became aware that they had an audience. Now that all danger had passed, a few of the other motel denizens were peering warily out of their cracked doorways at them.

"Let's talk about this back inside. I'm feeling a little exposed here," he said.

Esmeralda followed his gaze to take in the open doors and the peeping eyeballs. "Gotcha."

They hustled back into Luke's room. He put his hammer away in his tool case, and then he wedged a piece of chipboard from the dresser under the door to hold it closed.

As he worked, Esmeralda leaned against the wall next to the door, her body a sinuous curve. "I just had a thought. Maybe those guys weren't after information. Maybe they were trying to scare you. Kowalski might have sent them as a warning."

Luke barely refrained from rolling his eyes as he stood up. "I know you're convinced that Kowalski is a big bad ivory smuggler, but he is not the type to send out thugs with warnings. Trust me on this. Besides, he doesn't even know I'm in town. The way I see it, whoever is responsible for this is either someone I met at your house or at the Castillo office building."

"Hang on. When did you go to the office?"

"I stopped by there yesterday to find out your home address. I also did a little temp work." Briefly, he told her about moving the poor parlor grand that had been left on the street. And delicately glossed over the stressed-out receptionist with the appetite for a long lunch.

"Wait, Roddy's keeping one of the pianos for display? That's strange. I thought he wanted to dump them all and pretend this never happened." Shrugging it aside, she said, "So anyway, why would anyone at the company send those men after you?"

"I don't think it was one of the office people. You said those two guys were asking what my name was, right?"

"Yes," she said warily.

"Well, the office people already knew my name. I gave them my card. They even cut me a check."

"So, what are you saying?"

"The only people I've met down here who don't know my real name are the people at your house."

He could practically see her missile shields go up, but he blazed on recklessly. "What if someone there knows I'm not Kowalski, and is trying to find out who I really am?"

"That's nuts."

"Here's another question," he said, blasting ever-deeper into hostile territory, "How did those guys find out where I was staying? You were the only person I told. Did you give out this motel address to anyone?"

Probably seeing where he was going with this, she reluctantly said, "No."

"Did you tell anyone besides Agent Truitt you were meeting me today?"

Even more reluctantly, "No."

"Then someone who was at your house yesterday must have overheard us making arrangements when we were standing in the entryway. Whoever it was had those men follow you here."

"That's not possible."

"The way you drive, I wouldn't think so either, but if Agent Truitt could follow you, so could those guys."

"Very funny. I meant, no one in my family would set lowlifes on my trail."

Based on what he had seen of her cousin, Luke was less than convinced about that. But, feeling bad about the driving crack, all he said was, "There were others in the house besides your family."

She slitted her eyes at him. "You'd better not be talking about Anita, because I'll have you know she is a mother to me."

The idea of the housekeeper in her bun and sensible shoes ordering around a couple of dirtbags for hire nearly made him smile. "Obviously not her. But what about your dad's bodyguard?"

"Ignacio Gorte?" She shook her head. "He's been with us a long time too, and he's dedicated to my father."

That didn't reassure Luke at all. "And what about that other guy, Juan?"

She gave a sniff of contempt. "I threw him out of the house, remember? He couldn't have overheard us."

"He said he was going to wait for your cousin. He could have gone back inside through another door and lurked around eavesdropping. Sound carries very well in that hallway. Anyone in a nearby room could have heard us talking."

She chewed on her pink lower lip, uncertainty creeping into her eyes. "You still haven't said why you think someone would target you."

"I ... don't know. It has to be either because I'm chasing Kowalski or because I let people think I'm interested in the Chinese pianos. Those are the only two things I've done that could possibly draw heat." *Besides getting involved with you.* Esmeralda Castillo could bring down nuclear fusion levels of heat, he had no doubt.

Her mouth tightened. "This is all just speculation. Have you considered that maybe you're building up conspiracy theories about a couple of random assholes? I mean, if there's any place to run across random assholes, it's here."

A hollow grating noise vibrated through the door. They both jumped as someone on the other side shoved it open as far as the chipboard wedge would allow. The motel manager poked his crumpled paper sack of a face through the crack.

"Speak of the devil," Esmeralda said.

The manager goggled back and forth at Luke and Esmeralda. "You say you go, but you stay. You make trouble."

"*I* make trouble! Did you not see us nearly getting assaulted in your parking lot?" Luke said.

"I see nothing! You not call police!"

"Maybe we should skip over the police and call ICE instead," Esmeralda said sweetly.

The man blanched and ducked back out the door.

Esmeralda slammed it closed again and leaned against it as the sound of running feet pattered away.

"I really should call the police to report what happened here," Luke said.

"And tell them what? That someone ripped up your clothes as part of a vast piano-related conspiracy?"

"Well, I wouldn't phrase it in those terms."

"And what can we actually tell the cops about those two guys in the parking lot? Just describing them won't help much. I didn't get their license plate number, did you?"

"No. I had other things on my mind."

"We can't give the cops a good reason to investigate them, either. There's no proof that they were the ones who robbed you."

"They could interview the neighbors. One of them had to have seen something ..."

Even as he said it, he knew how ridiculous he sounded. Those two could have announced the break-in with a billboard and a bullhorn, and no one living here would remember seeing or hearing a damn thing.

Esmeralda clearly thought so too, because she sent him a look that said, "You can't be serious."

"They nearly attacked you!" he said.

"They didn't make any explicit threats. And the only one who actually pulled a weapon was you, Luke." She paused to let that sink in. "The police are not going to take this seriously. They may even blame *you*."

"I can't just let this go, Esmeralda."

"No, you're right. We can't let it go. I'll call Agent Truitt. He *will* take it seriously. And if there's any chance that this mess is related to Kowalski, he needs to know."

"All right. We'll report it to Agent Truitt. But I'm going to be asking my own questions."

She started to say something, then stopped and nodded thoughtfully. "That being the case, maybe instead of finding a new motel you should come stay with me."

It took a few seconds for that sentence to register. "What?"

"If you're right and there's something weird going on here, then I want to get to the bottom of it, same as you. And I want to find Kowalski, the same as you. It'll be more convenient for us to work together on this if you're staying at the house."

"The house? Your house?"

She shrugged and nodded.

"You're inviting me to come stay at your house with you?"

"Like I said, it just makes sense. For the investigation."

He eyed her for a long moment, weighing his options against her motives.

On the one hand, she was right, to a point. Sticking close to her was still his best bet for finding the Piano Tuners Guild seal, just as he had figured yesterday. And it would be far easier for him to pursue the strange new turn his quest had taken if he was staying in the same house as the main targets of his investigation.

On the other hand, he suspected that her reasons for inviting him had less to do with convenience than with pity. She was looking at him with a guileless expression, but deep in her eyes lurked the same softness reserved for fleabitten mutts in rescue shelters.

On the *other* other hand, maybe she needed him at her house far more than she realized. If anyone there was in the habit of consorting with once and future convicts like the two men in the parking lot, somebody had to guard her back.

And that was why he was going to do this, he decided. At least, that was the excuse he was going to give himself. Though, in his deepest, darkest heart, he knew he would have said yes to her no matter what. He would have grabbed on to any chance to be near her, logic and pride be damned.

"Okay," he said, striving for a casual tone. "Thanks. That's very generous of you."

He thought he saw a flash of triumph in her eyes. "Not at all. God knows we have plenty of room." She reached for the door. "I'll go on ahead and tell everyone to expect you. Come to think of it, I have a lot of explaining to do where you're concerned."

"No," he said, thinking hard. "We shouldn't tell anyone at your house who I really am yet."

"Why not?"

"If I'm right, and someone at your house hired those thugs to find out my identity, we shouldn't just give them what they want. Keeping them frustrated might be the best way to smoke them out."

She huffed out a breath. "I still think you're being paranoid."

"Maybe I am. But please, humor me. Just for a few days." The deception couldn't last much longer than that anyway. All anyone had to do to find out his name was give his description to the office workers. Whoever sent the goons after him hadn't realized the piano-mover from the office and the "Brett Kowalski" who showed up at the house were the same man, but it was only a matter of time before they figured it out.

Esmeralda still looked troubled. "I don't like keeping this from Roddy. If it involves the company, he should know."

"So you trust him?"

"Of course. He's my cousin."

Luke was unimpressed with that reasoning, but he had sense enough not to say so. "I still think we should keep it between ourselves, because Roddy might tell people he trusts, like Juan."

She nodded, conceding his point. "All right. Roddy stays in the dark for now. What about Anita?"

"The less she's involved in any of this the better for her."

"Okay, you win. We won't tell anyone." Then her mouth curved in a mischievous smile. "So, for the time being, you're still Brett Kowalski."

"Argh. I changed my mind."

She laughed her husky laugh. "Too late. Now, I want to get out of here before that manager comes back with a shotgun. Sure you don't want help packing?"

"I think I can handle it."

"Suit yourself," she said, reaching for the door again.

Luke got there before her. "I'm walking you to your car."

She rolled her eyes, but didn't argue.

They made it to the Mini without incident this time. "Thanks again," she said, taking her sunglasses out of her purse. "It was sweet of you to look out for me." She slipped the shades on and looked up at him.

He almost shuffled his feet. "Anyone would have done the same."

"No, they wouldn't. No guy has ever ... well. Let's just say you're one in a million, Luke Hansen."

He looked down into her staggeringly beautiful face. Saw his stark features mirrored in her dark lenses. Below the shades, her pink lips curved in a maddening smile, as if she were about to whisper a secret, or blow a kiss.

In that moment, he vowed to whatever might be listening that nothing terrible would ever happen to her. He wouldn't allow it.

"I meant what I said," he blurted. "You're a pearl beyond price. Or an emerald beyond price, since that what your name means. In English. Some kind of jewel beyond price. I should stop talking now."

She was laughing, a lovely blush running over her cheeks. "Well then, you'd better go get your stuff and your godawful truck and drive to the house. I'll meet you there." She pulled her car door open and got in. Then she threw a smile out the window at him. "Or, you know, just stand there like a street lamp."

The Mini's engine revved, and Esmeralda zipped out of the parking lot and down the road.

Luke jogged back to his room, where for once in his life he tossed everything into his bags without pausing to fold or organize. Even his precious tools got packed in haphazardly. He loaded himself up with his stuff, and called out to the roach in the sink, "The place is all yours, pal."

He heard it buzz happily as he banged out the motel for the last time.

17

ESMERALDA WAS in the front hallway ready to pounce when Luke finally made it to her house. She pulled open the door just as he raised his hand to ring the bell and grinned up at him. "I was wondering where you were."

He let his hand fall and looked down at her, his mouth bending in one of his subtle smiles. "Not all of us can drive through heavy traffic at warp speed."

"A sad fact. Come in. *Bienvenido.*" She stood back to let him walk in. Shutting the door behind him, she said, "I called Agent Truitt and filled him in on recent events."

"That must have been a fun conversation."

It hadn't been a fun conversation at all, in fact. At first, Al had been inclined to dismiss the break-in at Luke's room as random crime. But an about-face came when she told him that Luke was moving in with her. Suddenly, the motel incident was clear proof that Luke was neck deep in ivory smuggling. Even though his preliminary background check had turned up nothing, Truitt reluctantly admitted, she was not to foolishly trust such an unreliable character. He concluded by forbidding her to let Luke in her door.

In reply, Esmeralda made static noises in her phone, told Al she was losing the signal, and hung up.

She smiled cheerily at Luke. "He's on the case." She had a strong feeling that Al would double his efforts to find Kowalski if it meant evicting Luke from her house.

Whatever Al thought, she was highly pleased with herself for getting Luke here where she could keep an eye on him. If left to his own devices he would no doubt have landed in an even worse place than where she had found him. And now that he was involved in this ivory mess, possibly even in danger because of it, she felt responsible for him.

But she perfectly understood that his dudely pride wouldn't allow her to help him directly. Suggesting a loan had been a boneheaded move on her part, for sure. But with the excuse of the investigation, she could look after him without putting up his back.

Though he might not need as much babysitting as she had thought earlier. He had certainly handled himself well against the assholes in the parking lot. For a second there, with his hammer gleaming in his fist and a cold light in his eyes, he had lost every hint of his earlier gentleness and transformed into a warrior. The kind of conquering hero who could and would fight a battle for a lady's honor, and then proceed to screw the lady's brains out.

And for a fleeting moment, she, the lady in this scenario, wouldn't have minded getting brusquely railed by him. At all. *Dios bueno*, how messed up was that, she wondered with a rush of heat.

Cutting off that unproductive train of thought, she said, "You can leave your bags here for now. I want to take you in to see my father. He's out back by the pool."

"Will seeing me upset him?"

"No. I doubt he'll even remember you from yesterday. And he's just had his dinner, so his mood is as good as it gets. As long as you don't mention the bad pianos, you should be fine."

"All right then." He set his bags against the wall and started down the hall.

She touched his arm to stop him, and *wow*. It felt like touching a steel beam. She had noticed that when she had patted him at the zoo earlier. She would have liked to keep groping his arm for a while, but instead she took her hand away and said, "I have to warn you, I volunteered you to give a piano concert."

He stiffened. "You did what?"

"I'm sorry. It just popped out."

"How does a piano concert just pop out?"

"Well, you see, Roddy's having this cocktail party tomorrow night that I totally forgot about. He's wooing investors in Castillo Imports, and I'm supposed to be there to help host the thing, apparently. Papa and Ignacio were talking about it when I came home, so I got the idea to tell them I hired you to get the piano in shape and play it for the guests."

Luke just looked at her.

"I had to give them some excuse for why you were staying with us, since you won't let me tell them the truth. This was the best I could come up with on short notice. We didn't think this plan of ours out very well, you know." A sudden thought struck her. "You *can* play a piano, right? Not just tune it?"

A frown appeared between his blond brows. "I could manage a few scales. And 'Chopsticks'."

"Oh, *Dios mio*." She put her hand over her face.

"Relax, you're in luck. I actually have a Bachelor of Music degree in piano performance."

She peeked between her fingers to see the gleam in his gray eyes. Smiling back, she put her hand down. "You punk. A music degree, huh? That's impressive. You must be good."

He shifted, looking self-conscious. "I do all right. I'm no Martha Argerich."

She grinned. "No, you don't look like a Martha." She started walking down the hall again and Luke fell into step beside her. "So, you're okay with this plan? Playing for the party tomorrow?"

"Sure. It sounds like fun. I always did want to try playing professionally."

"Why didn't you? Why go into piano tuning instead?"

"Trying to make a living as a concert pianist isn't practical. Very few of them earn enough to support themselves, or a family." His voice took on a singsong quality, reciting something by rote.

She wondered who had put those disheartening words into his mouth. "Maybe you should go for it anyway. Practicality is overrated. Besides, you, my friend, are not a practical man. You're a dreamer, or you wouldn't be here in Miami. We've established that already."

He shot her a bemused look.

They had passed through the hall and into the large game room at the back of the house and were now standing at a set of French doors leading out onto the back patio.

Luke hadn't seen this portion of the house before, and as they walked outside she saw him take it in, clearly impressed. She followed his gaze without much interest.

A wide pavement of coral stone stretched across the back of the house and circled the swimming pool. The palm trees lining the property threw light shadows over the gleaming white tiles and glassy blue water. Beyond the patio and pool the crisply manicured lawn ran down to the dock where Roddy's sleek Coronet was moored, bobbing gently against the bright ocean waves and the Miami skyline in the distance. The soft sounds of the water and the breeze mingled with the music of a passionate Spanish ballad playing on hidden speakers.

Yeah, it was nice enough. And though she had lived with this kind of wealth and luxury all her life, she knew better than to take it for granted. But she couldn't make herself care about it very much either.

People were usually downright appalled to learn that she was turning her back on Castillo Imports in favor of zookeeping, of all things. But she had never shared Papa and Roddy's love of glamorous junk, something no one in her world seemed to understand.

She wondered if Luke got that about her, or if on some level he still thought she was the same spoiled rich bitch bimbo she must have appeared to him when they first met. Then she wondered why it mattered what he thought.

She said abruptly to him, "Let's get this over with." She led him across the patio to her father.

He was seated near the pool at a stone-topped table under a striped awning. As usual, he was dressed in beautiful clothes that showed subtle signs of disorder, the fine fabric sagging around his once-powerful shoulders. Ignacio sat across from him, his coat stripped off and his sleeves rolled up. A game of dominoes was scattered across the table between them.

Anita was standing to one side of the table, clearing the remains of a meal onto a cart.

All three of them looked up as Esmeralda and Luke

walked toward them. "Papa, our guest is here," she said, keeping her voice light and cheerful.

As Luke approached the table, her father examined him closely, his face a mask of arrogance overlying frightened confusion. "Who is this?" he demanded.

"This is Mr. Kowalski, Papa. He's going to stay with us for a few days and play piano for us."

Luke said, "Good to see you, sir. Thank you for having me. I'm looking forward to playing for your guests tomorrow."

Her father scowled. "He's a *gringo*. I don't like him. I don't like *gringos*. They don't make good servants. They think they're smart, but they always try to steal from me. He'll try to steal my ... my things." His fingers made agitated movements over the dominoes.

Luke said gently, "I only want to play music for you, sir."

"You like music, Papa," Esmeralda coaxed.

"I know I like music," he said sharply. After a moment, he picked up a domino. "He can play for me. But I wish he was a Guatemalan. Guatemalans make good servants." He placed the tile on his haphazard train.

"Yes, Papa," she said, relieved that the dominoes were staying on the table.

Ignacio, who had been watching carefully and silently, played a domino in turn.

Anita took the resumption of the game as her cue. She stacked the last of the dishes on the cart and hurried forward, saying in Spanish, "Maria Esmeralda, your Papa's had enough for now. Take your fellow up to his room to get comfortable, and then you bring him directly to the kitchen so he can eat his dinner. The poor boy looks famished."

Esmeralda said in Spanish, "He's not my fellow."

Anita paid no attention. She looked over Luke's strapping frame with a calculating purse of her mouth. "Tell him we will put some meat on his bones while he is with us. Go on, tell him."

Omitting the meat on the bones bit, she said, "Anita wants me to get you settled in your room, and then we'll see about dinner."

Luke had been wearing a guarded look, but at this, he perked up. "Dinner? That sounds fantastic. Thank you," he said to Anita. He thought for a moment, and added, "*Gracias*."

His Spanish accent was straight out of Sesame Street, but Esmeralda gave him props for the effort.

Anita seemed to agree, because she smiled up at him with an alarming new twinkle in her eye. Esmeralda hoped he was ready for the avalanche of food about to come down on him.

"Make sure you take your fellow to the blue guest room," the housekeeper said as she shooed them back into the house.

"He's not my fellow!"

Anita just smiled and closed the French doors after them.

Just before the doors shut, she heard Papa grumble, "Kowalski? What kind of name is that?"

18

LUKE FOLLOWED Esmeralda through the main hall to retrieve his bags, then up the grand iron-and-tile staircase and down another hall to a guest bedroom bigger than his entire studio apartment back in Minneapolis. It contained a king-size bed heaped with luxuriant blue bedding, a blue suede sofa in front of a jumbo TV screen, and a bathroom that was a cross between Versailles and Wet 'n' Wild Waterpark. For the tenth time since he had stepped through the front door, he wondered what in the world a guy like him was doing in a place like this.

He had no time to do more than stow his bags before she whisked him back downstairs and into a cavernous marble-and-stainless-steel kitchen. Anita bustled forward as soon as they appeared. She directed them to an alcove that would have qualified as a full dining room in a normal house but which here only made it to breakfast nook status. Inside was a massive wood-and-iron table set for two with china and silverware that could have come off a sunken Spanish galleon.

When they sat down, Anita made an array of heaping

bowls and platters appear before them like magic. Luke had a Midwesterner's healthy suspicion of seafood, and here on the coast he expected to be confronted with fish. But he was relieved to see that Cuban cuisine was heavy on pork and chicken, accompanied by mountains of rice, beans, sweet potatoes, and some other potato-like thing he was told was yucca.

He served himself up huge portions of everything and got down to business. And, oh, God, it was good. He could have cried actual tears it had been so long since he'd had a meal that didn't come out of a fryer.

When he finally came up for air, he found Anita watching him eat with critical assessment, like he was a prize steer she was fattening up for the state fair.

But Luke was awash in serotonin and couldn't possibly be self-conscious. He swallowed his mouthful of something delicious and said to Esmeralda, "Could you tell Anita that I think this is the most wonderful food I've ever eaten?"

"I think she gets it. The moaning kind of gave you away," she said, smiling at him over her own minuscule portion of rice, beans, and vegetables. But she obligingly translated for him, whereupon Anita smiled, vanished, and then reappeared with a heaping bowl full of rice pudding, placing it in front of him.

He cast her a look of what was probably bovine adoration and dug in. She all but patted his head before bustling off and leaving him and Esmeralda alone.

She had pushed her plate away and was watching him with a smile lingering on her lips. She had changed her clothes before he had arrived that afternoon, and was now wearing dark Bermuda shorts and a lacy tank top that clung to her astounding torso like plastic wrap. Her feet were bare, and he had noticed earlier that each of her toenails was painted a different rainbow color, like Skittles. God help him, he wanted to taste every flavor.

He put his spoon down and looked away from her, out of one of the nearby windows into the back yard. The sun was only just starting to sink behind the distant skyscrapers of the city, turning them into fountains of molten gold that poured their reflections across the water of the bay. The patio was empty. Castillo and Ignacio had come inside at some point.

"So what would you like to do now that your hunger is satisfied?"

He looked at her sharply, wondering if he had just imagined a smoky note in her question. Or was it a test of some sort?

He wasn't about to play a game he couldn't win. He looked her in the eye. "I believe we ought to concentrate on Kowalski and the pianos tonight, since neither of us will have much time for it tomorrow."

Her eyebrows rose. "You want to work on the investigation?"

"That's why I'm here, right?"

"Right, right. Right. Well. Hmm. How do you suggest we do this?"

"Uh ..." What would a detective do? He tried to channel Humphrey Bogart in *The Maltese Falcon*, but couldn't quite get into it. Not when he felt more like Peter Sellers in *The Pink Panther*.

"I think ... I think we should gather up every piece of information we have so far and compile it. I'd also like to talk to Roddy again. Maybe he knows something that could explain what happened today."

"It would be easier to find out what he knows if you just

told him what you were doing straight up and asked for his help."

She still didn't want to suspect her cousin of wrongdoing. Fine. He'd indulge her for now. "I might do that, but not yet. I don't want him accidentally giving anything away to Juan."

"All right," she grumbled. "Roddy's been working late recently. We can ask him some questions when he gets home tonight."

"In the meantime, is there any other source of information on these pianos we could look into?"

She considered for a moment, then brightened. "Maybe. Come on." Luke reached out to pick up his dishes, but Anita swooped in and chased him out of her kitchen with a volley of Spanish. Esmeralda came flying out hard on his heels.

"Good grief. I could have lost a hand," he said when they were safely in the hallway.

"Yeah, I should have warned you not to mess with Anita's kitchen."

She led him down the hall to a closed door. "Now, this is a long shot, but maybe we'll find something about Kowalski or the pianos in here." She opened the door to reveal a home office. It was decorated in men's club style, with wood paneling, leather furniture, massive antique desk, and shelves of books that had probably never been read. Like the rest of the house, it was caked with deposits of decorative objects. Strangely, there was no computer anywhere in sight.

She said, "We can go through Papa's office and look for clues."

He smiled down at her. "Clues? *Clues?* You mean a

hidden passage behind a bookcase or a secret drawer in the desk?"

"Though that would be awesome, I had something less Scooby-Doo in mind. I thought we could sort through his papers."

"What kind of papers?"

"Personal stuff, mostly. Roddy moved all the company files to the main office last year when Papa started to show signs of illness. But I think business papers or a phone call might have gotten through to him anyway. Something that would explain why he has such a horrible reaction to the mention of the pianos."

"What makes you think that?"

"Well, about two weeks ago, Juan was over for dinner and he and Roddy started talking about this shipment of pianos with ivory keys that they had bought. Roddy wanted to sell them offshore without reporting them to Fish and Wildlife, which you have to do by law when you're importing exotic animal parts. Roddy could have gotten into a lot of trouble if he was caught.

"Since I knew Agent Truitt through my work at the zoo, I convinced Roddy to let me tell him about the ivory myself, kind of smooth the way."

By which she meant charm and bullshit Truitt into letting her cousin off easy, Luke thought.

She went on. "The next day, when I went to report the ivory to Fish and Wildlife, my father dumped out all the papers in his filing cabinets and tossed them around the room." She gestured to a handsome set of cabinets behind the desk, the drawers open enough to show empty shadows inside. "He smashed his computer, too. It was a huge mess. He kept saying, 'The keys, the keys ...' Well. You heard him."

"No one knows what set him off?"

"Roddy thinks it was my fault. I insisted we get the law involved in the business instead of letting him hush the whole thing up."

"But no one actually saw what happened?"

She frowned. "You know, I never did get the specifics. Roddy, Juan, Ignacio, and Anita were all here when I came home from talking to Agent Truitt. Everyone was so busy yelling at me that I didn't find out who was where and when."

"We need to ask them what they remember."

"You're right. In the meantime, there's the paperwork," she said, pointing to half a dozen cardboard boxes stacked along one wall. "When we cleaned up, we just stuffed all the papers in those cartons over there. I thought I might as well go through everything before I filed it away again, but I haven't got around to it yet. And now, after everything that's happened, I wonder if there's some kind of memo or invoice related to those pianos in there. If maybe my father was looking for something specific when he emptied out his files."

"Huh," Luke said, thinking that a confused act of rage was a more likely explanation.

"Like I said, it's a long shot. If you don't want to—"

"No, no, you're right. We might find something useful." Data compiling was his idea in the first place.

At his capitulation she rewarded him with another one of her devastating smiles. His endorphins soared, a purely Pavlovian response. A few more rewards like that, and she'd train him to be a paperwork fiend, he suspected.

She said, "Thanks. Between the two of us, this job should go really quick." Crossing the room to the boxes, she sank down gracefully to sit tailor-fashion on the floor and opened the nearest box.

Luke drifted toward her, magnetized by the way her shorts rode up the taut curves of her thighs. He imagined running his thumb along the line the hem made over her silky skin. Instead of doing that, he sat down facing her and pulled out a box of his own.

She paused, eying him. "You're okay with sitting on the floor?"

"Why wouldn't I be?"

"You seem kind of, umm ... formal. Maybe it's the tie."

He loosened his tie, and even undid his collar button. "I crawl around underneath pianos all the time. I can handle a little informality."

She aimed a hint of her smoky smile at him. "Groovy."

That settled, they dove into the sea of files. Soon they were surrounded by drifts of papers sorted mostly by whether they were going in the shredder or not. The shredder pile quickly grew into a sizable peak.

It seemed Eduardo Castillo had kept every inconsequential scrap that had ever crossed his path. Luke sifted through sheaves of instruction manuals for obsolete gadgets, fundraising letters from the Republican Party dated 1987, and newspaper clippings and import trade journal articles going back even farther. Not quite as ghastly as financial or tax records, but close.

But the drudgery of sorting was soon enlivened when he pulled out a thick stack of photographs of nubile young women in various states of undress.

Esmeralda looked up and was caught by what must have been his dumbstruck look. She said, "Aha. You've found some of Papa's wives and girlfriends. All models, you know. We models like to give our photos to whoever can advance our careers. There are even a few of my pictures lying around here somewhere." She cast a vague glance around the room and shrugged. "I guess Papa kept those for sentimental reasons."

"Yes, I see how these would stir the finer feelings." Then something she'd said struck him. "Some? How many wives and girlfriends did your father have?"

"Four wives. And dozens of girlfriends, but he stopped marrying them after number four. Cheaper, you know. Papa always had an eye on the bottom line."

"And your mother ..." he drifted off, unsure how to finish his question.

"Was wife number two. And the longest lasting. Six whole years, until the day she died."

Luke stared at her in shock. He'd assumed her mother was divorced, not dead. "Your mother died? That must have been terrible."

"I don't remember her well. I was four."

"Can I ask what happened?"

"Sure. Medical complications from too many designer drugs and too much plastic surgery." Her eyes went distant and she shuddered slightly. Then she focused on him and said with a smile a little too bright, "That's why I don't do either drugs or surgery."

Luke's gaze went involuntarily to her chest. Her amazing, astounding, mind-blanking chest. He drew a breath but, coming to his senses in the last instant, he clenched his jaw shut and shuffled the photos into a pile instead of asking an unforgivably tacky question.

She said, "Yes, they're real. One hundred percent organic, no fillers, additives or preservatives."

Luke could feel himself turning red. "I didn't ... I wasn't—"

"And I applaud your restraint. But it's an FAQ I thought we should get out of the way."

He thought about how many men would have had to ask her if she had to make it a Frequently Asked Question, and had a disturbing urge to thump every one of them. He rifled through the pictures of polished beauties in his lap. Plenty of basketball-sized knockers there. And trout-pout lips and sliver noses.

"Did they treat you well, all of these stepmothers?" He shuffled them back into their folder and put them aside.

"Hah! Not one of them would appreciate being called a stepmother, let me tell you. We more or less ignored each other."

"That sounds rough."

"Not at all. I had Anita and my *au pairs*. I have nothing to complain about." She thought for a moment. "And Cerise was cool. She was Papa's girlfriend when I was eighteen. She's the one who helped me get into modeling. Introduced me to the right people, showed me how to avoid getting conned or whored out, that kind of thing."

There was nothing but casual annoyance in her voice as she said, "conned or whored out," like she was talking about a bad sunburn.

"Does that happen to models a lot?"

"Oh, yeah. Some modeling agencies are nothing more than escort services, and some only exist to suck the money out of naïve young girls who pay for portfolios and clothes and makeup. You have to learn how to protect yourself fast in this business or you end up writhing naked around a pole in some dive next to the airport. I've seen it happen more than once."

"And your family was okay with you taking those kinds of risks?"

She just laughed. "Considering Papa's history with models, he didn't have much room for disapproval, did he? Anyway, he and Roddy never cared what I did as long as it didn't affect Castillo Imports. They both wrote me off as a bad investment a long time ago, I'm afraid. Especially after I made it clear that I had no interest in going into the import business or marrying one of Papa's friends."

Christ. His opinion of the men in her family was sinking into the briny depths. But, amazingly, he couldn't detect any bitterness in her tone, only fond exasperation. He said, "Seems Roddy is pretty important to your father. I thought he was only your cousin."

"He is, but my *Tio* Gerardo, my father's brother, died when Roddy was a baby. Ever since then Papa has treated him as a son."

"Your uncle died too? How?" he asked before he could think better of it.

"In a boating accident." A troubled look crossing her smooth forehead. "At least, that's what everyone always says. But ..."

"But what?"

She shifted around to lean her back against the wall where the boxes of papers had been stacked, stretching her legs out in front of her. "I've always had the feeling that there was more to the story. That maybe *Tio* Gerardo was carrying something on his boat that he shouldn't have been, and that's why he ended up dead."

It took him a moment to get it. "Your uncle was a smuggler?"

"I don't have any real reasons to think so. It's more a feeling I get from things people say, or don't say, or the way they look when certain topics come up. You know how it is with family skeletons."

"Yeah, I guess. But, you know, sometimes those little secrets can blow themselves way out of proportion. I have an aunt my mother refused to talk about for years because she said she was a dirty hippie. We thought she was growing marijuana or something. Turned out she was an organic cookbook writer."

Esmeralda laughed again, that wonderful low chuckle. "Your family is pretty straight-laced, I take it?"

"Straight as a Lutheran ruler."

"Are any of them musicians, like you?

"Only my dad. He's a piano tuner too. Or was, until he retired. Mom was a nurse. My brothers and sisters all took after her. They're nurses and paralegals and insurance salesmen. Very practical."

"Practical. So that's where that word comes from. I wondered why it mattered to you so much. But I get it. Family's family. Their opinions are important to you."

He started to nod in agreement, but then stopped, thought, and realized ... No, actually. No, their judgment didn't matter that much to him anymore. In fact, the mere idea of another helping of family opinion like the one he'd been treated last Christmas was enough to make him break out in hives.

Last December, divorced, unemployed, and houseless, he'd stepped through the door of the family home in St. Paul into a fog of pine-scented candles and disapproval. His parents, who usually had all the pep of wet tissue paper, had summoned up enough energy to make their disappointment clear. And his three older sisters and two older brothers, each happily married and gainfully employed, had helped them stage a full-scale intervention.

They had settled him down on his parents' plaid sofa and gathered around him like a class full of med students dissecting a cadaver. His father had gently pointed out that piano tuning was no longer a realistic way to support a wife and family, as it had been in his day. His mother had sorrowfully taken the blame for letting him throw his college money away on a music degree instead of insisting on pre-law or computer programming.

His siblings had urged him grow up, shoulder some responsibility, and take a job as a gofer at his brother Pete's life insurance firm. "In a few years," his older though shorter sibling had jovially said, "you might even qualify for a company 401K, just like me!" And that was when Luke had run away so fast he'd nearly left a cartoon-style hole in the door.

When Esmeralda started laughing, he realized he had been telling her all of this out loud.

"You're always laughing at me," he said, a faint smile on his own face. "I ought to be insulted."

Still chuckling, she said, "Don't tell me you don't think it's funny, because I won't believe you. You laugh to yourself all the time."

At his startled silence, she said, "That's right, I've got your number."

"I ... No one has ever accused me of having a sense of humor before."

"Then I guess no one knows you as well as I do."

Luke nearly did laugh then. This girl, who he had first met a little more than twenty-four hours ago, understood him better than people who had known him all his life? Ridiculous.

Everyone he had ever met expected sober dependability from him. Friends, family, casual acquaintances ... Even Kowalski had tried to play on his stolid nature.

Only Esmeralda saw him differently. She thought he

was a dreamer, for God's sake. A dreamer with a sense of humor, no less. The man she described was almost a reverse image of the man he'd always thought he was.

So why did that man also somehow feel ... real?

Maybe, possibly, it was because she actually did see something in him that no one else ever had. Maybe, as crazy as it sounded, after a little more than twenty-four hours she really did know him well after all.

19

AT SOME POINT he wasn't even aware of, he had moved to lean against the wall, and now he was sitting shoulder to shoulder with her, his legs stretched out next to her. Her feet were as finely made as the rest of her, slender, high-arched, with delicately curling toes. And those Skittles-colored toenails ... dear lord.

His gaze traveled up her smooth, endless legs, over the dips and curves of her body, and up to her smiling face turned toward him.

Their eyes locked, and once again the sensation of falling into soft darkness folded over him. Her smile faded until she looked almost solemn. Her lips parted, about to speak, but instead her little pink tongue wet her lips, like she was readying them for a kiss.

Something beastly roared up inside him. He wanted to kiss her. He had to kiss her. He knew he shouldn't, but the reasons why not were burning away like tissue paper in a bonfire. And he was leaning down to her until her soft breath brushed his lips. Her eyelashes drifted down, half veiling her gaze. He could feel the heat of her skin, so close.

Smell the ocean scent of her. One more second, and he would be past the point of no return, and nothing on earth would stop him. One more second—

"*¡Hola!*"

Luke and Esmeralda jolted as Anita popped her head into the room, her sparkling black eyes moving back and forth between the two of them.

"*Hola Anita*," Esmeralda said, a little too brightly.

Luke surreptitiously checked to make sure the pile of papers was covering the bulge in his lap as the little housekeeper said something in a brisk voice.

Esmeralda blushed, cleared her throat, and said, "Anita wants to know if you would like some coffee."

The expectant way the older lady was watching him made him wonder if this was a trick question. "Ah ... yes?" he finally said.

The black eyes narrowed and the wrinkled mouth pursed.

He looked back at a now-grinning Esmeralda. "Was that wrong?"

"Afraid so. You see, when a Cuban offers you coffee, they're actually giving you a hint that it's time to go. Anita is being *mi abuela*. My chaperone. She wants to send you off to bed before you can defile my honor."

"Defile?"

Her grin turned dangerous. "You know. Get me all dirty."

Luke swallowed, unable to not think about defiling Esmeralda. Right here and now. Rolling around amid the drifts of papers, defiling and defiling—

Anita coughed sharply and said something to Esmeralda, who sighed. "I have to help Anita get the coffee." She got to her feet and stretched with a catlike arch to her back.

Luke wrenched his eyes away from her and grabbed another paper. He stared resolutely at the expired warranty for a vacuum cleaner in his hands.

"I'll be right back," she said, and followed the housekeeper out of the room.

"Take your time," he called after her. He shuffled the warranty off. With nothing better to do, he picked up another paper, glanced over it, and sailed that into the shredder pile too.

Paperwork was a lot more tolerable with a beautiful woman nearby, he found. It occurred to him that Esmeralda might have been right when she had said he was lucky Kowalski had snaked the Guild Treasurer's office out from under him. He would have been lousy at the job.

Anyway, this paper-sorting was proving a total bust as far as finding clues went. He scooped the files on his lap together and shoved them onto the shredder pile.

The sudden movement dislodged a sticky note, which fluttered to the floor. He picked it up, glancing at the spidery scribbles on the little square. At the top of the note was a big letter Z, circled once. He looked closer and made out the words, "Lamborghini Aventador SV," and, "Range Rover."

He frowned. Range Rover…

Luke heard a shuffle by the door and looked up eagerly. But it wasn't Esmeralda with the coffee. Cousin Roddy was back. And he wasn't happy.

The guy stomped into the room and looked around, his eyes hard, his jaw jutting. He saw Luke sitting on the floor and recoiled, like he had almost stepped in something a cat horked up. "So it's true. You managed to worm your way in here after all."

That didn't sound terribly welcoming. But a guest had

to be polite to his host, even when the host acted like he was up for the Golden Buttmonkey award.

He rose from the floor, shoving the sticky note into his pocket. "Hi. Esmeralda invited me to play piano at your party tomorrow—"

"Yeah, yeah, Ignacio told me. But let's cut the bullshit, all right? I know why you're really here."

"Is that right?" he said softly. Had Roddy found out his real name? Maybe the office people had finally told him. Was he going to admit setting the thugs on him at the motel?

"Yeah, that's right. You think I don't know a hustler when I see one?"

Hustler? So he didn't know who Luke really was. Or if he did, he wasn't admitting it. Luke breathed out, gathering patience. If Roddy was responsible for the break-in, he wasn't going to give away his game so easily. And if he wasn't responsible, if he still thought Luke was Kowalski, he couldn't really blame him for acting like a tool. Much.

"You think I'm buying that big dumb farm boy act?" Roddy said.

"Actually, I'm from Minneapolis. It's a city of half a million, none of them cows or chickens."

Roddy ignored that. "I know you're trying to weasel money out of Ez. But you're SOL, friend. Everything she makes on her photos goes to that elephant crap of hers. You'll never be able to talk her out of a cent. Nothing comes before those stupid animals for her, believe me." He sounded so resentful Luke had to wonder if he had tried to get money out of his cousin himself, and failed.

He said, "I'm not interested in Esmeralda's money."

"Well, don't think you can use her to get at my uncle's accounts. She's not one of his trustees."

"I don't want anyone's money!"

Roddy sneered. "Right. And you're not rifling through my uncle's office because you're looking for financial papers, either. Too bad for you I took those away months ago."

"So Esmeralda told me. For your information, I'm here because she asked me to help her sort these files, no other reason. And speaking of which, do you know why your uncle threw them all over the room?"

Taken off guard by the sudden attack, Roddy spluttered, "What? No! How the hell should I know?"

"Were you here with him when he had his fit that day?"

"No, I wasn't—and what the hell business is it of yours?"

"It's my business because Esmeralda needs to know, and I'm here to help her."

"Oh yeah? Why are you so keen on *helping* Ez? If it isn't money, which I don't believe for a second, maybe you think you'll help yourself up her skirt?"

Luke didn't answer.

Roddy laughed, a corrosive noise. "Don't be stupid. She knows better than to waste herself on your kind. My cousin is way out of your league, *gringo*."

Now, that drew blood, because it was something Luke already knew perfectly well. But he'd be damned if he'd let this raging dickwart see how deep his knife had sunk. He said, "Your cousin is an exceptionally intelligent woman. She can decide who she wants to spend time with all by herself. From what I've heard, she's had to do that her whole life, since you've never bothered to look after her until this moment."

A guilty flush spread over the guy's face. "That's bullshit. You don't know anything about it."

"He doesn't know anything about what?" Esmeralda said.

They both turned to see her standing in the doorway with a coffee service tray in her hands and a dark expression on her face. She looked back and forth between them, then focused on her cousin. "Roddy, are you being a jerk to my guest?"

Roddy's face switched from abashed right back to belligerent. "I was explaining to your *guest* that whatever scheme he's working here is not going to pay off."

"Scheme? That's ridiculous. There's no scheme," she said. "He's doing us a favor by playing piano for us tomorrow, so I offered him a place to stay while he's in Miami on business. It's as simple as that. Scheme. How silly." She marched into the room, carrying the tray toward the desk.

"That's another thing. This is my first party as the CEO of Castillo Imports. Do you think I want it ruined by some overgrown dirtball playing 'Twinkle, Twinkle'?"

Esmeralda set the tray down on the desk with a loud rattle. "Roddy! I can't believe you're being so rude!"

"This overgrown dirtball mostly plays the nineteenth-century French Romantics," Luke said.

Roddy sneered. "How fucking precious."

"Papa certainly thinks so," Esmeralda snapped. "You know he loves music. He hasn't had a chance to hear a concert in years. Do you really want to take that away from him?"

Roddy growled. "Fine. I'll allow him to play at my party, as long as he isn't a complete embarrassment. But only for *Tio*'s sake. And I want him gone after tomorrow." He pointed a finger in Luke's face. He had to reach up pretty high to do it, though, which made the gesture less than intimidating. "You do the job we hired you for. You entertain our guests like a good performing monkey, and then you get out. Understand?"

Esmeralda said, "Ignore him, Luke, he's hysterical. You can stay as long as you need to."

"I'm not running a homeless shelter!" Roddy said. "I want him out of my house, Ez."

"This isn't your house, Roddy. It's Papa's and mine, and I say he stays."

Roddy snapped his jaw shut and turned tomato red. "This isn't over," he snarled. With a last malevolent glance at Luke, he turned on his heel and stormed off, all but slamming the office door behind him.

"Twerp," Esmeralda said. She turned toward Luke, her mouth tight. "I'm so sorry about that. Don't pay any attention to him, Luke. He's being a brat. He's just under a lot of pressure now that he's running the business without Papa."

"Forget it." Luke scraped up some generosity and added, "It's understandable if he wants to protect his family from a stranger. He's afraid I'll try to take advantage of you."

She huffed. "As if I'm stupid enough to let myself get took. Roddy ought to know me better than that." She set about busily pouring coffee from a silver pot into paper-thin china cups. She handed him one, grace and class in every move she made. In his mind, a hateful voice whispered, *Out of your league.*

"Thanks." He took the cup in his big, callused hand. An awkward silence fell. The searing energy that had leapt between them just moments ago was jangled beyond recognition.

What in all universes was he doing in this place, with this woman? He stared down into the thick brew like he might see the answer there.

But it was simple, really. She needed him here, whether she knew it or not. After the brangle with her cousin, he was more convinced than ever that there was something wrong in this house. So he would stick it out. But, damn, he might as well have volunteered to be the test subject for new waterboarding techniques.

"Cream or sugar?" she asked.

When a Cuban offers you coffee, it means it's time for you to go. He shook his head. "No, thanks." He took a token sip and said, "It's been a long day. I should turn in."

She looked at him for a moment, then nodded, a troubled line between her eyes.

He carefully set down the delicate little cup. "Goodnight," he said. He turned and went to the door.

"Goodnight, Luke," he heard softly behind him.

He didn't dare look back at her.

He walked through the vast house, the echo of his footsteps muffled by the priceless treasures lining the walls. He went up the grand curving staircase and down the hall to the guest room. He would try to sleep on the huge, soft bed there, and try not to dream of things he could never have.

20

IN HIS EFFORT not to dream of Esmeralda, Luke totally failed. He knew this because the next morning he woke up fucking his mattress.

His hips were rolling, pushing against softness. His breath was sawing hard. His eyes shot open.

No dewy skin and wicked smile. Just a high-thread-count pillowcase. "Shit," he said. He rolled onto his back, sweat beading on his bare chest. His cock throbbed angrily against his stomach. *You couldn't have stayed asleep for thirty more seconds?*

He got out of bed and strode to the window. Even though the room temperature was perfect due to the top-of-the-line air conditioning, he felt stifled. He shoved the window open and leaned on the sill. Dragged a breath into his lungs and stared blindly out across the bay.

The dawn light washed the skyscrapers of Miami with pink and gold and shimmered over the dark water.

He heard a faint splash and looked down at the azure swimming pool right below his window.

Esmeralda was down there doing laps. She swam to the far end of the pool, touched the wall, and then flipped over and shot back. Each slender arm lifted and dipped in a smooth rhythm, her body gliding through the water as silkily as a dolphin. When she reached the end of the pool closest to the house, she launched herself out of the water in one elastic movement and stood.

Luke nearly went to his knees.

She was wearing the tiniest bikini imaginable, four triangles tied together with strings. Each triangle was an ice-blue color that seemed about to melt off her golden skin. The morning sunlight poured over her upturned breasts, skimmed the deep curve of her waist, and trailed down the smooth length of her legs.

Lucky, lucky sunlight.

She raised her arms and caught up her long inky hair and wrung it out, then shook it behind her in a scatter of crystal drops.

He must have made some sound then, because she looked up, her delicate spine arching. She spotted him. Slowly, she smiled. "Hi."

Luke actually felt the wood of the windowsill creak under his clenching fingers. "Hi," he said. The word came out as a growl. He cleared his throat. "Nice view. Of the bay, I mean. Beautiful morning." He tried to look like he had been innocently admiring the landscape instead of ogling her like a cretin.

"Yes." Her voice curled up to him like smoke. "But it'll be scorching hot later on."

Luke swallowed.

"Come down to the kitchen in twenty minutes. I'm making breakfast."

"Okay."

She did a turn and strutted out of his sight under the portico, the light winking off the peachy globes of her ass before she vanished into the shadow.

Luke turned and knocked his forehead repeatedly on the wall, groaning, "Why does she do this to me?"

Exactly twenty minutes later, freshly showered, shaved, and sporting a mustard-yellow tie, he marched downstairs with the grim determination of a man about to face a firing squad.

He stepped into the gleaming kitchen and found Esmeralda already there, whisking eggs in a bowl. She had changed out of her bikini and into a fresh zoo uniform. Her still-damp hair was drawn back in a ponytail.

She looked up at him and smiled. "Did you sleep well?"

"Yes. Thank you." Aside from the dream that had woken him up to such crushing disappointment, he'd slept like the dead. The exhaustion of the last several nights must have finally caught up to him. And it had felt too good to be lying in a bed without his feet hanging over the end for once.

"Good," she said. "I have to go to work, but I couldn't leave without making sure you had everything you needed for the day, including breakfast." She looked him over thoughtfully and then cracked two more eggs into her bowl.

He sat on a stool at the counter. "I thought Anita cooked for you."

"Usually she does, but I made her take the morning off so she can rest up for Roddy's party this evening. She's not as young as she used to be. I've been thinking she ought to retire, but she's been the general of this house since 1981 and no one's going to tell her to hang it up until she damn well pleases."

"She's been here all this time and she hasn't learned any English?"

"Nope. She insists she doesn't need to, because she'll be going home to Cuba as soon as the Communists are ousted. She's been saying that for nearly forty years, I'm told."

"So will she? Go back, I mean?"

"Frankly, unless she finds a time machine that will take her back to 1959, I don't think she'll be going anywhere. But she'll still refuse to learn English."

She poured the egg mixture into a smoking omelet pan, sprinkled fillings, folded, plated, garnished, and served it to him, all with the flair of a Food Network starlet.

It was perfectly golden, oozing with cheese and bulging with savory vegetables. He picked up the fork she had set out for him and took a bite. He almost groaned, it was so good. "My God, this is delicious. You are an angel of a cook."

She smiled. "Now, see, that's the kind of shameless flattery that makes cooking fun. That's also what gets you more cooking, for future reference."

"That was my plan. Is it working?"

She laughed. "Stick around and see."

As he ate, he watched her mix, sprinkle, and fold her own omelet with the same culinary precision. She plated it and carried it around the counter to sit next to him. Her body was warm next to his, and fragrant with her ocean and sunlight scent.

She said, "So tell me something. What will you do once you find Kowalski and get your seal back? Go home to Michigan?" She forked up a bite of her omelet.

"Minnesota," he corrected absently. He almost said, sure he'd go home. Except ... her words from yesterday replayed in his mind, impossible to get out, like a splinter. *A man like you should have gotten out of there years ago.*

Ridiculous, of course. Total nonsense from someone who hadn't known him for more than a couple of days. But …

What reason did he have to go home? Really?

There was no wife or house or steady job there. There was in fact nothing to tie him to Minneapolis except the Guild and his family. And maybe those ties could do with a little loosening.

"I don't know," he finally said. "I have to return the seal to the Guild, but after that, I think I might try somewhere new for a while. Like Chicago."

He looked up and saw her watching him. A shadow of something flickered in her eyes. She smiled, and whatever it had been vanished.

"Seems you've acquired a taste for adventure here in Miami."

"I wouldn't go that far. Adventures are uncomfortable things. They make you late for dinner."

Her jaw fell. "*Por Dios*, you're a *Hobbit* fanboy!"

"I told you I like the classics."

She gave him the slitty eye. "The book, not the movies, I hope."

He recoiled. "What kind of nerd do you take me for?"

She laughed, and he had to laugh too. It was impossible not to. She drew it out of him as easily as a kid yanking on a pull toy. They sat smiling at each other until that solemn look came over her again. Their eyes locked, an electric charge filling the air.

He turned away first. Too much, too dangerous, and her face tipped up at him was too infinitely kissable. "Is there any coffee?"

She leapt up from her stool. "Of course! Let me get you a cup." She dashed around the island to the coffeemaker, where a full pot was perking. "Black, right?" she said brightly.

"Yes, please."

She poured the coffee into a decent mug this time instead of a dainty china eggshell, and reached it across the counter to him. He made sure their hands didn't touch.

She got herself a cup too, and they sipped in silence.

"Good coffee," he said.

"Thanks. Listen, I've got to get going."

"I'll clean up. I insist."

"Fine by me. Unlike Anita, I'm happy to let you do the dishes." She pulled her phone out of her pocket and checked the time. "In fact, I would have drafted you if you hadn't offered. I'm running late."

"Go on." He stood up and gathered their empty plates. "I'll take care of things here until you get back." He took the dishes to the sink and turned on the faucet. He grabbed a sponge and the dish soap.

She stepped toward him and reached up a hand to cup his neck. He let her pull his head down, and she went up on her toes and brushed his cheek with a whisper of a kiss. "Thanks," she said. Then she was gone in a breeze, across the room and out the door, leaving only her sun-drenched ocean scent behind.

He stared after her, his sponge dripping onto the floor, his cheek burning from the touch of her lips.

He heard the front door close softly.

He was about to turn back to the dishes when he saw a figure step in front of the kitchen door. It was Roddy, suited up in business wear. He looked down the hall after his cousin for a long moment. He turned into the kitchen, his gaze raking over the remains of Luke's and Esmeralda's shared meal. "Having a cozy little breakfast?"

Then his eyes moved to the sponge in Luke's hand and the sink full of soapy water. "At least you're earning your keep. When you're finished, go see Anita so you can help her get ready for my party. And you'd better not screw up. I've got important people coming tonight, and if they're not happy, I'm blaming my new houseboy."

Luke indulged a brief fantasy of tearing his sponge in two and shoving one half up each of the guy's nostrils. "What's the big deal about this party, Roddy? You trying to charm some investor into saving your uncle's company?"

"It's *my* company, and it's doing fine. What would penny-ante trash like you know about what it takes to run a multi-million-dollar business?"

"I guess that's a yes." Luke turned back to the sink and got started scrubbing plates. Roddy ranted something else insulting, but Luke didn't bother to listen, going over the tricky *presto* section of Chopin's *Ballade* No. 1 in his head instead.

Roddy stomped off down the hall and slammed his way out the front door.

Luke finished up the dishes just as the last echo died away and the last frilly notes rang through his inner ear. Time for him to go to work too, because Roddy had given him an idea. A low, sneaky, underhanded, dishonest, dishonorable idea that he was totally going to carry out the second he got the chance.

While Anita and Ignacio were busy downstairs getting ready for the party and looking after Castillo, he would search the bedrooms upstairs and see what he could find.

His missing stuff from the motel, maybe, or a receipt for two Rent-a-Thugs. Or a hint of why the Chinese pianos were causing so much trouble. Something, anything, to justify hanging around this house like Esmeralda's stray mutt.

But first, he had another task to finish.

21

LUKE COLLECTED his tool case from his room and went to reacquaint himself with the forlorn piano in the library. He opened the lids, a little thrill of satisfaction running up his fingertips as he stroked the satiny wood. "Hello, beautiful," he said. "Let's finish what we started, shall we? It'll be you and me tonight. We have to get you sounding spectacular."

His tuning program set up on his phone, he placed his hammer on the pin where he had left off two days ago and stroked the note. Rich, vibrant, but half a tone flat. He tweaked the pin, listening for that perfect bright golden pitch. Another tweak, and there it was, the pure sound hooking into the place inside where the music lived and pulling a smile out of him.

Soon he was lost in the familiar lovely sounds of his work, the rest of the world fading to a haze in the background. At some point, he heard Spanish voices and the clatter of mops and vacuums echoing down the hall outside the room. In the corner of his eye, he saw a cleaning crew passing by the open hallway door. Aside from a few quizzical glances into the room, they paid him no mind.

An hour or so drifted by as he worked, polishing each pitch of every string until he could almost taste the honey of the notes he played.

And then he was done. He put his tools away, limbered up his fingers, and made a running leap at the opening of Chopin's "Octave Etude" just like he did every time he finished a tuning. The furious music thundered up and down the keyboard, pouring from the piano and crashing through the house until he slammed his fingertips down on the last chord and let it die away. Then he heard a tentative flurry of clapping.

He looked around and saw a small crowd of cleaners standing in the doorway, peering at him over each other's shoulders. But in the center of the group was Eduardo Castillo, his gaze no longer vague but focused intently on Luke. Behind him, as always, was Ignacio. The bodyguard had his usual impassive expression on, though eyebrows were possibly raised a millimeter or so.

"Wonderful!" Castillo said. "You are brilliant!"

"Thank you." Luke self-consciously smoothed his tie.

"You must play for me! You must! I'm going to ... to sit outside. I want you to bring the piano out to the salon where I can hear it from the patio, and I want you to play for me. I like music."

"Excellent idea," Luke said immediately. The acoustics would be a lot better out in the big back room than it would in the overstuffed library. And, he suddenly thought, if he was playing out there tonight, he'd have an easier time keeping an eye on the party guests.

The older man smiled, his dark eyes sparkling, and

Luke was struck by how much he resembled his daughter in that moment. He said, "Good. Good. Ignacio will help you."

"That's all right. I don't need any ..."

Castillo's attention drifted away and he shuffled off down the hall. The cleaning crew dispersed in his wake, leaving Ignacio standing there watching him.

"... help. Okay, I guess I'm getting help."

The bodyguard came to stand by the piano, silently awaiting instructions.

Luke said, "The best way to do this would be to take it through the French doors and around the outside of the house."

Ignacio favored him with a slow blink. Man of few words, was Ignacio.

"All righty then. I'll just go get my moving gear."

The bald head tipped a fraction in assent.

Luke went out to his truck and hauled out his piano trolley. This piece of equipment was a hundred-sixty-pound chunk of steel consisting of three telescoping arms extending out from a central hub, like half an octopus. At the end of each arm there was a wheel on the bottom and a cup on the top for holding the piano leg. With the trolley, he could push the instrument around without taking it off its legs and putting it up on its side.

This wasn't going to be a difficult move at all. Which was fortunate, because Luke could concentrate on a different problem—how to ask his new assistant if he had sent that pair of assholes after him yesterday. Ignacio, the paid muscle, would no doubt have plenty of contacts on the shady side of Miami. And he had definitely been in a position to overhear him making plans with Esmeralda.

He carted the trolley back to the library and set it down

on its wheels in front of the piano. His potential suspect hadn't moved at all. Possibly he hadn't even breathed. Luke extended the wheeled arms, saying, "One of us needs to lift up a corner while the other positions the trolley underneath ..." Ignacio was already lifting up one side of the instrument, his only sign of effort a low wheeze like a hydraulic jack.

"Great. Thanks." Luke rolled the first cup into position and the bodyguard carefully placed the leg in it. They moved to the next corner.

Time for a little subtle interrogation.

"So," he said as they set the next leg in its cup, "Esmeralda said you've been working for her dad a while."

The guy grunted.

"Is this a good place to work?"

"Better than some."

Actual words. This was progress. "You know anything about pianos?"

"No." They put the last leg in the trolley.

Luke stood up. "Well, you're doing great so far."

Another grunt.

Luke pushed the piano out through the French doors and down the walkway, the wheels shushing along the coral stone. Ignacio followed, carrying the bench.

Trying to sound idly curious, Luke said, "Do you live here at the house?"

"I have an apartment over the carport."

So searching his room was out. Damn. They rounded the corner of the house to the back patio and headed for the doors.

Castillo was sitting at the table where he had been yesterday, absently fiddling with the dominoes. He watched with a bemused frown as the piano sailed past.

Luke wheeled the instrument into the salon and positioned it near the wet bar in a spot where the acoustics could carry the music through the house and out across the patio. Without being asked, Ignacio set down the bench and went to lift up the left corner of the piano so that Luke could move the trolley out from underneath the leg.

"Thanks for your help," Luke said, moving the first arm of the trolley out.

"It's my job." Ignacio moved to the right side and lifted.

"Is it?" Luke took a couple of steps, bent, and pulled the second arm out. "What exactly *is* your job? Butler? Bodyguard?"

Ignacio let the leg down to rest on the floor and looked at him with total and utter boredom. "I do whatever Mr. Castillo wants me to do. He says, 'Move that piano,' I move the piano. He says, 'Break that *gringo*'s legs,' I break the *gringo*'s legs." He went to the back end and lifted.

"Ah," Luke said. He'd never been so casually yet professionally threatened before. He had to admit, the guy had a certain flair. "What about Roddy? Do you do whatever he wants you to as well?" He knelt, pulled the trolley completely out, and started telescoping its arms together.

Ignacio's expression didn't change as he set the leg carefully down. "Roddy's not the one who pays me."

Luke stood, hoisted the hundred-sixty-pound chunk of steel up and rested it on his shoulder, bracing it with one hand. He straightened to his full height and looked steadily at the other man. "And Esmeralda? How does she fit in to your job?"

In no way intimidated by Luke's weightlifting display, he said, "She doesn't pay me either. But she doesn't have to. See, for her, I'd break legs for free." With a hint of a smile, he sauntered off through the doors to join his boss at the domino table.

Luke was absurdly pleased. "Good answer," he said under his breath.

The inscrutable Ignacio gave no sign if he heard him or not.

22

"FOOT, RAJ," Esmeralda said, holding up a brush and a hose.

Raj lazily turned around and lifted his back foot up to the bars for her inspection.

She examined the pad for sores and embedded stones. "Looks good to me," she told him.

He flapped an ear in response.

She gave the foot a squirt from the hose and a brisk scrub with the brush, took out her file, and filed down his thick toenails. They followed the same procedure for the other three feet, and after each Raj snuffed in appreciation.

"You're welcome," she said absently, putting her grooming tools away in her cart and winding up the hose. It was a soothing, familiar ritual she had performed hundreds of times. Only, today the rhythm of it felt just the tiniest bit off.

Raj could tell, of course. When he turned back around, he fixed her with a dark, concerned eye.

"I'm sorry I'm spacing out on you, Raj," she said. "It's just ..."

It's just what? For half a minute, she tried to convince herself that it was this pain-in-the-ass ivory/Kowalski mess that was chafing her brain like imaginary sand in her mental thong. No use.

She admitted, "It's Luke. The guy you met yesterday. He's been distracting me." In fact, from the moment he had sneaked into her house and started messing with her piano, her usual thought patterns had been ... unruly.

And it couldn't have happened at a worse time. She needed to stay target-locked on the India study, like she had been for every moment of the last year or so. Instead, Luke was unsettling her. And she couldn't quite figure out why.

Yes, he was smart and funny. He was also way hot, though amazingly, he didn't seem to know it. And he had the rare qualities of courage and integrity. But she'd met a few other men who fit that description, and none of them had inspired her to swoony introspective bullshit like this.

So what was it about him? What was this affinity, this familiarity she couldn't quite name, but sensed whenever she was near him?

The first moment she saw him flashed into her mind, the almost fierce smile on his face as he listened to the single note of music hanging in the air. What was that look? Something bright and passionate shining from inside him.

Passion, that was it. That was what she recognized. He had an intensity that resonated with her because she felt the same devotion to her own work. She might not know music any more than he knew elephant care, but the love she understood completely.

Had he seen their alikeness as well? She doubted it. He was too restrained to easily connect with that part of himself. She had caught it flickering in his eyes once or twice since the first time, but mostly he kept it well hidden.

And she could guess why he hid it. Most likely because he had been told such powerful feelings weren't "normal." He'd probably been trained from very early on to be cautious in all ways. A creature his size and with that hint of wildness in him would no doubt have made people extremely nervous. They would have set about taming him for his own good, naturally.

Raj nudged against her, sensing how far her thoughts had wandered. She ran a hand over the bristles along his trunk, but her mind stayed on Luke. Thinking about what it must have been like for him, having his true nature gently, relentlessly crushed by his well-meaning friends and family.

She had been lucky in that way. Her papa had never tried to destroy her dreams. Mostly because he hadn't cared enough to bother, but still—

Suddenly a muscular length of elephant trunk wrapped around her hips, hoisting her into the air. Startled, she looked into the long-lashed eye shrewdly trained on her.

"Raj! I'm all right, I promise. I was just thinking."

He flapped an ear to encourage her to go on.

But she was curiously reluctant to tell her big friend her thoughts today. Not until she'd gotten them sorted out in her own head. And figured out what to do with this curious sense of disloyalty.

Just then, Celeste puttered up in a mule towing a wagon full of hay. She turned off the motor and crossed her arms on the steering wheel, shaking her head at the sight of Esmeralda dangling from Raj's trunk. "Raj, put the Cuban Barbie down. You don't know where it's been."

"I've been nowhere you haven't been many, many times before," she said as she hovered midair.

"Probably true, unless you've been rolling around on a

pile of Olympic swimmers in a Tijuana bar. I won't get around to that until next month."

As Esmeralda laughed, Celeste climbed out of the mule and started pitchforking hay at Raj's feet. The elephant immediately set Esmeralda down so he could use his trunk to stuff his breakfast into his mouth.

"So how did your sting operation go yesterday? You bag your man?" Celeste asked as she worked.

Esmeralda grabbed another pitchfork and got busy working alongside her. "Not exactly. It got complicated."

"Oh yeah? Spill. I bet Raj would like to hear it too."

Raj let out a subvocal rumble of agreement as he ate.

Esmeralda launched into a recitation of the previous day's events, and watched Celeste's round blue eyes get rounder as the tale went on. She tried to stay strictly matter-of-fact when she mentioned Luke, but some of her confusion about him must have slipped through. Because when she was done talking, the older woman exchanged a look with Raj, leaned thoughtfully on her pitchfork, and said, "So this Luke of yours sounds pretty interesting. And brave. And, as I recall, he's a total hottie. Tell me more."

"I get sucked into a criminal investigation and all you want to hear about is the hot guy?"

"Well, yeah. I've got my priorities. If I were twenty years younger, I'd consider poaching him myself. So, he's shacking up with you now, is that right?"

"No! What? No. It's not like that. I told you, he needs a place to stay for a few days while he tracks down this seal thing of his. I thought I might as well put him to use while he's in town to solve my own problem. It's practical."

"But you like him."

Esmeralda shrugged uncomfortably. "Yeah, sure I like him. He's a likable enough guy."

"No, you *like* like him."

"What is this, fifth grade?"

"You like him even more than Raj."

"I do not!"

Raj took a break from eating to snuff in agreement.

"Wow. A man you like more than elephants. That's amazing. I never ran across one of those before myself. That's why I keep getting divorced." Celeste was divorced four times and counting.

"Celeste," she said warningly.

"Esmeralda," she mimicked. "Admit that you like this guy."

Esmeralda reached through the bars and patted Raj's shoulder restlessly. "It doesn't matter whether I like him or not. In a few days, when we have this mess with the pianos sorted out, he'll be headed back to the North Pole and I'll be off to India. You know my dissertation is all I have room for in my life right now." Though, for some reason, talk of the future she had worked so hard for didn't bring up the bright and shiny feeling it usually did.

"Besides, I don't think he wants to get involved with me. He's never made so much as one pass." Which might possibly be unique in all her experience of men, now that she thought of it. So why was this particular man acting so different?

Maybe Luke, closet romantic that he was, didn't indulge in no-strings sex, which was all there could be between them. Maybe he wanted an emotional connection with a woman he slept with.

Now, if she stripped naked and crawled into bed with him, she could change his mind about that, no question. His physical interest in her was obvious.

Por Dios, was it ever.

This morning, when she had finished her daily laps in the pool, she had sensed she was being watched like a gazelle senses a lion at the waterhole. She had looked up at him standing at his bedroom window and seen a vision of ripped shirtlessness that had almost made her purr with pleasure.

Thick, hard, no-nonsense slabs of muscle over his chest and stomach. Ropes of more muscle over huge shoulders and down the long arms braced in the window frame. Dark bronze hair curling over his pecs and arrowing down his abs to disappear in tantalizing shadows. Here in the land of the sleek and manscaped, he was a brute.

And the look in his eyes was absolutely primal. For a second there, she had thought he might leap down from his window and ravish her on the spot.

She had kind of hoped he would, actually.

She drifted out of her thoughts to find heat blooming over her skin and her breaths coming a little too fast. Celeste was watching her, a knowing smile in her eyes. Even Raj had paused in eating to chuff at her meaningfully.

She cleared her throat. Yeah, yeah, he wanted to do her. So did everyone. So what. What she wanted to know, what she would really like to believe just once, was that he found her interesting on any other level. So far, the answer was a decided meh. What a lowering thought.

She said firmly, "We have a professional association. That's it."

Celeste gave her a long look. "Professional my *tuches*. Now pay attention, kiddo, because I know what I'm talking about. From what I can tell, this Luke Hansen of yours is one of a rare breed. He's solid. Men like him won't wander across your path very often, so make sure you know what you've got before you throw him away."

"I haven't *got* anything. Like I said, I don't think he's interested."

Raj gave her an exasperated nudge.

Celeste tipped her head back and laughed. "Just think about it." She plucked a shovel out of the mule and handed it to her. "And while you're thinking, you can scoop up the pile of crap Raj unloaded by the east boundary."

23

WHILE ESMERALDA WAS SHOVELING and thinking, Luke was stowing his moving equipment in his truck. When he returned to the house he found Anita waiting for him with a plate of pork and ham sandwiches in one hand and a book of music by Cuban piano composer Ernesto Lecuona in the other.

He ate the sandwiches while he rifled through the yellowed pages of music, and started to get excited. He had only a glancing familiarity with Lecuona, but a swift read reassured him that that he could stumble his way through well enough if he had time to practice.

He sat down on the bench and turned to "Vals Crisantemo," and after a couple of fits and starts, the sweet, carefree notes poured out of the piano as easy as the ocean breeze until the last resounding chord.

"*Brava*," Castillo called through the French doors from his seat by the pool. Ignacio flicked his eyes at him once, which he took as the equivalent of a standing ovation.

Luke waved to them and started in on "Crisantemo" again. Then he played it eight more times, each time getting a little more smooth and free. After that, he moved on to play the next piece ten times. And so on, working his way through the music book. At every pause, Castillo would call, "*Brava*" with the same amount of enthusiasm.

He'd say this for the man, he didn't mind hearing a little repetition. It probably helped that he'd forget he'd heard a piece the second it was over.

An hour slipped by, and then another. He kept playing steadily, making good progress. He had just finished "Malagueña" for the tenth time when a gentle snore drifted through the French doors. He shot a glance at the domino table. Castillo and Ignacio were slumped back in their seats, chins on their chests.

The time had come to put Operation Invasion Of Privacy into action. With the two men dozing and the rest of the household engulfed in the chaos of the party preparations, he figured he might have half an hour before he was missed.

He moved swiftly through the house and up the staircase to the second floor, soft-footing it to the end of the house where he guessed the master suite would be. He didn't expect to find much in Castillo's room, so he'd get them out of the way quickly before Ignacio came looking to give him a demonstration of his leg-breaking talents.

He opened the door to find a masculine room lavishly appointed in expensive fabrics and dark wood, and crowded with Castillo's ubiquitous doodads. Like the man's clothes, the room showed signs of his illness. Some of the things were stained, some were broken, and some were piled oddly on top of each other or squirreled away in corners.

There was the usual detritus on the dresser and the nightstand. A battery of serious-looking medications crowded the bathroom medicine cabinet. Nothing but the possessions of a sick and elderly man.

My moral compass is pointed straight to hell, he thought as he returned to the main hall. He opened the next door.

He found a bedroom designed in a light and airy style, but swamped in an advanced state of slobbiness. Books, papers, clothing, and miscellaneous junk was scattered liberally across the floor and the unmade bed. This had to be Roddy's room, he thought. Only a young guy would surround himself with such chaos, surely.

His gaze landed on a nearby bookcase with big, wide shelves crammed to bursting with books. He picked his way through the mess close enough to read the titles. Biology textbooks and peer review journals, mostly. But stuck haphazardly in with the big, serious texts were thick paperbacks with frayed covers. *Song of Ice and Fire. Wheel of Time. Earthsea. Lord of the Rings*. He reached out and ran his thumb lightly over a cracked spine.

He had indulged in these very books, once upon a time. Losing himself in daring-do somewhere far away from the real world.

He frowned. Biology textbooks and pulp escapism seemed out of character for Roddy. He'd expected douchebaggy business titles. *The Zen of Boardroom Conquest* or something.

He took a closer look around the room. Then he saw the tiny blue bikini dangling over the back of a chair.

He swallowed, his heart hammering. Not Roddy's room. Esmeralda's. He suddenly had a sense of her presence, lounging on her messed-up bed, watching him with a wry, laughing look in her eyes.

Just great, Hansen. Now you're rifling through a girl's

stuff like a pervert on a panty raid. Cheeks burning, he scooted out of her room and closed the door.

What was he supposed to be doing again? Oh yeah. Investigating. He took a moment to catch his breath, then resolutely opened the next door down the hall and looked inside.

It was another bedroom, this one much neater and full of expensive-looking stuff of the high-tech and black leather variety. Now this was definitely Roddy's room.

He inspected the bathroom but found nothing interesting. Nothing interesting in the closet or the dresser. Nothing in the bed, the sofa, or the entertainment unit. Nothing in the nightstands except a stack of model photographs that the guy must have filched from his uncle's stash, a jar of Vaseline, a package of tissues, and a box of condoms still in its plastic wrap. Poor Roddy.

Stymied, he stood in the middle of the room and took a square of paper out of his pocket. It was the sticky note he had found the night before in Castillo's office, with "Range Rover" and "Lamborghini Aventador" scribbled on it along with the big, dark "Z." It wasn't Castillo's handwriting, which he had seen on several documents yesterday. But, as he compared it to the signature on a credit card receipt he had found on the dresser, he thought it might possibly be Roddy's. He couldn't tell for sure.

He had already met the Range Rover. He wondered when the Lamborghini would appear. And who or what was "Z"? The cars, the pianos, the Castillos ... all the elements floated together in a confusing potpourri that was sending up a distinct scent of menace. What any of it might mean, he still had no earthly notion.

He left Roddy's room disheartened. So far Operation Invasion of Privacy was failing to justify itself. He figured he might as well look into the rest of the rooms on this floor, just in case. He opened the next door, but inside was no bedroom.

It was only a shallow space that had probably been a linen closet at one point, but had been emptied out leaving only a single shelf. This was covered in an embroidered silk cloth and crowded with a variety of objects. There were thick candles in ornate holders, scattered pennies, a half-burned cigar, an open bottle of rum, bowls of flowers and fruit and shells, statues painted in eye-searing colors and patterns, and, in the very center of the altar, a binder with a man's tie wrapped around it.

The tie was a navy-on-navy striped one in a durable synthetic fiber. It looked familiar. Because it was one of his, he realized with a start. He picked up the binder to untangle the strip of fabric from around it. When it was loose, the cover fell open to reveal a high-grade photograph of Esmeralda in a swimsuit.

The book in his hands was her modeling portfolio.

Everything else immediately forgotten, he started flipping through the pages. He saw Esmeralda kneeling in foaming ocean water, her hands lifted to hold her black curls against the wind. Esmeralda on her stomach on the sand, her supple limbs gleaming in the sun. Esmeralda spread out over a red Ferrari, looking over her shoulder, the line of her back sleek enough to make the car's designers weep with envy.

He studied every curve of her body, every plane of her face, trying to see the anchor point of his fascination. Was it the vital energy in the set of her limbs, which made her look like she was in motion even when she was perfectly still? Was it the intelligent humor in the sweep of her upper lip, or the challenge in the slant of her eyelid?

If questioned by the Spanish Inquisition, Luke might possibly have admitted that Esmeralda's face didn't have the classically molded perfection of a Greek statue. But that didn't matter. Hers wasn't the kind of beauty that refreshed a man's aesthetic sensibilities. It was the kind of beauty that wrapped around a man's dick and gave it a long, slow squeeze.

He was sweating, his hands shaking. He had to take this portfolio back to his room to investigate it more thoroughly—

"*Ejem*," a voice by his elbow said.

He jumped a clear foot in the air. When he landed, he came face to face with Anita.

He slammed the book closed and held it in front of him. "Hi, I was looking for the bathroom and I just, uh ..." He shut up as he realized that not only was his excuse amazingly lame, but he was reeling it out to a lady who didn't speak English.

Anita merely smiled, a satisfied little purse of her lips, as if she had just been proven right about something. He wondered how long she had been watching him.

"*Tú le gustas a los santos. Ellos dicen que eres el hombre perfecto para ella.*" She plucked the binder and tie out of his nerveless hands, wrapped the tie around the binder, and replaced them on the shelf exactly as they had been before.

"But that's mine," he said, not sure what he was referring to.

She just closed the door to the shrine and looked up at him with her twinkling black eyes. With one gesture of her thin hand, she ordered him to follow her, then turned and marched down the hall toward his room. He trailed along, bemused.

She opened his door, gesturing inside. He looked in and

saw the best clothes he had with him laid out on the bed. By some quirk of fate, his blazer and his good wool slacks had survived the mauling at the motel, and Anita had apparently cleaned and pressed them for him, along with his newest white shirt.

He looked down at the old lady smiling up at him through her network of wrinkles. It seemed she was not going to defenestrate him after all.

Cautiously, he said, "Thank you. *Gracias.*"

"*De nada. Debería estar guapo esta noche.*"

Luke stared blankly.

She clicked her tongue in fond annoyance. "Joo be 'andsome for Maria Esmeralda." With that, she turned back toward Castillo's room, and he swore he felt the lightest pat on his butt as she bustled past him and vanished down the hall.

24

ESMERALDA LINGERED over saying goodbye to Raj, so she was late getting home. The daylight was burning out of the sky by the time she wheeled the Mini into the carport.

She sprinted into the house, up to her room, and through her shower. She slapped on some smoky eye makeup, styled her hair in loose curls over her shoulders, and hustled into a sleeveless blue silk dress. There. Done. Slightly winded, she checked out the mirror, pronounced herself in decent enough shape for cocktails, and stepped through her door.

She heard the distant racket of the caterers setting up in the kitchen, the hum of Spanish voices, and above it all, a ripple of music floating lazy and sweet on the air. Not her father's romantic singers, but piano music. She followed the thread of sound down the stairs and through the hall to the big back room where she found the piano, and Luke.

The last golden light of the day flooded through the glass to illuminate the strong, clean lines of his profile as he bent over the keys. It scattered and tangled over his fingers as they moved, weaving the rays into the notes.

Esmeralda knew passion when she saw it. She could see it in Luke, in the set of his shoulders as he leaned into the instrument and the mastery in every move of his fingers over the keys. And on his face was that fiery little smile.

She drifted closer to him, netted and reeled in.

Her movement must have caught his eye, because he looked up and saw her. The music crashed to a stop mid-note. He went frozen and wide-eyed for a second, a deer in the headlights deal. Then he scraped back the bench and stood. "Hi," he said, his voice a little rough.

His studliness was on excellent display tonight in gray slacks and a blue sport coat, the fine cloth molding over the amazing width of his shoulders and skimming his narrow waist and hips. The clothes looked hand tailored, which was probably a necessity for a guy his size. He was daringly tieless this evening, his collar button undone.

She smiled to herself and walked over to him, putting a little slink in her step, 'cause she was bad like that. "Hi, Luke. You look ..." *Yummy.* " ... very nice."

He ran a hand down the front of his coat, a blush running over his hard cheekbones. "Thanks."

Silence. His eyes were locked on hers like blue-gray lasers.

"This is where you say I look very nice too."

He shook his head. "You know that wouldn't be accurate."

"I don't look good?"

"Like I told you yesterday, you're the most beautiful woman in the world." And once again his voice held a hint of exasperation that he had to restate a well-known fact.

And now *she* was the one blushing. Time to laugh lightly and change the subject. She reached out to touch the smooth curve of the piano lid. "What's that you were playing? It sounded really, ah, sweet."

"It's called 'Noche Azul'."

"Blue Night. Pretty. Too bad I'm too tone deaf to enjoy it properly," she said with real regret. Music was a foreign language she didn't understand. The modeling life had subjected her to enough club music to get a decent sense of rhythm thump-thump-thumped into her, but nothing had yet made a dent in her natural tin ear.

"Unless you're actually deaf, you can learn to appreciate music just fine." He adjusted the bench and sat down on the right end. "Come here, I'll show you," he said, patting the seat beside him with his left hand.

She raised an eyebrow. Well, well, could Mr. Hansen at long last be showing some game? With any other guy, she'd give that a big fat yes. But Luke was proving a rare beast indeed. Maybe he wasn't angling for a chance to feel her up. Maybe, stunning thought, he actually wanted to teach her about music.

Ah, what the hell. If she was being honest, either one would be fine with her. She settled onto the bench next to him, her leg and shoulder lightly pressing against his.

He drew in a sharp breath, and she could see his pulse pounding under the collar of his shirt. But he steadfastly avoided her gaze. He placed his right hand on the center of the keyboard. A strong, callused hand, and yet capable of such amazing precision and grace. "Put your hand on mine."

She reached out and aligned her fingers on top of his. Thumb, pointer, middle, ring, pinky. Her fingertips stroking lightly over his neatly cut nails. She was struck by their differences—her honey-colored skin against his pale, her slender fingers against his huge ones. She leaned into his shoulder, enveloped by the heat of his skin and his clean wood-and-sunlight scent. "Like this?" she said.

There was the finest tremor in his hand beneath hers. "Y-yes. Just like that. Now close your eyes."

She did.

"Whatever you do, don't think. You have to feel. Thinking comes later. Just open yourself to the sound. Let it touch you. Let it deep inside."

He fell quiet and still for a time except for the rise and fall of his chest against her shoulder as he breathed and the beat of his pulse under her hand. The domestic noises of the household, the busy din of the world outside slipped past her ears and faded away. Then, slowly, she felt his fingers move, hers riding along on top. A slow note curled up through the silence, then another. Then more, sounds swirling and mixing together into something so rich she wanted to open her mouth and taste it.

"There." His voice was a low rumble in her ear, his soft breath on her temple. "Do you feel it?"

Her lips parted on a little breath. "Yes." She felt it. Beauty conjured into the air with the touch of a fingertip.

A dissonant jabber of voices blared in from the hall, shattering the spell.

She snapped her eyes open and snatched her hand away from Luke's as Roddy and Juan came tromping through the door. They were dressed nearly identically in black slacks, black jackets, and black silk shirts unbuttoned at the throat. They caught sight of her cuddled up with Luke at the piano and stopped short.

Juan nudged Roddy and whispered something in his ear. Esmeralda looked at him narrowly. The consultant had the kind of shiny-eyed, jittery energy about him tonight that she could tell instantly was chemically induced.

Her gormless cousin either hadn't noticed or didn't care. He glowered at her. "Where have you been? My guests will be showing up any second now. You're supposed to be helping me greet them, not slumming with the hired help."

She felt Luke stiffen beside her.

She jumped up from the bench and stalked over to him. "Keep this crap up, Roddy, and watch the two of us walk right out the door and take ourselves off to the movies for the night."

Roddy saw that she was serious, and his eyes widened in what looked like panic. He cast a frantic look at Juan.

Juan stepped forward. "Look, Easy, let's not get hysterical, okay? This is no time to throw a temper tantrum. Our most important business partners are coming tonight. We have to show them that Castillo Imports is still a good investment now that Roddy's in charge. So can you get your head in the game here? We need you—ah, need a united front tonight, for the sake of the company."

"And that matters to me why? I'm not part of the company. Besides, I hear *The Smurfs Five* is out, and I've got to say that sounds infinitely more fun than watching the two of you smarming for investors all night long."

"*Tio* will get upset if tonight doesn't go smoothly," Roddy said. "This is a chance for him to have a good time with all his old friends. Do you want to mess that up for him?"

Esmeralda pressed her lips together.

"And what about me?" Roddy went on. "I've never hosted a party like this before and I've got a lot riding on it. Me, personally. If I'm going to take over the company, I have to impress *Tio*'s connections and convince them to trust me. I need your help, Ez. Don't you care about me at all?" And he looked at her with the big, dark eyes of the boy he'd been not so long ago.

Feeling herself weaken, she said, "All right, I'll stay. But no more rudeness out of you, got it?"

"Fine. I'm sorry," he said unconvincingly. "Can we get ready now, please? I want us to make a good impression on *señor* Zapata when he comes. And I know he's looking forward to meeting you."

"Zapata?" Luke suddenly said. "Did you say Zapata? With a Z?"

Roddy answered him with a dirty look, but Juan said slowly, like he was talking to a toddler, "That's right. Zapata with a Z."

"Who is he?"

"No one you would know."

"Just answer the man, Juan," Esmeralda said. "Who is this Zapata person? I'd like to know too, since he wants to meet me so much."

"Crissake, I've only told you a hundred times, Ez," Roddy said. "Important businessman from Columbia? Real estate in Bogotá? Luxury goods? Politically connected? Ringing a bell yet?"

"Does he fund any wildlife conservation efforts? No? Then he's not going to ring any bells of mine."

"Well, he's a potential investor in Castillo Imports. Can you remember that at least?"

"So he's the one you're trying to talk into saving your company?" Luke cut in.

"That's bullshit. I don't need Zapata to save me," Roddy said, a little too quickly. His belligerent pose fractured and he shot an anxious glance at his consultant. "We're just ...

putting the final touch on a mutually beneficial business relationship. He wants to get a foothold in the Miami import trade, and we could use his help with some of our cash flow issues."

"That's right," Juan said. "In fact he's already been incredibly helpful. He's fixing your screwup for us, Easy. He's taking the Chinese pianos off our hands. Be sure to show him some gratitude tonight."

Before she could tell Juan where he could stick his gratitude and what direction he could stir it, Luke said, "So Zapata is your buyer."

Juan smiled unpleasantly. "I'm afraid he beat you out, Mr. Kowalski."

"What's he going to do with the instruments?"

"How the hell should I know?" Roddy said. "They're not my problem anymore."

Luke looked thoughtful. "What kind of car does he drive here in Miami? Is it a Lamborghini Aventador?"

Juan narrowed his eyes.

Roddy said, "Yeah, it is. How'd you know?"

"Lucky guess," Luke said. Without another word, he turned back to the keyboard and started playing something loud and dramatic. The boys had clearly been dismissed.

Esmeralda cast a thoughtful eye at him and said, "Roddy, I just remembered, you might want to go check on the caterers. I think I heard them drop something large and breakable earlier."

"¡Mierde!" Roddy stormed out the door toward the kitchen.

Juan sniffled and cast her a suspicious look before following Roddy.

When they were alone, Luke shot her a faint grin and

eased up on the volume. "You're shameless," he said in a low voice.

"This is true. So what were all those questions about?"

In answer, he took a little square of paper out of his pocket and handed it to her, then went back to playing. Covering up their conversation, she suspected. She squinted at the note and read aloud, "Z. Range Rover. Lamborghini Aventador SV."

"I found that last night in your father's office. I wanted to ask you if you recognized the handwriting."

"No," she said slowly. "It looks kind of familiar, but I can't really tell. Whoever wrote this must have been in a big hurry. Or extremely drunk. What's this about?"

"I think this Zapata and his Lamborghini are connected with the pair of assholes in the Range Rover who accosted us yesterday. And all of them are involved with someone who had access to your father's office at the time he had his episode."

"That's an awfully big leap based on something as flimsy as this," she said, flipping the paper square against her fingers.

"Maybe." He took back the note and put it in his pocket with hardly a pause in the music. "Do you know anything about this deal Zapata has going with your cousin?"

She shook her head. "I didn't think the pianos were important once the ivory was taken off. And I never pay any attention to Roddy and Papa's wheelings and dealings. In fact I actively avoid them."

"A sound policy. But I think you should suspend it for tonight. We need to find out everything we can about this Zapata guy."

"Leave it to me. I can play detective tonight. When I put my mind to it, I can get anyone to talk."

"I don't doubt that for a second. Just ... be careful. I don't like the feel of this situation."

"Relax, Luke. It's a cocktail party on Di Lido, not a meth orgy at a biker bar. How dangerous could it possibly get?"

25

AN HOUR LATER, Luke had discovered that the prime danger of a Miami cocktail party was torture by yammering twits.

From his position at the piano he had so far overheard some idiot's five-year plan for enlarging his mistress's fake boobs, a borderline racist rant over various forms of domestic help, a long whine about doctors who wouldn't feed a prescription drug habit on the cheap, and a minutely cross-referenced dissertation on who among these winners was currently fucking whom. But no mention of Zapata.

Just when he was starting to wonder if the guy was going to show up at all, he heard an excited murmur ripple through the room. Whispers sliced past his ears. "Zapata ... Carlos Zapata ... Colombian ... rich ... OMG, like, super rich ..." Then the man of the hour stepped through the door.

He was medium tall, but fat in a congealed kind of way. The cut of his light-colored suit, though expensive, was doing absolutely nothing to flatter the spindly little twizzle-stick legs propping up his beer-keg girth.

His face was middle-age ordinary. Jowly, with dark little

eyes and a pouty little mouth. His most arresting feature by far was the combover construction of hair piled atop his fleshy noggin. Colored the shiny black of industrial-strength lacquer, it swept up from the sides of his skull and over from the back, weaving strands together to dip and swirl over his forehead and then wave back along the scalp in a mesmerizing vortex that obeyed no known laws of physics.

Overall, he gave the impression of a man shoved up hard against sixty who still saw a thirty-year-old when he looked in the mirror.

A step behind him was a musclebound bodyguard type, who looked over everyone in the room with the fish-eyed stare of a psychopath.

Roddy, Juan, and a few other men scurried alongside the great man, yipping and panting and all but wagging their tails. Every skeletal blond in the room homed in on him like their bullet-shaped breasts were seeking a target. He promenaded to the French doors, within earshot of Luke.

"… so great of you to come all this way, *señor* Zapata," Roddy was saying.

The great man waved his hand, which had surprisingly stumpy little fingers, and said in a heavy Spanish accent, "It was a good excuse to sail on the yacht." He cast a bored glance around the large, lavish room, his eyes passing right over Luke as if he were part of the piano bench. He said abruptly to Roddy, "Your *prima*, your cousin *la Esmeralda*. Where is she?"

"She's out there, by the pool," Juan said, making a "ta da!" gesture toward the French doors.

Zapata glanced to where Juan was pointing. A wolfish smile full of bleached teeth appeared. He said to Roddy, "Ah, there she is. Your girl *está muy buena*. Very beautiful."

"I'll go get her. She'll be so excited to meet you," Roddy said, and scampered off.

Zapata turned to his crowd of fans and said, "I love the women. It is good I took a mint, because when I see her I will kiss her. I always kiss the beautiful women when I see them. They love it. When you are rich like me, *mis amigos*, the women let you do whatever you want to them."

"Whatever you want?" one dimwit inquired.

"Whatever you want. You will see. I could grab her *puta*."

Obnoxious laughter followed.

Esmeralda stepped through the doors, an eager-eyed Roddy at her side. She had been towing around a conga line of priapic elderly men all night, but now they were nowhere to be seen. She took a look at Zapata and deployed a smile that Luke thought was incredibly brilliant and totally fake. "*señor*. Welcome," she said.

"*Bella*." Zapata stepped forward, his arms outstretched. Was he actually going to carry out his threat to kiss her?

But Esmeralda quickly grabbed his right hand, shook it stiff-armed, and then dropped it. "Let me get you a cocktail, *señor*. This way," she said, beckoning him toward the bar out on the veranda.

He chuckled indulgently. "Ah, she plays the game," he said. "The drink, then, *mi amor*."

With a smile nailed in place, Esmeralda guided her new guest along while somehow retaining a groping buffer between them at all times.

Luke watched until the crowd closed around them and they were out of sight.

Until this moment, Luke had thought that only Brett Kowalski had the ability to pitch him into psychotic fury, but

Carlos Zapata had just left Kowalski in the dust. He realized he was playing the *Andalucía* suite *molto furioso* in lieu of wrapping his hands around Zapata's fat head and squeezing.

When he caught sight of Esmeralda again, she and her new guest were walking along the pool with glasses in their hands, he talking animatedly, she nodding at intervals, a wide-eyed look of interest on her face.

He watched as Zapata tried to slide a pudgy hand over her hip. But, in a choreographed dance move she had performed a thousand times before, she nimbly sidestepped so that the groping paw landed on thin air. Then the crowd shifted and he lost them once more.

He played through *Andalusia* twice more without catching sight of them again. At the exact moment that he decided he couldn't stand it anymore and was about to get up and go in search of them, he heard voices drift in from the patio. Esmeralda's husky tones and Roddy's rough tenor.

He played softer, straining to hear over the piano.

"... thought you'd like him." Roddy sounded perfectly bewildered. "He's rich, and he's got class and connections. Why don't you like him?"

"You're kidding, right? The man is past fifty, he's stuffed into his suit like a chorizo, and he's got that— that molting skunk perched on his head. He's revolting."

"Appearances aren't everything," Roddy said, his tone virtuous. "I didn't think you were so shallow."

"Right, Roddy. Because it's super deep to lust after his bank account instead, like you?"

"I don't— Argh! I'm just saying, you could do a lot worse than Zapata, Ez."

"How, *por Dios*?"

"How about screwing around with a broke *gringo* piano man?"

Luke fumbled a chord change.

"You leave him out of this, Roddy."

"Look, I didn't want to get into this with you, but I think you should know. The fact is I'm at a delicate stage of negotiations with my lenders right now, and Zapata is deciding whether or not to help me out with them. We need to stay on his good side, so you have to be nice to him, Ez."

There was a pause. In a voice like the winds of Antarctica, Esmeralda said, "Exactly *how* nice do you want me to be to him, Roddy?"

Not sensing the danger, Roddy went on blithely, "We thought maybe you could go out with him while he's in Miami. You know, show him around, make him feel welcome. We already set up a late dinner reservation for you two tonight at that hot new place at the Marlin."

"You did, did you?" Esmeralda said, each word now as sharp as an icicle.

Finally cautious, Roddy said, "Well, yeah. What are you giving me that death ray look for? It's not like it's a big deal. Juan thought—"

"Juan. Of course. So this is the real reason you wanted me be here tonight. I'm the party favor, is that it?" Luke could practically see frost forming on the French windows. "You know, Roddy, I've had agents, magazine editors, and fashion designers try to pimp me out before, but I've got to say I never expected it from my own family."

"Now, Ez, it's not like that. It's just a date. It's for the company—"

"I don't care about the *carajo* company, and I don't care much about you anymore, Rodrigo. If you want Zapata's business so bad, you can suck him off yourself."

"Ez!"

Angry footsteps snapped on the pavement, and then Esmeralda burst through the doors, her cheeks blazing. Her eyes caught on Luke's, but then she spun away and marched through the crowd to the buffet table.

Luke had abandoned the piano and was following her before his conscious mind knew what he was doing.

She stopped short in front of a display of champagne flutes. Luke came to stand next to her. He could almost feel the outrage crackling off her skin. "You okay?" he said.

She looked at him out of the corner of her eye as she picked up a glass. "Heard all that, did you?"

"Yeah."

"That *mamalon* Roddy." She took a hearty slug of champagne. "This is all Juan's fault. I know Roddy didn't think that idiotic scheme up by himself. You'll never believe it, but he used to be a decent guy before that *pendejo* got his meathooks into him."

Luke said nothing.

"I mean, he never treated me like a hooker before. I never thought he'd ... I'm not a hooker, *por Dios*. I'm not a *thing* he can just hand off to whoever he wants to impress." She knocked back the rest of her drink. Her eyes were suspiciously bright.

"I know that," Luke said. He had figured that out within seconds of meeting her. Her dunce of a cousin should have known it too. Maybe it was time he had it explained it to him, and his favored guest.

He said, "You need to stay away from Zapata for the rest of the night."

"Believe me, I'd love to kick his *culo* out of here right now, but I haven't gotten him to talk to me about the Chinese pianos yet. I'm supposed to be playing detective tonight, remember? So far, he's told me all about his yacht, his cars, his mansions, his clothes, his golf courses, his money, more about his money, and his stupid freaking watch, but nothing about the pianos. I need one more shot at him to get the answers to our questions. Then I can ditch him."

"No way," Luke said rashly. "I've had a bad feeling about this plan of yours from the start, and I was right. I don't want you tangling with that guy, Esmeralda. I'll question him, and your idiot cousin too. I'm not letting you go anywhere near him again."

She spun to face him square on, her eyes glittering. "Listen up, Luke. You seem to think that what I do is your decision to make. It's not. I've been handling the Zapatas of the world for years on my own. I don't need your help. And as for Roddy, he's my family. My business. He's none of yours."

He fell back a step. Felt the blood rush out of his face.

He said, "You're right. I'm sorry. I'm just the trained monkey hired to play the piano. Didn't mean to get above my pay grade."

"*Por Dios*, that's not what I meant."

"Forget it." He turned sharply and went back across the room to the piano. He sat down and launched into a Shostakovich piece he had learned in his rebellious sophomore year, the furious ache in his chest moving down his arms and pounding out of his fingers in a melodic tirade. He tried to let the sound drown out the voice in his head telling him again what he had always known.

She would never truly be his business.

As he played, he saw Esmeralda hovering at the edge of his vision. After a moment he saw her whirl toward the patio doors and vanish back outside into the night.

26

ESMERALDA HATED, *hated*, being treated like a thing. An object to be acquired and positioned and carefully guarded from thieves. She'd had enough of that *mierda* over her years as a model, and she was not going to take it one single second more. Especially from a man she had hoped might ... see her. The real her.

Whatever he may or may not have seen in her, Luke had let his King Kong impulses get the better of him. But she was not going to indulge his mantrum.

She stalked off to let him work out his snit on his own and went back to her duties as hostess, which were finally, thankfully, drawing to a close.

Guests started trickling out of the front door and into their cars, and she smiled and waved them off. Her father had long since gone upstairs, squired by Ignacio. The house emptied out, except for Zapata. He stayed. And stayed. And *stayed*.

But this was good. In spite of her defiant words to Luke, she had found herself avoiding the man. Now she had one last chance to get information out of him before she kicked him out of her house and, hopefully, out of her life.

In preparation, she went to the bar out by the pool and grabbed a bottle of some violently red drink mixer, pouring a healthy glassful. There. She was suitably armed to do battle with a swinish suitor.

She found him inside near the buffet table, where he was amusing himself harassing the catering staff. The two women were wisely keeping the table between themselves and any wandering stubby fingers.

She quickly scoped out the lay of the land. Zapata's bodyguard had joined Ignacio and Anita in the kitchen some time ago, and distant voices from the front hall told her that Roddy and Juan were seeing off the last straggling guests.

Luke, soldiering on at the piano, was the only other person in the room besides the caterers. He shot one impassive glance at her as she stepped through the back doors, then locked his attention on his sheet music.

He was still sulking. Fine. She tipped her chin up and advanced on her target.

"Señor," she said. "Did you have a good time this evening?"

"Ah, niña," Zapata said. He turned toward her, flinging his arms wide. He had achieved the bright-eyed and boisterous level of intoxication, she saw. Just as well. It would be all the easier to milk him for information.

When she didn't walk into his sweaty embrace, he gestured expansively. "The night is still early. There is much time for us to spend together. Very much time."

"Right." She caught herself staring into the depths of his hair vortex, but she quickly refocused her gaze on his chins before it could drag her past its event horizon. "Señor, you never did get to tell me about your new business venture here in the States," she said, channeling the brainless admiration of the bimbette.

A flash of something unnerving crossed his face so fast she wondered if she had imagined it. "That is nothing for a beautiful woman to think about," Zapata said, waving his little hand in a kingly fashion.

"But I'm so interested in your business success," she burbled. "What made you give us *yanquis* the opportunity and the blessing to serve you?"

For a second she worried she might be slathering on the bullshit a wee bit thick, but his pouty little lips spread in a fat smile. "It is simple, *querida*. I had reached the top of the game in my home, and grew bored. A man must find new worlds to conquer always to keep his strength and vigor."

"Like Alexander the Great! Or Napoleon Bonaparte!" she cooed.

He squinted a look of piggy-eyed confusion. "No, no. Like Pablo Escobar. He was a man. He never stopped fighting. Always he made new conquests. Always he had the love of the people and the beautiful women," he finished with a leer.

In Esmeralda's opinion, Columbia's infamous drug kingpin was a strange choice for a role model. Especially since he had died in a hail of bullets as he ran from the police. But there was something in Zapata's voice as he spoke about his idol that told her he was serious. In fact, it might be the most genuine thing he'd said all night. She smiled gamely and said, "How fascinating! But tell me, how did you pick my cousin to get the honor of helping you with your new conquest?"

"A business like his is useful in many ways. And his new shipment was a perfect opportunity for me."

"Of course! The Chinese pianos. You were brilliant to pull off such a coup. How did you find out about the ivory key tops in the first place?"

"I have good people to keep watch on these things," Zapata said vaguely. "Very good people. The best people. But it is not right to talk to a woman about business. The beautiful women are like beautiful cars. They are for pleasure. Like you." He smirked at her. "You like the Lamborghinis, baby?"

She ground her teeth in an effort to keep her smile. "No. I've had to sit on top of too many of them."

Zapata, apparently not hearing a word, said, "*Bueno*. It is a great car, the best car. We go for a ride in my Lamborghini up the Miami Beach. Then we eat," he said, with a leer down her cleavage, just in case she didn't get the innuendo.

For a fraction of a second, Esmeralda considered going along with his agenda for a bit in hopes of ferreting out his secrets once he was drunker. But she hadn't avoided rape by entitled asshats for this long by frolicking off with them whenever they asked her.

So, after due consideration, she admitted defeat. Her superpower of getting men to talk had met its match. She had gotten Zapata to talk about himself—boy howdy had she—but the information she needed was a mere drop in the vast sea of his self-absorption, impossible to filter out. The best she could hope for now was to extract herself from this situation without a scene.

Holding the tumbler full of red stuff in front of her, she said loudly and clearly, "I'm sorry, *señor* Zapata, I'm afraid I can't go out with you tonight. I understand Roddy set us up for a dinner date, but that was a mistake. He didn't realize that I already have plans. And I have plans for the rest of the week, too," she added.

Zapata just smiled. "No, you don't."

Esmeralda blinked. "Yes, I do."

"No, you don't."

"Yes, I do."

Zapata's smile finally hardened. "No, you don't."

"Yes, I do!" She all but stamped her foot.

In the background, the piano music abruptly stopped.

Zapata stepped closer to her. "Perhaps you do not understand. Your *primo* and I made a deal, *niña*. It was a good deal for him, a tremendous deal."

Keeping a white-knuckle grip on her civility, she said, "But as you said, I'm only a woman, so I can't have anything to do with my cousin's business, can I?"

Zapata flicked his hand in dismissal, the light glinting on his heavy gold watch. "The deal is made. It is too late to renegotiate. So I think you do not have plans, *si?*"

"*Señor,* I'm not going to continue this ridiculous argument—"

"*Bueno.* I become bored. We will go to my car now, and we will not argue." He clamped a sweaty hand hard around her elbow and started to drag her toward the door.

She promptly tossed her glass of red stuff all over him.

He jerked back, his chins dropping in disbelief as he looked down at his ruined suit.

"Oops, so sorry, but you shouldn't have jostled me like that. I'll have someone show you to the kitchen so you can get cleaned up." She looked around for one of the servers who had been clearing the tables, but they had already gone to ground. Canny bitches.

Zapata's shellacked head came up. An ugly expression

twisted his pouchy face. *"¡Perra!"* he spat. He raised his hand to slap her, watch flashing.

Suddenly a massive hand shot out and grabbed Zapata's out of the air. Luke.

A big blond wall of muscle and testosterone had somehow materialized between Esmeralda and the other man. Luke's pale eyes were flat as glass and his mouth was a thin, hard line as he crushed the stubby fingers in his fist like a pizza box in a trash compactor.

Zapata's gaped soundlessly up at Luke, his face going gray.

"Time to call it a night, *señor*," Luke said quietly.

The other man's answer was only a tiny *squee* of air as he feebly tried to pry Luke's fingers off with his other hand.

Just then, Zapata's bodyguard, Ignacio, Roddy, and Juan all tumbled into the room, looking between the three of them with various degrees of suspicion, confusion, and hostility.

Without missing a beat Luke plucked out Zapata's silk pocket square and dabbed at the stain on his coat, while still hanging on to the man's other hand. "Go out the door and get in your car without a scene or I'll break your wrist," he said in a low, hard voice. Out loud he said, "I think *señor* Zapata has had a little too much to drink. It's time he went home." He yanked him helpfully toward the hallway.

"Is everything all right, *señor* Zapata?" Roddy said as he stumbled along in front of them, bowled forward by Luke's relentless progress.

She saw Luke's fingers flex in warning.

"*Sí*, it is fine," Zapata squeaked, his eyes rolling in Luke's direction.

Esmeralda found her voice. "That's right, everything is just great. Open the door, won't you, Roddy?" She hurried behind them as Luke dragged a stumbling Zapata toward the front door.

Zapata's bodyguard edged up to them, his eyes wide, his hands twitchy, but suddenly Ignacio was there pacing beside him, as solid as a granite bolder. Juan trailed along in the rear, far enough back that Esmeralda couldn't quite catch his expression.

Suspicion battled with confusion across Roddy's face as he opened the front door.

Luke walked Zapata out of the house and headed straight for the yellow glare of a Lamborghini Aventador parked obtrusively to one side of the front walkway.

He marched his captive around to the passenger side of the car. When Zapata unlocked it, Luke opened the gull-wing door and shoved him down into the seat. Only then did he release his hand.

Zapata snatched his hand back and cradled it against his chest. *"¡Malparido!* No one does this to Zapata! You have made a bad mistake," he hissed. In the harsh glare of the outside lights, Esmeralda saw spittle gathering at the corners of his lips.

"Yeah, I've done nothing else for the last week," Luke said, and slammed the door shut.

The bodyguard, escorted closely by Ignacio, got into the driver's seat. Everyone backed away. The car roared to a start and peeled off down the street in a yellow blur.

Luke stood straight, watching it go. He shook his hand out once, turned, and walked back into the house like he was the boss of the whole goddamned place.

Esmeralda drifted along behind him, towed by his wake. Behind her, Roddy and Juan were engaged in a heated discussion. Ignacio gave Luke and her a slight nod as they passed.

But she couldn't make herself pay attention to any of that.

When she entered the house, she heard her father's querulous voice upstairs, but she ignored that too.

She felt seriously weird. The air was curling over her heated skin like cool silken veils. Her heart was thundering, and every step she took was slippery liquid.

Good lord. She was turned on. She was more turned on than she'd ever been in her entire life.

He had saved her again. Protected her. Fought for her. And now ... now she wanted him to take his reward.

It was primitive, bestial impulse and so, so wrong, but utterly impossible for her to resist. She wanted this man inside her, taking her with all of his magnificent strength, and she wanted it rightthefuck now.

She followed Luke's tall, broad shadow down the hall, back into the big empty room where it all began.

He went to stand by the piano and gazed off through the French doors, his strong face in profile to her.

She shut the doors to the hall behind her and walked toward him, her knees trembling, lightning bolts of want forking through her belly. "That was—" *the hottest thing ever!* She cleared her throat and tried again. "I—" *want you to do me right now! Nownownow!* "Um—"

"I'm sorry," he blurted.

"Ah ... what?"

"I've never done anything like that before." He tottered to the piano bench and sat, his face white as milk.

A rush of concern finally cooled her off enough to make her function. "Hey, are you all right?"

"I haven't actually hurt anyone since I accidentally gave Brian Eberhart a concussion in fourth grade," he said, his Adam's apple bobbing.

She let out a long breath. Great. She wanted to leap on him like a starving ocelot on a porterhouse steak, and he was having a crisis of conscience.

Oblivious, he said, "I don't know what happened. I saw him about to hit you and I just— I went crazy."

"Luke ..." She paused. When she was certain she was in no immediate danger of tearing his clothes off, she eased up next to him and put her hand on his rock-solid shoulder. "I'm sorry you had to do that. But I'm very glad I didn't get hit. You did a good thing, saving me. And, frankly, I can't think of any better guy to bust your badass cherry on than Zapata."

His gray eyes finally focused on her, and he flashed a slight smile. Then he went serious again. "I know you didn't want my help, but—"

"No, I obviously needed it, no matter what stupid stuff I said earlier. And I couldn't have hid my brass knuckles in this dress, anyway. So, thank you."

"You're welcome," he said, his voice a deep rumble.

Their eyes locked. She saw his pupils go wide and dark. Carefully, she took her hand away from his shoulder and stepped back.

He stood up, towering above her, his chest moving with fast breaths.

She tipped her head up to him, parting her lips in anticipation.

"It's late," he said.

A fist of icy, spiky disappointment grabbed her heart and squeezed. She swallowed hard to get her voice working. "Yeah. Been a long night," she finally said.

"We should get some rest," he said.

"Right."

"Well."

"Well. Goodnight," she said.

"Goodnight," he said.

She half turned away.

She said *"Cojeme"* at the same time Luke said "Fuck it," and they threw themselves at each other, bodies pressing, arms tangling, lips fusing together in a ferocious kiss.

27

HE WAS LOST. Decorum, common sense, basic sanity. Gone.

It was like he had never kissed before, he was so shocked by the wonder of it. She was looping her arms around his neck, shoving her fingers through his hair as she made an eager sound against his lips.

He cupped her silky head in his hands and deepened the kiss, delving his tongue into her mouth. She opened for him, kissing him back until everything else faded and stilled and there was only this moment unwinding forever. The slickness of their mouths together, the hot thunder of his blood, the magic of her, here in his arms.

She slid her hands over his shoulders and down his chest. Her little fingers moved over his buttons, and then slipped inside his shirt, touching his skin.

More. He had to have more. He picked her up, her bottom round and resilient under his flexing hands. She instantly wrapped her legs around his waist, not pausing a second in their kiss. Her hair tumbled around them in a fragrant curtain.

He walked a few blind steps, desperate to find a couch, even a wall. His thigh brushed the curved rim of the piano. *Perfect.* He set her down, the lid at the exact height to align her cleft with the ridge of his erection.

Her thighs opened wider, and his breath stopped. *Holy fuck.* He could feel how slippery wet she was against his shaft, even through the layers of clothing between them. He bucked into her, following a brutal instinct.

She cried out against his mouth, a shocked stutter of pleasure.

He wrapped one arm around her back to crush her softness against him while his other hand slid up the sweet curve of her thigh.

"Yes, touch me," she said against his lips before lapping at his tongue again.

God, he wanted to slide his fingers into her pussy, wanted to feel that wetness on his skin. But his hips had their own agenda, flexing, pumping, shoving his steel-hard cock against her and forcing those little moans out of her. Her legs were locked around his waist, winding tighter with each thrust.

So instead he tore down her bodice and the lace of her bra, freeing her breasts. He cupped one, as perfect in his hand as he'd dreamed. He squeezed and rubbed, pinching her beaded nipple until she made that little sound of want again. He needed to lick her there, spend hours kissing her sweet flesh, suckling, biting, but he couldn't end their kiss, not for anything. Her tongue was in his mouth, twining with his in time with their bodies rocking together. Her fingers sank into his back. Her scent washed over him.

"Don't stop," he felt her lips say as she kissed him.

Like hell he'd stop. He growled and shoved against her. He was so sensitized he could feel it each time his cock rode over her clit. Squeezing tighter, moving faster, harder. Hot and slippery and filthy.

There was that shocked little catch deep in her throat, and he knew. She was going to come. And, God, so was he. About to come in his pants. Harder than he'd ever come in his life. He was going to—

"What the fuck do you think you're doing with my cousin, *gringo*?"

They froze. Like they'd been blasted with a snow machine.

His eyes snapped open. In the corner of his vision, he saw that Roddy had shoved open the door to the hall and stood framed there, Juan slinking behind him.

He wanted to throw his head back and roar in sheer frustration. It sizzled across his nerves, along with a full voltage shock of possessiveness and protectiveness. Every muscle in his body locked with a primitive, snarling urge to guard her from the others, keep her to himself. Finish what he'd started.

Esmeralda was the first to break the trance. She yelled, "Are you crazy? Get out!" She pushed him back with one hand and yanked at her neckline with the other, all the while sending a murderous glare at the intruders.

Juan leered over Roddy's shoulder. "Real classy, Easy, screwing the hired help."

"You're the hired help, and I'm not screwing you," Esmeralda shot back as she tried to shove her skirt back down over her legs.

Juan sneered something in Spanish, but Roddy ignored them both, his eyes blazing at Luke. "Look at me when I'm talking to you, *cabron*."

With every ounce of control he possessed, Luke carefully lifted Esmeralda off the piano and set her on her feet.

Only then did he turn to face the men in the doorway. He started to cover the front of his pants, but there was simply no hiding his monstrous erection. He opted to brace his hands on his hips instead.

Roddy and Juan stared at his crotch, momentarily cowed. Roddy recovered first. He tore off his jacket and tossed it aside. "First you insult my friends, and then you put your hands on my cousin? Outside, now, *puto*. I'm going to teach you a lesson."

"Don't be an idiot, Roddy," Esmeralda snapped. "You can't fight Luke. He'll take you apart."

Luke was strangely gratified at this, and more than half ready to prove Esmeralda right. Never before had he considered ripping someone's arms off and beating him to death with them, as the MMA fighters he guiltily watched liked to say. But, jacked up as he was on testosterone and adrenaline, he was considering the shit out of it now.

Reason briefly tried to reassert itself. *He's the relative of your hosts*, Reason said. *And you've never actually been in a fight before.*

But one glance around the room told him that Reason was about to tap out. Roddy was puffed up in outrage and getting puffier by the second. Juan was twitching eagerly behind him, ready to goad him on and to take a few shots at Luke, if he could do it without any danger to himself.

And then there was Esmeralda. Incredible body held straight with pride. Gorgeous face shining with absolute certainty that Luke could defend her against anyone and anything.

He folded his hands into fists. *Thumb goes on the outside of the fingers*, he reminded himself.

"¿Qué está pasando aquí?" came a sharp voice from the hallway.

Everyone jolted as Anita bustled through the door behind Roddy and Juan. She whacked them both and they jumped out of her way.

She stopped in the middle of the room, raked her gaze over all of them, and launched into a Spanish diatribe that nearly peeled the paint off the walls.

After two minutes Roddy was red-faced and Juan was pinch-lipped. But neither said anything except, "*Sí, señora. No, señora.*"

This did not pacify the *señora*. She kept at it for a good five minutes more. Then she turned her gimlet eye on him and Esmeralda, and continued on until Esmeralda was miserably intoning, "*Sí, señora. No señora.*"

Finally, the tirade reached a thundering crescendo. "*¡Qué vergüenza!*" rang through the room.

Everyone stared at the floor.

Anita sniffed. Then she pushed her way between Luke and Esmeralda and took each of their arms in an iron-clawed grip. Her chin lifted high, she marched them past Roddy and Juan, out of the room, down the hall, and up the stairs.

When they reached the second-floor landing, she released Esmeralda while retaining a firm grasp on Luke's bicep. She said something in a tone that allowed no argument.

Esmeralda dutifully translated. "Anita says you played beautifully tonight, and that you must be exhausted, and that you should go straight to bed."

He looked down at her, the most beautiful woman in the world. Her hair and dress were tousled from his hands, and her lips were red with his kiss. He wanted to howl in agony. He nodded, not trusting himself to talk.

Esmeralda shifted from foot to foot. Shot a glance at

Anita, who looked back, as immovable as a tiny Mount Everest. She said, "Well, goodnight then. I'm sorr— uh, thanks—" She blushed. Then she spun on her heel and stalked off down the hall to her room. She closed the door behind her with a snap.

Anita hauled on his arm with every one of her ninety-five pounds and eventually got him turned around and pointed toward his room. She towed him along the hallway to his room and propelled him inside with a firm "*Buenas noches.*" She shut the door behind him.

Luke did not take her advice to go straight to bed. Instead, he went straight to the shower, where he furiously jacked himself off to a release that was so powerful it wrenched his spine, and yet was completely unsatisfying.

28

THE NEXT MORNING, Luke had to drag himself out of bed and down the stairs to breakfast by force of will. His mood was vile, an adrenaline hangover blazing behind his eyes. Flipping the switch between "fuck" and "fight," and then getting neither, was hell on the endocrine system, he was learning.

When he entered the kitchen he dimly registered that Anita was at the stove cooking something wonderful, but his attention immediately locked onto Esmeralda. She was sitting at the counter over the remains of her breakfast and doodling a spoon in her coffee cup, her expression pensive. She was wearing a pale pink sleeveless shirt and tan Bermuda shorts. The morning sunlight coming through the window was eagerly licking over her face and body. Bastard sunlight.

She looked up and their eyes met.

His breath stopped for an endless moment as a kaleidoscope of emotions flashed over her face, until she finally settled on ... caution.

Luke's heart folded in half, then again and again, until it

was a tight lump in his chest. His vision went gray around the edges. He now had the answer to the question he'd been afraid to even think about asking.

She didn't want him. Whatever mercurial impulse had taken her over last night when she had thrown herself into his arms, it had vanished in the bastard sunlight of morning.

Had he really expected anything else? He'd be an idiot if he did. A stupid, sniveling fool who'd forgotten the real reason he was here.

He was supposed to be protecting this woman, not entertaining impossible notions about getting her for himself. Her safety was all that mattered, not his ridiculous feelings.

And oh, yeah. Finding the Guild seal. That job he'd been ignoring. He had to stop this crazy distraction, buckle down, and do what he came to Miami to do.

So instead of running out of the house to his truck and driving back to Minneapolis, he walked to the island and sat down next to her, folding his hands on the counter and keeping his head down.

"Good morning," she said, her voice wary. She was expecting him to pounce on her or propose marriage, no doubt. Like every other sap she'd ever met.

"Morning," he growled.

A heaping plate of ham and eggs appeared under his nose, along with a big mug of coffee. Startled, he looked up to see Anita's smiling face, and got a ghost of a wink before she hustled off again.

He picked up his fork, wondering how she was so damned chipper this morning, since she'd spent the night sitting in a chair outside his door. At least, that's where she'd been when he'd tried sneaking out of his room around one o'clock.

Next to him, he felt Esmeralda relax slightly, now that he'd demonstrated he wasn't going to act out any crazy stalkerish obsession with her.

Well, she didn't have to worry. He could control himself. As long as she didn't try to make him talk about it.

"We need to discuss last night," she said.

Oh, good God. "Last night was a mistake," he said with absolute finality. He hoped.

No such luck. "Oookay," she said, "What part of last night are we talking about?"

He forked up more breakfast instead of answering.

"The part where you stuck your tongue down my throat, felt up my tits, and almost gave me an orgasm?"

He choked, and had to gulp down scalding coffee to get his ham and egg down the right pipe.

"I'll take that as a yes." She drummed her fingers on the counter. Then she smiled brilliantly. "You're right, of course. That was all just crazy emotional nonsense that got out of hand. Looking back, it was a good thing we stopped when we did."

"Yeah, good thing," he said dismally. By the time they'd stopped, he'd learned that a kiss and a grope with her was better than all the sex he'd ever had combined. He shoveled in more food, though it had turned to gooey sand on his tongue.

"But anyway, that wasn't what I wanted to talk to you about last night. I wanted to discuss Zapata."

"Oh." The hottest encounter of his life, and she didn't even care enough to force him to have an awkward conversation about it.

"I think you were right about him," she went on. "There's something incredibly shady about that guy's business, and I'm not only saying that because he's a giant buttmunch. I can't think of a single legitimate reason he'd involve himself in my cousin's affairs. I don't know a lot about the company, but I do know it isn't a huge draw for international investors. We need to find out what Zapata is really up to here in Miami, aside from toying with Roddy."

"Yeah." She was right on all counts, damnit.

"Luckily, Saturday is my off day. No zoo, no modeling. We can spend all day investigating Zapata."

He stole another glance at her. Her eyes were shining at him eagerly.

He downed more coffee, thinking. Letting her get anywhere near Zapata again was out of the question. Ignacio would look after her while she stayed in the house, he felt sure. But Luke had to get away from the magnetic force of her personality, her voice, her scent. She was going to drive him into a psychotic break if he didn't.

"That's a good idea. I'll track down Zapata's hotel and talk to a few people about him. You can stay here and research him online."

She frowned. "I don't think—"

He never found out what she didn't think, because at that moment Roddy strode into the kitchen. He aimed a razor-sharp eye at Luke, and then smiled. "Good morning, sunshine," he said in dulcet tones.

Luke turned back to his breakfast, determined not to let the jerkoff get his goat. But Esmeralda eyed her cousin with suspicion.

"All right, what's going on?" she said.

Anita appeared with a coffee cup and a frown for Roddy.

He took the cup, ignored the frown, and blinked innocently. "What do you mean?"

"I didn't think you'd be quite so cheerful today, seeing

as how your big plan to pimp me out to that block of moldy spam last night was such a total failure."

Roddy's eyes flashed. But he sipped his coffee and said, "I'm just happy someone finally had that piece-of-shit truck that was parked on the street in front of our house towed. It was really bringing down the whole neighborhood."

Dead silence rang through the air. Then Luke dropped his fork and bolted out of the kitchen and down the hall to the front door, Esmeralda hard on his heels.

He threw open the door and ran up the drive toward the street. But it was far too late. His loyal truck was long gone.

Esmeralda appeared next to him and said something in Spanish, her tone thoroughly unladylike.

"Uh oh," came a voice from behind them. "That wasn't your piece-of-shit truck, was it?"

Luke turned on his heel to see Roddy sauntering through the open front door.

Luke took one step toward him.

Roddy raised his hands quickly, though his smug smile was still in place. "Hey, it wasn't me who called it in."

"Then who?" Luke said quietly.

He shrugged. "Anyone on the island could have called in a beater like that, right, Ez?"

Esmeralda set her jaw, but she didn't disagree. "Roddy," she said calmly, "did you happen to see the name of the towing company?"

"Try Pierre's Auto Parts." With that, Roddy moseyed off to a BMW parked under the carport, got in, and zipped away.

Esmeralda ran into the house, instantly reemerged with her gigantic orange purse, and said to Luke, "You look up the address for Pierre's Auto Parts. I'll drive."

29

THERE WAS a certain tension in the car as Esmeralda blasted the Mini down 112 toward Hialeah, an iron-jawed Luke hunkered in the seat beside her.

The strain had begun the instant he had appeared the kitchen this morning, blank-faced and cinched into an awful maroon tie. She'd been braced for the usual protestations of worship, the demands that she become his wife/girlfriend/fuck trophy. Instead, he'd bluntly said that kissing her last night was a mistake.

Which was a relief, obviously. Adorable as he was, and their crazy hot make-out session notwithstanding, she was still going to India in a matter of weeks. She didn't need distractions, or the guilt of yet another broken heart. So, yeah. It was great he wasn't that into her. Perfect.

Funny thing was, she hadn't felt relieved in the moment. In fact, she'd felt ... kind of ... devastated. Out of sheer perversity, no doubt. The lure of the unattainable, blah blah.

At least she'd covered it well, changing the subject and babbling about this investigation. How embarrassing, to almost be caught crushing on him. Maria Esmeralda Castillo y Rosa did not crush on guys. So there.

She cast a defiant look at Luke, who merely raised a blond eyebrow and said, "This next exit. Slowly, for God's sake."

She whipped off the freeway, ignoring a whispered prayer from beside her as she barreled off the exit ramp to Hialeah. She wove through a series of streets at his barked directions until a high chain-link fence sprang up on the right. Beyond the fence they could see a big lot stacked with a rusty rainbow of flattened cars and a few unflattened ones awaiting their doom. Above them loomed the behemoth shapes of a magnetic crane and a car crusher.

She tucked the Mini into a tiny spot between a GMC and a Dodge and got out of the car before Luke could attempt to open her door for her. Because that was just the kind of gallant thing he'd do, the big dumb gentleman.

She regretted her independence the second she set her foot on the pavement amid a drift of litter. She regarded her now-grubby toes and vowed to wear her work boots instead of lime-green wedge-heeled sandals the next time she traipsed around a junkyard.

She got herself together, locked the car, and strode off along the fence. Luke wordlessly fell into step beside her.

They made their way over the pitted asphalt until they got to a big gate with a shack next to it featuring a grated window. They searched the shadows behind the grate for any sentient life lurking inside.

"Hello?" she called out.

There was a shuffling sound, and a stringy, dark-skinned guy wandered out of the dimness up to the window grille. He was dressed in a t-shirt bearing some indecipherable logo, was aged somewhere between thirty and sixty, and he was smiling. Grinning like Esmeralda and Luke were long-lost relatives who had just arrived with the secret to enlightenment and a winning lottery ticket.

"Can I 'elp you?" he said.

"I want my truck back," Luke said.

The guy trained a beam of excessive happiness on the air between them. *"Kisa?"*

Esmeralda decided to take the reins. She shoved in front of Luke and smiled a dazzling smile of her own at the junk man. It made no impact whatsoever. The zenlike demeanor never rippled. *Okay, that's just not natural*, she thought.

She forged ahead. "What my friend here is trying to say is that we're looking for a truck that came in early this morning from Di Lido. It was towed by mistake and we need it back."

"Di Lido ... truck ..."

"Ford F150. White. Moving equipment in the back," Luke said.

"Ah, *wi*. The truck. The white one. It is over there." He gestured vaguely toward the right side of the junkyard beyond the chain-link fence.

They carefully scanned the sad array of vehicles lined up for the crusher like cows in a slaughterhouse. "I don't see it," Luke said.

"It is there. Somewhere in the top layer."

They raised their eyes slowly to the wall of metal pancakes. Sure enough, resting on the top of the stack there was a white blob that used to be a truck.

"You mean it's already gone?" Esmeralda said, her voice high.

"Wi," the guy said, smiling ever so happily. "The man said to make sure it got compacted as soon as it came in. 'E paid double."

"What man?" Luke said very softly. "Who was it, exactly, this man who murdered my innocent truck?"

The huge smile faded. Luke was apparently harshing the guy's mellow. "*M pa konnen.* I don't know. 'E paid cash."

"You don't know? Someone just pays you to crush a truck, and you don't bother to find out who he is, or if he even owns the truck in question?" Luke's voice got louder and louder, and his fists bunched harder and harder at his sides.

The junk man stared at the fists, which were, to be fair, the size of roast turkeys, and squeaked, "'E paid cash."

Suddenly, a horrific noise sounded from deep within the junkyard, getting louder and louder. A smell like a burning Porta-Potty burst across Esmeralda's senses. A massive, filthy brute of a dog come charging from behind a pile of tires to fling himself at the fence in an enthusiastic bid to rip their faces off.

The junk guy's beatific smile reappeared. Over the sound of teeth gnawing on chain link, he said, "Etienne tells you *orevwa*."

"Okay!" Esmeralda chirped. She tugged hard on Luke's arm, trying to get him to move away from the junk guy, the fence, and the slavering hellhound.

Luke allowed her to pull him back down the street toward the Mini in silence. But when they got to the car, he said very quietly, "You know, I'm getting really, really tired of your cousin destroying my stuff."

"It might not have been him," she pleaded. "There are a lot of people on Di Lido who could have called in your truck."

He just looked at her.

"Okay. If Roddy was responsible, I will make sure he compensates you for the truck and the equipment."

"*If?* Who else could be spiteful enough to have it crushed? Or to have my motel room vandalized?"

Esmeralda opened her mouth to answer, then closed it. Family loyalty might demand that she stand up for her cousin's honor, but family loyalty had gotten the shit kicked out of it last night, and would need some time to recover.

"We'll pay you back," she said instead.

He laughed bitterly. "And I guess I'll have to take your money. I have no choice, if I want to make it out of this insane swamp and get back to the normal world." He put up his hands and laced his fingers behind his head, staring off across the junkyard at the corpse of his truck.

Esmeralda didn't know what to say with so many half-sentences of apology and comfort queuing up in her mouth. But a small, forlorn thought kept shoving to the head of the line—*You want to leave Miami? You want to leave me?*

That was the moment Esmeralda's phone started ringing in her purse.

Tearing her eyes off Luke, she yanked it out and put it to her ear. "Hello."

"Is this Esmeralda?" A rich, intimate voice oozed out of the phone at her.

"Could be," she said, ready to hang up at the first sign of telemarketing.

"Esmeralda! It's me, Brett. I've heard so much about you, it's good to finally talk to you in person."

She froze. Then she slapped her hand over the microphone and said to Luke, "It's him."

"Who?"

"Kowalski!"

Luke turned quickly toward her, eyes wide. "That ass-gerbil is calling now, of all times?"

Esmeralda flapped her hand at him and hit the speaker button. "Mr. Kowalski, I've been expecting your call," she said, holding the phone up between her and Luke.

"I sure am glad to hear that, Esmeralda." Kowalski said. "Or should I call you Easy?"

She could tell Luke was nearly biting his tongue in half keeping himself quiet. She shot him a warning look. "Esmeralda is fine."

"Easy by me," he laughed, apparently thinking this was wit. "I gotta say, you Miami folks know how to entertain high rollers in style. The cruise was a nice, nice touch."

"The ... cruise?"

"It was fantastic. Just the best. Won tons at the slots. All-you-can-eat lobster, I mean, my God. I totally don't even blame you at all for having to return to port early. I mean, how were you supposed to know about the salmonella outbreak?"

"What?"

"Yeah. Nasty stuff. Half of deck three started gacking up the place. You probably saw it on CNN."

"Oh ... right." She mouthed to Luke, *"What the hell?"*

Luke shook his head.

"Anyways, it's all been beautiful. You've convinced me you treat your customers right. I'm ready to cut a deal."

"For the ivory?"

"Yeah. Sure. For the *ivory*." A snicker dripped through his voice. She saw Luke's eyebrows draw together.

She said, "Okay! Great! Where are you?"

"I'm headed to your warehouse, the one where the, ah, *ivory* is stored. Wanted to see the merchandise for myself before I made any commitments."

"Wonderful! I'll meet you there in half an hour."

"I like the sound of that, sweet *chiquita*. Then we'll go hammer out the details in my hotel room, you and me."

You and me and my brass knuckles. "I'll see you soon, Brett." She hung up.

"Time to call Agent Al," she said to Luke.

"And here I thought my day couldn't get any worse."

30

"NOW REMEMBER," Agent Truitt said, "you're only going into the warehouse to make contact with Kowalski. You'll invite him out to the coffee shop we agreed on so that I can be on hand when you ask him questions. If he refuses to meet you in a public place, the interview is over. You come straight back here. Under no circumstances are you to put yourself in any potentially dangerous situations. Are we clear?"

"Crystal, Colonel Jessup," Esmeralda said as she adjusted the new transmitter in her bra. They were sitting in Truitt's Crown Victoria, parked just out of sight of the Castillo Imports warehouse in Doral. Truitt was in the driver's seat, Esmeralda in the front passenger, and Luke was spread out in the back. The Mini was parked behind them, waiting for them to finish up their scheming.

Esmeralda said, "Don't worry, Al. I'm just visiting my family's warehouse and asking a goober out for coffee. How dangerous can it possibly be?"

"I really wish you wouldn't tempt fate like that," Luke said in an undertone.

Truitt gripped the steering wheel and frowned. "I still don't like you confronting a suspect alone."

"We don't have any choice. I've called him ten times to try to change the plans, and he still hasn't answered. If we want to lure him out into the open, I have to go get him."

"Besides, she won't be alone," Luke said. "I'm going with her."

Agent Al, who had been pointedly ignoring him so far, turned his frown on Luke's reflection in the rearview mirror. "I shouldn't allow this. You might spook the target if he thinks you're after him for the money he stole."

"It isn't the money, it's the Guild se—" He stopped and shook his head. "I'll just tell him I've reconsidered his offer and I've tracked him down so I could get in on his money-making scheme. Lord knows he's dumb enough to believe me."

Truitt held his gaze in the mirror for a long moment.

"You know she needs backup, Agent," Luke said quietly.

Esmeralda rolled her eyes, but said nothing.

Truitt let out a breath. "All right. But what I said to Esmeralda goes for you, too. This isn't Mission Impossible. Don't get cute."

Luke stiffened. "I am never cute."

With a hint of a smile, Esmeralda said, "Trust me, Luke can take care of himself."

Luke couldn't help it. He puffed out his chest.

"And if all else fails, I'll scream real loud and you can bust down the door and rescue us." She patted her bosom near the transmitter. Al winced and touched his ear where the receiver was tucked in.

They got out of the Crown Vic and back into the Mini,

and Esmeralda tooled them down the street and around the corner to the warehouse.

Luke saw a number of cars in the parking lot as they pulled in. Esmeralda frowned at them. "Huh," she said as she wheeled into a spot near the front entrance and killed the engine.

"What?" Luke said.

"The workers are here. Usually there's only a security guard here on Saturdays. They must be doing some overtime because of the reorganization."

Luke shot her a glance. "Reorganization? That's one way to put it. The people at the office told me that the warehouse crew had all quit."

"I guess Roddy hired some new guys."

"I guess so. But ..."

"But?"

"But there's something ..." He shook his head. "I don't like the look of this place."

Esmeralda bristled a little at the slight on her family's property. "What's the matter with it?"

It was an ordinary warehouse, better maintained than some he'd seen. The aluminum siding was recently painted, the asphalt parking lot well patched. But by the clammy whisper on the back of his neck it might as well be a rotting gothic castle with the full lightning-and-crows accessory package. He shook the idea off. "Nothing. Let's go."

They got out of the Mini and walked to the front door. She punched the intercom. "Esmeralda Castillo and guest," she said. There was a long pause. Then the lock clicked quietly. Luke reached past her to haul open the thick glass door for her and followed her inside.

The front of the warehouse was partitioned off from the

main space beyond, with an office on one side and a break room area on the other. Windows lined the front of the building, letting in morning sunlight that was already doing battle with the air conditioning. They walked toward the office.

Three guys were in there, one of them sitting at a desk in front of a computer, the other two standing behind him where they could look at the screen. They were youngish, with tough-looking faces and brand new designer clothes. There was also something familiar about them, though Luke knew he'd never seen them before.

The guys turned their heads toward them as they approached, looking alert and watchful. Like meerkats. Evil meerkats. They slithered their eyes over Esmeralda, but then focused on Luke. They blatantly sized him up. None of them said a word, the silence broken only by the yowling of internet porn coming from the computer.

"Hi, I'm Esmeralda Castillo." All three of them switched their focus back to her. "I'm meeting with a Mr. Brett Kowalski. Is he here yet?"

They looked at each other, then back at her. "No, we ain't seen nobody," said the one sitting at the desk.

"I see." She glanced over at a row of metal chairs in the break room, then back at the guys. "I'm going to go show my friend around while we wait." She clearly didn't want to spend any more time around these cherubs.

She turned away and Luke followed her. He stole a glance back at the men in the office and saw three sets of eyes staring after them. It suddenly came to Luke why they looked familiar. They resembled the two guys in the motel parking lot. Good clothes, bad attitudes, and an agenda they weren't sharing.

Luke pressed his hand to the small of Esmeralda's back,

hurrying them through the inner doors into the main space of the warehouse. "Do you know any of those guys back there?" he said quietly.

"No, I've never met them before."

"They don't look like much of a crew."

"Yeah. Roddy must be desperate for help."

They wandered further into the building. It was forested with heavy racks containing crates of furnishings and art from all over the world. Glaring lights high above cast hard shadows on the floor. Voices echoed distantly among the metal rafters—more warehouse workers, he assumed.

They walked around a tall rack and abruptly came upon a big herd of gleaming black grand pianos, like great sleeping beasts. There were four rows of them, about fifty instruments to each row. They had been uncrated and their plastic wrapping had been cut off, but they were still up on their sides, the legs and pedal lyres in boxes in the curves of their rims.

Esmeralda looked them over. "So those are them. I wonder how many elephants died to make those pianos?"

"Not the pianos, just the keys," Luke said a bit defensively. He went to the nearest instrument and opened up the fall board, exposing the jagged wooden mess someone had made of the keys when they stripped the ivory off. "Where is the ivory now?" he asked.

"Gone to be crushed up, Al told me," Esmeralda said with satisfaction.

He nodded and closed the fall board. He stepped into the wide space between the ranks of pianos and walked slowly down the rows, Esmeralda following.

He reached out to run his hand along the rim of one as

he passed, the curve as deep and smooth under his palm as a woman's waist.

"You love them, don't you?" Esmeralda said.

He stopped and turned to look at her. It was an intimate question that should have been jarring in this cavernous, sharply lit place. But the walls of the pianos around them gave the illusion that they were enclosed in a quiet little wood-paneled room.

And she was standing close to him, waiting for his answer, her lips a tender curve, her eyes shining softly.

So he confessed. "I love everything about them. The way they sound, the way they feel. The way they respond to the lightest touch. The way they're so ..."

"Wonderful." She said the word in a way that gave it its original meaning. A thing full of wonder.

Luke nodded. She understood. Of course she did, he thought, remembering her at the zoo with Raj. She knew all about that kind of love.

They were quiet for a moment, looking into each other's eyes. She stepped even closer to him and, like yesterday morning, she went up on tiptoe and cupped her hands around his neck to pull his head down. She probably meant to brush his cheek again in another affectionate, chaste little peck.

Didn't work out that way. That one tiny spark was all it took to set off a firestorm. In a flash her slender body was wrapped in his arms and his lips were moving over hers in the hungry, frantic kissing that had gotten them into so much trouble the night before.

With a shocked, throaty sound, she arched her back, pressing her body against his. She twined her arms around his neck and kissed him back so hard he reeled. His elbow bumped against a sleek wooden surface, which wobbled dangerously.

"Woah," he mumbled, grabbing at the piano he had almost knocked over. They were panting against each other's lips. He grappled for some common sense. *Time and place, for god's sake! Time and place!* Poor Agent Al must be getting quite the earful from the transmitter now smooshed between their bodies.

He pulled back on a shaky breath and looked down at her. Her eyes were dreamy and dark, her lips open, moist, delicious—

"Luke," she whispered. Her fingers slipped under the collar of his shirt to touch his skin.

He groaned, about to dive back into the kiss and let time and place and Agent Al go screw themselves, when the lid of the instrument next to them made a cranky sound and fell open. Something soft and heavy plopped out onto his foot.

Glancing down, he saw that a desiccant bag had flopped out of the piano and onto his toe. The glued seam of the cheap fabric had split, showing a gleam of plastic wrap underneath, which had also torn. A drift of powdery white chunks had spilled out over his shoe, dribbling down to the floor.

He stared down at the gray bag, uncomprehending at first. Then, a rising tide of ice-cold dread slowly engulfed him, dousing every last flicker of heat. "That's not desiccant," he said.

"Mmm, desiccant," Esmeralda murmured into his neck. Then she stiffened and drew back, blinking hard. "What ...?" She followed his gaze down to the package. Her face went still.

Her hands slipped away from his shoulders. She knelt

down, dipped her finger in the powder and touched it to her tongue. "Nope. It's not desiccant, whatever that is. It's pure uncut cocaine. A full kilo, I believe." She stood, dusting her hands.

"You seem very sure."

She threw him a look. "I'm a model from Miami. I've seen every drug you can name and some you can't. Trust me, that's coke."

They were silent for a moment.

Luke gingerly toed the package off his shoe. They looked inside the open lid of the piano. Gray pouches lined the rim, nestled against the strings. "About twenty bags," he said. Just like the ones in the piano he had moved at the Castillo office building.

They looked around at the neat rows of instruments.

Esmeralda said, "A kilo per bag, twenty bags per piano, times two hundred pianos equals ..."

"A shit ton of cocaine."

"Two shit tons. About a hundred fifty million dollars' worth. *Coño.*"

More silence.

"Those new warehouse workers your cousin hired must be drug traffickers."

"Uh huh." She tipped her head toward the transmitter in her bra. "I hope you're getting all this, Al."

In Luke's opinion, a US Fish and Wildlife agent was not going to be much help with this particular clusterfuck. "Speaking of Al, I think this qualifies as a potentially dangerous situation and it's time for us to—"

"Run like hell?"

"Yep." He scooped the bag back into the piano and closed the lid, then ran after Esmeralda, who was already booking it back down the row, her wedges echoing on the concrete floor.

They made it to the door to the front rooms without seeing anyone. Luke tried to calm himself as they slowed to a walk. They both knew that if they wanted to get past the guys in the office without raising suspicion they had to act like they were still the same pair of clueless schmoes who had waltzed in.

Voices floated out of the opening as they approached. Esmeralda stopped him with a hand on his chest as she drew up, listening. Luke caught the murmur that sounded like it was coming out of a speakerphone. Carefully they edged toward the door so that they could hear without being seen.

"... Who it is with her?" the voice on the phone was saying.

One of the office guys said, "Don't know the name. Big dude, blond hair, stupid tie."

"Ah, *sí*, it is the man I want. Good," said the other voice, which was starting to sound very familiar. "I will be there soon. You keep them for me until I come. And you tell them —" The voice switched to Spanish.

Luke looked a question at Esmeralda.

As she listened, her eyes started snapping with rage. But the blood was draining steadily out of her face as the voice on the phone continued on and on in a horrible ripple.

Whatever he was saying, Luke hated it.

Finally, the voice stopped on an ugly laugh.

"*Sí señor Zapata*," the office guy said, sounding subdued.

Zapata. *Shit. Shit on a Dutch apple pie.*

Esmeralda went up on tiptoe to reach his ear. "Fire exit," she breathed.

Luke nodded. It would set off an alarm and bring the goons chasing them, but it beat walking into their arms.

They backed away from the door and turned around to find two of the office guys standing there, pointing great big fucking guns at them.

31

THE TWO GOONS, plus the third guy from the office, marched them back deeper into the warehouse, away from the windows in the front. But when they got them standing next to the pianos, they seemed at a loss as to what to do.

After a few confused looks between them, Thug Number One said, "Gimme your phones and wallets. Real slow."

Luke and Esmeralda complied, he handing over his phone and wallet and she giving up her purse to Thug Number One, who scuttled up to them cockroach-style to snatch away their stuff.

As the other two held them at gunpoint, Number One rooted around in her purse. "Oooh, *perra* got some hardware," he said, plucking out her pepper spray and brass knuckles along with her wallet and phone. But not, she noted with an intake of breath, her keys. He stuck the purse on a nearby crate. He said to the other two, "I'll go look out for *el jefe*. He's on his way. You keep *los pendejos* here." He looked at Esmeralda. "He said to tell you—"

"I heard him," she said.

The guy apparently didn't have the stomach to repeat Zapata's threats, because he just grunted and trundled off toward the office with their belongings.

She tried to catch Luke's eye. They needed out of here, now. They didn't have time for Truitt to call in the cavalry.

Luke didn't spare her a glance. He kept an unblinking stare on their captors. He was unnaturally quiet and still, his hands up, fingers relaxed. His face held no expression at all. But his eyes had turned glacial, the pupils black pinpricks.

A weird electrical sensation shot up Esmeralda's spine and vibrated on the hairs of her neck, slicing through her terror and fury. It was the same kind of awareness she had when in the presence of a large and dangerous animal.

Thugs number Two and Three seemed oblivious to the threat emanating from Luke. After all, they had the guns, didn't they? Guns they were holding sideways, like they were in some dumb Tarantino knockoff flick. *What a pack of amateurs. Is it too much to expect the drug cartels to maintain professional standards?* She fought a hysterical giggle.

The boys exchanged a questioning look. Then Thug Two stretched his lips into a profane smirk. "I wanna check the *perra* don't have no more shit like the knuckles." He stuffed his gun in his pants. He swaggered up right in front of her, that nasty leer twisting his face.

"Hey, man," Number Three said.

Very quietly, Luke said, "Don't." The single icy word hung in the air.

"*Cállate puto*," Number Two barked at Luke. He licked his sweaty upper lip, then reached out and grabbed Esmeralda's breasts in a hard, disgusting grope.

Esmeralda kept her arms held out as the bruising fingers dug into her flesh, unwilling to move an inch as long as there was a gun aimed at Luke's heart. All she could hope was that he wouldn't discover the transmitter in her bra.

Number Three was watching them, still nervous but now with a prurient gleam in his eyes. His gun was drifting slightly off its target.

Number Two, impatient with her shirt getting in the way, reached for her buttons. Panic closed her throat. If he tore off her clothes he'd find the transmitter for sure, and then they were both dead.

She risked a glance at Luke.

She saw him reaching out a hand, slowly, silently. He placed it on the piano he was standing next to, the first in a row. With an explosion of power from his shoulder, he shoved the massive instrument over.

It crashed into the piano next to it, the strings roaring and the wood cracking. That piano tipped and fell into the next one in line, and then the next fell, then the next, a row of huge and noisy dominoes. A deafening *BANG ker-THWANG* roared through the warehouse.

Number Three's gun wavered around as his gaze whipped back and forth between them and the toppling instruments. "You—"

He didn't get to finish his sentence. Luke took one step forward and shot out two massive fists. The left slammed down on the asshole's gun hand with a meaty crack. Before he could even draw breath to howl, Luke's right fist crashed into his face.

It was as beautiful a punch as Esmeralda had ever seen, two hundred fifty pounds of muscle and bone channeled into a few square inches of knuckle and delivered with the speed and precision of a machine to the point of the guy's chin.

The power of it slammed his jaw closed, snapped his

head back, and took him clean off his feet. He toppled to the floor like one of the pianos. His head *chunk*-ed solidly on the concrete, putting the finishing touch on the knockout. The gun bounced from his broken hand.

Number Two had time to fumble for the gun in his pants and open his mouth to curse, but that was all. Luke spun and slammed a gargantuan haymaker into the side of Number Two's head. It would have sent the guy sailing across the room, but Luke plowed a left hook into his gut and dropped him to the floor instead.

The entire beat-down took about three seconds.

"¡Coño!" Esmeralda choked.

Luke stood, massive and silent, and breathing just a little fast. He looked at the two unconscious men sprawled out before him. Then he looked down at his fists. A thunderstruck expression washed over his face.

Esmeralda decided that this was not the time for processing. She stepped over the fallen douchebag, grabbed Luke by the arm, and managed to shake him slightly. "Come on," she yelled over the din of the still-falling pianos. She ran to snatch her bag off the crate. Then she fisted her hand in Luke's shirt and hauled him toward the glow of an exit sign at the back of the building.

After a couple of stumbling steps, Luke got with the program. They ran headlong toward the side door, bursting through it into a narrow alley. Shouts, footsteps, and the wail of an alarm sounded behind them.

"This way!" She yanked at Luke to get him turned in the right direction. They ran along the side of the warehouse toward the front parking lot where they had left the car. As they rounded the corner, three more men burst out of the door behind them, screaming in Spanish.

They made it to the Mini just as Number One slammed

through the front door. Esmeralda threw herself behind the wheel and fumbled her keys out of her purse. "Hurry!" she screamed, cranking the engine.

"Trying," Luke said. He wedged his shoulders into the car.

The four thugs ran toward them, each one waving a big, black, scary gun.

Luke yanked his feet into the car.

Esmeralda slammed the gear into reverse, cranked the wheel, and spun the Mini to point it at the street.

Luke yelped and got the door closed as Esmeralda shot out of the parking lot. He grappled for the Jesus handle as the Mini tore up the road away from the guns.

She saw him look back through the rear window at the receding figures of the gunmen. "We're clear!"

"*Coño*, no we're not!" She smashed the brakes.

A block ahead, a sharp yellow shape flashed in the sunlight. Zapata's Lamborghini. He was here. And he had seen them.

The wicked yellow car prowled down the street toward them like a cheetah getting ready to eviscerate a rabbit.

Esmeralda whipped the Mini into a tight U-turn that smashed Luke up against the window and left a cloud of burned tire behind them. They tore back up the street in the other direction, only to see a mountain of a dark green Range Rover pull out in front of them, blocking the street.

The assholes from the motel. More of Zapata's gang.

"¡*Carajo!*" she yelled at the same time as Luke yelled, "Fuck!" She stomped the brake again and yanked the wheel right. They lurched into the mostly deserted parking lot across the street from the warehouse and raced through it, doing an end run around the Range Rover.

The big car blundered to a halt, then turned around just as the Lamborghini screeched past it.

Esmeralda forced the Mini over the low curb in between the parking lot and the street with a bone-rattling bump. She straightened out the car and took off, the Lamborghini and the Range Rover behind her. But that wouldn't last long. The other cars were too fast.

They got to an intersection and whipped left. Luke grunted as his shoulder slammed against the window again. "Where are the cops? Where's Truitt? Shouldn't he be sending the cops after us?"

"We're out of range of the transmitter," she bit out.

They got to another cross street. Esmeralda wheeled right. Luke yanked on the handle and coiled his body toward the door to keep from crashing into her.

She listened hard for any sounds of sirens, but there was nothing but the growl of big engines getting closer and closer. She risked a glance in the rearview mirror. The Lambo was making up distance, the Range Rover right behind.

"Get us to the freeway! There'll be cops there for sure. Turn right next chance you get!"

"I'm not racing a Lambo on the interstate! Are you crazy?"

"Yes!"

"Wait, I have an idea! Hold on!"

She cranked the wheel left again, the Mini's tires grappling with the pavement as they charged down a side street, straight toward a dead end at a derelict industrial complex. Shells of buildings rose up alongside them, blurring past their windows. A tall chain-link fence loomed directly in front of them at the end of the road. A loosely chained gate in the fence led to a berm rising up to a railroad track. They charged full speed at the gate.

"This is a terrible idea!" Luke yelled.

"You've got ten seconds to think of a better one!"

Behind them the Lamborghini roared up to lunge at their bumper, the Range Rover right behind. Esmeralda kept her foot to the floor. Chain link loomed up before them. Luke threw up his arm in front of his face. Then the Mini was crashing through the gate, and lurching and bouncing over the gravel and up the berm.

She wrenched the wheel to the right and hit the gas again, driving along the slope between the tracks and the fence.

Luke cranked around to look back. "They're still coming!"

32

THE LAMBO SCREAMED to a stop before it hit the gate. But the Range Rover roared around the other car and onto the railroad berm after them.

Beside him, Esmeralda's lips were drawn back from her teeth, her knuckles bone-white on the wheel as she forced the Mini along the rough terrain. The wheels jostled and rattled over the gravel until Luke's bones were bouncing around inside him like Powerballs. And they were at such a steep angle that he was half sitting on the door.

Luke kept his eyes pinned to the back window. The engine growled and the SUV leapt into pursuit.

A flash of yellow to one side caught Luke's eye. The Lamborghini was keeping pace with them, racing along the road parallel to the railroad tracks. But then it vanished behind a tangled construction zone and failed to reappear at the other end.

"I think we lost the Lamborghini! Get back on the streets so we can ditch the Range Rover."

"On it," she bit out. "Look!" She pried a finger off the wheel to point forward.

He looked to the front. A few hundred yards away, he saw the flash of cars speeding past. There was a street up ahead crossing the railroad tracks.

They barreled toward the opening, the Range Rover steadily gaining but not fast enough to catch them before they hit the street.

The berm leveled out enough for them to bounce up onto the pavement. Esmeralda whipped the car right, screeching into a gap in the sparse traffic. They were on a boulevard divided by a wide median planted with palmettos. They darted around and between cars, putting more distance between them and the Range Rover only just now blundering onto the street behind them.

Luke watched behind them. "I think we're losing them!"

Then, past the hulk of the SUV, Luke saw a familiar evil yellow gleam. "Shit! The Lambo's back!"

Esmeralda swore in Spanish and zipped around a mini-van. The Lamborghini swerved around the Range Rover and came slithering up through the cars behind them, closing fast.

Esmeralda squealed around another car, trying to make it to a turn-off onto a side street. But the Lambo blazed up next to them, cutting them off. The Rover clawed up to them, lunging for their bumper.

A bone-rattling jolt shuddered through the Mini as the SUV hit them. A girlish shriek sounded in Luke's ears, which he sincerely hoped came from Esmeralda and not him.

Through the back window he could see the shadowy faces in the Range Rover, eyes dark pits, teeth white snarls. The thug in the passenger seat stuck his arm out the window. The sunlight gleamed off a too-familiar black shape.

"Gun!"

"¡Mierda!"

Over the roar of the engines and the screech of the tires, Luke heard a bloodcurdling *plink plink plink*.

Then two holes blew through the rear window and the windshield, jagged cracks spiderwebbing across the glass.

Esmeralda screamed and yanked the wheel left. The little car swerved toward the median at a diagonal. It slammed up over the curb and into a thick stand of palmettos. Branches cracked and crashed, leaves sliced past the windows, and then they were out, bouncing into the oncoming traffic of the opposite lane.

Horns wailed. Esmeralda swerved right, avoiding an oncoming Mazda.

"We're going the wrong way!" Luke yelled.

"Put it in the no shit pile!" Esmeralda yelled back. She swerved left, almost trading paint with a Subaru.

"There!" Luke pointed to a street opening.

"I see it!" She yanked the wheel left and slung the car onto the new road as a Prius almost clipped the bumper. They tore down the street and screeched around another corner.

Luke strained to see through the lines of broken glass behind them. No sign of the other cars. "I think we lost them!"

"¡Coño! This is bad, right?"

Luke spun back around. Clouds of gray smoke billowed from under the hood and a burned-sugar stench invaded the car. "Hell. We must have cracked the radiator back there."

"So, bad?"

"Yes, bad!" A grinding rattle shook them. "Pull over!"

Esmeralda spun them into another half-empty parking lot attached to a warehouse. She slammed into a parking space behind a rusted-out delivery van just as the Mini's engine coughed its last smoky death rattle and quit for good.

They sat there for a full minute, panting, vibrating, and staring through the shot-up windshield at the row of rolling doors in front of them.

Luke eventually got his bone-dry throat working. "We need to get to a phone and call the police."

Esmeralda flexed her fingers, still clenched in a white-clawed grip around the steering wheel. "Yeah."

"But first we have to get away from here. It won't take them long to find us." He could almost sense the Lamborghini and the Range Rover circling and weaving through the streets around them like a pair of sharks hunting through the coral reefs.

"Yeah," Esmeralda said again.

He shoved open the door and pried himself out of the Mini for the last time. He walked around to Esmeralda's side, his breath stuttering as he saw the bullet holes in the metal and the crushed bumper. He wrenched his gaze away and went to open Esmeralda's door. He leaned down and held out his hand to her. "Come on."

She didn't move except to look up at him with big, unfocused eyes.

He crouched down and reached in and gently peeled her small hands off the steering wheel. They were cold. He warmed them in his, holding them like they were the most precious things in the world.

"Esmeralda, you know I will never let anything happen to you. You're my jewel beyond price, remember? My incredibly brave, crazy-driving jewel. I'll keep you safe. Consider me your personal Fort Knox."

Slowly, the shocked look seeped out of her expression. She blinked a few times and then wrinkled her nose at him. "You're cute when you start babbling."

He grinned in relief. "A compliment insult! You're going to be fine." He stood and pulled her up and out of the car. He wrapped an arm around her shoulders and turned her away before she could see the bullet holes in her poor brave Mini.

He hustled her through the parking lot to the nearest cross street. They had landed deep in a run-down industrial district where all the buildings were either empty or closed for the weekend.

"Do you know where we are?" he asked Esmeralda.

"I'm not sure— no, wait." Her eyes regained some sparkle. "I've been by that place before." She pointed at a sign about a block away in the shape of a rooster wearing chaps, a sombrero, and a toothy smile. Underneath the chicken was a black awning and a blacked-out glass door that signaled "nightclub" loud and clear.

"In fact, I have a friend, Marco, who works there on the weekends doing light and sound. He'll help us. We've got to get in there and talk to him. Only ..."

"Only?"

"I might have some trouble getting in."

"Why?

Ignoring his question, she tapped her lips thoughtfully. Then she turned to him with that brilliant smile he knew meant nothing good. "I have an idea." She reached out and started unbuttoning his shirt and pulling it out of his pants.

"What are you doing?"

"Listen, this place is kind of ... different. Just trust me, okay?" In a few quick moves she stripped off his shirt and wadded it into her purse. But she left his tie still knotted around his neck.

Luke looked down at the maroon ends of the tie trailing down his bare chest. "I don't object to you taking off my clothes in principle, but the time and place—"

Esmeralda, paying no attention, produced a lipstick and a pair of her ridiculously large sunglasses from her purse. "Hold still," she said, and with a few deft flicks of her wrists, she painted a scarlet cupid's bow on his mouth and perched the shades on his nose. As he stood gaping at her, she gave him a critical squint and a nod. "You'll do. Let's go."

"But—"

Esmeralda dashed off toward the chicken club, leaving Luke no choice but to follow.

They hurried down the street, sticking close to the buildings. When they ducked into the shadow of the awning, Esmeralda grabbed the end of his tie and held it, leash style. "Now, let me do the talking," she said.

"I'll have to. You're crushing my larynx," he said, yanking the knot at his throat.

She pressed the buzzer next to the door and smiled up at the camera mounted above. They stood there for a long moment, exposed in more ways than one. Luke tried to keep from crossing his arms over his naked chest as he listened for the sounds of two powerful engines getting closer. Esmeralda's smile grew tense.

Then, with a low shushing sound, the door slowly edged open.

33

OUT OF THE darkness within the nightclub appeared the bouncer of all bouncers.

He was enormous, nearly as tall as Luke and twice as wide. His head sat atop his shoulders with no intervening neck, as round, hairless, and white as an egg. He stared out of the shadows at them with the lashless eyes of a creature from the deepest bowels of the earth. He wore work boots, overalls, and a set of c-clamps attached to his nipples.

Esmeralda didn't so much as blink at his appearance. "Hi," she said, holding out her free hand for a business handshake. "I'm Desi Arnaz, talent manager. This is the one and only Lucille," she said, shaking the end of Luke's tie in her fist. "We're here to audition for the male review show. Piano act."

The bouncer's eyes moved over them with a lizardly flick.

Esmeralda withdrew her unshaken hand and rummaged around in her purse. "I'm afraid I gave out our last card this morning. Could you let Marco Cortez know we're here? He's setting up the light and sound for us."

The egglike head rotated toward Luke. The lipless mouth opened. In an accent he might have cribbed from *Downton Abbey*, he said, "We at Polla's Nightclub do not generally host many acts which require managers. Might I inquire what services Ms. Arnaz renders you in particular, sir?"

"Uh," said Luke, his gaze still riveted to the c-clamps.

"He's an idiot savant," Esmeralda said. "He can play piano like Beethoven, but he's got no brains. Needs someone to get him around, make sure he takes his medication so he doesn't go into mindless killing rages. You should see him on stage, though, he's an animal."

The bouncer stared at her for a long, uncomfortable moment. Then he let out a girlish titter. He moved aside and waved them through the door. They stepped past him into a foyer screened off from the main part of the club by a black velvet curtain. "You'll find Mr. Cortez on the stage conducting a lighting check for Goldy De Fur," the bouncer said.

"Thanks." Esmeralda pushed confidently through the curtain, tugging Luke along behind her by his tie.

"By the way, I loved you in 'Lucy and Superman,' Miss Ball," the voice fluted behind them as the curtain closed.

"You know what, I don't think he believed your story," Luke said as they walked down the short hall.

"Who cares? It got us inside, didn't it? You need to develop an appreciation for the fine art of bullshit, my friend," she said, releasing his tie.

"Clearly."

They stepped into the main room of the club. It was two stories tall, with a balcony floor above. On the lower level, a neon-and-mirror bar snaked along one side of the room. A stage featuring two fireman-style poles dominated the other side. Chairs and tables lined the walls, as well as a few cages, and a dance floor took up the middle.

The house lights blazed down from the tall ceiling, sparking glints off the disco balls above and casting knife-edge shadows along the edges of the room. Fortunately, Esmeralda's sunglasses protected Luke from the glare.

They headed for the main stage. There were two people up on the low black platform, standing between the fireman poles. One was a young guy with curly black hair wearing jeans and a wife-beater. He was fiddling with an iPad, which was controlling the stage lighting. Pink and blue lights were blinking on and off as he tapped on his tablet.

The other figure, in a red Scarlett O'Hara hoop skirt and a towering blond beehive wig, was lounging against a speaker and cleaning the nails of one hand with a wicked-looking folding knife. Luke hazarded a guess that this was Goldy de Fur. Goldy did a double take as they walked into the room, then settled in for a long stare at Luke's tie.

"Marco, hi," Esmeralda called out.

The curly-haired guy looked around and saw them. "Ez," he said, a smile in his brown eyes. He put the tablet down on a speaker and came to meet them as they stepped up on the low stage. "Ez, my darling nectarine, what are you ..." He caught sight of Luke. "Hel-*lo*." His eyes moved in the old up-and-down, and he grinned.

"Esmeralda, you divine kiwi, don't tell me you brought me a baby bear of my very own!" To Luke he said, "I'm Marco Cortez, but you can call me Papa."

"Pipe down, Papa," Esmeralda said. "This is my friend Luke Hansen, and he's not your type."

Marco looked back and forth between them with a keen glance, and grinned ruefully. "Yeah, I can see that. Hmph. It's not fair. All the good ones are straight. Well, Ez, if you haven't come bearing gifts, what brings you to my humble workplace?"

"It's a long story," she said. She drew Marco out of Goldy's hearing. In a low voice, she quickly ran down the high points of their day so far.

Marco listened carefully, his eyes no longer smiling.

Esmeralda wound her tale up, saying, "Not to put too fine a point on it, we need to borrow your car. These are some real bad dudes after us. We have to get out of here before they find us or the next time you see me they'll be cutting me out of a tiger shark in the Bahamas on the nightly news."

"I'd give you my car in a heartbeat, Ez, but I don't have it today. One of my partners took it to Orlando for MegaCon."

"Listen, we really have to find a car, because I'm not kidding about the tiger shark."

"Can you lend us your phone?" Luke asked. "We'll call the cops and they can come get us."

Esmeralda and Marco stared at him, then looked at each other, then back at him.

"What?" Luke said.

Marco said, "That could be a problem. You see—"

"All right, where's this new kid?" bawled a voice that sounded like it had been stewed in fifty years' worth of cigarettes, liquor, and grease in the back of a Brooklyn dive bar. "Oswald called up and said there was a new kid. Let's take a look."

Everyone turned to see a man waddling out of a door behind the bar. This, Luke presumed, was Mr. Polla, owner of Polla's Nightclub. He had the shape of a squashy pyramid with feet, and was dressed in a rumpled suit and plenty of gold jewelry. He rounded the counter and huffed across the open space to stand at the foot of the stage. He slicked a hand over the thin hair covering his liver-spotted scalp as he raked an appraising eye over Luke. Craned his neck to get an angle on his ass. Finally, he too homed in on the tie and leered.

"Not bad. Long and hard. Nice big basket. Beautiful skin. Got that tight-ass quality that drives 'em crazy. Solid nine point eight. Nine point nine if you like a little bit of hair, and baby, I do."

Luke had absolutely no response to that at all.

Esmeralda leapt into the breach. "Hi, you must be the manager. Thanks so much for giving us a chance—"

"Shut it, chick," the guy said, still staring at Luke's torso. To Luke he said, "You say you can play music too? Okay, show me what you got."

"I ... ah, where's the piano? I was told there was a piano. No? Oh well, I guess—"

"I'll go get the keyboard," said Marco, the traitor. He vanished backstage.

"Wait! Uh, Mr. Polla?" Luke said, looking a question at the manager.

The liver-colored lips twitched. "Sure, I'm Mr. Polla, yeah."

"Ah, okay ... Goldy here was just in the middle of a light check."

"Goldy don't mind taking a little break," Polla said with a flick of be-ringed fingers. "Right, Goldy?"

Goldy shrugged a well-muscled shoulder and whittled down another nail.

"There, see? Go for it, kid."

Luke said desperately, "I can come back another time. I don't want to mess up her rehearsal."

Goldy's knife stilled. Kholed eyes flashed up from

beneath the beehive wig. "Her? Did you just call me *her*? Do I look like a female? Huh? Do I?"

"Well—"

"I prefer the term 'ze.' That a problem for you?"

"Nope. Not even the slightest hint of a problem."

"Damn straight," ze said, raising the knife to dry shave ze's neck.

Marco reappeared with a keyboard and stand. As he positioned the equipment between the fireman poles and connected it with the sound system, Esmeralda and Luke huddled for a conference.

"We don't have time for this," Luke whispered.

"Then play something fast," Esmeralda whispered back. "We can't afford to alienate these people. Just think of it as a unique career-building experience. You said you always wanted to be a performing musician."

Marco tapped on his iPad, cueing up the sound system. "Ready," he announced. He, Goldy, and Esmeralda stepped off the stage and looked up at him expectantly.

Luke surrendered. He went to the keyboard and looked it over. It was a surprisingly decent piece of equipment. Marco obviously knew his stuff.

He called up a romantic piano sound and played an experimental arpeggio. Not quite right for this place. He shifted the controls until it had a grungy, distorted edge. Then he launched into a keyboard arrangement of Grieg's *In the Hall of the Mountain King* he had learned for Halloween a few years back.

The first slow, sly notes of the old warhorse wove through the air. Faster and faster they came, getting more and more dynamic. Soon the sound was crashing through the wide space, winding up and up and up. Then, the last dramatic smash of the keys echoing away.

Panting slightly, he looked over his audience. Esmeralda was wide-eyed, Polla was squinch-eyed, and Goldy had stopped shaving. Marco was grinning at him lustily.

He picked the keyboard up off the stand and lifted it over his head. "This is generally where I start smashing the equipment."

"No!" everyone yelled, throwing their hands up to stop him.

Luke docilely set the instrument down on its stand.

Polla lowered his hands and rubbed his jowls, eying him critically. "Okay. You're hot, kid, no doubt. And you got talent. But, gotta say, just being honest, don't have much call for piano acts these days."

"Shucks," Luke said.

"Don't suppose you'd want to come back to my office and convince me to give you a chance? Exchange some sweet nothings?"

Luke, guessing at what that entailed, said, "Ah, no."

"Didn't think so," Polla said glumly.

"Ahem," came an Edwardian butler's voice from the entrance hall.

Everyone turned to look at the bouncer, framed dramatically in the doorway.

"Yeah? What is it, Oswald?" Polla said.

"A pair of unsavory young Columbian expatriates just rang the door asking if we had encountered a lady and a gentleman answering to your descriptions," he said, nodding toward Esmeralda and Luke. "Naturally I saw no need to inform these persons of the comings and goings within the club. But I suspect that the gentlemen in question will not be propitiated by my explanations for very long. I strongly suggest that our guests should depart forthwith, should they decline to encounter these individuals."

Polla turned to Luke and Esmeralda and said, "I don't want no trouble with no Columbians. Sorry, kid, but the job's off the table."

Luke tried to look disappointed.

"You two heard what Oswald said. You gotta get out of here."

"Okay!" Luke said instantly. He got down off the stage and went to stand by Esmeralda. "Do you have a phone we could use? We need to call for a ride."

Polla gave him a strange look, no doubt wondering what kind of freaks didn't carry phones of their own. "Phone's over there," he said, pointing to the bar. "Use it and scram."

Esmeralda said in a low voice, "We can't use a rideshare or a taxi. If those guys are watching this place, they'll shoot us the second we set foot out the door. Probably the driver too."

Luke said, "We can call the cops and get an escort—"

"No way," said the manager, who had been blatantly eavesdropping. "No cops."

"It's the best option—"

"No cops!" His gold chains rattled and his fleshy face suddenly looked hard and dangerous. Oswald the Bouncer loomed closer in the shadows. Goldy paused in shaving ze's chest to eye them over the tip of the knife blade. Even Marco went tough and watchful.

"No cops," Esmeralda and Luke agreed in unison.

A tense silence descended.

So, Luke thought, *how do we get out of here without getting ourselves or an innocent Uber driver shot?* They needed a ride that could conceal them. One that could claim a legitimate excuse for showing up at this joint. And a driver who wouldn't flinch at a little life-threatening danger from psychotic lowlifes. Who ...? Where ...?

A bolt of inspiration struck him. "I have an idea. You got a Yellow Pages?"

A few confused minutes later, a dusty book was unearthed from behind the bar. Luke flipped through the As until he found the company he wanted. He punched a number into an antique corded phone as Esmeralda watched anxiously. After only a couple of rings, the line picked up.

"Help ya?" a familiar voice said.

"Hi," said Luke. "I'm calling from Polla's Nightclub. An alligator from one of the stage acts got loose. He's holed up in the loo. We need you to come fish him out before he gets hungry."

"Aw, not Polla's again," said Joe Bob of Joe Bob's Discount Gators, Inc.

A half-hour later found them standing in a gray, box-stuffed storeroom at the back of the club. The door was cracked so that they could listen for the arrival of Joe Bob, the fast and efficient remover of large creatures and possessor of an enclosed van. Perfect for their getaway driver, if he could be convinced to take on a pair of warm-blooded passengers.

"How do you even know this guy?" Esmeralda asked.

"It's a long story," said Luke, pulling on his shirt. He was saved from further embarrassing explanations by the rumble of an engine, then the squeal of the back service doors to the club.

A muffled voice said, "Hear you got a gator problem?" It was Joe Bob, all right.

They heard the murmur of Marco doling out some charming patter. Then the scuffle of feet.

Luke handed Esmeralda's huge sunglasses back to her and got his shirt and tie straight just as the door opened.

Esmeralda peeked around his shoulder as Marco led Joe Bob into the room.

The gator-catcher's eyes passed right over them as he looked around the floor for signs of a scaly beast.

"Hi," Luke said.

Joe Bob finally squinted up at him and frowned. "Hey. Uh, you got sumpin'," he said, pointing at his mouth.

"Jeez," Luke said, rubbing off the lipstick Esmeralda had painted on his lips.

The gator-catcher said, "Wait, I know you. You're that ol' boy who nearly passed out over that little bitty—"

"Yeah, yeah, you got me," Luke said hurriedly. "Listen, we need your help. We want to hire you to drive us out of here in the back of your van."

Grizzled brows rumpled up. "So, there's no gator?"

"No, sorry. Just us. We really need a ride."

Joe Bob folded meaty arms over his massive belly and glowered. "I ain't no damn Uber."

Luke said, "We don't need to go far. Just to ... ah ..." He realized then that he had no idea where to go next.

They couldn't go to Esmeralda's house, obviously. That was the first place Zapata would look for them. And something told him that asking Joe Bob to take them to the police would be an excellent way to get a shotgun pointed at his face.

"Take us to Zoo Miami," Esmeralda said, stepping out from behind Luke. "We can pay you." She gave Marco a meaningful look.

Marco sighed and pulled out his wallet. "I've got sixty-three bucks and a ten-dollar coupon for Dunkin' Donuts."

Joe Bob sniffed. "I'm strictly Starbucks."

"We'll give you the sixty now, plus another eighty when

we get there." She blinkety-blinked at him, smiled a vulnerable smile, and said, "Please, Mr. Joe Bob."

Joe Bob's mouth fell open a little. He shook his head, struggling to resist her spell. "Wait a sec, why do you two need me to drive you anywheres? What's the deal here?"

"A Columbian drug lord and his crew are after us," Esmeralda said seriously. "We need you to smuggle us to safety."

Joe Bob stared at her for a long, unnerving moment. Then his scruffy face lit up in absolute delight. "A Columbian drug lord? Hay-ell, why din't you say so?" His eyes took on a faraway glimmer and he murmured, "Just like the Okeechobee job in '87."

Luke and Esmeralda exchanged looks.

"All right, mister, you and the lady got yourselves a ride."

After a short strategy session, they all trooped out of the storage room to the service door that led to the back alley. Joe Bob peered through the door, saw no baddies, and went to open up the back of his van.

Marco was to stand lookout where the alley met the street and give them the all-clear signal if Zapata's cars were out of sight. Before he could slip away, Esmeralda grabbed him in a big hug. "Thanks for your help, Marco. I owe you."

"*No hay problema*, peach," Marco said, setting her away and smiling at her. "It's kind of exciting, all this daring-do. Arousing, you might say. You know, when you two are done running for your lives, you should give me a call. We could have a hell of a good time, the three of us." He leaned over Esmeralda's shoulder toward Luke and said in a throaty voice, "You could be the pork in a Cuban sandwich, baby bear."

"Marco!" Esmeralda said, stepping in front of Luke protectively.

"Kidding!" He mouthed at Luke, *Not kidding. Call me,* and waggled his thumb and pinky in the phone sign. With a last wink, he strutted out the door.

Esmeralda socked Luke in the stomach to make him quit laughing and dragged him into the alley.

Luke quickly sobered as he edged up to the van and looked apprehensively into the dark interior. It was a simple box with a few metal rings bolted to the floor, presumably for tying down large reptiles, and a thick plastic web separating the back from the driver's seat.

To Luke's profound relief, it was empty, aside from a coating of mud and alligator goo. But an astounding swampy stink lunged out at him and fastened its jaws around his sinuses.

"Nope. I changed my mind," he gagged.

Esmeralda poked him. "Don't be such a little girl. This was *your* plan."

"I'm leaving all future plans to you. I'm no good at them," he said as he climbed inside.

He helped Esmeralda scramble up into the van and closed the doors behind them. They crouched side by side against the webbing, trying to breathe through their mouths, while Joe Bob hoisted himself into the driver's seat.

Through the front windows they could see Marco casually loitering at the end of the alley, smoking something that might pass for a cigarette. After a little look-around, he flicked two fingers in a "come on" gesture.

Joe Bob turned a terrifyingly cheery grin on them through the mesh. "That's it. Hold on to yer tits!" He cranked up the engine, let loose an actual, real-live "Yee-haw!" and stepped on the gas.

The van lurched forward, the momentum sending them stumbling along its length to the back doors, where they landed in a pile, Esmeralda on top of Luke.

He grabbed a tie-down and wrapped his other arm around Esmeralda to keep them both from pinballing against the walls and doors as they wallowed around a series of corners.

At last they were out of there, barreling down a major road toward the freeway. Esmeralda wriggled her taught rear end around on his lap until she faced him, a dawning smile of relief on her lips. "I think we're in the clear," she said, wrapping her arm around his neck.

"Shh. *Do not* jinx this," he said. He clutched her to him harder as they swerved up an on ramp, and contemplated the fact that, even fleeing for their lives in a slime-coated gatormobile, she was still able to give him a mile-long boner.

34

JOE BOB DEPOSITED them at Zoo Miami's main gate in remarkably good time and only a little the worse for wear. Esmeralda was still as fresh as a flower, he thought, as he helped her climb out onto the pavement. Whereas he looked—and smelled—as if he'd been rolled in the flower's fertilizer.

Joe Bob waved away their offer of money, bestowed a gallant kiss upon the back of Esmeralda's hand, climbed back into his van, and rumbled off into the sunset.

Esmeralda turned to Luke with a faint grin. "Home free."

"Not until we get out of public sight," Luke said, starting for the gate.

"We should be okay now," she said, falling into step beside him. "Zapata will never think to look for us here."

Her cousin Roddy might, though, Luke thought. He wouldn't believe they were truly safe until they were behind the walls of a police precinct.

Dusk was coming and the zoo was only a few minutes

from closing as they hustled through the gate. The minute they stepped on the premises, the pavement at Luke's feet was swarming with ibises, all peering up at him worshipfully.

"Jeez, guys, I'm kind of in a hurry here," Luke said as they plowed through the fluttering birds.

"I told you, they're yours for life," Esmeralda said.

They finally managed to ditch the flock and make it into the administration building. After a stop at the main desk to get Luke another guest pass, they went to Esmeralda's locker. She rummaged around inside until she came up with an envelope full of emergency cash and a brand new prepaid phone.

"The state of Florida issued a bunch of these out to all state offices, including ours," she told him as she tore off the plastic case and switched the phone on. "Taxpayer money well spent, is all I've got to say."

"We can finally contact the police."

"I want to go see Raj first. We can call Al from the elephant barn."

Luke wanted to tell her that they'd already wasted too much time for another detour into zoological nuttery. But one look at the fragile lines around Esmeralda's eyes had him saying, "All right. Let's go say hello to your big friend."

Esmeralda drove them to the elephant barn in the mule, slowly for once, and in silence. When they got out, she called, "Raj?" her voice wavering.

The shadows under the barn's roof coalesced into a gigantic dark shape reaching out through the bars toward Esmeralda.

"Raj!" She dropped her purse onto the ground and ran to the elephant.

The big trunk scooped her up into a strange yet tender

interspecies hug. Then a gleaming eye turned toward Luke. That eye said, "What did you do to her, puny tennis ball man?"

Luke raised his hands. "It wasn't me, I swear."

Esmeralda nodded against the rough gray hide. "It's all right, Raj. He saved me. He's a good guy." She turned her head and smiled at Luke. "The best guy."

All on its own, Luke's hand went to a sudden sharp pain over his heart.

After a moment, Raj quit eye-stomping Luke and relaxed his hold on Esmeralda.

She dashed the back of her hand over her eyes and stepped away. She said to Raj, "I have a lot to tell you. But I have to tell Al Truitt as well, so I might as well do it all at once." She pulled out the new phone, punched out a number, and hit the speaker.

One ring later, the line picked up. "Truitt," a voice barked.

"Al, it's me. And Luke."

"Agent Truitt," Luke said curtly.

"Esmeralda? Where are you? Are you safe?"

"We're safe. We're at the zoo."

"Zoo Miami? What ... how did you end up there?"

"It's quite a story, Al," she began. As Luke listened to her narrating their recent adventures to the agent, he found himself newly astounded that they were still alive.

Raj seemed to feel the same. He kept lashing his trunk around in what Luke guessed was an elephant stream of profanity.

"... and so now we're at the zoo," Esmeralda finished up. "So. How have you been?"

"Crazy. I've been crazy," Truitt said. He told them that the instant he heard the word "cocaine" in his transmitter, he had sent out a system-wide call for help. The FBI, the DEA, the Miami PD, and various and sundry other law enforcement organizations had all shown up to storm the warehouse. Unfortunately, they had arrived on the scene a few minutes after Luke and Esmeralda had already made their escape. Zapata's crew had also rabbited off in a panic, leaving behind an unholy mess of drugs, guns, and smashed pianos, plus two unconscious guys who looked like they'd been run over with a tractor.

"You wouldn't happen to know anything about that, would you?" Truitt said casually.

"It was an accident," Luke said.

"It was amazing," Esmeralda said at the same time.

"It was totally reckless and irresponsible! You don't attack armed men. You wait for law enforcement to de-escalate the situation. Didn't I tell you not to play hero, Mr. Hansen? You could have gotten both of you killed!"

"He didn't have any choice," Esmeralda said. "They were searching me, Al. If they had found the transmitter they would have shot us anyway."

"Unlikely. Any sensible criminal would have used you as bargaining chips to ensure his own safety."

"If only we had kidnappers with brains! Instead we had a couple of amateurs auditioning for the drug thug cartoon hour," Esmeralda said.

"What do you mean, 'amateurs'?" Truitt said.

"Well, you've got to admit these guys have been pretty sloppy and bumbling for ruthless cartel soldiers. The flashy cars? Letting the cargo sit around in a warehouse for days? Come on."

"Amateurs," Truitt repeated thoughtfully. "Yes, that fits with what we've learned about Zapata's operation. It makes sense that he recruited a totally green crew."

"Why is that?" Luke asked.

"As far as we can tell, he's brand new to the smuggling game. Homeland Security found out that his real estate business has been in difficulties for some time. He couldn't get loans from legitimate banks, so he went looking for alternative capital streams. The cartel apparently thought a businessman of his supposed reputation would be a useful mule, so they recruited him."

"Big mistake on their part," Esmeralda said with satisfaction.

"And on Zapata's. His new bosses aren't going to be happy with him when they find out he lost a hundred fifty million dollars' worth of product. He'll be the luckiest son-of-a-gun in the world if we find him before they do."

"Why haven't you found him yet?" Luke said. "How is that possible? He's driving a bright yellow Lamborghini, for God's sake."

"This is Miami, Luke," Esmeralda pointed out. "Lambos grow like mushrooms here."

"And speaking of the incompetence of US law enforcement," Luke went on, "would you mind telling us how Zapata, the amateur, managed to smuggle two tons of cocaine past the customs officers in the first place?"

Truitt said stiffly, "Customs didn't put the shipment through the usual inspection process when it came into port because Fish and Wildlife had already taken legal custody of it. And we were focused on the ivory, so we didn't check it for anything else."

Esmeralda said, "So, those pianos fell through an interdepartmental crack? Is that what you're saying?"

Truitt said, "Actually they got shoved through the crack."

"What do you mean?"

He sighed. "We discovered that two individuals at DHS have been taking bribes to help importers find loopholes in the system that allow them to smuggle contraband. And there's more. We traced the most recent payoffs to Castillo Imports."

35

LUKE SAW Esmeralda's knuckles go white as she gripped the phone.

"Esmeralda, law enforcement needs to talk to your cousin Rodrigo Castillo, but we can't seem to locate him," Truitt said gently. "Do you know where he might be?"

Esmeralda's spine went as straight as a flagpole. "Roddy is not a drug smuggler. If someone from the company was manipulating the system, it wasn't him. He didn't want to go to Fish and Wildlife at all. He didn't even want to take possession of the pianos when they arrived in port. He was going to try to return them to China, or unload them offshore. I'm the one who talked him into turning the ivory in after Juan let the news slip ..." Her eyes widened.

"It's Juan Hernandez, don't you see, Al? He's your guy. He and Roddy were talking about the pianos at dinner the night before I came to see you. But it was Juan who brought up the ivory keys in front of me." Her delicate jaw clenched. "Because he knew what I would do. He knew I would turn the ivory in to Fish and Wildlife. Roddy was balking, so that *pendejo* used *me!*"

"We need to bring Juan in for questioning too," Al said diplomatically. "But they're both missing. Do you know where they might be hiding?"

"I have no idea, Al. I'd tell you if I did, because I know my cousin is innocent. But he's also a complete dumbbell, so I have no doubt Juan convinced him he had to go on the lam. I want to help you find him if only to save him from himself."

"Okay, good. We can go over any ideas you have about tracking him when I come to get you. I'm taking you into protective custody for the night. I'll be on my way to pick you up from the zoo the minute I file my report."

Esmeralda's chin tipped up in a gesture Luke knew all too well. "Still trying to order me around, Al?"

"Esmeralda, be reasonable. You need protection while Zapata and his associates are still at large. We already arranged a police detail for your family home, but it would be safer for all of you if you didn't return there for now."

"I know," she said, subdued.

"Usually this would be a job for the Federal Marshals, but they're scrambling for coverage. They won't be able to take over your security until tomorrow. Until then, you'll have to stay with me in a hotel room."

"The three of us in one room?" she said grumpily. "Can't the government spring for a suite?"

"Not the three of us. Just you and me, Esmeralda. I can only take responsibility for the safety of one person. I'll call the Miami PD for Mr. Hansen. They'll assign an officer to guard him at a separate location."

Every instinct Luke had instantly fired up. "No way. I'm not leaving Esmeralda's side while that psycho is on the loose. I promised her I'd keep her safe, and I will."

"She doesn't need you for protection," said Agent Al,

getting snitty. "She has me and Federal law enforcement for that."

"And quite the shit job you've done of it so far," Luke noted.

"Enough, guys," Esmeralda said. "Al, thanks for your offer, but until the Marshals can take over, I want to stay with Luke."

It was impossible for him not to puff his chest up. Who needed the cops, anyway? He wondered why on earth he'd been so keen to get to them before. He could protect her on his own, like he'd been doing since the day he met her.

She said, "Don't bother coming to pick us up from the zoo, because we won't be here."

"Esmeralda, this is not an offer, it's an order! Luke Hansen is a civilian. You belong in protective custody with trained professionals to guard you. Did you forget Zapata's threats in the warehouse? I have them recorded if you need to remember how serious this is."

"What threats?" Luke said.

Esmeralda said quickly, "Al, we'll call you later. Bye."

"Don't you dare—"

She hung up. "Well, that certainly was an interesting conversation," she said, her voice overly bright.

"Yes. What—?"

"Now we just have to find a place to hide out for the night," she said. "I'm going to call home and ask Ignacio to arrange a room for us. Don't worry, he won't snitch on us to Al or anyone else."

"I'm sure. But what—?"

"And I need to check in with Anita and Papa. They must be in a panic by now." She started to press the numbers on the keypad.

Luke reached out and covered the phone with his hand. "Esmeralda, what did Truitt mean about Zapata's threats?"

Not quite meeting his eyes, she said, "Oh, just that phone call we overheard in the warehouse. He was yapping a bunch of stupid tough guy *mierda*." She tried for a smile, but it wavered and died.

"Tell me what he said."

"Well ... roughly translated, he more or less said that he was going to ... to rape me until I bled to death, and then cut off your fingers and your penis and ... and make you eat them. Approximately."

Luke took a long, slow breath.

"Kind of over the top, right? The guy must be addicted to HBO." She went silent for a moment. Then she said in a high voice, "But, the thing is, I think he meant it. That sadistic *comemierda* actually meant it. If he had caught us, he would have ..."

Luke heard her as if from a great distance. Once again preternatural awareness flared through his every cell. He could see with crystal clarity how to manipulate his physical surroundings according to his whim. If Zapata were standing in front of him now, for example, Luke knew he would be able to move his hands and body in exactly the right way to twist that fucker's head clean off his shoulders. A crunch and a pop, like unscrewing a Coke bottle.

The weird, unbearable sensation of an impending lightning strike seemed to fill up the entire elephant barn.

Raj made a deep rumbling sound and waved his ears in a slow flap.

"Luke? Luke!" Esmeralda stepped toward him, her hands raised in a calming gesture, though he hadn't said a word or moved a muscle. "Please, don't get mad. You're making Raj nervous. He doesn't like angry men."

He blinked hard, spun, and paced a few feet away. He stopped with his face turned away from her, taking deep breaths, trying to find his way back to the normal world. Slowly the strange cold tide receded, leaving him shaken and appalled at himself.

He'd just had a good, long look at what he was truly capable of. What he'd never known was in him until now. And it was terrifying. "What's happening to me?" he said softly.

He heard Esmeralda say, "I'm sorry, Luke. I'm so sorry I dragged you into this ... this insanity."

Luke said nothing.

"You know ... none of this is really your problem. The Feds won't need you to stay here to testify, not as long as they've got me. And Zapata still doesn't know your name, so he couldn't track you down if you left. I'll be safe enough with Al, so you don't have to worry about me. I can get you a ticket on a plane out of Miami right now, tonight. You could go back to your normal life, just like you wanted to."

He turned and looked at her in amazement. She didn't understand at all. Concern for his own safety had never once crossed his mind. The only thing worrying him was how far he might go for her sake, and what he might do to keep her safe. But then, he already knew, didn't he?

Anything. He'd do anything and everything for her.

He went back to her and took her slim shoulders in his hands. "Esmeralda, you didn't drag me anywhere I didn't want to go. And I'm not leaving you until I know you're safe. And that's all there is to it."

She looked up at him with big eyes and took a quick little breath. "Okay. All right." Her lip trembled a little, but then she straightened up and smiled brightly. "In that case, let me call home, then we're out of here."

Right then, he wanted to crush her to him and kiss them both into oblivion, until the danger was far away and forgotten. But he knew that wasn't what she needed. She had to find her inner steel again before she went back out to join the battle.

Also, he wasn't entirely sure she wouldn't deck him if he tried anything right now. So instead of shocking Raj with a display of human mating rituals, he nodded and released her.

She took a moment to compose herself and called Anita, breaking into an excited Spanish conversation and pacing around the enclosure.

Her tone varied between abject apology and reassurance, until it veered off into wheedling. His mouth started curving as he listened to her work. She really had a natural genius for bullshitting.

Eventually she looked over at him. "Anita says Ignacio is going to get us a room at a hotel on Miami Beach. And he's sending a taxi to pick us up and bring us there."

"Okay."

"Anita also says to tell you thanks for saving my life, and ... ah ..." She blushed and put the phone back to her ear. She paced away, placating Anita in Spanish once again.

Luke was wondering exactly what else Anita had said to tell him when he felt a firm thump on his back, the heavy, rough weight of an elephant trunk. He spun around and saw that Raj had moved silently up behind him and was regarding him with a fathomless dark eye.

They looked at each other through the bars for a long moment. The big ears flared out. The long tusks gleamed in the gathering dusk.

Luke's skin bristled with a deep, animal awareness of danger. The elephant was close enough to throw him across the clearing if he wanted to. But Luke didn't move back. He looked steadily at Raj. "Don't worry. I'll take care of her, I promise."

A long, tense moment passed. Slowly, Raj reached his trunk through the barrier again and thumped him on the chest. And Luke knew that meant, "You'd better, kid, else I'll sit on you."

36

"I THINK NOW I can guess what first caused Papa's attacks," Esmeralda said.

Luke quit his own brooding and looked over at her in the seat next to him. They were in the back of the taxi Ignacio had sent for them, cruising over the MacArthur Causeway toward Miami Beach. Her face was washed with light, dark, light, dark as they passed beneath the street lamps.

She said, "Papa must have found out that the cocaine was hidden in the pianos. But he hates drugs and drug runners because of what happened to his brother, my uncle. Smugglers using his company for a front would definitely have set him off."

Luke remembered what Castillo had said during his episode on the day he had arrived in Miami. The keys, the keys, he'd said, over and over. At the time Luke had thought he was talking about the ivory piano keys, but he could easily have meant the slang term for kilos of coke instead. "That's a good guess."

"The only thing I can't figure is how he would have

known what was happening in the first place. He hasn't been involved with the company for a year."

"Remember the sticky note I found in your father's home office with 'Z,' 'Lamborghini,' and 'Range Rover' on it? I'll bet you someone was using that room to do business with Zapata, and your father overheard them."

"If you're right, that someone was Juan, not Roddy. There's no way Roddy was a willing part of this scheme."

"Are you absolutely sure? Roddy's pretty desperate to save Castillo Imports, and desperation can make people do crazy things." As he himself knew well.

Her lips set in a stubborn line. "Roddy would never smuggle drugs. After the way his father died? After the way my papa raised him? Not in a million years. He's a clueless dope, and Juan took advantage of him. Case closed. But now he's missing, and ... and if Juan convinced him to run, or worse, took him to Zapata ..."

He felt an unwilling pang of sympathy for the young dimwit. "If Juan wrote the note, and if he acquired those two cars for Zapata, there should be a paper trail to him that might clear Roddy. It might even help track them both down."

"We'll have to tell Al about your theory," Esmeralda said, but she still looked worried.

Aiming to distract her, he said, "I hope they devote some time to tracking down Kowalski too. How in the world did a bottom-feeder like him manage to get mixed up in a cocaine racket?"

"Maybe he's not. Maybe he really was just after the ivory. But if that's the case, I wonder why he didn't show up at the warehouse for our meeting?"

"It's possible he did show up, and then scurried to the nearest rat hole when the bullets started flying."

Esmeralda shrugged. "We may never know. Finding him is no one's priority now."

"Except mine. I came here to get back what he stole from me, and I'm not leaving without it."

Esmeralda looked at him as the lights passed over her face. She smiled, a little wistfully, he thought. "Well then. We'll find him. As soon as we're not in danger of getting machete-ed to death by a drug cartel."

Luke traded glances in the rearview mirror with the taxi driver, a middle-aged Sikh who was looking mightily concerned about the conversation in the back seat. He had driven up to them as they waited at the front gates of the zoo, taken one look and sniff at Luke's gator-stained attire, and had almost peeled off, stopped only by Esmeralda waving a fistful of bills in the windshield. He was now thoroughly regretting disobeying his instincts, if his muttered prayers were anything to go by.

Fortunately for the driver, his part in their adventure was about to end. The taxi turned left onto Ocean Drive and crawled through bumper-to-bumper traffic until it finally reached the front door of the hotel Ignacio had arranged for them. Spring break was still in full swing, which meant that the sidewalk restaurants lining the street were hosting a combo keg stand, karaoke competition, and stripper review.

Luke eyed the barrier of bouncing club kids between them and the entrance to the hotel, then looked down at his slimy duds.

"I suppose this is the only way in? We don't want to attract attention."

"I wouldn't worry about it." Esmeralda sent a glance toward a ... woman, maybe, who was strolling past them dressed in nothing but a strategically draped Burmese python.

"Right. What was I thinking?" Luke said.

Though Ignacio had already paid for the taxi ride, Esmeralda forked over fifty bucks from their meager stash in hopes that the driver would forget he ever saw them. Luke figured it might buy them a day of silence, tops. They got out and the taxi puttered away in prudent haste.

They did indeed attract notice as they battled through the sidewalk restaurant and into the hotel, but not for long. People looked at the luscious swimsuit model, then they looked at the huge guy covered up to his slightly crazed eyeballs in slime looming protectively over her, and then they looked away.

Inside they found a lobby decorated in white marble and white furniture that looked like an Art Deco suite squeezed through Tim Burton's brain. In one corner was a white lacquered piano.

As they walked in Esmeralda said, "We don't have our IDs, so I'm going to have to do some fast talking to get us checked in. Just follow my lead."

"Like last time, huh? Do I take my shirt off again?"

"Unfortunately, no."

At the front desk the concierge greeted them with the pleasant smile of a professional host and the glazed eyes of a taxidermy exhibit. He seemed completely unfazed by their appearance. But then, they probably weren't the weirdest sight he'd ever seen on South Beach.

Esmeralda's nose tipped up and she looked around the hotel with conspicuous boredom before her gaze finally fell upon the desk guy. "I," she announced, "Am Carmen Sandiego. My personal assistant Ignacio Gorte has purchased a room for me in your little ... establishment. You may have someone show me up now."

The desk guy smiled genially and consulted his computer. "Yes. Here's the reservation, Ms. Sandiego. Could I see some form of ID?"

"No." She tipped an eyebrow up, somehow conveying that she was embarrassed for the man at being so gauche as to ask such a question.

"I see. And the, ah, gentleman? Does he have any identification?"

Her face became a study in scandalized shock. "Do you not know who this man is?" she said in a stentorian whisper. "This is Mikhail Kyrscechevyscovich, of Gualeharyachevistovinia! The Miami Heat has spent the last year trying to recruit him for their new center!"

Luke turned to look at her.

She raised her eyebrows at him and tipped her head toward the desk guy.

He summoned up the sole German phrase he could remember from high school. *"Entschuldigen Sie bitte, wo ist das Badezimmer?"*

"Exactly right, Mikhail. Now then, I am Mikhail's guide to Miami and the chairperson of his steering committee. As you can see, we've had a difficult day. We had an unfortunate encounter at the Reptile Adventure Park when a crazed fan caused him to fall into the turtle pit ..."

As Esmeralda spun her web of preposterous nonsense, Luke's attention wandered over to the piano in the corner. Recent model baby grand Yamaha. Nothing special. Looked like it hadn't been touched in a while, but he might be able to get a decent tone out of it. He started to edge toward it for a closer look.

Esmeralda grabbed his elbow and hauled him back to

her side. "Focus, Mikhail," she whispered. "I know pianos really tickle your prostate, but try not to throw wood until after we get to our room. We're trying to be inconspicuous."

Luke gasped, laughed, and choked all at once, and ended up in a coughing fit.

She said out loud, "As you can see, Mikhail's health is on the line here. If you don't get us into our room right now, I will hold you directly responsible for losing us the championship this year."

The concierge was already clickety-clacking away at his computer, apparently having had enough of Esmeralda's brand of persuasion and hoping to get the large and stinky man out of his lobby as fast as possible.

When he handed over their key cards, Luke suddenly realized something. They had gotten *a* room. As in, one single room for both of them.

What did that mean? Probably nothing. Maybe she just wanted her *de facto* bodyguard close at hand. Maybe she just didn't want to spend the money on two rooms.

But would their room come with two beds, or would there be only one?

Esmeralda sniffed. "I see you have no gift shop. I demand you go and send someone to buy me a toothbrush."

"Every room comes with complementary toiletries," the desk guy said. He glanced back and forth between them. "And an intimacy kit. In the bedside table."

"Good to know. Come along, Mikhail." She traipsed away toward the elevators.

The concierge aimed his cast-iron smile at Luke. "Good luck in the playoffs, Mr. Kyrscechevyscovich."

"*Gesundheit*," he said, and went to follow Esmeralda. To his doom, no doubt.

37

THEIR ROOM WAS one of the hotel's best, on the top floor and facing east over Ocean Drive to the beach and the Atlantic glimmering under the moonlight. It was, however, tiny, with just enough room for a dresser, a chair, and a king-size bed.

A bed. One. Luke froze just inside the door, staring at it.

Esmeralda had no such hesitation. She darted for the bathroom, saying, "Oh, *gracias a Dios*! Dibs on the shower!" She dove in and shut the door. It was a narrow door made of frosted glass.

Déjà vu washed over him. He'd seen that frosted glass bathroom door before. Except it was splattered with blood. Then it hit him. "Wait a minute. This is the hotel where they shot the chainsaw scene in *Scarface*! You know, the one with Al Pacino playing the Cuban— uh, cocaine gangster."

"Yeah," she laughed a bit grimly from inside the bathroom. "Ignacio has an odd sense of humor." The shower hissed on. Through the rapidly fogging glass, he saw a slender golden shape shimmering. Esmeralda was taking off her clothes. He stared, heart hammering, until the clouds of steam obscured his vision.

In a daze, he wandered over to the window and looked out over the black shimmer of the ocean beyond the waving coconut palms. Nice view.

The water streamed and pulsed behind him. He heard a soft sigh.

He wheeled around and stared down at the bed. The single, king-size bed that they were apparently going to share tonight. *Was she actually thinking that* ... He swallowed.

He opened the drawer in the sleek white bedside table. As promised, inside was a cardboard box labeled "Intimacy Kit." He sorted through its contents with shaky fingers. A ten-pack of condoms, a bottle of lube, a pair of edible one-size-fits-most underpants, a couple of feathers, a blindfold, and a few lengths of silky material that were helpfully tagged, "Bondage Strips."

He heard the water shut off and quickly scooped everything back into the box and shoved it underneath the pile of pillows. He turned around just as the glass door opened. Esmeralda appeared in the midst of a cloud of fragrant steam, wrapped in one of the hotel's thick terrycloth robes. "Your turn."

"Right. Ah, thanks. I'll just go get cleaned up. Should be nice. Good soap here, I bet." He bit the inside of his cheek before he could babble anything further and edged past her to the glass door. The bathroom was a cubbyhole so narrow Luke's shoulders barely cleared it. Maneuvering carefully, he stripped off his stinking clothes, balled them up and tossed them into a corner.

He wedged himself into the shower and turned the water on to scrotum-crawling cold. It got him clean but did nothing to calm his dick, which kept getting harder with every beat of his heart.

He leaned his forehead against the tile, struggling to get control of himself. But that was simply not gonna happen. With the woman of his dreams literally an arm's reach away, there was no possibility that his ferocious erection was going down on its own tonight. Not unless he took things in hand right now. But he winced at the idea of rubbing one out like some creep while she sat innocently in the next room. And then, there was the slight chance that she ... that she might ... want ...

Want us! She might want us! his rampant member seemed to yell at him.

It was possible, wasn't it? She'd been into him on the piano last night. And today in the warehouse. He hadn't imagined it, had he? The way she had moaned and licked his tongue, the way she had arched her breasts into his hands, rubbed her soft, hot pussy against him ...

A groan ripped from his chest as he fisted himself.

"What was that?" Esmeralda called from the next room

He coughed. "Nothing. I'll be right out."

With shaking hands he shut off the water and got out of the stall. He dried off and wrapped the towel around his hips, holding it closed in front to hide his condition. He eased the bathroom door open.

She was standing by the bed, her face in profile, her hair drying in a rippling black curtain over her shoulders. So lovely. He took a step into the room, then froze when he saw her reach down to the bed and pick up the string of foil packets. He must have missed them when he was stuffing the intimacy crap back into the box.

She turned to face him, condoms in hand. "I don't know, Luke," she said, a troubled frown between her brows.

His heart plummeted so hard and fast it left him sick and shaking.

He stared blindly past her out the balcony window. So, rejection. What now? Run straight through the sliding glass doors and dive over the railing to plunge to his death? Seemed like the only reasonable plan of action at the moment.

Then she said, "I don't think ten is going to be enough."

His gaze shot back to her.

She continued in that same thoughtful tone, "You know what else? These aren't Magnums. Based on what I could feel last night when we were dry-humping on the piano, you definitely need Magnums."

His jaw fell open.

"You don't have any diseases, do you?" she asked

"N-no! Of course not."

"Me neither. And I have an IUD. So I vote we have sex without the condoms. Any objections? Speak now or forever hold your peace."

Luke couldn't move a muscle.

"Well then." She tossed the condoms aside. Her hands went to her belt, slipping the knot free. She opened the robe, one side at a time. With a shimmy of her shoulders, she let it slide off to pool on the floor. She lifted her chin and stood before him, splendidly, gloriously naked.

She was so perfect it hurt to look at her. Breasts high, firm, proudly upturned, tipped with tight dusky-rose nipples. Waist tiny, hips flaring in a curve like a mandolin. Arms and legs slim and strong. She had a Brazilian wax, because of course she did. Only the softest hint of hair shadowed the pink place between her thighs.

Then he raised his eyes to hers, and he knew it was a

dream. Because he saw desire there, for *him*. He didn't dare move in case he woke himself up.

Her brows took a quizzical slant. "Luke, are you nervous?"

"No," he croaked.

"You are! *Por Dios*, that's so—"

"Don't say it."

"—cute!"

"That's it." He dropped his towel, strode across the room, and scooped her up off her feet. He shoved his iron-hard erection against her belly and she gasped, eyes shining. "I am not fucking cute," he said, and crushed his mouth down on hers.

And he was lost. Swept away in a primal frenzy. He clutched her ass, grinding her against him in a brutal instinct. And she was climbing him like a tree, wrapping her long legs around his waist. Her fingers were twining in his hair, her tongue was in his mouth.

They tumbled onto the bed, and he only just managed to twist around so he landed on the bottom. Her hair fell around them as she kept kissing him. Her body pressed along him, her skin rubbing hot against his. She was wrestling him for the top, her lips and hands stroking him everywhere, but he put her under him and finally got his mouth on her breasts. He gripped them in his hands and rubbed his face against them, kissed them and sucked them until she was trembling and panting beneath him.

"Luke," she whispered. She pulled his head back up to her lips for another wild kiss. He scooped her against him and wedged himself against the wet place between her open legs. His hips jerked instinctively, lunging for the heat of her sex. A feral noise tore out of his chest, the sound of an animal caught in mindless rut. His cock demanded to be inside her, the tip slick with his excitement, ready to penetrate. He slid himself along her wet cleft again, and the hot pulse of her little clit against his naked shaft was almost enough to do him in. The knot of his orgasm pulled dangerously tight at the base of his spine.

"Oh, yes now!" she said against his lips. She grabbed his ass, urging him into her.

"No, wait!" He leaned up, peeling her hands off of his butt and pinning them above her head. Though it was very fucking hard, he pulled his dick back out of the danger zone. It bobbed and strained over her wide-open thighs, but he kept it under control, barely.

She went still. "What's wrong?"

"Nothing. It's— I want you so much— I have to cool it or I'm going to come the second I get inside you."

Her eyes flared with excitement. "That's okay. So am I." She wound her legs around his waist and rolled her pelvis up, running the lips of her pussy along his shaft in a long, wet glide, until his cockhead was wedged in the heat of her opening.

It was more than mortal man could bear. He thrust into her with a harsh groan, all the way in, and oh. God. *God*. It was more perfect than any dream. Better than life itself. He pumped into her again and again and again, enslaved to the wet slide and grip of her sheath.

A spark of fear flared that he was being too rough, but fuck! True to her word, her legs were twisting around his hips, her inner muscles clamping around his cock and she was gasping out an involuntary noise, an unmistakable sound of helpless, mindless pleasure.

Her animal cry, and that incredible quake and clench of her body tore his orgasm from him in a rush of hot bliss. She twisted under him, screaming out. And he came, and came, and kept on coming, until his vision flashed white.

A long time later, he opened his eyes, dazed to find himself alive. Breathing hard, he rolled them both to the side so he wouldn't crush her. But he stayed buried deep inside her body. He couldn't even think of leaving the heat of her. He never wanted to be anywhere else for the rest of his life.

Her smooth leg hooked over his hip, her breasts plumped against his chest. They lay face to face, panting and looking at each other in silent wonder. Stunned by what had just happened.

Luke could barely grasp what he was feeling, it was so shocking and new. It was like beams of pure joy were radiating up from his dick, slicing through his heart. He'd liked sex well enough before, but this ... her ...

He raised a shaking hand and sifted his fingers through the silk of her hair as she smiled at him, mouth a tender curve, eyes soft and shining. "Esmeralda, I ..."

Her fingertips trembled along his shoulder and up to his jaw. "Yes?"

"I ..." *Adore you, treasure beyond price.*

He almost said it. But a warning sounded in the back of his mind, a voice telling him he was teetering on the edge of the highest cliff in the world and if he leapt off, he might very well end up a ruined gory mess at the bottom. Better to back away. Safer.

Besides, something else was demanding his attention. "I think there's a problem."

"What?"

He pulled away slightly and looked down their bodies to where they joined. Astoundingly, his shaft was still as thick and hard and raring to go even though he'd just gone off like the cannon in the 1812 Overture. "It's not going down."

She smiled a devil's smile at him and squeezed her inner muscles tight around his dick.

He gasped, his eyes rolling back in his head.

"You're right. This is a huge, hard problem. Let me solve it for you."

38

ESMERALDA'S SOLUTION was another blistering hot fuck, this one lasting a good long time now that they'd taken the first desperate edge off.

After they'd both come their brains out writhing and screaming, they collapsed side by side, nearly glowing with radiant heat in the dim light. Luke groped for her hand, folding it in his. "Problem solved," he panted. But only temporarily, he was certain. Good thing he had another project in mind to keep him busy during his down time. The instant he caught his breath he rolled over and brushed a kiss over her lips.

She opened her eyes. "I'm starving to death."

"Me too," Luke said. He trailed kisses along her neck, moving down to her breasts.

She put her hand on his face and pushed. "No. No way. I have to eat before I do anything else." She wriggled around and leaned over to grab the room phone and hit the button for room service.

He growled, "I don't care." He wrapped his hands around her waist and flipped her onto her back, spreading her legs wide with his knees. She gaped up at him as he loomed above her, his eyes feasting on the wet pink flesh between her thighs. "I have to eat too," he said.

"Just one *carajo* minute here," she said, but then he heard a tinny voice coming from the phone in her hand. "Room service. How can I help you?"

She put the receiver up to her ear and said hurriedly, "Uh, hi, yes, this is room 501. What are your vegetarian options?"

Room Service started reeling off a list of dishes, but Luke dipped his head to lick the inside of her knee, then work his lips in a trail up her inner thigh.

Esmeralda said, "You know what, never mind. Just send up one of everything."

"Excuse me?" Room Service sounded politely confused. "One of everything? Are you sure?"

Just then, Luke's mouth made it to his destination. He slid his tongue hard over her clit and sucked it between his lips.

"Yes!" she screamed into the receiver. She threw it in the general direction of the bedside table and sank her fingers into Luke's hair.

Oh, God. She was a succulent, creamy, juicy feast. He kissed her lower lips, delved his tongue inside of her and tasted the bite of his own come. He groaned and shoved his newly hardened dick against the mattress, licking her plump little clit in a frenzy.

She kept her hands fisted in his hair, showing him exactly the way she wanted him to be, saying something in Spanish that sounded absolutely filthy. Her hips pulsed against his face, her body writhed, and she came, screaming, cursing, and gasping before she fell back on the bed, motionless and dazed.

He sat up, awed at her pleasure and extremely pleased with himself, and saw the phone receiver lying on the nightstand. With a shaking hand he picked it up to put it back in the cradle, only to hear Room Service say dryly, "You want drinks with that?"

Esmeralda got her revenge on him when Room Service arrived with one of everything plus drinks, in the middle of the best goddamn blowjob in the world.

Declaring that turnabout was fair play, she had pounced on him, pushing him over onto his back and scattering hot kisses over his chest and down his stomach, nuzzling the trail of hair leading to his groin and nipping little bites at his muscles.

She curved her fingers around his cock and pulled them up and down his length in long, leisurely glides. She slid her lips in a lingering kiss over his straining tip as he watched, her eyes locked on his. She stroked his shaft and balls with her slim hands, milking a drop of precome out of him. Her little pink tongue came out and licked it up, and she moaned like she thought he was the most delicious thing ever. She lapped at his cockhead with hot, wet strokes.

Then a knock sounded on the door.

"You'd better talk to them." She dipped the tip of her tongue into his slit. "My mouth's busy." She licked just under his crown.

He cleared his throat. "Please, uh, leave it outside, please, thank—"

She grinned and sucked him into her mouth.

"—you!" he gasped.

One of her hands stroked the base of his shaft, the other cupping his rock-hard balls in her palm while her clever finger rubbed the taut skin right behind them. Sucking.

Stroking. Rubbing. Then the finger moved lower. It twirled around his opening, once, twice.

He sucked in a breath, his hands fisting in the sheets. It was the most wicked thing any woman had ever done to him. "Wait, Esmeralda, I don't know—"

"Did you say something, sir?" said the voice beyond the door.

Luke could no longer answer. Her fist pumped fast over his shaft, her mouth sucked on his crown. Tight, wet, hot, driving him to the brink of insanity—

She twirled him again, the fingertip pressing firmly until it just breached him.

He roared, head shooting back, his back arching, his cock shoving deep into her mouth. Come pulsed out of him in a searing wave and that finger twirled and twirled. She swallowed, drinking every drop down, her throat closing on him, and he almost fainted.

When he came to, Esmeralda was still lapping at his shaft, softly, slowly, sending shudders down his legs with every lick. All Luke could do was pant and whimper.

At the door there was a sound that was suspiciously like a snicker. *Bon appetit*, sir," said Room Service, the punk. There was a clank of dishes and the squeak of a cart wheeling away.

Esmeralda sat up, bright-eyed, and licked her glistening lips. "Yummy, but not very filling. Let's have some dinner, shall we?"

When Luke had recovered enough to help her bring the food in from the hall, they laid out the feast on the floor and hunkered down amid the dishes. Esmeralda picked out the vegetarian stuff and Luke demolished the rest.

Eventually he was satisfied enough to slow down and

take stock. He swallowed the last of the prime rib and looked around in bewilderment. "This is not me."

Esmeralda looked up from the remains of her pasta primavera. "It's not? Then whose dick was I just sucking?"

He did a double take, coughed, and said, "I mean, all of this." He waved his fork to encompass their room, the hotel, and basically all of Miami. "Drug gangs and gay bars and alligators. Eating dinner on the floor, naked, with a supermodel. This is not my life."

"It is now. And what an incredible life it is, right?"

"Some parts are pretty horrific," he said, thinking of the man who had assaulted Esmeralda, the big black barrels of guns pointing at them, and his own scarily violent response.

"Oh," she said quietly.

"But when it wasn't awful, it was actually kind of ..."

"Exciting? Interesting? Orgasmic?"

"Fun," he said.

She grinned. "Stick with me, kid, and I'll show you Disney Worlds' worth of fun." Then she climbed on his lap and fed him key lime pie by letting him eat dollops off her breasts.

Dessert didn't last long before they found their way to the bed. There she pushed him onto his back and mounted up like a jockey at the Kentucky Derby, and they were off again, rolling across the mattress, hips pumping, arms and legs twining, lips fused, fucking each other like their lives depended on it.

39

WHEN ESMERALDA WOKE, it was morning, and Luke was touching her. Just her fingertips, brushing his own fingers over her hand as it lay palm up near her face. She watched him through her lowered lashes, keeping her breath even, letting him think her still asleep. She wanted to see what he would do next.

The room was dim, the curtains drawn against the daylight, but a few sunbeams spilled over the bed, painting their bodies with gold.

One ray found his face as he leaned over her on an elbow, lighting his gray eyes with wonder as he watched his fingers tangle with hers. Softly, he moved his hand to her wrist, stroking the skin there, smoothing his palm along her arm to her shoulder. He traced her collarbone, then dipped down between her breasts, brushing against the inside curves.

She heard his breath catch as he saw her nipples tighten to little points, and he rubbed his broad knuckles over them, one, then the other. She had to struggle not to arch her breasts into his hands.

He sat up and she almost moaned against the loss of his touch. But then his big hands were back, moving over her the way they moved over his pianos, deft and sure, playing her body with the same expert skill.

He was a marvel, a wonder. So strong, but with a sensibility, a fineness of touch that would never allow him to hurt her. His fingers slipped down her stomach, curved around her waist, shaped her hips, his calluses rasping pleasure over her skin. He cupped her thighs, his hands trembling slightly, and paused, his thumbs caressing the creases of her legs. His face was in profile to her now, and she could see his lips part as he looked at her sex. She was drenched with wanting him, quivering for his fingers to slip into her folds. But instead of touching her there he leaned down to draw his hands down, caressing the backs of her knees, circling her calves and ankles, until he cupped her feet in his palms.

Every inch of Esmeralda's skin was singing with pleasure, and she wanted to ripple and move with its music. Luke was cherishing her, as if she were the most precious thing he had ever held in his hands.

What she'd seen when he played his music, what she was feeling in his touch now, was true heart's passion. And that bright and steady fire burning in him was what she had always wanted.

She slipped her feet out of his hands and sat up, draping herself over his back before he could turn. "Shh," she breathed to him, stilling him with a hand at the nape of his neck. He obeyed, going quiet except for the deep rise and fall of his chest.

The soft strands of bronze hair tickled her palm, and she let her own hair drape in a shimmering black curtain over his shoulder as she leaned to breathe into his ear, "You play me like your pianos, Luke. Now it's my turn. Let me show you how well you taught me." She brushed her lips over the curve of his ear, making his breath stutter. Then she kissed the wedge of muscle where his neck sloped into his shoulder. Opened her mouth and took a soft bite. A small sound growled in his throat.

She slipped her hands over his shoulders, spreading her fingers over their colossal bulk. His skin was fair and smooth, as fine as a girl's, but the steely cables of muscle underneath were all man.

She eased her hands along the deep indentation his spine made between the muscles of his back, all the way down to the hard globes of his buttocks, watching as his skin rippled beneath her touch. He was so sensitive, her beautiful beast. She swept up his flanks to the brush against the hair under his arms, then eased forward, crushing her breasts softly against his back. She sifted her fingers through the curls covering the slabs of his pectorals, gently rasping the velvety circles of his nipples with her nails. She laid her ear against his back as she caressed his body, listening to the roar of his breath and the thunder of his heartbeat. She smoothed her palms down his ridged stomach and rubbed the iron strength of his thighs.

His hands were raised, hovering in the air, his control of them gone. A helpless sound escaped his lips, cut off as she slid her hands between his legs. His thighs opened and she slipped her fingers under his sack, cradling the ripe, heavy weight. She squeezed his balls lightly, rubbed her thumb along the seam between them. She could feel them draw tight as his pelvis started to clench and rock. He growled now, his hands moving to touch hers and then flying away again.

She circled the root of his cock with both hands and heard his growl turn into a groan. She traced each pulsing vein up the thick column of hot flesh until she reached the flare of his crown, swollen and slick with his excitement. She dipped one fingertip into his weeping slit, and he yelled, grabbing her hands. He folded one hand around his shaft. The other, he clamped over his heart. He pumped his hips, driving his cock through their joined hands as his heart pounded against her palm.

"Esmeralda," he said, like her name was a prayer.

Esmeralda was panting, melting. She was drunk with the power in her hands, under her cheek, against her breasts. She owned him. This huge, powerful, gorgeous beast was her prisoner, her slave, her possession. Now, what was she going do with him?

Her pussy clenched in a slippery knot of want. And then it came to her out of the kaleidoscope of possibilities. What she most wanted to do with her captive was blow his mind to pieces. Rock his world to dust. Show him that she was the woman of all his dreams, and always would be.

"What do you want, Luke?" Her voice was shaking. "Tell me. I'll do anything you ask. Anything you can imagine. What do you want?"

"I want— you!" He turned in her arms and grabbed her to him. His lips found hers in a frantic kiss, and he was bearing her down to the mattress and shoving her legs apart with his knees. Then he was inside her again, his hips rocking slow and hard, his back arching and rippling under her hands.

He kissed her thoroughly, mercilessly, until they were groaning into each other's mouths.

He leaned up on one arm, looking down into her eyes. "All I want is you." He bent his head and bit her softly on the throat. All the while his cock drove relentlessly into her. It was a dominating, possessive move and she fucking loved it. She arched her neck into his lips, opened her legs wide for him, giving him everything he wanted.

It was timeless, eternal. The shafts of sunlight moved over them like the fingertips of a god. The light was around them, inside them, roaring higher, burning hotter, until it consumed them.

40

LUKE CRACKED an eye at the clock. Way past noon.

He drew in a breath of sweet, clean woman. While he was passed out cold she had gotten up and taken a shower.

Not a bad idea. He himself probably smelled like a locker room full of horny highschoolers.

He eased out of bed and looked down at her. Her lashes fluttered on her smooth cheeks and she made a little breathy sound. One slim golden hand fell onto the sheets where he had just been. She was reaching for him in her sleep. Manfully resisting the urge to dive back in bed with her, he scuffed to the bathroom. He caught sight of himself in the mirror and paused to take stock.

Bites on his neck, fingernail scratches on his ass, hair standing on end, dazed look in his eyes, enormous goofy grin on his face. *Yep. There stands a man who has just had the fucking of a lifetime.*

He finally wandered off to the shower, humming Schubert's Piano Trio in E-flat major, the happiest of tunes. Because happy, yes, he was. Had never been so fantastic in all his life.

And he intended to stay this way. The practical details of the plan might be a bit hazy for now, but so what. He was living in the moment. And now Esmeralda was going to enjoy the full benefits of his new attitude.

He looked down at his already half-hard dick (really, this was getting ridiculous) and grinned. When he was clean he wrapped the last towel around his waist and stepped through the glass door into the room.

He looked up and saw that she was awake, sitting on the side of the bed, her new burner phone pressed to her ear.

She smiled at him, and he felt something move in his chest. His heart broke open and joy leapt out, singing its head off. He took a step toward her, eager to share his good mood and his latest erection with her.

But she said, "I'm listening to my voicemail. I switched the phone off last night to keep Al from bothering us. Turns out that was a smart move. He left twelve messages. Twelve. I think I've finally driven him off the deep end. But whatever, you've got to listen to this." She pressed a few buttons and held it out.

"Esmeralda," Truitt's voice buzzed on the phone's cheapo speaker, "you need to call me right away. There have been important developments in our case. We believe Zapata has left Miami and is hiding somewhere on the Gulf coast. Our sources say he's trying to find a boat to smuggle him out of the country. The FBI is closing in on him. They expect to have him in custody soon.

"You're no longer in immediate danger, but you and Mr. Hansen will still need the protection of the US Marshals until we get the all-clear signal from the FBI. If you hadn't been so hysterical and irresponsible last night—"

Esmeralda hit a button and Truitt's hectoring became a tinny drone.

"This is good news," Esmeralda said. "It looks like we'll still have to put up with protective custody, but hopefully it won't be for very long."

"Yeah, great." Luke was relieved. He really was. Zapata wouldn't be leaping out of the darkness like some boogeyman to snatch Esmeralda away from him. He hadn't even realized how much that terror had been weighing on his mind until it was gone. But ...

Now that his fear for her had lifted, a strange sort of resentment crept into the space it had left. Soon, she wouldn't need him to protect her. And then what?

Esmeralda's attention was caught by a new message on the phone, which Luke couldn't quite hear. "Wait a second," she said, a new spark of excitement in her voice.

She hit a few buttons and a bouncy Indian-accented voice filled the room. "This is Sanjay Ranganathan of the World Elephant Foundation calling to let you know that your grant has been approved ..." The voice chattered on, talking about funding and lodging and logistics, none of which Luke understood or gave a damn about.

But as he listened, he saw Esmeralda's expression lighting up. When the message ended, she raised glowing eyes to his. "Did you hear that? It's finally happened! I'm going to India!" She leapt up from the bed with a huge smile, her whole beautiful body vibrating, even her hair crackling with excitement.

Luke couldn't think. Because sudden, astonishing pain had blown a hole straight through him.

He had entirely forgotten about India. That whatever place he occupied in Esmeralda's heart, it ranked far below her love for her animals. That for her, last night was only a temporary detour on her way to somewhere else.

"Congratulations," he said.

She had taken a step toward him, like she was about to jump into his arms. But at the dry creak of his voice, she abruptly stilled. She stood looking at him, quicksilver expressions flashing over her face too fast for him to catch. Finally, she said, "Thanks." She grabbed up the robe she had discarded next to the bed the night before, and put it on.

Luke tore his eyes off her and looked at the bed where he had just spent the most incredible hours of his life. The sheets were tumbled in a white froth, a little world of clouds and dreams. One step out of that world and he'd smacked face-first into reality.

She said, "I suppose I'd better call Truitt and tell him where we are."

The pain drilled in deeper. But he nodded.

"Before he turns us in to the Marshals, I want to buy us some new clothes." She walked past him into the bathroom. She shut the door, and he turned to see her shape moving behind the glass, getting dressed again. She called out, "I saw a little gift shop next door to the hotel when we came in. I'm sure I can find something in there for us to wear." She emerged wearing the clothes she'd had on yesterday, a little limp, but not too bad, considering.

He tried to pull himself together. He cleared his throat. "You're right. Give me a minute to get dressed and we'll go."

"That ... might be a problem."

He looked at her. "What did you do?"

"I put your clothes in the laundry bag and set them outside to be washed. They probably won't be back until tomorrow."

His eyes narrowed.

"They stank!"

"Okay, fine. But I need something to wear downstairs besides a towel."

"No, you don't. This is South Beach. You might as well be wearing a tux." She sidled up to him and tugged playfully at the hem of his towel.

He retained a firm grip on the terrycloth. "I refuse to leave this room like this. And that means you can't go either. You're not going anywhere without me while Zapata is still on the loose. I'm going to call down to the front desk and have them go shopping for us."

"Luke, you're being ridiculous. You heard what Truitt said. Zapata and his gang are on the run. There's no more danger. Besides, I want to stretch my legs."

She wasn't hearing him. He said firmly, "You're not leaving this room. I won't allow it."

Esmeralda went still. Absolutely still. *Oh, shit* still. Then she said, "You won't let me leave?"

Luke realized he had stomped on a landmine. He raised his hands in a placating gesture. "Now wait—"

"You don't get to *allow* me anything, Luke. I'm not a *thing* you can put wherever you decide I should be. I go where I want, when I want, and I do what I want when I get there."

"I—"

"And right now, where I want to be is away from you." She pushed past him toward the door.

The hole in his chest turned into a pit. The swirling panic that he couldn't protect her, that he was losing her, drove him into a state of temporary insanity. That was the only excuse he could come up with for what he did next.

"Would you just listen for a minute?" He grabbed her arms, trying to hold her still, keep her safe.

Her slim body turned to steel. She looked down at his

hands, and the pure fury in her eyes was almost enough to blister the skin on his fingers. "Let me go."

He released her, lurching back.

She strode toward the room door and seized the handle.

"Esmeralda, I didn't mean—"

She shot a fiery glance over her shoulder. "Yes, you did. Get this through your head, Luke. I don't belong to you." She yanked open the door, swung through and shut it behind her.

Luke stood in the middle of the room, staring at the door and listening to the angry rhythm of her footsteps disappearing down the hall.

He sank down on the edge of the bed and leaned his forearms on his knees. Stared down at the floor between his feet. Wondered vaguely why he couldn't see his heart's blood dripping onto the carpet.

He'd lost her.

Lost her? You never had her. She just told you so. And how could he blame her? She was miles out of his reach in every conceivable way.

"Stupid," he said to himself. Stupid for imagining that their night together, so shattering for him, had been anything to her but a temporary fling. For letting himself care so much that the loss of her would rip him in half.

It occurred to him that in the last six months he had lost every single thing he had ever had. Wife, shop, house, truck, every stitch of clothing. And those losses had done a number on his pride, no doubt about it. What else was this whole crazy quest to get the Guild seal back about if not some kind of attempt to reclaim his pride? But he realized now that none of it, not even the end of his marriage, had really touched him in any way that mattered.

Losing Esmeralda—that mattered. More than anything had ever mattered.

His throat closed. His breath sawed in his lungs. He should never have come here. He should have forgotten about the stupid seal and gone about his business, grinding his way through his life, snatching glimpses of happiness in his music here and there. If he'd just tried to be practical, he would never have met her.

But he had come, and he had met her. And her presence had woken up a sense of joy and wonder in him that he'd totally forgotten, if he'd ever felt it at all. And now she was going to take it away forever.

He sank his head into his hands and sat that way for a long time.

Eventually he realized that he had been blindly staring at his tie, a maroon-and-gray striped one crumpled on the floor near the bed. Esmeralda must have dropped it when she'd bundled up his other clothes. He reached out an arm and picked it up, letting it dangle from his fingers. "Guess it's just you and me, pal."

41

ESMERALDA STOMPED into the gift shop, still flushed and scowling. The sales clerk at the counter looked up from her copy of *Ocean Drive*, let out a grunt, and stuck her face back into her magazine.

Esmeralda barely noticed, she was so furious. She was *carajo* sick of men treating her like she was a brainless *thing* they could do whatever they wanted with. A possession they kept to boost their macho status. Like a car. With boobs.

She'd thought Luke was different. But not only had he forbidden her to leave the room, he'd tried to physically control her. She'd hauled out her knuckleduster for the last guy who'd pulled that shit.

She heard the tromping of feet and a garble of voices in what sounded like Dutch as a pack of tourists filed into the shop behind her. She darted out of sight behind a shelf full of souvenir kitsch, still struggling to get control of her temper.

There was something else underneath her anger, something that confused and disturbed her. And, being a woman who aimed for self-awareness, she tried to figure out what it was. Luke had pulled a stupid move, yes, but there was more to their fight than that.

Okay, yes, possibly she had overreacted. Now that she was calmer she could see how Luke's douchey order to sit and stay might not have been a bid to control her but a misguided attempt to keep her safe. He had never treated her like a car with boobs before now, so maybe he deserved the benefit of the doubt.

But she hadn't given it to him. Instead she had stormed off into what he thought was danger just to spite him.

Mierda. If she saw a chick in a horror flick act like that, she would be the first one to throw popcorn at the screen and cheer when the psycho killer came a-chainsawing.

The thing was, she had little experience with men who had her best interests at heart. Letting her guard down for him instead of flaming up in defense was tough. But shouldn't she have tried?

She knew Luke wasn't an asshole. She wouldn't have had the hottest sex in the universe with him if he was. She also knew she could train him to quit the Tarzan routine. So it wasn't really the power play he'd pulled that had sent her running out of the room.

She absently fingered a shot glass in the shape of a thong-clad butt as she considered what else was bothering her.

He had never asked her to marry him. Which was weird. Guys were always asking her to marry them, or at least trying to set her up in a condo. She had rarely spent more than a few hours with any man before getting a proposal of one sort or another. But she'd been with Luke for days without even a hint that he wanted to put a claim on her.

If there was one thing the modeling life had taught her, it was that her looks were a commodity that men valued and would try to acquire, much like the latest Audi. Sooner or later they would want to trade her in for a newer model, of course, so she never bothered to play that game. She always dumped them first.

But Luke never even gave her the chance to dump him, because he never tried to get her in the first place. She had been the instigator of all their sexytimes, she realized to her mortification. And not once had he talked about a future with her. When he'd heard the call from India, he hadn't objected to her leaving. All he'd said was, "Congratulations."

Could it be ... was it possible that ... he just didn't want her?

Sure, he wanted her body, if all those orgasms they'd just had were any clue. But maybe he didn't want the rest of her, the person with flaws and ambitions and a life beyond the bikini.

She pressed her hand against her ribs as something twisted in her side and squeezed up into her throat. That, then, was the heart of the problem.

All of a sudden, the memory of the morning seized her. Him inside her, looking into her eyes, wrapped in each other, rocking together, until she didn't know where she ended and he began, the two of them consumed in the light of the sun. For a moment she'd thought ...

Obviously, it hadn't meant anything, she thought with a hitch in her breath. But wasn't that for the best? In a few weeks she'd be on the other side of the world. She wanted to avoid messy entanglements before she left, didn't she? And she wouldn't even consider the possibility of staying here for his sake, betraying her elephants, abandoning her life's work, would she?

Would she?

Her eyes blurred. No, it was impossible. All of it, impossible.

Didn't matter anyway. He didn't want to be with her. And why would he? She'd been nothing but trouble for the guy from the second they met. And yet he'd supported her and protected her and understood her. He'd done his best for her. But he didn't want to deal with her *mierda* forever. He wanted to go back to his normal life. He'd said so over and over.

It wasn't his problem that she'd started to hope for more with him. It was her own fault that she was lurking in a hole-in-the-wall tourist trap, about to start sobbing into a shelf full of obscene shot glasses.

She angrily brushed tears off her cheeks and looked around in dismay. While her emotions had been having their free-for-all, the Dutch tour group that had come in behind her had descended on the clothing racks like an infestation of grasshoppers and stripped them bare. She got herself together enough to pick over the remains, but now the choices were slender indeed.

She made her purchases and went to the dressing room to change into her new clothes—a blue fitted t-shirt and tan Bermuda shorts. Then she trudged back up to the hotel room, a little wiser, a lot more depressed, and completely unsure what to do next.

She found Luke sitting on the bed, stone-faced and dignified in his towel. "No trouble?" he said.

She shook her head and saw his shoulders slump a little in relief.

She opened her mouth to say ... what? *I'm sorry? I still want to screw you blind? I lo—*

She nearly choked on a rush of pure terror at what she'd almost thought. "Here," she finally said, holding out the bag of clothing for him. "These should fit you."

He got up and took the bag from her, making sure their fingers didn't touch, she noticed. "Thank you," he said very politely, and he wedged himself into the tiny bathroom to change.

Dios, this was awful. A few hours ago she'd had her tongue in every one of the man's crevices, and now he couldn't even get dressed in front of her.

As she was pondering how to fix this, she heard him say, "Jeez! You've got to be kidding." The glass door flew open and he stomped into the room, wearing his new clothes, a pair of neon-yellow board shorts and a muscle shirt printed with kissy lips.

Personally, she thought he looked pretty smokin', what with all the rippling muscles in his arms and legs. But Luke was apparently feeling exposed.

"I know you're pissed at me," he said stiffly, "But if it's revenge you're after, I'd rather you beat me up. Or doxxed me. This is just inhuman."

She dragged her attention off his biceps. "It's the best I could do," she said. She told him about the Dutch horde that had swept through the gift shop like the Visigoths sacking Rome and made off with all the extra-extra-larges.

Luke's mouth twitched, but then he straightened it out. "And what's your excuse for not getting me any underwear?"

"You're supposed to go commando in board shorts. In fact, to be really fashion forward, you're supposed to pull them low enough to show crack."

He instantly hiked the waistband toward his armpits. "There will be no crack." But his mouth twisted in a reluctant grin.

And that was all it took. The wild emotion that had taken them over last night blazed up between them again. They looked into each other's eyes with naked yearning.

Panic seized her. She had the sudden feeling that might happen in the next few seconds, what she did, what she said, could change the whole course of her life.

He took half a step toward her. "Esmeralda—"

At the same time, she said, "Luke, I—"

Her phone rang.

"*Cojeme!*" She yanked it out of her pocket and looked at the screen, but didn't recognize the caller. "It has to be either my family or Truitt. They're the only ones who have this number," she said. And only they had such lousy timing.

"You'd better answer," Luke said. Every trace of emotion had flickered out of his eyes.

A little shakily, she hit the button. "Hello?"

"Ez, it's me."

"Roddy!" She wheeled around and put her hand on the wall. "Where are you? Are you all right?"

"I'm fine. I'm at the office."

"*Gracias a Dios!*" she said, dizzy with relief. "I've been so worried! Have you called Anita? She's been scared to death—"

"Ez, I need to talk to you," Roddy said, sounding ragged.

"You need to turn yourself in as soon as possible, is what you need to do. Running and hiding only made you look guilty. What were you thinking?"

"I can explain everything. But I have to see you in person. And your friend Kowalski too."

"What are you talking about?"

"I have some, uh, evidence I need to show you."

"Evidence? What—?"

"I can't talk about it over the phone, okay? Just come meet me at the office right away. I'll tell you everything then. But Ez, you can't call the cops. Do you hear me? Whatever you do, *do not* call the cops."

He sounded so panicky that she found herself saying, "All right, Roddy, I'll come. We'll talk things over. We'll figure it out."

"The office, right now. No cops. I'm counting on you, Ez. We all are, *Tio*, me, the company. Don't screw this up." The line went dead.

"*Mierda*, Roddy, a little more drama, please." She returned the phone to her pocket and said to Luke, "I have to go talk my idiot cousin into turning himself in. He's holed up in the office building."

Luke's mouth had flattened out. "And Agent Truitt?"

"I'll call him from the office when I've calmed Roddy down."

"We'll call him, you mean. I'm coming with you. Unless you don't want me to." She saw a flash of confusion and pain before he hid it behind his Stoic The Viking face.

"No, I want you to come," she blurted. If he wasn't there, watching her back, talking over ideas, making her laugh, she didn't know what she'd do. He'd become an absolute necessity for her.

Twenty-four years of self-reliance, and after less than a week, he'd somehow turned into a support pillar of her life.

She said, "I want ..."

Well, what do you want? You don't even know, do you?

"... some company," she finished lamely.

He nodded, his big shoulders easing a little. He was still worried about her, she realized.

"This will just be a quick detour. We go in, we get Roddy, we call Al. What could be easier?"

"You really have to quit saying stuff like that. Really."

42

THE TAXI PULLED up to the Castillo office and idled. As Esmeralda paid the driver, Luke raked a careful gaze over the place. The fading daylight washed gold over the thin lines of windows up the front. Beyond the glass doors, the interior was saturated with shadows. It was Sunday evening, so the rest of the businesses up and down the street were closed and dark. The sidewalks were empty.

He suddenly wondered why the cops weren't watching the building. Wouldn't staking out a fugitive's office be an obvious step for them to take? But then, with the manhunt moving out of Miami to Florida's west coast, maybe they didn't want to waste resources on round-the-clock surveillance here.

Still, foreboding ghosted across his skin. He said to Esmeralda, "Tell me one more time why we're not calling the police and letting them deal with Roddy."

"Because I promised him I wouldn't. Let's go talk him off the ledge, and then we'll call Al. Scout's honor." She raised her right hand with three fingers up.

Luke reached out and bent down one finger. "That's better. I was a Boy Scout, you know."

She grinned. "Of course you were. Because you're just that c—"

"Don't even think it."

They got out of the cab and it drove away. Luke turned toward the looming building. Esmeralda stood quietly next to him.

"I guess we should go in," she said. She started climbing the steps to the glass doors, but Luke got there first. He looked carefully into the lobby, but all was quiet and dark. He pulled the handle. The door was unlocked.

He stepped through the opening and looked around. The overhead lights were off. Only the slanted evening light through the windows illuminated the space, washing over the empty reception desk and throwing the shadows of the many potted plants across the tile floor.

He looked up at the mezzanine level curving along the shallow arc of the back wall. One of the doorways leading back from the balcony was lit up. The rest were in darkness. The decorative objects and display cases were muffled in shadow. The dark shape of the Chinese piano stood upright on its side near the glass half-wall, exactly as he had left it less than a week ago.

"Hello?" he called out. His voice echoed through the shadows and died away. He listened hard, and heard a faint rustling coming from the mezzanine. "Hello! Roddy, are you there?"

A muffled voice floated down. "Up here."

Esmeralda shoved impatiently at his shoulder, so he reluctantly moved aside and held the door for her.

She marched inside. He let go of the door. It shut with a quiet hiss.

She nodded up at the lighted door. "That's one of the conference rooms. Let's go on up."

He said, "I'll go first." He didn't let her argue, but strode toward the stairs that ran up the right side of the atrium to the gallery above.

His eyes constantly moving, he climbed up to the second story, Esmeralda's light footsteps echoing behind him. At the head of the stairs, he paused. The lighted doorway up ahead beckoned them.

He looked over his shoulder at Esmeralda and said, "Stay here for a second. I'll go see if he's in there."

"Why—?"

"Esmeralda. Please."

She must have seen something in his face, because she said, "All right."

He walked quietly along the curve of the terrace toward the light. He passed a door cracked open to show darkness inside, and display shelves full of expensive junk. The lit-up room was just ahead. Obeying some deep-down instinct, he kept his body behind the wall and darted a look around the doorframe.

He saw a typical conference room with a long table surrounded by sleekly uncomfortable chairs and a projector and screen at one end. It was empty.

His neck bristled in warning. He turned back to hustle Esmeralda the hell out.

She had followed him halfway down the hall, her lips parted to ask him a question. She stepped in front of the first doorway.

An arm shot out of the dark and grabbed her.

He lunged for her on pure reflex but drew up short as a meaty fist shoved a gun at her head.

She didn't even have time to gasp before men piled out

of the door, surrounding her, pointing guns in every direction.

There were three of them, and they all looked awfully familiar. The one who had hold of Esmeralda was Zapata's bodyguard from the party. The other two were his old friends Fatty and Skinny from the motel parking lot.

The bodyguard tilted his bullet-shaped head toward the doorway and said something in Spanish.

Zapata strolled out of the darkness within. He too had a gun, and a smile on his blimp of a face. "*señorita* Castillo. You will accept my invitation now, I think."

"You make a persuasive case." Esmeralda had gone ashen, but she was gamely ignoring the gun barrel against her temple. "Where's Roddy?"

"Do not fear. You will see him soon." Zapata turned toward Luke.

The erstwhile tycoon wasn't looking so good. His suit was limp and wrinkled. His face was grayish, deep lines carving into the hardened fat of his jowls. His carefully engineered combover had devolved into a few lank strands swirling over his gleaming scalp. Finding himself in the crosshairs of US law enforcement and psychopathic drug cartels had evidently been stressful.

But at the moment Zapata was wearing a horrifically satisfied grin. "I am happy to have the company of *la Esmeralda* for a little while. But I am more happy to have yours, Mister Luke Hansen."

"Those two idiots finally found out my name, then?" Luke said.

Zapata flicked a glare at Fatty and Skinny, who cringed. "*Sí*. Castillo's people told us. They said also that you were the man who moved that piano." He wagged his gun at the parlor grand standing quietly by the glass wall. "There was a million dollars' worth of my *coca* in that piano. It is not there now. And who knows where it is but you? You, the man who attacked me. The man who betrayed me to *la policía*." His voice was rising, his face turning uglier.

Luke quickly said, "If you want to know where your drugs are, I'll be delighted to tell you. But the girl doesn't know anything. She's not a part of this. Let her go, and we'll talk, you and me."

Esmeralda jolted in her captor's grip. "No!"

Zapata ignored her. His capped teeth gleamed in a smile. "You will tell me it all. But first, we will make you watch while we fuck *la puta*." His men all laughed. "Then we will cut you until you beg to die. Then, I will let you tell me what you know. And then I will kill you."

"Yeah, no. I gotta say I'm not in favor of this plan of yours."

Zapata gave him a strange look.

Esmeralda said, "You don't have time for your little rape and torture fest. We called the police before we came. They were going to meet us here to take Roddy into custody. They'll be here any minute."

Fatty and Skinny started to look a wee bit freaked, but the bodyguard's expression stayed empty.

Zapata narrowed his eyes at her. "I think you are lying."

"I'm not," she lied. "Shouldn't you run while you still can? Avoid the humiliation of being caught by the cops? Or maybe you're hoping to get shot in the head like your hero Pablo Escobar?"

He grabbed Esmeralda's hair close to her scalp and yanked, wrenching her head back.

She let out a cry, quickly stifled.

"Pablo Escobar never let himself be taken by *los tombos*. And I will not. We are going, and you are coming with us."

To the other two goons, he said, "Bring the piano man." He and the bodyguard started dragging Esmeralda toward the stairs.

The two remaining thugs raised their guns and came for him.

Luke wasn't worried, because it had happened again.

From the instant he saw the gun pointed at Esmeralda's head, the world around had gone cold and still. He saw the positions of every object around him. He saw the inevitable paths of movement like lines on a blueprint. And he saw exactly what he had to do.

Eliminate the men. Get to Esmeralda. Simple.

The two gangsters tasked with taking him down weren't so aware. Fatty had moved ahead of Skinny, lining up instead of separating and coming at him from two angles. Which made Luke's next move easy.

He grabbed a stone statuette off a display case next to him on the wall and whipped it at Fatty with all his strength.

Luke's aim was never good, but at that range a man's torso was hard to miss. The statue cannoned into the guy's sternum, sending him wheeling back into Skinny.

In the second it took for the dirtbags to disentangle themselves, Luke spun and threw himself at the grand piano standing on its edge near the glass wall. Shots tore through the air around him.

Fire slashed along the left side of his body. He'd been hit. He ignored it.

He ducked behind the five-and-a-half-foot barrier of the piano, crouching and plastering himself against the back of the instrument.

Bullets slammed through the case and into the iron plate

at his back. The piano screamed in a musical outrage of splintered wood and broken strings. More shots blasted through the chest-high wall next to him, blowing holes in the thick glass panel and sending long cracks throughout the surface.

"*¡No lo mates, idiotas! ¡Lo quiero vivo!* Alive! Alive!" Zapata yelled from down below.

The gunfire ceased. The silence roared.

Zapata didn't want them to risk killing him, not before he'd told him where his drugs were. That gave him an advantage.

In his mind, the space around him spread out in a perfectly realized diagram. He calculated the paths Fatty and Skinny would have to take and where they would have to move. All he needed to know was when. It was a matter of timing.

He heard the soft scuff of footsteps on thick carpet, creeping closer.

Closer. Closer. Now.

He lunged out from behind the left corner of the piano and shot out his left arm, grabbing the skull he knew would be there. He twisted, powering the head into the piano case with a solid *chunk* and the crackle of a breaking nose. The instrument rocked. The guy's hands flailed wide, the gun flying off.

As Fatty's head bounced off the piano, he staggered backward into Skinny.

The canny little bastard whipped aside, but he couldn't get his gun up and aimed before Luke brought his fist around for a monster right hook.

Luke saw he had miscalculated the angle, and instantly corrected. Instead of a face, his fist smashed into the arm of the thug's gun hand.

A yelp of pain. Another gun spinning across the floor. Skinny wheeled back, clutching his arm to his body.

The first guy was staggering and moaning, his face sheeted with blood. Luke slammed his elbow backward into the side of his head.

The guy flew into the piano and collapsed against it like a pile of lumber. The instrument rocked dangerously again.

Skinny darted in and leapt onto his back like a spider monkey. A ropey arm snaked around his neck and cinched tight.

He grabbed the arm and yanked, but Skinny was hanging from his neck, using his entire bodyweight to squeeze his windpipe shut. Blood rushed in his ears. He had only seconds of consciousness left. If he tried to fall backward to crush the guy, he risked breaking his neck. Only one chance.

He plunged to the floor, landing hard on his ass. At the same time he jackknifed his body forward. The abrupt change in balance hurled Skinny over Luke's shoulder. He crashed into the piano headfirst and instantly went limp. The piano, battered by another head, rocked back even further than before.

Luke shoved the guy off him and sat up with a harsh gasp.

"¡Idiotas! What is taking so long?" a voice yelled from below.

He glanced past the instrument, down through the shattered glass wall. Zapata stood directly beneath him, head tipped up at the balcony, a sneer on his pouty lips.

The piano in front of him continued rocking up, up, up, until it teetered on the very slimmest edge, all eight hundred pounds of it perfectly balanced on an axis for one infinitesimal moment in time. It could fall one way. It could fall the other.

In that crystal cut moment, he saw everything. Exactly what would happen with just one push.

He reached out a finger to the smooth black lacquer. He pushed.

The piano tipped over, crashed through the bullet-riddled glass wall, and sailed into space.

43

WHEN THE BODYGUARD started dragging Esmeralda down the stairs she went limp, trying to slow him down. Didn't work. He picked her up and slung her over his shoulder like a sack, knocking the wind out of her lungs.

The world tilted into a crazy kaleidoscope as he carted her down the stairs. A fusillade of shots and yelling broke out. She struggled to drag in enough breath to scream.

The bodyguard got to the bottom of the stairs and loped across the atrium toward the hallway behind the reception desk, Esmeralda bumping along on his back. She caught glimpses of Zapata following behind, gun in hand.

"*Espere*," Zapata said sharply.

Her captor stopped and dumped her on her feet. He grabbed her arm in a bruising grip, all that stopped her from falling.

They were standing just underneath the mezzanine. Strange clangs and cursing and thumps echoed down from above. Zapata backtracked, walking a few steps out from under the upper level. Frowning, he craned his neck up to see the minions trying to hurt Luke. "¡*Idiotas!* What is taking so long?" he yelled at them.

A crack splintered the air. Flashing shards of glass hailed down.

Esmeralda had one split second to see Zapata's eyes widen in surprise. And then a piano landed on top of him.

Thunder blasted through the atrium as eight hundred pounds of wood and iron detonated a few feet away from her. Esmeralda and the bodyguard threw their arms over their heads.

Echoes rang on and on, dying away into dumbfounded silence. They straightened up, staring in sheer disbelief at the shards of wood and tangled metal piled where Zapata had been standing. A piano leg fell off the balcony, bounced off the remains of the case, and rolled to gently bump up against Esmeralda's toes.

"*¿Jefe?*" the bodyguard peeped.

"Esmeralda!"

She and the bodyguard spun and looked up at the balcony.

Luke's face appeared over the edge, white with fear.

The thug raised his gun to point it straight at Luke.

Esmeralda scooped up the piano leg that had landed at her feet and swung it at the bodyguard's head. It landed on the side of his skull with a solid *thwock*.

The blow staggered the thug. But he didn't go down.

He lurched around toward her. His face was rabid, though his eyes were crossed and his gun was wavering around like he was aiming at multiple Esmeraldas. He fired, his shot smashing into the glass reception desk behind her.

Fuck this mierda, Esmeralda thought. She twisted into a backswing and chunked the leg into the man's head again.

That did the trick. The bodyguard's eyes rolled up and he keeled over in an unconscious heap next to the fallen piano.

"Esmeralda!" The edge of her vision caught Luke's big shape running along the balcony and hurtling down the stairs.

"I'm all right!" She concentrated on unclenching her fingers from around the piano leg. It dropped to the floor and rolled off.

And then Luke was there. "Are you hurt? Did they hurt you?" His hands were all over her, running down her arms, up her back, over her hair.

"I'm fine. I'm okay. Luke, it's ..." She caught sight of the side of his muscle shirt, soaked with sticky red. "*¡Por Dios!*" she shrieked. "You've been *shot!*"

Their hands tangled up in each other as she tried to pull up his shirt and he patted her down for injuries. Finally she slapped his hands away and yanked the fabric up over his head.

While he flailed to get the shirt off, she took the chance to get a good look at his wound. It was low on his left side, a long, angry welt.

A bullet had grazed him, breaking the skin, but nothing more. The bleeding was already slowing, in fact.

She wilted against him in relief, hanging on to his shoulders. He threw his shirt on the floor and wrapped his arms around her in a bone-crushing hug.

After a long while, she gulped in a breath, rubbed her tears off against his bare pecs and pushed back. He let her move away a few inches.

She lifted her hands from his shoulders to cradle his massive jaw and looked into his eyes. "Luke."

"Esmeralda."

"You threw a piano on Zapata."

"It was an accident."

"Right. Okay. But, Luke, there's ... fluid ... seeping out from under it."

They both looked down to where a red puddle was slowly spreading toward their feet from beneath the pile of broken wood and iron. Luke's Adam's apple bobbed. "So there is."

"And I think I'm going to be sick."

"Yeah. Me too. How about we go outside and throw up while we wait for the cops?"

"Great idea."

They started toward the door, the glass shards from the shattered balustrade crunching under their feet. Luke frowned down at Esmeralda's open-toed sandals. "Be careful of the glass—" He stopped short and she saw his eyes widen in a hunter's stare.

Esmeralda followed his gaze along the floor.

Near one of the clumps of potted plants scattered around the lobby was a satchel. Next to it, a man's shoe was just peeking out from behind a cluster of potted palms.

Luke eased forward, a big predator quietly stalking his prey. He shot an arm behind the thick greenery. There was a shriek, and he hauled a smallish, lumpy figure in a wrinkled suit out from behind the plants by his neck.

Luke dragged the man upright with one fist twisted in his collar, and looked down into his face.

The lumpy guy gaped up at Luke. He said, "Luke! Bro!"

Luke said, "Kowalski!"

"Kowalski?" Esmeralda said. "That's Kowalski?"

The guy smiled shakily at her over the top of Luke's fist, exhibiting an array of white and shiny dental work. "That's me. You must be Esmeralda." He stuck out a soft little hand.

She ignored it. "What are you doing here?"

"I saw you come in, so I followed you. I thought I'd get my good buddy Luke here to introduce us."

Luke said, "I'm not your buddy," at the same time Esmeralda said, "You were watching the building?"

"Yeah, but not for long. I didn't see Zapata and his crew go in," he said to her quickly. "I didn't know all hell was going to break loose in here. I just wanted to find someone to finally make a deal!"

"For what? The ivory, the pianos, or the cocaine?"

"Any of them! I gotta get something. I made some promises. Owe some people some money." He slid a quick glance at Luke, from whose fist he was still dangling. "Yesterday, when I saw the cops crawling all over the warehouse, I thought I was fucked, pardon my French. But then I saw you with my buddy Luke, and I thought, jackpot, baby."

He tilted his head toward her confidentially and said in a plummy voice, "I'm the treasurer of the Minneapolis Piano Tuner's Guild, so I'm kind of like Luke's boss—"

Luke twisted both huge hands into the front of Kowalski's jacket, picked him completely up off the floor, and shook him until his head bobbed around like a dashboard ornament.

By the time he was done, Kowalski's eyes and mouth were as round as satellite dishes. "What the hell, dude?" he gasped.

Luke's bare, muscular chest, streaked with sweat and blood, heaved. "Please excuse me, Brett. I've had a stressful day. But I need to ask you something, and you're going to give me the right answer or the next piano I throw is going to land on you. Got it?"

Kowalski nodded energetically.

"Good. Now, where's the seal, Brett?"

"Seal?"

"The official Guild seal!" Luke roared, bobbling him. "The big stamp that you put on your stupid prospectus! The thing I came here for! The thing that started this whole insane mess!"

"It's ... in ... the ... bag!" Kowalski squeaked as he jolted around in Luke's grip. He flailed an arm toward the satchel on the floor.

Luke slammed Kowalski's feet to the floor, lunged for the bag, and tore it open. He delved in a hand and pulled out a polished wooden handle topped with a gleaming brass head. He raised it up to the light like it was the Holy fucking Grail.

"That's it?" Esmeralda said.

"That is it." Profound satisfaction rang through Luke's every word.

A new voice said, "I hope it was worth it, dipshit."

44

LUKE WHIPPED AROUND to see a figure stalk out of the shadowed doorway behind the reception desk. A big black gun jutted from its fist as it moved around the desk toward them.

The figure stepped into a splash of light falling from the front windows, revealing a familiar face.

Esmeralda gasped. "Juan?"

It was indeed Juan, looking unnaturally pale and hollow-eyed. The gun jittered in his hand, his pupils were as big as manhole covers, and he kept smacking his too-dry lips. He had obviously neglected Notorious B.I.G.'s advice not to get high on his own supply.

"Juan, my man!" Kowalski said, his voice smooth as Vaseline. He stepped forward, teeth gleaming, arms spread for a bro hug. "I was wondering where you were, homie!"

"Shut up, you useless dickwad," Juan said.

Kowalski's grin turned confused.

Luke felt Esmeralda's fingers curling around his arm in a convulsive little movement. She at least understood how serious this was.

As for Luke, his world had gone cold and calm one more time. But now there was a spark of fear flickering in a corner of his mind that had never been there before. Because, amazingly, this was the worst situation he had been in yet.

Juan was either smarter or more cowardly than the rest of his gang. He was keeping himself well out of Luke's reach, but he was still plenty close enough for an accurate shot. His hot eyes were locked on them, and he twitched with the slightest movement. If Luke tried to rush him, Juan would kill him, no question. Then Esmeralda would be at his mercy.

The other men he had faced had been distracted, undisciplined, and focused on capturing them, not killing them.

Juan just wanted them all dead. That was bona fide hatred gleaming in his eyes. He was only barely restraining himself, because he wanted to get something from them first. That was Luke's only advantage. And the seal in his hand was his only weapon.

Juan read his mind. "Drop that thing. Right now." He aimed his gun at Luke's heart.

"Okay, you betcha." Luke bent slowly and set the seal on the floor, handle up. He straightened and raised his empty hands. "Now let's just talk for a minute."

"Yeah, let's start with what you did with the twenty keys of coke that were in that piano," Juan said, jerking his chin toward the pile of wood, metal, and thug on the floor a few feet away.

"Zapata told you about that?" Luke said, stalling for time.

"Zapata didn't need to tell me anything! He was just the face. I was the brains." He blinked hard. "The coke in the pianos was my plan. Mine! I'm the one who found out about the ivory keys. I'm the one who set up the deal with the cartel. I'm the one who bribed the Feds. I'm the one who—"

"Leeched on to my cousin so you could use my papa's company to smuggle your drugs?" Esmeralda said.

"You shut up!" He jabbed the gun at her. "All you had to do was turn the pianos over to Fish and Wildlife, but you had to keep poking around in my business, dragging all your idiot boyfriends along with you!"

"Hey, I've only got one idiot boyfriend," she snapped.

"Shut up! If you say one more fucking word, I'm going to shoot you right now!" He licked his lips. "Mouthy bitch. I was going to enjoy watching Zapata teach you some manners."

Esmeralda lunged at him. "*Hijo de puta!* I'll show you manners!"

Luke caught her and shoved her behind him, keeping her there with one arm. "Wow, you must be really, really smart to come up with such a brilliant plan," he said to Juan, since that seemed to be the point the guy had been driving at.

"Smarter than you! I had your room trashed and your truck smashed, but you couldn't get the hint to fuck off back to where you came from. I guess pussy turned you stupid."

Luke flushed. "You! You killed my truck!"

"What about me, buddy?" Kowalski broke in. "You said we were partners! You said we were going to get rich!"

Luke couldn't stand it. "You were never going to get rich, you unbelievable waste of skin. You were going to get fed to the alligators. You were Juan's patsy."

"But ... but he sent me on a complementary cruise," Kowalski moaned.

"He wanted you tucked away somewhere safe until he was ready to make his play. When you got back to Miami, he was going to skim the drugs in that piano and throw you to the cartel to cover his tracks. Isn't that right, Juan?" Luke said.

Juan shrugged. "Useful idiots don't fall into your lap every day."

Esmeralda said, "The cops will be here any second, Juan. Just forget about us and go."

"I'm not running before I collect what you owe me."

"The twenty bags of coke, right?" Luke said. "I can tell you what I did with them. Why don't you let these two go on out, and we'll talk."

"No! You tell me now or I'll start shooting kneecaps. Hers first." He aimed his gun at Esmeralda's legs.

"All right! I'll tell you."

Juan twitched like an overmedicated Chihuahua.

"I put them in the trash."

Juan stared at him for a moment. Then he shrieked, "You threw a million dollars' worth of cocaine in a dumpster?"

"No. I put them in the trashcan. That one up there." He pointed toward the mezzanine level, but Juan didn't take the bait.

His pupils like black holes, he aimed his gun at Luke's center mass. This was it. Juan was going to kill him. He tensed to shove Esmeralda away while he made a last, desperate lunge.

A scuffle of feet echoed behind the reception desk. A figure streaked out of the shadows, arms pinned behind it, a silvery strip of tape over its mouth, more tape flapping from his ankles. In a flash, Luke recognized Roddy.

Esmeralda's cousin rushed straight at Juan, shoulder tilted like he was sacking a quarterback.

Juan jerked around, his gun arm tracking. A shot

cracked the air just as Roddy rammed into his former friend and bowled him to the floor.

Juan heaved, cursing, desperate to get his gun arm out from under Roddy's weight.

Roddy heaved around, trying to knee Juan in the junk and headbutt him at the same time. But Juan writhed in a coke-fueled frenzy, dodging Roddy's convulsions.

Luke scooped the seal up from where he'd put it next to his feet and took two strides to the men tussling on the floor. He reached over Roddy's shoulder and tapped Juan smartly on the forehead with the brass head.

Juan instantly disintegrated into a boneless sprawl. Roddy collapsed on top of him, sucking air and making furious noises through the tape on his mouth. Luke grabbed him by the back of his shirt and helped him scramble to his feet.

He ripped the tape off the guy's lips.

"Ow! Watch it, you prick."

"You've got some fucking gall." He spun Roddy around and yanked at the tape around his wrists. "You lured us into a trap."

"I did not! I was trying to send a message, dumbass. This is all her fault!" Roddy pointed a newly freed finger at his cousin.

"My fault?" Esmeralda yelled.

"Yeah, yours! Why didn't you call the police, stupid?"

"Uh, because you told me not to?"

"That was code! Duh!"

She threw up her hands. "Well, how was I supposed to know that 'don't call the cops' actually meant 'call the cops'?"

"Because you always do the opposite of what everyone tells you!" Roddy yelled, also throwing up his hands. "The one time you follow orders and you almost get us all killed. It figures. It just fucking fig—"

"Shut the fuck up before I tape your mouth closed again," Luke suggested, feeling his knuckles for damage.

Roddy shot him a pale look and subsided.

Sirens suddenly wailed through the darkness outside the building, screaming to an eardrum-shattering height. Lights splashed through the glass doors, painting the room in lurid red and blue.

The doors flew open and a herd of cops stampeded into the room, swarming up the stairs and spreading out through the lower level. A few gathered around the destroyed piano sitting in a blood puddle, gun arms drooping in bemusement.

Then Agent Truitt strode through the entrance, slowing down to glare in disapproval at the chaos around him.

"Al?" Esmeralda said. "What are you doing here?"

"Rescuing you," Al said. "We found out that Zapata had his people lay a false trail up the coast. We determined he was still in Miami, hunting for you. So I called in everyone to help bring you in," he said, waving at the small army milling around.

"You're late, as usual," Luke said.

Truitt tried ignoring him. "Where's Zapata?"

"Under the piano," Luke told him.

Truitt stared at the pile of gore and wreckage in the center of the atrium and turned slightly green. "I see."

"It was an accident," Luke said.

Truitt looked up at the ruined upper balcony, then back down to the mess on the lower level, and sighed. "Of course it was. This whole ridiculous saga has been a Charlie Foxtrot from beginning to end." He cast a hopeless gaze at Ezmeralda.

"How did you find us?" she asked.

"I went to the zoo and tracked down the phone you were using. Once I learned it was issued by the State of Florida it was easy enough to ping it." His gaze skated over Juan and the bodyguard, still sprawled amid the wood splinters. "Although I think it would have been even easier just to follow the trail of unconscious guys and destroyed pianos."

"Cheer up, Al," Esmeralda said. "At least we caught the bad guys." She turned toward the clump of potted plants nearby. "Isn't that right, Mr. Brett Kowalski?"

A whimper came from behind the foliage. Kowalski, Luke realized, had dived back behind the plants for refuge when fists and seals and bullets started flying. The little guy crept out of the greenery and tried on a sickly shadow of his salesman's smile. "Agent Truitt! It's a pleasure to meet you. We spoke on the phone—"

"Indeed we did, Mr. Bart Calamari."

"Aw shit."

Luke said, "Explain, please."

"Gladly," Truitt said. "The US Marshals finally gave me the file on Mr. Calamari's real name and history. He's been in the witness protection program for the past two years, which is why we couldn't find him in our usual databases. He took the second chance the government gave him and started flirting with organized crime again."

Luke turned on Kowalski/Calamari. "Again? You've pulled this same crap before?"

"Back in New York, okay? I was running a piano showroom for the mob. Washing money, you know? I tried to work a few deals on my own, but the Don got pissy. So then I had to turn state's evidence and I ended up in bumfuck Minnesota selling pianos to yahoos."

"I don't believe it," Esmeralda said. "You managed to piss off the Mafia *and* the cartels?"

"I'm just trying to make a living, Chiquita," Brett/Bart said. "You're a working girl. You understand."

Luke and Esmeralda both started for him.

Truitt grabbed their arms and yanked them to a stop. "Whoa, there. I think you've caused enough mayhem for one evening, Mr. Hansen."

"Hansen," said Roddy, whose brows had been rumpling in ever-deeper confusion. "So ... you're not Kowalski?" he said to Luke.

"God, no."

"Who are you, then? What are you? FBI? DEA?" demanded Roddy.

"No, I'm only—" He stopped. He cast a glance over the cops milling around them, the sprawled forms of the enemies he had vanquished, and Juan's lolling forehead, emblazoned with a welt in the shape of a crossed tuning hammer and tuning fork.

He smiled. "I'm the piano man."

He bent and scooped Esmeralda into his arms. Ignoring Roddy's curses, Truitt's spluttering, Kowalski's whining, and Esmeralda's command to "Put me down this instant!" he crunched through the broken glass to the entrance, kicked open the door, and strode out into the Miami night.

45

THIRTY-SEVEN HOURS LATER, Esmeralda and Luke walked out of the lobby door of a budget hotel a few streets away from the Dolphin mall. Esmeralda was wearing a cheap sundress, and Luke had on a pair of cargo shorts and a t-shirt with an alligator in sunglasses printed on it. Each of them carried a plastic bag containing the toiletries and extra clothes provided for them courtesy of Federal law enforcement. Also in the bags were their wallets and phones and Esmeralda's brass knuckles, all recovered during the raid on the warehouse.

Aside from a brief stop at the hospital to get Luke's gunshot wound stitched up, they had spent most of the previous day and night being interviewed in their hotel rooms by the entire alphabet soup of Federal agencies. Fish and Wildlife, DHS, FBI, ICE, ATF, DEA, and, hell, probably the IRS and USPS were in there somewhere too. Truitt hadn't been kidding when he had said he'd called in everyone. Now the government was finally through with them.

They trekked across the asphalt desert of the parking strip to the oasis of a waffle house. At this early hour, it was the undisputed turf of a gang of octogenarians. A mass of frosted heads turned toward them suspiciously as they pushed through the tables to a booth. Luke ordered one of everything, and devoured it. Even Esmeralda threw her carb count to the wind and ate a tall stack of pancakes.

Then, while Luke gulped down a pot of coffee, Esmeralda shoved the pile of empty plates aside and spread out a copy of the *Miami Herald* she had snagged off the newsstand by the door when she saw the headline, "Miami Business District Erupts in Drug Violence."

The photo with the story showed none other than Agent Truitt standing in front of a piano full of coke like a safari hunter with his trophy beast. His face had been blurred out, but Esmeralda could see a shadow of his chiseled Superman chin. He stood with his hands on his hips, displaying his gun holster in classic G-man style.

She turned the paper around and showed it to Luke.

Luke raised his eyebrows. "Looks like Agent Al did all right for himself."

She folded the paper and shoved it aside. "So did you, Luke. You got something out of this adventure, didn't you? Besides a badass scar, I mean."

He brushed a hand over the slight bulge in his t-shirt where a bandage covered the bullet wound along his side. "Badass, huh?" His cheeks went ever so slightly pink.

"Baddest ass evah."

"Well." He cleared his throat. "To answer your question, you're right. I got this." He dug into his plastic bag and took out the Piano Tuners Guild seal. He set it on the table, handle up.

"You've certainly earned it. You know, I think Zapata and Juan would have gotten away with everything if you hadn't come down here looking for that thing."

"Maybe."

"So? Was it worth it?"

His eyes stayed locked on the seal. "Generally? Yes. Protecting you and stopping Zapata and Juan was worth it. But personally? Well ... I did what I set out to do. That counts for a lot. But not enough for the price I'll be paying."

She had no idea what he meant by that last part, and was afraid to ask. She said, "So what's the story you're going to tell your piano tuner friends?"

"The Guild will get the PG-rated version of what happened. That's all they can handle. They'll have enough trouble just dealing with the fact that their treasurer got put in the witness protection program and shipped off to Alaska or wherever."

"Lord, yes. Poor Kowalski."

Luke finally looked at her, a wry gleam in his eyes.

"What? The guy's such a nub, I can't help feeling sorry for him. I hope they do send him to Alaska, purely for his own sake. How much trouble can he possibly get into up there?"

"I don't know. But if the Inuit have a mafia, I'm sure he'll find a way to run afoul of it." He sat back and studied her. "And does Juan get your sympathy too?"

"Not at all. Even if that *comemierda* actually manages to cut a deal with the Feds and squeals on the cartels, he'll still spend the next twenty years hiding in a penitentiary in Bismarck, North Dakota. That's what Al Truitt promised me."

"And you believe him?"

"He's come through so far. Admit it."

Luke tilted his head in reluctant acknowledgement, which was all she could hope for. Luke and Agent Al would never be buddies.

But Al, the straight arrow, had still helped Luke, Esmeralda, and Roddy file the claim on the reward money that was due them as informants in a successful bust.

And it turned out that the reward for busting two thousand kilos of drugs was substantial, even split three ways. It was more money than she'd ever made working as a model. Probably more than Luke would make tuning pianos, if she had to guess. It might even be enough for her cousin to haul Castillo Imports out of the financial tar pit, if he got himself some decent advice for a change.

"And Roddy turned out to be innocent, just like I told you," she said.

"Okay, you were right. He saved our lives, and I'm eternally grateful. Happy?"

"I am. My cousin may be a douchebucket, but in the end he did the right thing, so my family's honor is salvaged."

"Hooray. Well, if he's learned his lesson, then I guess I wish him luck."

"Very magnanimous of you."

"I thought so too. So, what are you going to do with your share of the reward?"

"Pay back Marco, first of all. I still owe him sixty-three bucks and a Dunkin' Donuts coupon. After that, I'll supplement my grant money. I can expand my study, hire an assistant maybe. There's no end of good I can do with that money when I get to India."

India. In her mind, the word resonated with a strange echo. She would be going there in a few weeks. Without Luke.

She blurted out, "And you? You've got a nest egg now, so what are you going to do with it? Go back to Madison to tune more pianos?"

He cast her a patient look.

"Okay, okay. Minneapolis. So? Are you going back?"

He said slowly, "I don't think I can go back. Not for good. Things have changed too much. Or I've changed." He ran a finger over the seal's shiny wooden handle. "I have to return this to the Guild, but after that ... I don't know. I'm kind of at a loss."

"Well. I hope ... I hope you find what you're looking for."

His dark blond lashes lifted over his beautiful gray eyes, and he looked straight at her, like he could see into her and read everything written on her mind.

Could he? Could he really see ... her?

A long moment passed. He didn't say anything.

She swallowed. So this was it. This was really happening. They were going to say goodbye and continue along their paths in life away from each other, probably never to meet again.

It was hard to speak, but she somehow forced out a normal tone. "Are you going straight to the airport from here?"

"I could. There's nothing keeping me here."

A shocking pain shot through her, like at the gift shop but even worse. Her hand was pressing against her ribs again. She shoved it back to her lap. "Well. Then. I ... should go too. I need to— to give a full report to Anita, check on Papa. Get started on the preparations for India."

She looked into his face, searching. But all she could see was heartbreak barreling toward her. A Mack truck o' misery about to plaster her all over the highway of life in an undignified mess.

She tossed some money onto the table, grabbed her plastic bag and her orange purse, and scooted out of the booth. He hastily stuffed his seal into his bag and stood as well, towering over her.

Say something, she silently begged. *Give me a reason not to go.*

He said, "Will you stay in touch? Friend me on Facebook? So I know you're all right?"

"Yeah," she made herself say. "Of course I will."

He made an uncertain motion to maybe draw her into a hug.

She stepped forward and, careful of his injury, wrapped her arms around his waist. She leaned her head on his solid chest, listening to the deep beat of his heart. His arms came around her, holding her with all that power he controlled so well. She breathed in the warm, clean scent of him one last time.

She would miss him so much, she thought, her breath hitching. She would miss his sly sense of humor, and his methodical intelligence, and his rock-solid decency. She would miss his big, beautiful body, and the light in his gray eyes when he smiled. She was going to miss his amazing cock, to be sure. And she was going to miss the way he kept trying to protect her from anyone and anything.

Most of all, she would miss the bright, passionate spirit that she had never seen in any man before, and might never see again.

She loved him. There was no other explanation for the way her heart was tearing itself up in her chest. She had let him *see* her, the real her. He was the only man she had ever let in. He knew her like no one else did.

But he didn't want to keep her.

She pulled away, bowing her head. If he looked in her eyes, or went in for a kiss, she'd lose it for sure.

"Goodbye, Luke," she whispered.

His arms slipped away from her.

She turned and made herself go down the aisle of booths toward the door, a rip tide sucking at her feet with every step as she walked away from him.

Through a sheen of tears she saw the door wavering in front of her. She had to open it up and go through it. Get into the rental car the Feds had provided and drive to a place she could sob her heart out in private.

She was not going to have a waffle-house breakdown.

She reached for the door handle.

"Esmeralda!"

46

ESMERALDA'S SLIM SHAPE FROZE, her hand hovering over the door handle. Luke had a vision of running to her, throwing himself to his knees and clutching her leg, begging for her not to leave. And he'd probably do it, too, if he thought it would work. He had no pride whatsoever where she was concerned.

"Wait," he said.

She lowered her hand and turned slowly toward him, her face a beautiful mask.

He strode through the restaurant toward her. "Let me go with you to India."

Her lips parted, but before she had a chance to say no, he rushed ahead. "You need someone to watch your back, just in case you run into any more drug lords or ivory smugglers. And knowing you, you absolutely will. Let me come with you, and I'll keep you safe. You know I can."

Her lashes flicked down, then up again. "You're volunteering to be my bodyguard for the next two years?"

He nodded. "Whatever you need, for as long as you need."

Her dark eyes searched his face. "India is a long way from home. Are you sure you want to go that far just to look after me?"

"Doesn't matter. I want to go with you. Wherever you are."

"Why?" she asked softly. "Forget about what you think I need for a second. Why do *you* want this?"

Deep inside him, a spark of hope lit. She wasn't saying no. What would convince her to say yes? "It isn't because I think you can't take care of yourself," he rushed to say. "And it isn't because I think you're my trophy or possession. And it isn't because of the sex, though God knows I want to have it with you all the time."

She blushed a little, but said steadily, "Why is it, then?"

"It's because ..."

"Because ...?"

"Because I love you. Because I need you so much, I think I might actually die if you say no. Really. Keel right over and die, here and now."

A geezer sitting at the table next to them promptly moved his breakfast away from Luke's fall zone.

He said, "You're the answer to my prayers, Esmeralda. You're every dream I've ever had. When I'm with you, I'm the man I want to be. So I'm yours now. I always will be. That's why."

She blinked up at him.

He held his breath.

She said, "Okay. You can come to India with me."

"Great!" he said, dizzy with relief. He'd laid his heart at her feet, and she hadn't crushed it. "That's ... good! Great! India, here I come. Bet they have a lot of pianos that need tuning there." As relief ebbed, he tried to feel excited and enthusiastic.

This was what he wanted, right? He was going adventuring in foreign lands with the most wonderful woman who ever lived, who might possibly continue having sex with him. That was exactly what he wanted. Exactly. More than he had been hoping for. It was absurd to feel let down.

Esmeralda was still watching him expectantly. "So ..."

"Ah ... so?"

She huffed. "So are you going to ask me to marry you or not?"

The world, which had just started turning normally again, tipped crazily around him. Marriage? Her? *Him?* "But, I ... uh ..." He groped around for words. "But I thought you hated it when guys asked you to marry them."

"Not a guy who actually loves me."

Somehow he kept it together, saying gravely, "But you said that twenty-four is too young to get married."

"I'm getting older by the second here," she said, tapping her foot.

"But ..."

"But what, *por Dios?*"

"But you never told me that you love me back."

"Well, of course I love you! I fell in love with you the minute I saw you! Couldn't you tell?"

He shook his head, too poleaxed to speak.

"Well, I did! I saw you, and I knew, right here," she said, tapping her heart. "I knew you were the sexiest, sweetest, most magnificent man I would ever meet in all my life. I love you, love you, love you, Luke Hansen. And I absolutely cannot live without you. So, are you going to give me *mierda* all day or are you going to propose?"

He was so stupefied that it took him a few seconds to notice that everyone in the dining room was avidly training their bifocals on their little drama. For this next part, privacy was definitely in order.

He scooped his arm around Esmeralda's waist and half-carried her through the door. He whisked her around a corner of the building out of view of the street and leaned her up against the brick wall near a big plate window.

He looked down into her face. Her cheeks were glowing, eyes sparkling with a galaxy of stars.

He said, "Marry me," and kissed her.

Wonder blazed into the world around them, flaring out from where they touched. Her lips, hot. Her body, soft. All of her, as much a part of him as his own beating heart. "Marry me." Kiss. "Marry me." Kiss, longer, deeper. "Marry me, jewel. Please."

He tried to pull back to see her answer, but her fingers wove into his hair and she pulled him back into the kiss, her lips moving against his, saying, "Yes."

The sun bathed them in light. The air sang to them. Time folded in on itself in an endless loop until there was only this. Their kiss.

Dimly, he heard a *chink, chink* sound interfering with his communion with the universe. He opened his eyes and saw a row of faces smooshed up against the long window nearby, watching them. Somebody's oxygen tank was clanking against the glass.

He broke the kiss and said, "I feel like a feature on the *Today* show."

She looked over, groaned, and bowed her head into his chest.

A few steps away, the waffle house doors swung open and a couple with matching walkers came out, their facial wrinkles bunched up into smiles.

"Nice to see the young people can still be romantic," the old lady warbled as they inched past.

Her gent murmured, "It's downright inspiring. Let's head back to the double-wide, sugar. I've got a little blue pill with your name on it."

"Well, all right. Do you remember where I put the handcuffs?"

Luke and Esmeralda looked at each other and burst into laughter.

A good five minutes later, she wiped her eyes and gasped, "Okay, okay. So, if you're sure about this getting married thing, then I've got a new plan."

"Uh oh," he wheezed, leaning on the brick wall.

"No, no, wait. You'll like this one. So, okay, first, we go to the courthouse and we apply for a marriage license."

"Uh huh. And then?"

"And then we go to my house and tell Anita and Ignacio and Papa the good news."

"All right."

"And then we find a hotel room and order room service and have more crazy hot jungle sex."

He grinned. "Okay."

"And then we sort the rest of it out tomorrow."

"Sounds good."

"Great. I'll drive."

"Not a chance in hell." He bent, wrapped his arms around her hips, and picked her straight up off her feet.

"What do you think you're doing? You'll tear your stiches," she said, whacking him on the shoulder.

"Don't do that, you'll hurt your hand." He started carrying her across the joined parking lot to the hotel, where the Feds had left them a workmanlike Ford Escape.

"Oh, I see how it is," she said as he marched her along.

"He singlehandedly takes down one drug gang and all of a sudden he thinks he's Robocop. Well, let me tell you something, mister, you'd better not get in the habit of muscling me around. We zookeepers have ways of keeping our critters in line."

"I'm sure you do." He deposited her on the ground at the passenger side of the car and held out his hand for the key. She gave it to him and he unlocked the door and politely opened it for her.

"Yep. I'll have you trained in no time." She slid into the passenger seat. "And you're going to love the reward system I have worked out for you." She shot him a wink, thoroughly addling his wits, and grabbed the key out of his hand. She scrambled across the car to the driver's seat and cranked on the engine.

"Hey!" He dove into the passenger side after her and got the door closed just as she stomped on the gas, whipping the car out of the parking lot and into the Miami morning.

EPILOGUE

Mysore, India, nine months later

FOUR MEN WALKED into the dusty hall where he was practicing on the new Kawai, their shadows long and dark against the scuffed wood floor.

"It's over there," he said, nodding toward the hulking shadow of the old piano in the corner. It was a no-name instrument which he knew for a fact had not been touched since the end of the British Raj.

The concert hall's owner, gleeful over the appearance of a trained pianist willing to work for next to nothing, had sprung for a brand new parlor grand and hired him to play it. But the corpse of the hall's old piano was still in need of removal.

Which was where the four guys came in.

Without a word, they crawled under the piano, one at each corner. Then, at a signal from their leader, they all stood up at once, the six-hundred-pound load balanced on their heads. They started to walk the instrument out of the building.

Though he had never seen a piano moved in this particular fashion, he had the professional courtesy not to interfere with the process in any way. So instead he launched into a practice run of Dvořák's seventh Humoresque.

At the first few notes the four guys stopped in their tracks. As one, they shuffled around so that they were all facing his way, their eyes rapt on him, the piano still firmly positioned on their heads.

Not knowing what else to do, he continued through the whole piece until the last cheerful note rang through the room. His audience burst into a gratifying round of applause. The piano on their heads didn't move an inch.

When the last clap died away there was a beat of awkward silence. The guys kept standing there under the piano. He said, "Thanks, friends. Come to the concert tonight." Or so he tried to say. His grasp of the local Kannada language was still iffy.

The four men waved their hands at him, though, so at least he probably hadn't insulted their mothers. They shuffled around so that they were facing the door again and marched through it, quickly merging with the rest of the foot traffic down the street until only the piano gliding along on top of the crowd was visible.

He shrugged and got back to practicing, running through his usual eighteenth- and nineteenth-century repertoire, plus a selection of Bollywood tunes he had learned for spice.

He worked in a satisfied haze until another shadow darkened the door. A shadow belonging to the most beautiful woman in the world.

He always knew when that woman was near. He always would.

He started playing "As Time Goes By." "Of all the gin

joints in all the towns in all the world, she walks into mine," he said.

"You're going to say that every time I come in here, aren't you."

"You betcha."

Esmeralda Castillo Hansen walked further into the concert hall, a wide grin lighting her gorgeous face.

His wife. To everyone's perpetual astonishment. Especially his.

And yet it was true. Nine months and one week ago they had gotten married at the Miami Beach District Court —though only after Esmeralda had spent a few days talking Anita down from a full Catholic ceremony. A vague but genial Eduardo Castillo had given away the bride while a sulking Roddy, a weeping Anita, and a slightly smiling Ignacio looked on.

After the wedding they had gone straight to the zoo so that Raj could hug Esmeralda and glare threateningly at Luke. Then they were off to Minnesota for a lightning-quick visit.

There, Luke had finally returned the Piano Tuners Guild seal to the Guild president. The elderly gentleman had accepted the seal and politely listened to his tale of how it had been recovered, all the while regarding him with the look reserved for possibly dangerous crazy people. Which, Luke had to admit, was not too far off the mark.

His quest at last complete, he had gone to present his family with his new bride and announce their departure for India. His parents had been shocked. His sisters had been shocked and scandalized. His brothers had been shocked, scandalized, and so jealous they had nearly combusted right there on their mother's plaid sofa.

Luke was compelled to acknowledge a slight amount of

smugness about this. Which had only been compounded when his father had shaken his hand and given him a broad wink as he and his new wife went out the door. Then it had been on to India, and the Nagarhole National Park.

They had settled into a cabin-villa type thing near Mysore. From their home base, Esmeralda herded elephants and Luke tuned and played pianos. Of which there were a surprising number, each one in desperate need of him.

It was an all-around wonderful life. Though one he never would have dreamed of for himself, if not for Esmeralda.

She walked toward him with that amazing catwalk strut, a holdover from her modeling career that would probably be with her the rest of her days. "You're sounding good, Maestro."

"Thanks. What brings you back to town so early, jewel? I thought you'd be in your jungle for a few more hours."

"I had to come show you the newest baby video."

He pushed back his bench and rose as she came to stand by his shoulder, tablet held out so they both could see it. "Just look at him, Luke. Isn't he beautiful?" She gazed down at the baby on the tablet, her lips softly parted, her eyes gooey and lovestruck.

On the screen, a slightly fuzzy gray shape scampered around a forest clearing waving his trunk and flapping his ears before scrambling back to his mother, a formerly captive young cow named Pari who had been reintroduced to the Nagarhole park only three years before. The pair twined their trunks together in an elephant hug and disappeared into the trees.

"Now, that's cute," Luke said.

"I'm going to call him Raj Junior."

"Excellent choice. So, Pari is adapting well to life in the park?"

"Yes indeed. Running wild and free suits her."

"It suits all of us, doesn't it?"

She clicked off the screen and smiled up at him, her eyes moving over him in a way that never failed to rev his engine. "You betcha," she said. She reached up and curled her fingers around his tie.

The tie, a wedding gift from his bride, was blue-gray to match his eyes, she'd told him, and printed with little elephants marching in lines. He wore it loose around his neck with his collar unbuttoned these days, but he would never think of going without it. It was too convenient a handle for his wife to grab onto. She tugged on it, a determined glint in her eyes, and he yielded with a smile, letting her pull his head down for a thoroughly uncivilized kiss.

The End

If you enjoyed this book, please leave a review at your online bookseller of choice. Thanks.

Sign up for my newsletter at jbcurry.com to get sneak peeks, special offers, and news about the next book in the Pianos Wild series.

ACKNOWLEDGMENTS

For the excellent care given to their animals and to novelists with oddball questions, I would like to thank the staff of Zoo Miami. Any mistakes made depicting the care of elephants are entirely my own.

For their dedication to protecting American wildlife and the American public, including novelists with oddball questions, thanks go to the United States Fish and Wildlife Service.

Many thanks to Diane Tobio for translating my Spanish phrases and for your important work in teaching.

Thanks to the Romance Writers of America, the best professional writer's organization there is.

An enormous thank you to the Bookies, Ann Clement, Julia Gabriel, Victoria Hanlen, and Anna James, for your encouragement and good advice. I could never have written this book without you.

Endless thanks to my husband Chris for your expertise in all things musical, and for providing so many bizarre yet true piano stories for me to write about.

And finally, thanks always to my family for your love and support.

ABOUT THE AUTHOR

J.B. Curry is an artist and writer. She has traveled to every corner of the United States, but currently lives in beautiful New England with her family and her vast collection of houseplants.

Follow her on Facebook. Visit her at jbcurry.com to sign up for her newsletter and get news, sneak peeks, and special offers.

Made in the USA
Middletown, DE
05 July 2019